COLD
BURN

Also by A. J. Landau

Leave No Trace

COLD BURN

A National Parks Thriller

A. J. LANDAU

MINOTAUR BOOKS
NEW YORK

First published in the United States by Minotaur Books, an imprint of St. Martin's Publishing Group

www.minotaurbooks.com

Design by Meryl Sussman Levavi

The Library of Congress Cataloging-in-Publication Data is available upon request.

ISBN 978-1-250-87736-9 (hardcover)
ISBN 978-1-250-87737-6 (ebook)

Our books may be purchased in bulk for promotional, educational, or business use. Please contact your local bookseller or the Macmillan Corporate and Premium Sales Department at 1-800-221-7945, extension 5442, or by email at MacmillanSpecialMarkets@macmillan.com.

First Edition: 2025

10 9 8 7 6 5 4 3 2 1

To Keith Kahla and John Talbot: Thank you for your friendship and support, and for making our dream a reality.

In wilderness is the preservation of the world.

—Henry David Thoreau

COLD
BURN

GLACIER BAY NATIONAL PARK AND PRESERVE, ALASKA

"Watch your step, everyone," David Lees said through the bitingly cold and shrill wind that had seemed to whip up out of nowhere. "We're here to measure the ice, not fall through it."

The remark from Lees, a United States Geological Survey team leader, was meant to be humorous, but the expressions on the faces of his fellow staffers and the students accompanying them showed anxiety and concern. And with good reason. The Lamplugh Glacier had been the site of a catastrophic incident in June of 2016.

Normally, violent landslides and avalanches were caused by overly abundant amounts of rainfall, earthquakes, and volcanic eruptions. But the 2016 avalanche was believed to have been caused by ice that had melted inexplicably faster than any other such occurrence on record. Scientists at the USGS only knew it had happened because the incident was captured on seismic instruments that put the result as roughly equivalent to a five-point-two on the Richter scale.

Lees assumed the team's three college interns—all majoring in some combination of climatology, geology, and environmental science—knew all that. They had come here as part expedition and part work-study program to bear witness to the devasting effects climate change was producing on glaciers in general and in Glacier Bay in particular.

The interns didn't know the true purpose of the USGS team's exploration, what they were actually looking for with their probes of the relative thickness of ice and potential degradation of the permafrost.

"Why are we spending all our time down here?" asked a kid named Bellows who played football at Brown University. "Why aren't we where the action is?"

"You're referring to the north- and northeast-facing slopes, right?"

"I guess so. That's where the landslides took place."

"Because those areas are subject to mountain permafrost. Mountain permafrost is the ice in the cracks and crevices between the rocks that holds them together and helps stabilize steep slopes. Once the permafrost melts, the cohesion that had existed for thousands and thousands of years is jeopardized."

"So we're safe down here," assumed a female student from the California Institute of Technology named Shayna.

"Relatively. But we're here because research studies have revealed a dramatic drop in the thickness of the ice, even on the south-facing slopes."

Lees' remark seemed to reassure her. They had carried only light equipment with them from base camp located on a ship anchored in Glacier Bay itself. Each day, they had taken careful measurements at various levels toward scrutinizing the rate and severity of the ice melt. So far, the results had proven far more dramatic than Lees had been expecting. The situation had grown significantly direr since he had last explored the area two years before, further convincing him that estimates by top climatologists dramatically underestimated how fast the entire ice shelf was degrading and the devastating effects it would have on all life on the planet. And yet this reality raised the odds of the team being successful in its greater purpose of uncovering a secret buried in the ice for millennia, a secret that could change the world for the better.

"Ever get caught in a landslide yourself, Doc?" the kid named Bellows asked him.

"Yes, and it's an experience I have no desire to repeat," Lees said. "That's why we're in what's considered a safe zone."

He thought the rumbling he felt in the next instant was a product of his imagination. The looks on the faces of the others, though, told him they had felt it, too. Seconds later, Lees felt the frozen ground shaking beneath his feet. While the eyes of the rest of the team members looked toward him, he turned his gaze up toward Mount Cooper, a six-thousand-foot behemoth that dwarfed the glacier in its shadow.

A thick white cloud was rolling downward, expanding by the second until it seemed to stretch across the entire width of the mountain itself. It was at the first stages of a massive rock avalanche, boulder-sized chunks encased in ice taking on more mass from the snowpack clenching tight as the momentum gathered more and more steam.

"Everyone, follow me! *Run!*"

Lees failed to keep the panic from his voice. Gone was the excitement of the conditions being right to succeed where all other USGS teams working in these parts had failed. Gone was any thought other than finding some way to survive the thundering slide of rock, snow, and ice barreling toward them.

"Stay close! Run in pairs! Keep the person next to you in sight."

The thundering sounds drowned out the last of his words. The land beneath Lees seemed to be shaking, then alternately lifting and falling like some twisted amusement park ride. He had survived the last landslide he'd nearly been trapped in by squeezing into a crevice and holding his breath while praying he wouldn't be entombed there. He very much doubted any such crevice existed here on the southern slope of the Lamplugh Glacier, never mind one deep enough to fit all six members of his team. There was no way they could possibly outrun the avalanche, so they had to try to find some form of cover or shelter, which meant heading upward into the avalanche itself.

Just when the first of the rolling cloud's icy white tentacles reached them with a feeling like needles being scraped across their skin, he spotted a dark chasm amid the white-tipped tundra of the lower slope of the glacier, up a natural winding trail carved by runoff.

A cave! It had to be a cave!

"There!" he cried out, even though no one could hear him.

He steered toward the mouth of the cave, feeling the crunch of snow and ice beneath his boots without hearing it. He was aware of the others nipping at his heels, led by Bellows, the football player. He could feel the heat of panic and terror wafting off their bodies to challenge the frigid mist that had enveloped them.

Lees began blowing an emergency whistle as hard and loud as he could, so the team members would be able to follow if he was lost to sight. The grade leading up to the cave's mouth was steeper than he had expected, and he pressed on with no real concept of how close the rolling blanket of promised death was drawing toward them. Two of his charges went down, injured, but were quickly scooped up by rescuers. One of the rescuers, he saw, was Bellows.

They reached the mouth of the cave moments before the thundering force of the avalanche rolling down Mount Cooper was upon them. Lees maintained the presence of mind to herd the others into the cave before he lunged in after them, feeling a great wave of relief that all five were accounted for, though two were clearly hobbled.

The group lurched backward from the cave's mouth as the dark wave splattered with white rolled on just before them, sounding like piles of loose change jangling together. A few seconds more and they all would have been dead. The cloud pushed inside through the cave's mouth, freezing when it touched the team members' skin even through their clothes, which Lees knew would be damp, sodden, and quickly frozen. He and the other USGS professionals had all toted emergency heaters in their packs that would keep them alive long enough to await rescue. Those emergency, but powerful, Lixada propane heaters could provide comfort even in an icy environment like this for hours, especially if employed judiciously.

It was in that moment a rancid stench turned Lees' stomach, bitter and rotten at the same time, like a festering wound. He also detected a sound like a low, harmonic growl from somewhere well back of the cave's mouth—a trick of the wind, he hoped, since he couldn't contemplate escaping death by one form of nature, only to face it from another.

"Lights!" he ordered, through the near total darkness, the day beyond cloaked by the rolling pile of debris that measured in the tens of thousands of metric tons.

Four flashlights switched on almost immediately, catching Bellows and another one of the student interns still fumbling in their packs. Lees swung his beam toward the cave's rear where it fastened on something black, like a blanket of molten darkness.

The growling sound he still hoped was the wind grew deeper as his flashlight caught a massive, hairy shape directly in front of him.

PART ONE

—◆—

National parks and reserves are an integral aspect
of intelligent use of natural resources. It is the
course of wisdom to set aside an ample portion
of our natural resources as national parks and
reserves, thus ensuring that future generations
may know the majesty of the earth as we know
it today.

—President John F. Kennedy

—◆—

CHAPTER 1

ICY STRAIT, ALASKA

More than 60 percent of the world's population of humpback whales migrate to this area every year from Hawaii.

"Set depth at one-zero-two, zero bubble."

A twenty-year Navy veteran and a submarine captain for half of those, Captain Jack Fincic of the USS *Providence* SSN-812 had seen war up close and personal, often on missions no one outside a select few would ever learn about. He had faced off against Soviet subs, looking to make a name for themselves, and had been forced to sink one when it strayed danger-ously close and refused to give way. But he found nothing as stressful as a new sub's initial training voyage where a mistake could lead, in this case, to a $6 billion loss of the Navy's newest, biggest, and fastest submarine ever built.

"Aye, sir. One-zero-two, zero bubble."

The *Providence* was the thirty-seventh entry in the Navy's Virginia-class fleet to be commissioned, and Fincic's job was to make sure all the bells rang and whistles blew as they were supposed to. So far, the vessel's first two full weeks at sea had gone off without a hitch. The training mis-sion was currently taking the sub through Alaska's Icy Strait, waters that were home to large pods of both whales and sea lions. Just minutes be-fore, they had passed George Island. A World War II history buff, Captain Fincic had already regaled much of the crew with tales of the island being home to a living artifact of that war in the form of an eighteen-ton, long-range gun. The Navy had actually had to build a road from one side of the island to the other that was big enough to accommodate it. That gun had only been fired in practice and never in combat, a deterrent as much as anything, just as Fincic hoped would be the case with the *Providence* itself.

The most important feature of the ship's two-week training mission was testing the ultra-top-secret stealth technology that made the *Providence* undetectable to surface ships and even rival subs. The stealth technology was designed to render all incarnations of sonar and radar moot, so she would have free rein of the sea. Accordingly, the *Providence* could approach, sneak up on, or take up position in range of any target on land or at sea without her presence ever being detected.

"Con, sonar! We have a surface bogey slowing above us!"

"Coordinates," Fincic said into his headset.

"Twelve hundred meters ahead. Stopped in the water."

"Can you identify?"

"A trawler or salvage vessel based on the size and signature."

"Marine or environmental science?" Fincic quizzed, since such excursions were common in these parts.

"No way to be sure, sir."

"No naval vessels on station in the area," reported his executive officer, the ship's second-in-command.

"Stay on course. Maintain heading, Chief," Fincic ordered the chief of the boat. "Descend to one-zero-zero and resume zero bubble."

"Aye, sir, one-zero-zero meters. Resume zero bubble."

He felt the hairs on the back of his neck warming, the first sign that his defenses had been alerted. "And I want an ID of that ship over us. I want configuration, armaments, registry, and I want it five minutes ago. Clear?"

"Clear, sir," said the chief.

Fincic turned his gaze involuntarily upward, picturing the vessel almost directly above them as he felt the *Providence* level off at a depth of one hundred meters.

‡‡‡

"Rover One has located the target, Captain!"

Captain Barbara Larson of the *Salvor* watched as the World War II mine took shape on the bridge monitor before her, courtesy of the underwater ROV's high-definition camera. It was formed of black steel with a pair of ridged bands wrapped around its circumference. Larson knew the mine was circular in design, but the angle of the ROV's camera made it appear oblong. It weighed a thousand pounds, around half of that comprised by the still-live explosives packed within, rigged to detonate when it came into contact with a vessel cruising near the surface. The floats keeping it buoyant had long since deteriorated, accounting for it sinking to the bottom to join a graveyard of unexploded World War II ordnance that remained a great danger to anything that came into contact with them.

Larson had never commanded her own boat while serving in the Navy, though she had served as the executive officer on both a destroyer and a guided missile cruiser. The *Salvor*, a rescue and salvage–class vessel, had originally been commissioned by the Navy in 1986. The ship had performed her duties admirably for more than twenty years before being decommissioned in 2007. Fifteen years later, she was retrofitted for her current purpose of locating and dredging unexploded World War II explosives that continued to litter the seas. Upon leaving the Navy and assuming her first command, Larson was pleased that the ship still carried its original name, though all naval markings had been removed. The *Salvor* was now the property of a private contractor the government retained to do the job.

Larson watched as the ROV operator adroitly manipulated a pair of joysticks that controlled the actions of Curly's fully articulable arms and pincers. "Curly" was one of three ROVs on board the *Salvor*, the other two appropriately named Moe and Larry.

On-screen, Curly wrapped steel cable around the mine and then attached a thick eye hook through which to thread a thinner, Kevlar-wrapped cable in order to haul the mine to the surface where it would be raised aboard the *Salvor*. Detonating the mine where it lay was strictly against protocol, due to the potential of doing damage to the existing ecosystem and unsettling the resident population of marine life. Procedure dictated that the mine be safely detonated once it reached the surface instead.

"Target secured," Curly's operator said to Larson.

With the tug cable in place, there was only one thing left to do.

"Then let's bring the son of a bitch up."

‡‡‡

"Goddamnit!"

Second Class Petty Officer Tom Massick, one of the machinists aboard the *Providence,* was still wondering how he ended up with the job of draining a clogged auxiliary condenser that circulated pumped-in seawater to cool the ship. That was as standard a process as could be, except when something went wrong, like today. It was a simple fix, but a horrible job given the stench-riddled muck sure to pour out once he cleared the clog, and the rubber apron he had donned was ill-suited to keep the discharge off him.

"Goddammit," he said again, as he twisted open the valve and pulled it off to reveal a mass of clenched seaweed infused with ocean refuse and waste matter up close and personal.

In Massick's mind, some whale had taken a shit that had washed into the *Providence* with the huge volume of seawater that was drawn in continuously as a part of the ship's cooling system. So here he was, senior man of the group, drawing a job that belonged to a rookie. The problem was, there weren't any rookies with the required experience aboard the ship's test voyage under the sea, which left Massick playing the role of a deep-sea Roto-Rooter man with tools not unlike the plumbing variety belted around his waist.

His snake tool cut through the clump that was clogging up the works, but it was wedged in too tightly to extract no matter how hard he tugged. Massick twisted the snake tool free and went to plan B: effectively, a grabbing device with multiple fingerlike prongs that would close on the clump to give him the leverage he needed to yank it out of the condenser and free the clog.

The stench was nauseating, not something anyone could ever get used to, especially in the barren environment of a submarine's interior, which seemed to have no smells at all. Massick's stomach turned and he held his breath, as he worked his grabber tool into the clump and then squeezed the handle to clench the prongs together.

He added a second hand to the first to close the device with enough of the clog snared to yank it out. Even then, Massick figured it would take several yanks to do the job, given the size and concentration of the clump. He held one hand on the handle and the other on the extension rod.

"One . . . two . . . three . . ."

With that, he yanked. Incredibly, the clump came free on the first tug, dragging with it tentacle-like strands that smacked him in the face and ended up in his mouth when it dropped open to cry out in surprise. The clump was followed by a multi-gallon flood of water that had been trapped behind the clog, now freed to burst out in a stream powerful enough to nearly knock Massick from his feet. Though left standing, he was now soaked from head to toe in rancid water and muck that coated him in a stench that left him retching.

"Shit, shit, shit!" Massick screeched, suddenly feeling nauseous.

Which was pretty much what he was covered in.

‡‡‡

"Con, sonar. We have two bogies on-screen rising fast!"

"Rising? From where, sonar?"

"The bottom, sir."

In times past, Fincic would have assumed those bogies were some species of marine life. The *Providence*'s state-of-the-art system, though, was able to distinguish between organic organisms and foreign, potentially adversarial objects.

"Con, sonar! Two hundred meters and closing!"

"Chief, evasive maneuvers. Right full rudder. Increase to max speed."

"Con, sonar! One hundred meters and closing!"

"Aye, sir. Evasive maneuvers. Right full rudder. Increase to max speed."

"Configuration?" Fincic demanded, anxiety growing in him over this potential threat. "Signature?"

"Undetermined, Captain. The objects are too small to get a clear reading on!"

"Con, sonar! Fifty meters and closing!"

Fincic could feel the *Providence* bank sharply to starboard. Because he had no real-time visual of the closing object, he couldn't know whether the maneuver would be enough to steer clear of whatever it was. He rejected the notion of an attack as quickly as he'd considered it. No one, including naval command, knew their position and barely a handful of people knew of their mission. But the Russians were known to frequent these waters on provocative missions of their own, and Fincic couldn't help but recall reports of a Typhoon-class Russian sub being detected in the area just a few days ago.

"Chief, set battle stations. Condition red."

And with that, a new alarm began to sound.

‡‡‡

The winch drew the unexploded World War II mine closer to the surface. Captain Barbara Larson was able to follow the progress on-screen thanks to Curly's camera making sure they had a clear glide path to the surface.

Suddenly, the screen caught something silhouetted in the upward glide path, something long and cylindrical like a giant bullet traversing the sea.

"Oh my God . . ."

Larson didn't need twenty years in the Navy to know what she was looking at, any more than she could fathom why neither the *Salvor*'s radar nor sonar systems had picked up what was clearly a naval attack sub.

"Stop the winch!" she ordered.

"Winch stopped, Captain!"

"Release the tether."

The tech behind Curly's control worked the joystick. "Tether, released."

"Give me visual."

The momentum the mine had gained kept it propelling upward, straight on line with the submarine, which was taking evasive maneuvers that might not be enough to avoid an apparently inevitable collision.

"Get Curly to the mine. We've got to stop it!"

Larson knew the ROV was too far away, knew it could never get to the mine in time, but she had to try, had to do something. The tech controlling the ROV complied, his motions belying the fact he knew the task was hopeless.

"Brace for explosion!" Larson ordered.

‡‡‡

The blast shook the *Providence* to its core. The first immediate effect of the damage sustained was a reactor SCRAM in which the engines ceased running, cutting off propulsion. The sub's lighting flickered, died, and caught again when the emergency generators kicked in. Fincic felt the sub seem to hang in the water briefly before beginning its descent to the bottom of the sea.

A mine, it must have been a mine!

In that moment, it all became clear to Fincic. The ship on the surface could only be some sort of salvage vessel, a modern-day mine sweeper cleansing the seas of World War II relics.

From what the LED readouts monitoring the ship's multiple systems told him, there had been no catastrophic hull breach or anything that might place the *Providence* in further peril. Without power, though, the ship's atmospheric control equipment would be rendered inoperable, shutting down the oxygen generator and its accompanying carbon dioxide scrubbers. Breathable air would now be supplied by oxygen candles to supplement the oxygen already present in the air.

Fincic could feel the collective anxiety and fear of the crew around him. No matter how much elite training submariners aboard a ship like this received, it was never enough to prepare for a moment like this, a moment seldom experienced by a modern submarine crew, particularly a Virginia-class vessel.

"Depth two hundred meters . . . three hundred meters . . . four hundred meters . . ."

Just after that, Fincic felt the thud of the *Providence* rocking to a stop on the bottom of the sea, just over thirteen hundred feet down. The sub seemed to shift slightly before settling in the silt.

Fincic knew damage-control parties were already checking the area close to the ship's bow where the explosion had taken place. The damage at this point seemed limited to the propulsion system and the engine room itself, nothing that would imperil the crew so long as the oxygen candles kept functioning, which would be for four days. The nearest naval base capable of mounting a rescue with submersibles rigged for evacuation was outside of Seattle, twenty hours away. That meant the entire crew could be offloaded, and the process of raising the *Providence* begun, one day from now. There remained only one last thing for Fincic to do.

He grasped a standard mic from the console before him, pressed the proper keys and switches to activate the ship's emergency communication system. While running silent and deep, submarines maintained no contact whatsoever with the surface, either incoming or outgoing. A ship like the *Providence* existed in an entirely self-contained world, until an emergency like this occurred. Emergency procedure dictated that Fincic record a message onto a device that would then be dispatched to the surface, which was the only way communication was possible with the overwater world, and then only to transmit.

"Naval command, mayday, mayday! This is the *Providence*. We have suffered engine and propulsion damage from contact with a World War II mine lifted by a salvage ship and are currently resting on the bottom on emergency power. Request assistance and rescue. Coordinates follow."

Once Fincic had provided those coordinates, he launched the ship's SLOT buoy. SLOT was short for "Submarine-Launched One-Way Transmitter," and once the buoy reached the surface it would automatically transmit his message via a secure channel to naval command, at which point rescue ships would be scrambled out of Naval Base Kitsap. Meanwhile, following protocol, he would launch another buoy every hour until the rescue team arrived on-site.

Until then, all Fincic and the rest of the *Providence* crew could do was wait.

—◦—◦—◦—

CHAPTER 2

MS EURODAM, SITKA, ALASKA

**Sitka National Historical Park was redesignated from a
national monument on October 18, 1972.**

"I'm going to kill your ass."

Michael Walker had no idea how the song "I'm Going to Kill You" by
Wesley Willis ended up on his playlist, but he was new to Apple Music and
seemed to be making a habit out of downloading the wrong songs.

"So kiss this earth goodbye."

Michael hit pause on his iPhone's music app, pulled the buds from his
ears, and stuffed them in the pocket of the jacket he'd donned to ward off
the chill rising from the Gulf of Alaska. He stood on the deck of the Holland
America cruise line's MS *Eurodam*, its pace slowing to a crawl as it approached the dock in Sitka, Alaska, for a scheduled stop.

He'd boarded the boat at the Alaskan cruise's point of origin in Seattle,
Washington, overlooked by Mount Rainier. Normally, the mountain
would be covered in clouds, rendering it invisible from the dock's vantage
point. But on the morning of his departure the mountain was out and
crystal clear, looking like a picture lifted from a postcard. The beauty was
lost on Michael, whose mind imposed a snow-swept landscape onto the
scene, lifted from the day his fellow park ranger wife, Allie, had lost her
life and he'd lost his foot.

The MS *Eurodam* bucked slightly against the current, as the dock crystallized into view. Mist-shrouded hills colored a rich emerald green hung
over the scene, blocking all but a smattering of buildings just off the shoreline. He turned his focus from memories of that day on Mount Rainier
back to the investigation he'd been assigned to lead that explained his presence undercover on the ship.

Artifacts from the native Tlingits, who were indigenous to the area, were disappearing at an alarming rate. (While the tribe's name was spelled with a *T*, it was actually pronounced *K*lingit.) Possessing little monetary value and attractive only to what were known as "curiosity collectors," these Tlingit artifacts nonetheless made for vital keepsakes of Alaska's primitive history dating back long before civilization had found its way here. The fraught relationship between the tribe and the outside world in general, as well as the National Park Service in particular, made this case a priority all by itself. Add to that the fact that the Park Service was responsible for maintaining some of the museums and historical locations, and was thus suffering the ignominy of the thefts taking place on its watch, and his investigation became a *high* priority.

The investigation on Mount Rainier more than four years before had been about poachers, a low priority in contrast, except to his wife, Allie. And then it turned out not to be about poachers at all, but killers who were responsible for Allie's death.

Whenever the memories of that day resurfaced, Michael felt the phantom pain of his missing foot. He'd been warned to expect it as a common occurrence that may or may not diminish over the years. The only time he ever felt that pain, though, was when he revisited that day in his mind.

Surgery saved his foot, at least temporarily. When a combination of time and physical therapy failed to restore his mobility or forestall an endless series of infections, Michael opted for amputation in order to be fitted with a state-of-the-art prosthetic that would restore a far greater measure of his mobility and independence. Because his knee and much of his ankle had been spared damage, he learned to walk without a limp and found in recertifying to become an Investigative Services Branch special agent that he could do almost everything he could before, just not quite as well or as fast.

The prosthetic had restored a surprising degree of form and function, but not enough to handle the rigors of patrolling a park. That explained why he had chosen to become what was essentially a detective, working both in and out of uniform for the ISB to investigate crimes that took place within the grounds of any property under the domain of the National Park Service. The training had proven rigorous for even a fully nondisabled man. Michael was neither granted nor sought any quarter. If he couldn't cut it anymore, so be it. The thought of a desk job was more than enough to motivate him through those arduous months.

His former boss, Angela Pierce, had been recently appointed to run the National Park Service, but many of his assignments still came directly from or through her. Her last action as Special Agent in Charge of the ISB's Atlantic field office was to name him a special agent at large. That allowed Angela to personally assign Michael cases of particular interest due to their political sensitivity or the severity of the particular crime.

Angela had given him the stolen artifacts investigation because of pressure from the congressional delegation of Alaska. He would be starting at ground zero since no one had any idea of the methodology behind those thefts, which had been occurring over a three-year period. They had been increasing, and several theories had been put forth regarding the potential perpetrators. One theory, advanced by the congressman from Alaska, was that the Tlingits themselves were responsible. There was no proof of that and the congressman was an oil man who'd fought his share of court battles with the tribe over drilling, which made it even more important to get to the bottom of things before the relationship between the Natives and the NPS frayed even more.

Michael had started his investigation a few weeks back. He considered any number of scenarios but kept coming back to the notion of Alaskan cruise ships offering the perfect means to smuggle the artifacts out. There weren't a lot of other options, none in fact, that could explain the frequency of the thefts. Michael's review of the incident reports revealed what could only be a very well-orchestrated criminal organization involving multiple parties. And there was also the fact that the only sites reporting multiple thefts were located in ports of call visited by cruise ship lines. Even if his initial assumptions were true, though, this brought Michael no closer to the perpetrators or their precise methodology—how they were managing to steal the artifacts off museum shelves or from storage areas, and how those perpetrators were getting them off the cruise ships back in Seattle or some other port of call.

With twelve cruise lines, both big and small, exploring Alaska's vast area, Michael's initial efforts had proven laborious. Given that he had served as a law enforcement park ranger prior to moving into the ISB, he much preferred working in the field. That's when he felt he did his best work and felt the closest to his late wife, Allie. Sitting behind a desk all day came with the job of an Investigative Services Branch special agent more often than he'd expected. Angela Pierce was relying on him to avoid a political kerfuffle, and the fact that she always had his back made her the last person Michael wanted to let down.

He was in his element now, enjoying the cold clean air and even the chill that permeated his clothes and made his skin feel clammy while he stood on deck. The postcard-perfect backdrop of trees dominating the landscape of Sitka grew larger as the *Eurodam* edged closer to the dock.

Criminals, in his experience, never expected to get caught. They always considered themselves smarter than their pursuers and inevitably believed their machinations were too well planned to give them up. In this case, they were almost right.

Almost.

Michael started his investigative process by creating a spreadsheet listing every known theft over the thirty months since the plotters had abandoned all attempts at subtlety. During that period, just over one hundred pieces had been stolen from five different museums and the Sitka National Historical Park, which housed the artifacts given or loaned by the Native tribes. The museums were small in scope and displayed the items on a rotating basis, some of those items ultimately being returned to the tribes in question. The Tlingits were threatening to pull all the artifacts, a major embarrassment for the Park Service and a certain setback to the improved relations the NPS was trying to foster. Angela had fought to remove fishing limits and ease movement across these protected park lands, but her efforts had been stymied by politicians who watered down the loosening of restrictions to the point of being ineffectual.

Next, Michael created a twin spreadsheet that focused on the park rangers on duty at the time of the thefts, as well as the ones in charge of inventorying all incoming items and storing those that had rotated out of display. He found nothing of note when it came to the rotation of rangers, but plenty on the inventory of artifacts itself. His findings revealed that most of the stolen artifacts had been in storage at the time of their theft, though somewhere around a quarter of them were actually stolen while on display. These tended to be the most valuable of the bunch. Michael's research indicated that curiosity collectors were known to pay anywhere from five thousand to as much as fifty thousand for select items, though the bulk of the sales were made closer to the lower end.

The key to his investigation was a close inspection of the Alaskan cruise lines' manifests to create a database that would match passenger names to thefts. He'd started by eliminating families and focusing only on individuals or couples. But when that failed to yield any discernible results, Michael did what the investigators who'd preceded him never had:

He started looking into families.

In the past three years, five different families had each taken between four and six Alaskan cruises, spread out between the different lines servicing the route. Not a single one of the parents or kids had a criminal record at all and no hint of anything remotely associated with smuggling. Since neither the bags of passengers nor their persons were searched upon returning to the ship from a port of call (beyond a simple metal detector and X-ray scanner), all they'd need to do after taking possession of a stolen artifact was bring it back on board disguised as a souvenir.

One of the families Michael's investigation had identified, the Morgans, had boarded the ship in Seattle as was their custom for their third voyage in the same calendar year, though this was the first time they'd booked with Holland America. They had reserved a signature stateroom suite, so their twin thirteen-year-old sons would have somewhere to sleep. Their cruise application listed a home address in San Diego and Michael's interest in the Morgans had piqued further when it became clear this wasn't a school vacation week.

Michael had spent the first days of the voyage north familiarizing himself with the Morgans and the placement of their suite. He had arranged for his simpler accommodations to be located on the same deck to facilitate his being able to observe them at meals and during activities on board the ship, like evening entertainment selections and stops in the gym. Nothing made someone stand out more than a prosthetic limb, but fortunately Michael's was anything but obvious, so long as he didn't wear shorts—hardly a burden in this weather.

Only Holland America executives at the company's home office knew of his presence on board, since he had no idea if a crew member, or members, might be involved. He had followed the Morgans off the ship at the *Eurodam*'s first stop in Ketchikan and had kept eyes on them through the entire visit ashore. The Tongass Historical Museum was well lit, but the family split up once inside and it was hard for him to keep track of the parents and their kids, so he focused especially on Olivia Morgan since her shoulder bag would be perfect to stash a good many of the artifacts displayed within, though its contours were already stretched by whatever she had left the ship with. Her husband, Steve, carried nothing with him but a black plastic bag in which he'd stuffed a pair of newspapers and two paperback books.

He was confident they hadn't stolen or been passed anything while inside the museum, but back on board he used a passkey the home office had provided so he could search the Morgans' quarters once they headed to dinner. After thirty minutes, he left the suite confident there was nothing incriminating among the Morgans' possessions.

Michael wasn't discouraged, since the pattern indicated only one or two museums were struck during any given cruise and sometimes none at all. There were still four more stops with museums coming, starting with Sitka today. And, just as he formed that thought, the Morgans emerged from an elevator and took their place in the line of passengers waiting to disembark. He spotted Steve Morgan say something to his wife. He wrapped an arm around her waist and she adjusted her ever-present brown leather shoulder bag. It looked lighter than normal from what Michael had observed, enough to get his heart rate to pick up a few beats.

Michael turned back to the view beyond the deck rail to wait a few moments before taking his place in line behind the other passengers. He cast his gaze forward to find the Morgans heading down the gangway toward a waiting bus he'd be boarding just after them.

CHAPTER 3

———○———

EVERGLADES NATIONAL PARK, FLORIDA

Everglades National Park was authorized on May 30, 1934, as a conservation site, but not for tourism.

"There's not much left of the body," Law Enforcement Park Ranger Clark Gifford said to FBI Special Agent Gina Delgado. "But, as you already heard, we still got lucky."

"Lucky enough to know we're looking at a murder here," she told him. "Anything more on that count I should know?"

"No precise determination of the actual cause of death yet, but we're looking at blunt force trauma to the head, a single stab wound from a blade that penetrated the thorax before lodging in the heart, and ligature marks that suggest strangulation."

That was enough on its own to give Gina a chilling assessment of the murder itself. A single stab wound, delivered the way Gifford described, strongly suggested a professional armed with a blade that could slice through bone and cartilage. Stabbings almost always involved multiple points of entry, pointing to either a crime of passion or an unskilled killer. Similarly, Gina assessed the blunt force trauma as having been what had first incapacitated the victim and the ligature marks could mean torture had preceded the murder. She'd have to wait for the entire autopsy results to come in before her assumptions were confirmed.

"Solid work, Ranger," she complimented.

"I did some background on you," Gifford said, tightening his gaze on her. "I see you've got some experience working joint investigations with the National Park Service."

"You might say that." Gina nodded, not elaborating since she wasn't sure how much the ranger knew.

"You worked with Michael Walker from the ISB on those domestic ter-
rorist strikes. Not much I could find about how the two of you managed
to close the loop on that."

"We did our jobs, Ranger. Enough said."

"Meaning you've said as much as you're allowed to say."

Gina let his statement hang in the air, moving back to the subject at
hand. "What else have you got for me?"

Gifford wore his hair short, not quite military high and tight, but close-
cropped enough to suggest he'd served—in the Army, if instinct and intu-
ition served her well. He had broad shoulders and thick fingers that she
noted were nonetheless nimble and lithe when he started to rummage
through the folders stacked on his neatly arranged desk.

Gifford stopped that process suddenly, between folders.

"What's the FBI's interest in this anyway? I expected someone from the
ISB, given the body was found inside a national park. I thought that maybe
Michael Walker would show up, not his partner from the Bureau."

Gina let that comment stand. The truth was she didn't know herself
why she'd been dispatched down here. She was a "roving special agent,"
assigned to no specific FBI office after three years as the Assistant Special
Agent in Charge, ASAC, of the New York field office. With an impressive
list of commendations, she was on the fast track to becoming a SAC, Special Agent in Charge, or an assistant director at headquarters in Washington, D.C. While on the surface some might see her current assignment
as a demotion, a slightly deeper dive would reveal she received her cases
directly from the White House, sometimes from the president herself. For
obvious reasons, Gina had assumed her investigations would continue to
focus in the terrorism realm. Although not a single one had come her way
yet in her new role, the four cases she had worked on all involved national
security in some respect.

Which begged the question what the remains of a murder victim found
in Everglades National Park had to do with national security. The president's
new chief of staff, Daniel Grant, had not elaborated on that other than to
leave her with a cryptic thought when she pushed for more information.

*"The president considers this case to be of the highest priority, Special
Agent Delgado. She also hopes that she's wrong."*

Cryptic indeed. Gina figured she wasn't being provided with any further
specifics because, in the event she came up empty, the White House would

have shared nothing that might result in blowback. In Washington, some-times what you don't say is more important than what you do.

Gifford finally found the file folder he was looking for. He opened it and, instead of passing it across the desk for Gina to inspect on her own, began to read from its contents.

"The victim was a white male believed to be in his early- to mid-twenties." He peered over the desk at her again. "The full autopsy results aren't back yet, but we should be grateful for the fact there were enough remains recovered for one."

"Not what whoever dumped his body was expecting," Gina noted, again wondering what about this case made it a priority for the White House and the president herself.

Gifford leaned forward in his chair and laid his arms atop the desk. "Why do I get the feeling there's plenty you're not telling me?"

He was a law enforcement ranger assigned to park headquarters at the Ernest F. Coe Visitor Center, one of a half-dozen such rangers assigned to the sprawling Everglades National Park, which covered over a million-and-a-half acres and nearly twenty-five hundred square miles. As a law enforcement ranger, Gifford wore the same uniform as a regular park ranger, only with a nine-millimeter pistol holstered on his belt and a badge pinned to his lapel.

"This isn't my first experience with a dead body turning up," Gifford continued, "just the first time the FBI ever showed up before we even made an ID."

"Then we can assume it's for a good reason," Gina offered, because it was the best she could do. "Meanwhile, the briefing I received stressed the fact that we caught a break, a big one, besides the fact the body was found intact."

"When I heard you were coming, I did some checking," Gifford told her, instead of elaborating on Gina's prompt. "Turns out we've got something in common: we're both Army and we both served in Iraq during the Surge. I was Eighty-second Airborne out of what's called Fort Liberty today. How about you?"

"Corps of Engineers," Gina told him, keeping it simple.

Gifford seemed impressed. "Interesting work."

"Sometimes," she agreed, not bothering to elaborate on how her tour in the Army had morphed into something else altogether.

The Army had offered Gina an opportunity to hone the skills she loved the most and wanted to make a career of. She deployed to Iraq to help rebuild the country as part of the Army Corps of Engineers. And she excelled to the point that when a Special Forces A Team demolitions specialist rotated out, she was assigned to the team on a temporary basis, effectively to blow up bridges and roads instead of building them, for what turned into six months.

"Look, Ranger, if you don't mind . . ." Her tone had become terse, impatient, stoked by memories of an experience that left her unsettled to this day.

Gifford looked perturbed by her appearing to exert her authority over him. "Sure, no problem. Where were we?"

"Discussing the break we caught."

"Right. I mentioned that this wasn't the first set of remains I ventured into the Everglades to retrieve. But it was the first time those remains were pretty much whole."

Gina didn't bother to ask Gifford to explain the "pretty much" part.

"The gators and crocs, not to mention the lesser waterborne predators, normally don't leave much of a corpse behind. The Everglades isn't a very forgiving place."

"What about the snakes?"

"Since the big ones swallow their prey whole, it's hard to know for sure how many disappearances end up in their digestive tract. The point is this time we got lucky because the body must have drifted in the storm we had a few days back, the kind that sends the gators and crocs burrowing for safety. The overflow must've pushed it up into a hardwood hammock where it got snared in some bramble thick enough to keep it from washing back out."

"Hardwood hammock," Gina repeated.

"Little known to anyone outside these parts, Agent. Like a tropical oasis amid all the beautiful muck that defines the Everglades. The hardwoods are broad-leaved trees that grow well here. If you were to look straight up, you might have trouble seeing the sun and sky because of all the trees growing so close together. Their branches and leaves crisscross so much they create a canopy, or cover, above your head. That's where we found the body. It was pretty chewed up, thanks to the smaller predators, but there were enough fingers left to lift prints."

"Get a match?"

"Unfortunately, no, and there was no wallet on his person to make our job easier."

The lack of a wallet, or any other personal items, found with the remains suggested they had been removed before the victim's body had been dumped. The fact that this was almost certainly a murder explained why the FBI would be called in, since Everglades National Park was federal property, though not why she was dispatched here by the White House.

She remained silent, waiting for Gifford to resume.

"But the biggest break we caught," he said finally, "was that the victim still had his shoes on and nothing munched on them. So when they were removed, we found this."

Gifford held up a sealed plastic evidence bag that held a rectangular plastic object inside:

A hotel key card.

> < ⊷ ○ ⊷ >

CHAPTER 4

SHELDON JACKSON MUSEUM, SITKA, ALASKA

Sheldon Jackson started collecting and purchasing artifacts from the indigenous people in the late 1870s.

"If you don't mind moving along, sir."

Michael nodded apologetically to the guide leading the tour that had reached the Sheldon Jackson Museum, where fifty historic artifacts had been stolen over the past three years. He fully expected the next item on that list to end up in the roomy leather bag currently hanging from Olivia Morgan's right shoulder.

The guide leading the tour had met them on the dock where the sixty passengers who'd signed up had crowded aboard a tour bus. Michael maintained a discreet distance from his quarries but was careful not to lose sight of them at any point just in case the transfer of goods actually took place outside the museum. He grew suspicious of the fact that the Morgans' twin teen boys slid off on their own on a few occasions during the stops the bus made throughout the historical park itself, the guide never missing a beat with his well-rehearsed narration stating the significance of whatever it was they were seeing.

The last stop prior to reaching the museum had been on the grounds of the fort the Native Tlingit tribe had built to help withstand the onslaught of Russians, mostly fur traders, onto their ancestral lands. Built near the mouth of the Indian River, and confirmed to be the location in 2021, the fort must have once made for an imposing sight. That didn't stop the Russians from overrunning it and forcing the vanquished Tlingits to flee in the culmination of 1804's Battle of Sitka. The Tlingits of today were very much the same underdogs as their ancestors, only these days their battle was against the government in general and the Park Service specifically.

Michael knew that was especially true of the Park Service thanks to its claiming much of their ancestral land as part of Glacier Bay National Park. The only way the tribe could fish the waters they'd accessed for centuries was to get a permit. That led the Tlingits to withdraw even more, growing more insular and militant, while proving extremely hostile to anyone who ventured or strayed onto their land.

The museum on this tour was not actually maintained by the Park Service, but contained nearly 250,000 items in its inventory, and most were culled from the personal collection of the museum's founder and namesake, Sheldon Jackson. Highlights of the collection include totem poles, Chilkat weaving, Tlingit oral history recordings, raven masks, nineteenth-century Russian furniture, Russian Orthodox icons and vestments, and over a thousand original glass plate negatives by Sitka photographer E. W. Merrill.

The extensive inventory the museum maintained meant that almost all fifty items from its extensive collection of artifacts had vanished before the facility realized it was being victimized. Of the missing items, around half possessed great historical value to the Tlingits, further exacerbating the friction between the tribe and the Park Service to the point where the tribe had hired a lawyer to force all of their previously donated possessions to be returned.

Michael fell in with the group behind the Morgans, discreetly passing through the main entrance of a building that looked like an old elementary school. It was the oldest museum in Alaska as well as the state's oldest concrete building. It didn't look that big from the outside, but the interior turned out to be far more spacious than he'd been expecting, crowded with various exhibits of Native life going back centuries that were neatly housed behind a combination of glass counters and standing glass display cases.

It would have been easy to let himself get distracted by the living history before him, but Michael kept his focus on the Morgans, especially Olivia, waiting to see at what point the artifact they'd come here to collect ended up in her shoulder bag. He didn't expect for one minute that Steve, Olivia, or one of their sons would simply open up one of the displays and lift an item from inside. There had to be a methodology to the practice, a tried-and-true procedure behind the rash of thefts.

He wasn't sure what he was looking for, because any number of means could be utilized for the transfer. The most obvious, and easiest to track, would be a museum or tour guide, even a ranger, passing the pilfered item to the courier in question—the Morgans, in this case.

Again, their teen boys wandered away from them and Michael wondered if this might be meant as a distraction in case anyone was watching the couple. Or, perhaps, the boys were actually involved in the theft. Who would suspect kids of being the conduit between the source of the theft and their courier parents? That would explain why the kids had accompanied the Morgans on all their cruises up here, not just to provide obvious cover, but also as participants. Who knows, maybe the proceeds from this were intended to pay for their college educations? At this point, given the gravity and endurance of the ring at large along the Alaskan coastline, nothing would surprise Michael.

He lost sight of Olivia Morgan somehow when the flow of the group reached an L-shaped break in the museum's floor plan just before a glass display case full of ornamental Tlingit masks. She was nowhere to be found and an anxious Michael felt his heart begin to pound, concerned that the Morgans were somehow onto him. Then Olivia Morgan reappeared, coming across the floor from the left where her husband and sons were camped in front of a counter display of Tlingit knives and spears.

Once she rejoined the rest of the family there, Michael noticed the distinct bulge in her shoulder bag, something pressing out from the bag's contours that clearly had not been there before. Michael couldn't tell its precise size or shape from this distance or angle. He cast his gaze in the direction from which Olivia Morgan had come and spotted a small alcove with an embroidered sign that read RESTROOMS above it.

So that was the methodology at work here . . .

At least today, and likely on plenty of other occasions, someone on the inside had planted the artifact in either the men's room or, in this case, the ladies' room. Maybe hidden in the refuse of the trash can or in some kind of crawl space or beneath a floorboard. There would be time to figure all that out later. For now, Michael finally had one of the perpetrators dead to rights, perpetrators who'd have to talk and give up the whole process behind this or orphan their children while they were in prison. He felt the buzz of excitement, needing only to continue keeping eyes on the Morgans the whole way back to the *Eurodam*. He wasn't sure from that point whether they would bring the stolen artifact off the ship in their luggage or, more likely, pass it to a crew member to facilitate off-loading it when they returned to Seattle. And, at the end of that criminal chain, there was very likely a wealthy collector.

Michael was jostled by a man taller and broader than he was pushing his way forward. He got a cursory look at the man, enough to tell Michael the man hadn't been a passenger on the bus and he didn't recall ever seeing him aboard the *Eurodam* either. He seemed to be moving straight for the Morgans, who were still in front of the display of Tlingit weapons.

Something flashed in the big man's hand.

Michael saw him raising a semiautomatic pistol with a squat silencer attached and was in motion before he could even form his next thought.

The pistol was still coming up, even with Steve Morgan's head when . . . *Pffffft* . . . *Pffffft* . . .

Two shots. It looked like Olivia and Steve Morgan had the floor pulled out from under them. They crumpled like puppets released from their strings.

Michael dropped low to draw his own pistol from his ankle holster, the panicked flow of fleeing tour patrons already starting to storm past him. He was vaguely conscious of the big man stripping the leather bag now containing the latest stolen Tlingit artifact from Olivia Morgan's shoulder, then rising and resteadying his pistol on the nearest of the Morgans' sons.

Michael somehow recorded the icy emptiness of the man's stare, as he steadied his own SIG Sauer, hesitating when he was jostled by a fleeing bystander. Michael wasn't the greatest of shots under the best of conditions, much less with bodies rushing at him from all directions. He didn't dare fire, opting for the next best thing instead by throwing his shoulder into the first in a neat row of standing glass display cases. It toppled sideways and then, like dominoes, all the others followed, crashing to the floor in a successive torrent of noise and flying glass.

Impact knocked the big man off his feet just as he was about to fire. Michael's gaze froze on the Morgans' teen boys now kneeling dazed over their parents' bodies, as he burst into motion. As far as he could tell, impact from the cascading display cases had pinned the big man with debris while the Morgan boys remained frozen, thin shards of glass shining atop their hair. Instead of slowing to aim and fire his pistol, Michael sped up, jammed the pistol in his waistband, and scooped the boys up in either arm, just as the big man was pushing the debris off him.

He dropped down with the boys behind the cover of a heavy wooden display partition and felt it hammered almost immediately by the big man's gunfire. He could feel the percussion of the impacts with his head pressed against the half-wall, cradling the boys before him to further shield them with his frame. He had his SIG Sauer palmed again in the next instant, peeking out and firing blindly toward where he expected the big man to be.

Instead, he glimpsed the blur of his shape charging outside through the now abandoned museum with the strap of Olivia Morgan's shoulder bag clutched in his grasp.

"Are you okay?" Michael said to the boys. "Are you hit?"

They looked at him blankly, shaking horribly, both in shock.

He could tell they weren't bleeding, knew the best thing he could do for them right now was catch the man who had killed their parents.

A pair of shots rang out, echoing from somewhere ahead of him as he ran through the museum in the big man's wake. A third shot reverberated through the air, coming from outside the building, Michael realized.

He burst through the entrance to find a park ranger from the Sitka National Historical Park feeling the tour guide's neck for a pulse. He had just started administering chest compressions when Michael noted the blood staining the left side of his uniform where a bullet must have grazed him.

"Which way!" Michael demanded. "Which way did he go?"

The ranger pointed breathlessly toward a trail that broke toward the deepest woods of the park.

Michael looked back down at the tour guide. "There are two boys inside who need help. They weren't hit but their parents were murdered."

The ranger nodded grimly, and Michael raced off onto a trail that sliced through the nearby woods.

CHAPTER 5

‣-•-◦-•-‣

EVERGLADES NATIONAL PARK, FLORIDA

Over half of the Everglades ecosystem has vanished in
the last two hundred years.

"Please step back from the door as soon as you use the key card," Gina told the hotel manager. "And don't follow us inside."

Even though they had the room's actual key card, the manager needed to use his electronic master to preserve chain of evidence. Of course, since this investigation had been assigned to her directly by the White House, she wasn't sure what protocol exactly she needed to follow.

The door clicked open. Gina and Law Enforcement Park Ranger Clark Gifford slid past the manager into the room.

‡‡‡

It hadn't taken a trained investigator to figure out the origins of the key card, since it was imprinted with the logo of the Tru chain by Hilton, and there was only one of those in close proximity to where the young man's body was found amid the reeds and bramble of the swampy lowlands of the Everglades.

Gina accompanied Gifford on the roughly fifteen-minute drive to the hotel on Florida City's North Krome Avenue in his ranger-issue white SUV, with a green stripe and the National Park Service logo on each door.

"Windows or AC?" he asked respectfully, as soon as they set out from the park's ranger headquarters next to the Ernest F. Coe Visitor Center.

Gina grinned. "I'm from the north and didn't bring an extra shirt, so AC all the way."

Gifford smiled back. "I'm from the south and have two extra shirts in the back, but I'm AC all the way, too."

Gina used the drive time to email an update to the chief of staff's office. The White House's involvement was enough to tell Gina they didn't want the investigation to be handled by the book by regular detectives, agents, or even law enforcement park rangers. When she had accepted the president's personal offer to be a roving FBI agent without portfolio, a posting, or a partner, she'd never considered a case proceeding minus the protocols that accompanied every investigation she'd ever been involved in during her dozen years with the Bureau, starting with reporting her findings directly, and only, to Chief of Staff Daniel Grant.

After arriving at the hotel, Gifford had grabbed his green ranger jacket from the back seat and slung his arms through the sleeves in spite of the heat. She thought maybe it was part of the particular protocol of the Park Service's law enforcement arm. Or it could have been to cover up his pistol, since hers was concealed by the tight-cut blazer she'd left on through the duration of the drive, thanks to the cool blast coming from the air-conditioning vents.

Gina followed him through the door and let him lead the way to the front desk and identify both of them to the clerk, before requesting to see the manager.

"How can I help you?" the manager, whose name tag read JARED MAN-HEIM, greeted, eyes flitting between two of them as if to assess the odd-looking partnership.

Gina and Gifford both flashed their ID badges and Manheim stopped assessing.

"This was found on a body that washed up in the Everglades," Gifford said, producing the plastic evidence bag containing the Tru by Hilton key card. "He wasn't carrying an ID on him, so we need to know who he is and see the room in which he was staying."

Gina gnashed her teeth over Gifford having provided more information than he'd needed to. The manager looked toward her, as if to get her consent. Clearly, an FBI agent carried more weight than a park ranger, law enforcement or otherwise. She nodded just once, so as not to appear she was superseding her de facto partner.

"The card's going to have to come out of that baggie, so I can pull the information you need."

Gina pulled a pair of plastic evidence gloves from her pocket. "Please put these on before handling it and I'm going to need to record everything you do in order to preserve our chain of evidence."

Manheim nodded as if he understood. She was about to ready her phone to record him handling the evidence for the record, when she spotted Gifford positioning himself with phone already in hand. She nodded his way, impressed by his initiative and knowledge of crime scene procedures. She changed her assessment of him; he might not have done his law enforcement training at Quantico, but he clearly knew how to investigate a case, even a murder.

"Your victim was staying in room four-sixteen," Manheim said, consulting the computer screen after plugging the key card into a slot with a gloved hand. "He'd been with us for just under six weeks and his stay was open-ended."

"Is that unusual?" Gina asked, no longer content to leave the floor to Gifford.

"Somewhat, but not entirely. We get a lot of young people down here to study the Everglades, work on this project or that, sometimes serve as an intern for one of the scientific study groups based in the area. The Tru is normally one of the hotels recommended to them."

Gina and Gifford both waited for the manager to continue on his own.

"The young man's name is, or was, James Bidwell, but he signed in as Jamie. Age twenty-six, from Bethesda, Maryland, according to his registration. We have a picture of his driver's license on file, if you'd like it."

"We would," Gina told him.

"Be just a moment . . ."

Manheim pressed a few buttons on a keyboard, then fished a single sheet of paper from a nearby printer.

"Here you go."

Gina regarded the license quickly and then handed the page to Gifford. Jamie Bidwell of Bethesda, Maryland, looked younger than his twenty-six years. He had long brown hair that looked like something you'd see on a nightclub stage. His eyes were listed as blue, his height as five-foot-ten, and weight as one hundred and seventy pounds. Gina wondered how much of that hundred and seventy pounds remained after at least some of the wildlife that called the Everglades home had had their way with him.

"We'd like to see his room now," Gina told Manheim.

‡‡‡

The Tru's exterior had a faux art deco feel to it, both in color and a design in which the hotel's black façade extended above and beyond the sides of the actual structure. This single room with a king bed played off that motif, boasting the same blue hues mixed with a mauve color. It was pretty much like every other hotel room Gina had seen, except for the spacious windows currently covered by the drawn curtains. The bed was neatly made, making her think that the room hadn't been touched since the maid had last cleaned it. She made a mental note to ask the manager for the housekeeping schedule, figuring she and Gifford would need to interview whoever was responsible for this room. Though time of death wouldn't be firmly established until they got the results of the autopsy, the condition of the body suggested Jamie Bidwell had been dead for less than twenty-four hours when his body was found. That meant that in all probability he'd last been inside this room two, but more likely three, days back.

Still wearing evidence gloves, Gina's initial sweep of the room left her with the distinct feeling that someone had been here before she and Gifford. There was nothing concrete to suggest that off the bat, except for those closed curtains. Upon closer inspection, Gina saw they'd been drawn over the sheers.

"Mr. Manheim," she called to the manager, "could you come inside here, please?"

Manheim entered the room in stiff and tentative fashion.

"A question for you," Gina said to him. "Would your housekeeping staff have drawn the curtains and the sheers?"

Manheim noticed the potential anomaly for himself. "Er, no. Ordinarily, unless otherwise instructed, they would draw only the sheers to let the light in but keep most of the heat out."

"And when was the last time this room would have been serviced?"

"I'd have to check at the desk, but I believe Mr. Bidwell requested maid service every other day."

In Gina's mind, that meant the room had likely been serviced yesterday. Then, sometime between the time the maid had left and now, someone else had searched the room, closing the curtains to hide their work from any curious eyes beyond. Totally unnecessary, unless you were taking extra precautions to avoid being spotted. As soon as she and Gifford were finished here, Gina would arrange to have the room dusted for prints through the FBI's Miami field office, though she wasn't expecting that process to yield anything, given that professionals appeared to be responsible. Then her eyes strayed to the cords that drew the curtains back and forth. She'd heard of more than one case where a criminal had taken every precaution imaginable, only to leave his prints on something mundane like that and she made another mental note to inform the Miami field office to make sure to dust those cords.

"Why don't you check?" Gina said to Manheim. "And could you also please see if the maid who last serviced this room is currently on the premises? We'd like to speak with her."

"Of course. Anything else right now?" he asked subserviently.

"Just the fact that you're going to have to take this room offline for a stretch, because it's officially a crime scene."

"Hey," Manheim said, trying for a smile that didn't quite flash, "the kid's on an open-ended stay. That means we keep getting paid until he checks out."

"I think you can consider him checked out, Mr. Manheim."

When he was gone, Gina and Gifford set about conducting a careful search of the room. As she began her efforts by wading through the drawers containing the victim's clothes, Gina was struck as usual by the sense she was violating someone's privacy. Also as usual, she had to keep reminding herself it was for his own good and necessary to bring his killer to justice. Still, the thin supply of fresh clothes indeed suggested a shorter stay than the six weeks Jamie Bidwell had already been here. She made another mental note to check laundry records to see if the victim was having his clothes cleaned, which would explain the relative emptiness of his drawers. And there were several gaps in the drawers that indicated clothes he'd brought with him were missing.

Next, Gina moved to the closet where she found a selection of casual slacks and jeans, along with a couple of light jackets and a zippered hoodie. The shelf held an additional pillow and blanket, along with a steam iron. The accompanying board was attached to a bracket on one of the closet walls. She stepped back and looked at the closet from a different perspective, struck by the sense she was missing something, but nothing stood out from that viewpoint either.

Gina trusted Gifford's skills enough to let him search the area of the bed, the window, the desk, and the in-room refrigerator, while she focused on the bathroom, closet, and drawers.

"We've got an open bottle of water in here, half full," Gifford reported from eight feet away. "Five more unopened and still held together in the plastic."

That meant they had an object they'd likely be able to lift fresh prints off of, compared to the rest of the room where Bidwell's fingerprints would have been dusted or cleaned off by the maid. It was one thing to know who someone claimed to be, sometimes quite another to see who they really were once their fingerprints were run through the national database.

"Let's bag it," Gina said to Gifford, and proceeded to watch him do so as professionally as she would have.

The rest of the room yielded nothing of substance, including both small trash receptacles. Gina knew they'd be empty because of the housekeeping service, but wondered if there was any possibility the trash from this room might still be salvageable. She sincerely doubted it, but it was definitely another question to pose to the hotel manager Manheim.

The more she probed through the room, the more she became convinced that someone else had been there before her. She couldn't say exactly what led her to that conclusion, beyond those drawn curtains, but she couldn't shake it.

As soon as she was done, Gina conducted a second sweep of the room, this time with a different agenda. The fact that the room contained no personal items whatsoever, including something as innocuous as loose change or a pack of gum, strongly suggested that Bidwell had been grabbed somewhere outside the hotel. That or whoever had swept the room ahead of her and Gifford had taken anything that even qualified as innocuous with them. Maybe both.

When she completed her second sweep, Gina moved on to the bathroom. The young man didn't have much beyond a toothbrush, toothpaste, shaving cream, a disposable razor, and deodorant. She checked the shower for the first time and saw a bar of soap in a slot carved to accommodate it and a pair of unopened hotel-sized shampoo and conditioner plastic bottles.

Again, nothing.

There was a hair dryer under the sink with the cord still wrapped in place, either left that way by the maid or indicative of the fact that Bidwell hadn't been using it on his wavy, shoulder-length hair. There were two extra rolls of toilet paper and a small box of tissues sized for the wooden receptacle on the vanity. Gina then eased the door inward and saw a pair of gym shorts hanging from the hook, musing that Bidwell had perhaps neglected to include them the last time he bagged up his laundry.

The thought brought her back to the closet, having realized what she had missed the first time.

CHAPTER 6

SITKA, ALASKA

The city was ruled by the Russians from 1799 to 1867.

Michael's prosthetic foot wasn't designed for anything beyond a short burst or steady jog as opposed to an all-out run. He could feel his leg straining under the effort, saved only by the flat nature of this trail that cut like a ribbon through the evergreen and spruce trees that dominated Sitka's natural landscape.

Michael spotted the big man putting more distance between them before the trail banked sharply to the left a hundred or so yards in front of him, no idea whether he knew Michael was in pursuit. He had to slow his pace to avoid snapping the housing on his prosthetic.

His mind had cleared, now processing what had just occurred. A killer who was clearly a pro had murdered the couple responsible for stealing artifacts, which he had then stolen from them. It made no sense. Or, alternatively, the sense lay in something Michael and everyone else had been missing here. He needed to catch up with the big man to have any hope of finding out what that might be, though catching up with him promised to be only the first challenge given the man's superior size and skill level. Michael's presence inside the museum must have surprised the big man almost as much as the reverse. Whatever was happening now was clearly not according to whatever the plan had been.

The big man had been ready to shoot the kids, too. . . .

Why? It could only be because he thought they might be in league with their parents, loose ends as far as the theft of the artifacts went. But what sense did that make?

Michael continued on at a jogger's pace, clinging to the edge of the trail to make himself less of a target and be closer to the thick brush of the forest rim to dive into if the big man doubled back and reappeared before him. He reached the break in the trail, where the big man had swung down an equally level path. He heard rushing water and spotted the contours of a normally placid river now raging with overflow from a combination of heavy spring rains and snowmelt. A shot rang out, chipping the bark from a tree just over his head, and Michael spotted the big man just short of a wooden bridge that spanned the river to the other side.

Michael burst back into a near sprint, reaching the nearest end of the bridge just as the big man leaped off it on the other side and veered right. On the other side of the bridge, he spotted a sign that read DANGER! TRAIL CLOSED DUE TO STORM AND WIND DAMAGE! That hadn't stopped the big man, and it didn't stop Michael either.

A hundred feet in, the debris strewn across the trail began to thicken. Toppled trees, broken branches, and scattered brush were everywhere in his path, forcing Michael to slow his pace yet again, this time to avoid a fall that would end his desperate chase here and now. It was like negotiating an obstacle course.

In addition to the awkwardly laid obstacles, the trail ground was littered with depressions from falling rocks. It made for a treacherous slog the big man had somehow managed without breaking stride.

Michael panted, heaving for breath while nonetheless pushing himself on, motivated by the frozen memory of the big man having been about to shoot two thirteen-year-old boys. The trail thickened more with debris the farther he drew along it, becoming as much a maze as an obstacle course. He followed it as the trail banked to the right, down a relatively clear stretch, and ground his shoes to a halt, jostling his prosthetic.

Because the big man had frozen seventy feet before him, and as Michael's vision tightened, he saw why: a brown bear was lumbering across the trail about ten yards in front of him. He was paying the big man no heed at all, but remained an imposing sight certain to freeze any man nonetheless. Michael could see Olivia Morgan's leather bag was now slung from the big man's left shoulder, his right hand still clutching the silenced pistol.

Michael stepped all the way out into the center of the trail and steadied his SIG Sauer in both hands, about to shout out something when the big man suddenly swung around, pistol sweeping with him. Michael started firing and didn't stop until the SIG's slide had locked in place. He thought the big man might have gotten off a shot, maybe two, before he caught bursts of red mist staining the air. Four, he thought, at least three, all torso and chest hits. The big man dropped to his knees, then shed the pistol he was still holding before keeling over to the ground on his right side.

Michael jogged toward him, pistol held at the ready just in case. But the big man wasn't moving and, as Michael drew closer, he saw his eyes were locked open and sightless. Still, he kicked the silenced pistol farther aside and stooped to unsling the leather bag from the killer's shoulder.

He unzipped it to find the only contents, aside from a few sundry items, to be a weather-beaten urn that reminded him of the kind a deceased person's ashes were stored in. He recalled a Tlingit tradition of burning the departed to ease their passage into the afterlife. But he'd never heard of Tlingit ashes being stored this way.

He could feel something shifting about inside the urn when he removed it from the bag. Not believing the museum would display one with human remains still inside it, he turned the top gently until it came free. He moved the urn into a shaft of light streaming down through a break in the canopy of evergreen trees overhead to better view what was inside.

"What the . . ."

He nearly dropped the urn when the cell phone vibrating in his pocket startled him, shocking him back to reality. He eased it out in a trembling hand to see **ANGELA PIERCE** lit up in the caller ID.

"Boss," he greeted, his voice dry and scratchy.

"Michael, what's going on? I've got reports of a shooting in the museum. A local ranger ID'd a man matching your description chasing the killer. What the hell happened?"

"I, er, I, I . . ."

He couldn't find any words and took a few deep breaths, finally composing himself.

"I killed him."

"Who?"

"The gunman. I chased him into the woods. I didn't have a choice. He fired first."

"Are you okay, Michael? Tell me you're okay."

He looked over at the man he had killed. "I'm fine. A little shaken, but fine."

"Okay. Catch your breath. Get yourself settled. I want you to stay exactly where you are, with the body. Can you do that?"

"Yes," Michael managed, gazing at the contents of the urn and wondering how to explain what he was seeing to Angela. "But there's something else I need to tell you."

"Tell the reinforcements from the Alaska Bureau of Investigation who are en route," she informed him, when his voice trailed off again. "Wait until they arrive to secure the scene of the shooting and then head back to the museum. An emergency has come up and I need you someplace else in Alaska. But only if you're up to it. That's your call and nobody else's."

"Yes, I'm up to it," Michael said. "Where's this emergency?"

"Glacier Bay National Park, Michael. A U.S. Geological Survey team up there has disappeared."

CHAPTER 7

EVERGLADES NATIONAL PARK, FLORIDA

The area provides drinking water for over 8 million residents of South Florida, courtesy of the Biscayne Aquifer.

Not one anomaly, but two . . .

In addition to a dearth of clothing, the standard room-issue laundry bag was missing from the closet. For Gina, that confirmed Jamie Bidwell had indeed filled the missing bag and brought it down to the front desk, or had it picked up, to be laundered. Since he'd been here for nearly six weeks, it was more than possible Bidwell had made use of the hotel's paid laundry service several times.

Gina and Gifford found Manheim dutifully still in the hallway when they finally left the room.

"We won't strip crime scene tape across the door, so long as you take this room offline," Gifford told him.

"FBI crime scene techs will be here tomorrow to do a more thorough inspection," Gina added.

Manheim nodded.

"Two other things, Mr. Manheim," she continued. "We'd like you to run the log of every time the door was opened in the past week. Can you do that?"

"Yes. The system may only go back seven days. Will that be good enough?"

"It should, yes. Also, we think James Bidwell may have sent some clothes down to be laundered. Can you check on that for us?"

"For sure. Any idea of the time frame?"

"Start with the day before yesterday," Gina instructed, based on the timeline she'd already roughly established. "Any chance the clothes haven't been cleaned yet?"

"We send all our laundry out and, since yesterday was Sunday, it's possible, yes. Let's head back downstairs to the front desk. I can handle both these tasks best from there."

‡‡‡

Gina laid the room entry log on the front desk counter so she and Gifford could read it together, while Manheim was on the phone with someone to determine whether their murder victim had sent down clothes to be cleaned. The log listings for which housekeeping service was responsible were denoted by a bolded *H*.

"You seeing what I'm seeing?" Gifford noted.

Gina pointed to the second to last entry, theirs being the last according to the time stamp. The room had been entered yesterday evening at eight o'clock, after Jamie Bidwell's body had already been discovered in the Everglades.

Manheim hung up the phone and looked across the counter. "You were right about the laundry bag," he told Gina. "It was logged into the system Saturday and should still be on the premises. They're going to call me back once they confirm that."

"How many key cards did you make for the guest in question?" she asked Manheim.

Manheim moved behind the computer monitor and punched in a few keys.

"One," he responded.

Since that key had been recovered inside the corpse's shoe, whoever had searched the room last night had used another means to get inside. Only professionals wouldn't let such technological inconveniences deter them, which was starting to suggest to Gina why this investigation had been assigned to her. Not only did that suggest the White House knew more than Grant was saying, it also strongly confirmed they wanted to keep the loop as small as possible.

What is it they're not telling me?

"Can you bring up the security footage for the elevators and the fourth-floor hallway from yesterday evening starting at seven-fifty?" Gina asked Manheim, figuring a ten-minute window was more than enough to determine who had accessed the room.

She watched him work the computer again. He stopped briefly, then seemed to repeat the same process. Manheim's brow furrowed and his eyes narrowed to little more than slits, clearly not liking what he was seeing.

Or not seeing, as it turned out.

"I don't know what to make of this," he said, shaking his head. "The footage is recorded in three-hour loops, kept for seven days, and then automatically deleted. For yesterday evening, the five to eight P.M. and eight to eleven P.M. loops are missing. The footage is gone."

Gina was dismayed, but not surprised. "Deleted?"

"Or a system malfunction."

"And how often do such malfunctions occur?"

"In the four years I've managed this place, twice—both because of power failures caused by weather events—you know, hurricanes."

Which had obviously not been the case last night. Gina figured the system must have been hacked from the outside, not a hard task for the kind of professionals it was clear were involved here. Before she could press Manheim on the issue further, the phone by his side buzzed and he drew the receiver to his ear.

"We got lucky," Manheim said, holding the phone against his shoulder. "The bag with this guest's laundry got misshelved after it was dropped off on Friday and hasn't been picked up yet."

"Can you have it brought up here?" Gina requested. "And remind them not to open it or touch any of the contents."

Manheim nodded and relayed those instructions to whoever was on the other end of the line.

Five minutes later, a man wearing a hotel maintenance uniform appeared carrying the laundry bag in question. It was overstuffed and Gina spotted what looked like the drawstring for a pair of lounge pants protruding from a small gap in the knot keeping it closed.

They adjourned to Manheim's private back office to inspect the contents. Gina donned a fresh pair of evidence gloves and used the desktop to slide out James Bidwell's laundry one piece at a time. A pair of jeans, the bulkiest item of all, was the last item she pulled out, added to the collection of socks, underwear, a few shirts, and workout clothes that smelled of stale sweat. The jeans stuck for a moment, as if something had snagged on the bag's interior.

"Holy shit," said Gifford, spotting the same thing Gina did hanging from a rear pocket when the jeans finally emerged.

CHAPTER 8

ICY STRAIT, ALASKA

The Cape Spencer Light, a lighthouse next to Cross
Sound and Icy Strait, was constructed in 1925.

The nearest naval station to Icy Strait, Naval Base Kitsap, was located nearly a thousand miles away outside of Seattle, Washington. Kitsap served as host command for the Navy's fleet throughout the Pacific Northwest and was also home to the Puget Sound Naval Shipyard.

As soon as the *Providence*'s distress signal reached naval command via the SLOT buoy, a fleet of ships were appropriately loaded and dispatched to deal with the crisis. Since it would take upward of twenty hours for those ships to reach the site, the Coast Guard scrambled cutters out of Ketchikan, Sitka, and Juneau Stations, as well as choppers out of Air Station Sitka to provide a real-time view of the scene.

Admiral Ben Mosely happened to be on board the *Reef Shark,* the first cutter to arrive on the scene. The commercial salvage ship *Salvor* had remained on station to fulfill the proper protocol at sea. Mosely was previously acquainted with the ship's commander, Barbara Larson, and knew she would have stayed there even if protocol hadn't dictated it.

"Why didn't she show up on our screens?" she asked Mosely, when they made contact over the radio while the *Reef Shark* steamed toward the scene.

"Need to know, Commander. Loose lips and the like."

"Well, loose lips didn't sink this sub—a World War Two mine did, on my orders."

"This wasn't your fault, none of it," Mosely assured her. "My orders are to establish contact as soon as the *Reef Shark* reaches the coordinates, not hang you from a mast."

"Can't miss it, sir. Just look for a salvage ship with an embarrassed captain at the helm."

"Aye-aye, Commander."

Ten minutes later and nearly two hours after getting the call from Kitsap, the *Reef Shark* came to a stop close enough to the *Salvor* for Mosely to see Barbara Larson standing on deck with a pair of binoculars pressed to her eyes. She lowered them and saluted, and Mosely saluted her back from the bridge.

Since the fleet of ships steaming north from Naval Base Kitsap were still more than half a day away, naval command took the extraordinary step of giving the Coast Guard operational command of what was fast showing signs of becoming one of the worst naval disasters in history. Part of that might have been due to the presence of Admiral Mosely, and his requisite security clearance, on the scene, but the rest was the desperation arising from what was clearly an unprecedented situation.

Naval Admiral Jock Wendall, head of operational command for the Navy's fleet of attack submarines that included the Virginia-class, hailed him personally on the bridge of the *Reef Shark*.

"Am I on speaker, Admiral?"

Mosely nodded to the young ensign manning communications. "Not anymore. Headset only."

"Two things you need know, Ben. The first is that there's been a change of plans. The convoy out of Kitsap has been slowed by a storm, so we're air-lifting an SRDRS and crew to the scene. The second is I need you to remain on station and, right now, get to a secure location where nobody can hear your end of the conversation. We're entering uncharted territory."

"Roger that, sir. But we're already there."

‡‡‡

The *Reef Shark* was part of the Heritage-class of Coast Guard cutter, the latest and most advanced ship the Coast Guard had ever sailed. Longer than a football field, it was also the biggest and best armed, outfitted for a modern fleet charged with major drug interdiction operations at sea and for joint missions with the Navy in American territorial waters. That said, there were extraordinarily few true areas of secure privacy on board, so Mosely adjourned to his quarters, contacting the bridge on the fully-functional com gear built into the wall.

While making the fast walk there, Mosely reviewed what he knew about the Navy's state-of-the-art Submarine Rescue Diving and Recompression System that had replaced the now retired, last generation DSRVs. Since that wasn't much, he figured being ordered to his quarters to speak to Admiral Wendall where no one else could hear them must have involved something else entirely.

Mosely fit his headset into place.

"Get Admiral Wendall back on the line and transfer it to my quarters via a secure frequency," he ordered the young ensign.

"Aye, Captain. You'll hear a buzz when he's on."

The buzz came fifteen seconds later.

"We're lucky you're on board, Admiral Mosely. Not sure I could do what I'm about to do with a junior officer. The first thing you need to know is that the *Providence* was supposed to launch a SLOT buoy every hour on the hour with an update on her status."

"I understand, sir."

"Good, because the second thing you need to know is that after the first three status updates were received without a glitch, there's been no contact for the past four reporting cycles. In other words, Admiral, she's gone dark."

The admiral stopped purposefully to let that statement sink in. Mosely felt cold and clammy all of a sudden.

"We did catch a pair of major breaks in this regard," Admiral Wendall resumed. "The first is that an officer of your reputation and experience is on station. The second is the fact that the *Reef Shark* is part of the new Heritage-class of Coast Guard cutter. That means your com system is compatible with the *Providence*'s."

Mosely nodded to himself, aware that had been a purposeful design addition to further enable joint missions at sea between naval and Coast Guard forces.

"You have the standard ship-issue Dell laptop in your quarters, I assume."

"I do, sir, yes."

"Fire it up. I'm going to direct you to a secure Department of Defense site and provide you a code to access it. Are we clear, Admiral?"

Mosely had already switched on his laptop. "We are, sir."

"Tell me when you're booted up and ready to go."

"Ready now, sir," Mosely said, as his home screen appeared and he jogged it to his military browser.

"Here's the site . . ."

Mosely went to it. "I'm there."

"And the access code . . ."

Mosely entered it. "I'm in. It's asking for a secure designation."

"Our next step. The designation I'm about to give you will take you inside the *Providence*'s system. The system automatically engages in the event of an emergency, like a reactor SCRAM, but can be remotely accessed only by a rescue team once on station. Given the circumstances, we no longer feel we can wait that long. Now, fingers on the keyboard, Admiral. Enter the characters as I give them to you."

There were thirteen in all, a strange choice, Mosely thought.

"Done, sir."

"When you press enter, you're going to access the *Providence*'s onboard cameras that cover a great portion of the ship's most vital areas. They were designed and installed to provide Operations with real-time situational command and control in the event of an emergency. Enough said. When you press enter, you'll see a long menu of choices listed both numerically and alphabetically."

"I'm there, sir."

"Zero-zero-one is the ship's bridge. I want you to enter that and then forget everything you just did."

"Aye, Admiral. Consider it forgotten," Mosely said.

And then he hit entered 0–0–1 on his keyboard, bringing up the camera focusing on the *Providence*'s bridge.

"Tell me what you see, Admiral."

The screen came to life, and Ben Mosely's breath caught in his throat. His heart skipped a beat and for a long moment he literally forgot how to breathe.

"Admiral," Wendall said, his voice cracking, "what do you see?"

Mosely finally found his breath, his voice emerging scratchy and broken. "They're all dead, Admiral. Everyone on the bridge is dead . . ."

CHAPTER 9

⊢•⊷•⊶•⊣

ABACO ISLAND, THE BAHAMAS

The area offshore, known as the Marls, is distinguished
by a three-hundred-square-mile flats fishing paradise
within the bend of Great Abaco, and is one of the most
celebrated spots for bonefishing.

From the raised platform, Axel Cole's guide, Walter, poled the flats boat slowly through the mist-riddled waters, pointing directly ahead.

"Bonefish, mon, lots of 'em, at twelve o'clock," Walter called out. "Look at 'em all! We finally got lucky, mon!"

Cole cast his gaze forward from the bow and caught a dark splotch riding just beneath the surface of the Abaco Bay shallows and cast his line through the air straight ahead. An instant before his lure plopped home, the school of bones seemed to veer right on a dime.

"Bones at ten o'clock, mon, forty feet away," his native Bahamian guide, Walter, said from the perch.

Cole turned to the port side of the boat, made a few back casts, and stepped on his line. The fly fell short, allowing no opportunity for a hookup.

"It's okay, mon. Don't worry yourself. Bones at eight o'clock now, forty feet away. Get 'em, mon, get 'em!"

Cole cast his rod back and forth again, and this time he stepped in between the line and got it wrapped around his legs.

"Careful there, mon, careful. Just be patient. The bones, they be biting!"

He and Walter were alone on the flats boat that featured a unique design, with gunwales a foot off the water and big casting decks, a small center console, and wide platform in the stern. Most flats boats, like this one, boasted poling platforms that were fiberglass boards perched on top of a shiny chrome scaffolding. That vantage point allowed guides to see the fish from a distance, and then steer stealthily in that direction.

Meanwhile, three sleek cabin cruisers motored in easy rhythm a hundred yards behind the flats boat, carrying the security team that had accompanied Cole to the Abaco Island in the Bahamas. They were armed with fully automatic M4 assault rifles, wore body armor, and each boat had a Stinger missile on board in case of an attack from the air.

Cole had a lot of enemies. And although few had the resources to mount such an attack, he was a man prone to taking great risks, but never chances. It was one thing to fly on the maiden voyage of the first of his christened rocket ships, but quite another to venture into the open without being protected. At this stage of his life, just past fifty with three children given him by the woman of his dreams, he had one goal and one goal only: to become the world's first trillionaire, his collective list of companies growing more influential and powerful than all but the world's greatest powers, his worth greater than the GDPs of France and Italy combined. And now, incredibly, he was on the verge of making that happen.

A naturalized American citizen, Cole had been born in Norway under a different name and heritage. His parents had emigrated when he was a young boy to flee that heritage Cole had in recent times come to embrace. It helped him understand his own nature, the importance of being formidable above all else and finding an advantage to exploit over anyone he dealt with. He had read Sun Tzu's *The Art of War* so many times, he'd practically committed it to memory. The less people knew about him beyond the gossip and social media posts, the better. Cole found it far more preferable to be seen as more myth than man. An enigma others judged based on their own perspective of the world.

When you've accomplished everything, it's hard to find where to reach for more. Cole had spent a large portion of the past four years prepping for one of the greatest adventures in the history of mankind: the first manned voyage to Mars.

Much of that period had been dedicated to overseeing construction of a prototype of the actual space vehicle itself, as far advanced beyond the space shuttle as the shuttle was from a model airplane that flew on battery-powered remote control. Unbeknownst to the naysayers and critics who deemed his quest a fool's errand and a pointless vanity project, Cole had discovered his own version of battery power in a fuel source capable of getting a crew all the way to Mars and back. According to his admittedly optimistic timetable, he estimated that civilians would be forking up somewhere in the area of $100 million to make a 300-million-mile trip he similarly estimated would be sixteen months round trip, with an additional one month spent exploring the planet itself. The cruise phase would begin after the spacecraft separated from the rocket carrying it soon after launch, after the spacecraft departed Earth at a speed of about 24,600 mph.

The process and the anticipation had left him an obsessed basket case who could neither slow down nor unwind. That explained why Cole had taken up fly-fishing at the urging of his wife, a hobby that would take him away from boardrooms and the social media he so obsessed over. Especially the posts he made on his own site about anything that popped into his head, expressing especially his intolerance for anything and anyone that went against the core beliefs he'd come to adopt as his personal dogma. Fly-fishing was a way to commune with the great outdoors and get his head in a different space, where he could think of something other than the miraculous fuel source his efforts had uncovered, following a cryptic tip he'd been provided. The fact that there was no way he could know for sure whether such a fuel source even existed proved only a minor impediment. Axel Cole had never let himself be stopped by something deemed impossible. Because the impossible only existed until someone discovered a way to change that.

Which he had.

"Bones at two o'clock, twenty-five feet away. C'mon, mon, cast, cast, cast!"

Axel Cole stood in the bow of the flats boat off the coast of Abaco Island and cast his line into the air, only for it to land short.

"No, mon," Walter said, the patience ebbing from his voice, "you not doing it right there."

Walter's nagging was beginning to plague him. He'd never met the man before this morning but had promised his wife he'd seek a normal, regular fishing experience. As a local Bahamian and likely poorly educated, Walter probably had no idea who Axel Cole was. A man who'd never owned a share of stock in his life and who thought the Dow Jones was a guest at a neighboring lodge, though the three boats with gunmen manning the decks must have given him some idea Cole wasn't an ordinary fisherman. But now Walter was on the verge of ruining his attempt to focus on something other than his everyday obsessions, as he'd promised his wife he would, by annoying him so much the sea didn't feel calming at all.

"Get ready to try again, mon."

Cole recalled the basic lessons a well-paid expert had provided on his last fishing jaunt. You fished from the front of the boat, the bow, while the guide poled and spotted from the stern, calling out targets by location. *Three o'clock* was directional code for off your right shoulder, *nine o'clock* meant off your left shoulder, and *six o'clock* was directly behind you. The communication was supposed to help an angler get into a rhythm. But all Cole was getting today out in the mist-shrouded flats was frustrated.

Abaco was located in the northern Bahamas and was comprised of two main islands, Great Abaco and Little Abaco, which were surrounded by about a dozen smaller islands, the entire area having been a hot spot for serious fishermen for decades. Cole had rented out all eight rooms in the Abaco Lodge to ensure he had enough space to house his security team, some of whom were on duty twenty-four hours a day to guarantee no one outside his party ventured close. As an added feature, he flew in his own private chef for the weekend because that man was the only one who knew the particularities of how Cole liked his food cooked. They wouldn't be eating any bonefish because the lithe, muscular bodies offered little meat and were foul tasting at that. Accordingly, traditional practice when fishing for bones was to release them back into the water, though that made no sense to Cole. For him, the fun of fishing was the catch and the kill, all the better if he could watch his prey die.

Walter poled slowly and pointed out ahead. "Bonefish, lots of 'em, twelve o'clock. Look at 'em all!"

This time, Cole managed a perfect cast. The bonefish, a three-or four-pounder, raced up to the fly and looked at it. Cole held his breath while the fish seemed to contemplate the situation. Then he saw a puff of sand kick up and his fly disappeared.

At long last, he had finally hooked a fish!

Cole pulled hard to set the hook, and in an instant the fish was peeling off line in a mad dash. The rest of the school scattered, with some racing away while others closed in on his fish as if to see what was going on. The line was going out fast, and Cole lurched sideways several times to keep from stepping on it and breaking the fish off.

Walter moved the boat while he reeled in the line. Just as soon as Cole got the line back on the reel, the fish would turn and go racing out again, fighting him every step of the way. Cole liked that; it would make the kill all the sweeter and he'd have this bone mounted fittingly to memorial-ize the battle between man and fish. This bone wasn't tiring very easily and was already into a third long run. Fishermen lived to hear their drags whine and their lines rip through the water, and Cole was certainly getting his money's worth here. He wasn't used to being challenged and yet here was a three- or four-pound creature giving him all he could handle.

"Reel him in, mon, reel him in!" Walter said, cheering him on.

Cole's satellite phone rang and he switched his rod to a single hand to answer it.

"What you doing, what you doing? You going to lose him!"

"I'm busy," Cole greeted the extremely well-paid and loyal employee who headed up what he liked to refer to as the Special Projects Division of Cole Industries.

"We have a problem in Alaska."

With Cole no longer reeling him in, the bone extended the out line farther and farther.

"Talk to me. Fast. I've got a fish on the line."

"The couriers are dead, shot in the museum after making the pickup."

Cole waited for the man to continue, as he started to simmer. That pickup was another in a chain crucial to his becoming a trillionaire.

"Who was the killer? What do we know about him?"

"Nothing besides he's dead, shot by an ISB agent."

"A what?"

"Investigative Services Branch."

"What the hell's that?"

"The Park Service's version of the FBI. He was undercover, by all indi-cations, and ended up with the artifact."

"Which means he also has its contents," Cole said, stating the obvious, which made it no less impactful.

The man in charge of his Special Projects Division didn't respond, be-cause there was no reason to at that point.

The dank sweat coating Cole's body seemed to freeze in that instant. He suddenly felt the day's chill in his bones, while his skin felt superheated with the rage building inside him.

"I need more details."

"We're working on it."

"You need to also work on recovering the contents. There's got to be a way. Don't let anything stop you. Use any resources and means necessary to get them back."

"There's more, sir."

"Not that blogger again . . ."

"He plans to post something we can't allow."

Cole knew it could only be one thing. "Set up a meeting with this blogger. It's time we dealt with him once and for all."

Just then, Cole's line lost tension and he saw his fly flopping across the gray sea surface, the bone having somehow managed to spit out the lure.

"No, mon, what you doing? You lost him, you lost him!"

Walter's tone pissed Cole off to no end. He'd had it with this guy. Maybe a thousand guides in these parts and this was the best the Abaco Lodge could do? The man on the other end of the satellite phone was blabbering on with his report about this Alaskan mother of a mess, and Cole found himself blaming Walter for that, too.

"More bones at two o'clock, mon, twenty-five feet away. C'mon, cast, cast, cast!"

Cole hung up and pocketed the phone while the man on the other end was still speaking. Then he set about reeling in his line to try another cast.

"What are you doing, mon? They're getting away. Listen to me, forty feet away now at four o'clock!"

Walter didn't know Cole's future as a trillionaire could be in jeopardy, didn't know about the problems that had surfaced in Alaska. Didn't know the truth about the contents of that burial urn. Didn't know what this set-back might do to his Mars project. Didn't know this meant there was an enemy out there who must have somehow caught on to the truth behind his smuggling operation, which placed all his plans in peril. And in that moment, all of that became Walter's fault, because Cole needed someone to blame, someone to punish, someone over which to exert his dominance.

"Come on, you're gonna lose them again. Cast! Cast! Cast!"

Cole back-cast his line, and it lashed through the air straight toward Walter. He heard a scream.

"Hold, don't pull. You got me in the—"

Axel Cole pulled and felt something rip.

Walter screamed again, only this time the scream dissolved into a screech. The fly plopped down on the edge of the bow, a meaty hunk of the guide's cheek attached to the hook.

Walter was wailing constantly now. "I need help, you gotta help me, mon!"

The guide was now alternately sobbing and whimpering.

"Please, mon, please! I'm bleeding here! You hooked me!"

But all Axel Cole could think was that it had been his best cast of the day.

PART TWO

———◆◆———

Who will gainsay that the parks contain the highest potentialities of national pride, national contentment, and national health? A visit inspires love of country; begets contentment; engenders pride of possession; contains the antidote for national restlessness. . . .

He is a better citizen with a keener appreciation of the privilege of living here who has toured the national parks.

—STEPHEN T. MATHER, NATIONAL PARK SERVICE DIRECTOR, 1917–1929

———◆◆———

···o···

SITKA NATIONAL HISTORICAL PARK, ALASKA

President Benjamin Harrison designated this park
on June 21, 1890.

"What do we know?" Michael asked Angela Pierce, as the body of the killer he had gunned down continued to leak blood into the dirt.

"Not much beyond their last known location on the south side of the Lamplugh Glacier."

"Which is roughly the size of a town."

"According to reports, the area was struck by an avalanche, a big one, right around the time they went missing this morning. If they had a tracking beacon with them, it wasn't on, and since we haven't heard a word from them, they could have been buried alive for all we know."

"And if they weren't?"

"They could have taken refuge in a cave or someplace where they had no signal. They had nothing for com gear beyond walkie-talkies and cell phones. The south side of Lamplugh is normally safe."

"Not anymore apparently. This doesn't look good, Angela. They've been missing for how long now?"

"Just over twelve hours since their last contact."

"Can we get a rescue team in?"

"That's the rub, Michael. According to the recent agreement the Park Service struck with the Tlingit tribe, the area in Glacier Bay National Park, where the Lamplugh Glacier is located, was returned to their territorial lands. No one from the government on or off without permission."

Michael saw where this was going. "Don't tell me, the United States Geological Survey never requested access for the team that's gone missing."

"Correct. And, as a result, the Hoonah Tlingit tribe based on a nearby island that's also part of the park is not being cooperative at all. If we don't want to risk squandering all the progress we've made in our relations with them, we need permission to mount a rescue. And even if we could get a rescue team in, they don't know the terrain or where to look, not to mention the snow squalls and fog banks that could make approach by chopper a suicide mission. I think we're going to need to enlist the Tlingits' help in bringing the members of that team home. That's why I need to send you there."

"Because of my diplomatic skills? Tell that to the man I just killed," Michael told her, still eyeing the body before moving his gaze back.

"Speaking of which, I'm trying to expedite your dealings with the Alaska Bureau of Investigation."

The ABI was part of the Division of Alaska State Troopers, men and women who had to work in tough conditions, often in darkness and isolation.

Michael's eyes fell again on the urn he had resealed and returned to Olivia Morgan's brown leather shoulder bag. "Before the ABI takes over the case, Angela, there's something you need to know . . ."

‡‡‡

"You're suggesting it's not really the artifacts that are being smuggled?" Angela asked him, after he had described the contents of the urn that were clearly not human remains.

"There's something I should have realized before, but didn't, specifically that almost all of the stolen artifacts were big enough to hold something else inside them."

"And you think that this black powder you noticed when the urn's lid came free is that something else?"

Michael knew Angela was coaching him to avoid a possible break in the chain of evidence. "Right," he said, instead of belaboring the issue. "That's exactly the way it happened. And I know I said 'powder,' but that's not really accurate. It's more like the size and consistency of freeze-dried instant coffee—less granular and more like tiny crystals."

"Tiny crystals," Angela repeated. "And these crystals are being smuggled out of Alaska in ancient Native artifacts."

"Unless today was an anomaly."

"You don't believe that for a minute."

"Any more than I believe a pro would be sent to kill an entire family over an artifact, Angela."

"Do you think this couple knew the truth about what they were smuggling?"

"I doubt it. They were just couriers. Doing what they were paid to do and waiting for the next trip." Michael took a deep breath that left his ribs aching, he assumed from all the tension and exertion. "I'm sorry I missed the inconsistency in the smuggling. There were a few trinkets, pieces of jewelry and that sort of thing, but that was just to throw anyone who looked deeper off the track, which it did. It shouldn't have, but it did."

"These black crystals—drugs, you think?"

"Not like any drug I've ever seen."

"How much do you think we're talking about, given the frequency of the thefts over the past three years?"

Michael was of no mind to try calculating that in his head right now. "I have no idea. I'd have to review the inventory of the stolen artifacts and try to estimate their size. I'd say there's about two pounds of it inside the urn. If we assume an average of one pound each theft, we'd be looking at somewhere around one hundred pounds."

"The FBI's already mobilizing out of their field office in Juneau. Let them sort it all out for now. How much do you know about the Tlingit tribe?" she asked him, switching back to the subject at hand.

"Not a whole lot, besides the fact that pretty much everyone they've ever dealt with has taken something from them, starting with their land and way of life. You can't blame them for not being very cooperative with the Park Service."

"That's why I'm glad you happened to be up there. It seems to be your specialty."

"I didn't know I had one."

"Dealing with bad things, Michael, really bad things."

He pondered that briefly. "And you believe that's the case up in Glacier Bay."

"Nobody's heard from the USGS team since they went dark twelve hours ago. The only question is how bad."

CHAPTER 11

DANIEL BEARD CENTER, EVERGLADES NATIONAL PARK

The U.S. Geological Survey location that studies
ecological changes as a result of invasive species and is
a part of the Fort Collins Science Center in Colorado.

With her evidence gloves donned again, Gina tugged gently on the black round cord lanyard that extended from a rear pocket of the deceased Jamie Bidwell's jeans. Something on the other end snared on the fabric briefly, ahead of a laminated ID badge emerging from the pocket.

"United States Geological Survey," said Park Ranger Clark Gifford, noting the name and logo at the top of the ID. "They're based at the Daniel Beard Center, right near Lake Eaton in the Ocala National Forest on the eastern edge of the Everglades. A half hour or so from here."

Gina looked back down at the ID badge, which featured a better picture of Jamie Bidwell than the one on his driver's license. "Let's get going."

"We planning to call ahead from the road?"

The FBI rule book in such situations was to go in cold, a strange way of putting it given that they were headed deep into the Everglades. "Let's see how they react when we just show up."

‡‡‡

"Jamie's dead?"

Since it was closing in on four o'clock, Gina had called the Daniel Beard Center to make sure whoever was in charge was still on the premises and would be able to see her before the center closed for the day. The director, Rosalee Perry, said she would stay as long as necessary.

"When was the last time you saw him?" Gina asked from her chair next to Law Enforcement Park Ranger Clark Gifford's in front of Perry's government-issue steel desk.

Perry looked both shocked and perplexed, obviously her first time dealing with such a situation. She had short, spiky hair and a faded tan born of someone more comfortable in the outdoors but who currently spent too much time chained to a desk writing out reports and budgets. Gina spared Perry the bulk of the details at this point, saying only that Jamie Bidwell's death involved suspicious circumstances.

"Does that mean he was murdered?" Perry concluded on her own. "That's what you're suggesting, isn't it?"

Gina glanced toward Gifford, who was remaining deferential to her, before responding. "By all accounts, that does appear to be the case, yes. Now, when did you last see him?"

"Let's see," Perry pondered. "Friday, I saw him on Friday."

That jibed with the rough timeline Gina had assembled in her mind. Working backward, and considering that the body had been found yesterday, she believed it had been dumped the day before and that James Bidwell had been murdered the day before that. So it figured that the last time Perry would have seen or spoken to him, with today being Monday, would have been Friday, the same day Bidwell had brought his laundry to be cleaned at the Tru Hotel.

On the drive down here, Gina had learned that Perry had been with the United States Geological Survey team for six years, the last three serving as a team leader here at the Daniel Beard Center. As far as she knew, the challenges faced by Perry's USGS team assigned here were limited to the infestation of the Everglades by non-native species, primarily Burmese pythons and the Argentine tegu, a similarly large-bodied lizard that had become another out-of-control, invasive animal in the region. But Gina sincerely doubted invasive species had anything to do with Jamie Bidwell's murder.

There was something odd about Perry's tone, but Gina elected not to press her on something that felt awry. "Do you recall that conversation?"

"Not all of it, but he did say he'd be in by ten o'clock."

Again, something felt strange about Perry's tone.

"And then he never showed up?" Gina prompted.

Perry shook her head. "He came in right on time, but left a bit early. We were supposed to talk later, but—"

She stopped abruptly, clearly holding something back.

"No further word from him after that, Rosalee?"

"None."

"Could we ask your assistant or secretary to be sure?"

The woman behind the desk chuckled. "I run a U.S. Geological Survey team. I don't have an assistant or a secretary unless you count our interns."

"Like Jamie Bidwell?"

"Yes."

Gina thought for a moment. "Had he come in on Saturdays in the past?" she wondered.

"Every single one since we accepted his application," Perry said, "except for this past Saturday."

"Would it be possible for me to see that application?"

"Yes. It's filed in that cabinet over there," Rosalee Perry said, rolling her chair backward to stand up.

"Let's keep talking, if you don't mind," Gina said, not wanting to break the momentum of their conversation and waiting for Perry to push her chair back in before resuming. "Let's get back to the timeline, Rosalee. The last time you saw him, on Friday, did he seem nervous to you?"

"No," Perry said, picking up again as soon as she finished. "Did he have reason to be nervous? Did he know he was in danger, Special Agent Delgado?"

"We've found no evidence to suggest that, ma'am," Gina started. "That's why I asked if you noticed anything that might have suggested he was anxious or scared."

"I didn't, nothing. So his death could have been random," Perry said. "Wrong place at the wrong time, that sort of thing."

"Of course."

Gina pretended to make some notes in order to gather her thoughts. Rosalee Perry's last conjectures had sounded like wishful thinking to her, as if she was afraid that the team's work might somehow be to blame for the young man's death.

"Director Perry, you said Jamie Bidwell was part of an eight-person team."

"Yes."

"Have you been in touch with the other seven?"

"It's only six. I'm the eighth. And yes, I saw all six today. Three were collating material here in the office and the other three were back in the field. They'll go straight home from there. The others have already left."

Gina knew she'd have to interview all of them to learn everything she could about the young man whose remains had been in Everglades National Park. For now, she was still unsettled by something Perry wasn't telling her.

"Director Perry," she resumed, "my investigation has revealed that Jamie Bidwell was down here for six weeks at minimum. Does that sound correct to you?"

"It sounds about right, but I'd have to check to be sure."

"And did his work center on any one particular project or several of them?"

Gina could see Perry hedge and was certain that she'd struck some kind of nerve.

"One project," she said, leaving it there. "It made for a solid fit for his interest and expertise level."

"And what would that be in?"

"Climate change."

"Pretty big field."

"One area in particular, Special Agent Delgado."

"Could you be more specific, ma'am?"

Rosalee Perry fixed her gaze on Clark Gifford, instead of responding.

He rose, a bit put off. "I get it. Something you don't mind sharing with the FBI, but not the Park Service, even though the USGS is working here under our auspices."

"I'm sorry," Perry said, not bothering to dispute his point.

Gifford left the office and closed the door behind him.

"The project we're working on down here might well foreshadow the kind of cataclysmic event not seen since the last ice age. Because our work is in the preliminary stages, protocol dictates we don't discuss it outside of a very tight circle—those orders come directly from the White House. But that protocol says nothing about what to do when the FBI comes knocking, so I want to be of as much assistance as I can to help you find whoever killed Jamie. He was a good kid and a hard worker, really solid in the field. If what he was working on has anything to do with his death, that's something the USGS needs to know and I don't want to wait to get their permission to figure that out. I can't risk putting any more members of my team in danger."

Gina remained silent, waiting for Perry to continue on her own.

"Operation Cold Burn," she said finally.

CHAPTER 12

SITKA NATIONAL HISTORICAL PARK, ALASKA

Residents have given the park nicknames like Lovers' Lane and Totem Park.

Michael gave Angela the precise coordinates to pass on to the Alaska Bureau of Investigation people so they could find him here. He could not leave the crime scene unsecured, especially the body, on the chance it could be disturbed by wildlife or the elements. Knowing there might be no time for a stop back on the ship, which would be held in Sitka while the ABI searched the Morgans' cabin, Angela also assured Michael she'd have his belongings packed up and brought to him on land. Since the temperature farther north in Glacier Bay could be fifteen to twenty degrees cooler than here, he'd need heavier clothes and Angela said she'd have a local ranger take care of that as well.

He didn't have a pair of evidence gloves with him but couldn't resist at least feeling about the man's pockets for some ID, travel documents, or anything else that could help identify him. Not surprisingly, he wasn't carrying anything on his person at all, other than a contact lens case and a box of toothpicks.

It was another hour before he heard the approach of what sounded like three or four men, based on muffled voices and footsteps thrashing through the wind-strewn refuse, coming from around the top of the bend.

Michael rose to await their arrival, only to realize he couldn't be sure those approaching were actually from the ABI. They could just as easily be reinforcements dispatched by whoever had hired the killer. So he ducked back behind the nearest cover he could find, a sprawling spruce tree, and snapped a fresh magazine into his SIG Sauer pistol before holding it low by his hip in the ready position.

Then he peeked out from the cover of the tree, just as four figures turned onto the trail, passing the spot from where he'd fired three bullets into a dead killer's torso. All of them were wearing uniforms in the brown and khaki colors of the Alaska Bureau of Investigation. He had been expecting plainclothes detectives along with forensic techs wearing the kind of initialed windbreakers he was used to seeing at crime scenes. Apparently, the ABI had its own way of doing business.

Michael stuck his pistol back in his ankle holster and stepped out from behind the tree with hands raised even with his head. His sudden appearance seemed to startle the approaching officers, one of whom he saw now was carrying what looked to be the kind of case that would hold the tools of a crime scene tech's trade.

"You Walker?" the lead ABI officer called to him, coming to a halt.

"Michael Walker, Investigative Services Branch of the National Park Service."

The man before him started onward again, the three men behind him following in place. "Captain Innik Yazzi, Alaskan Bureau of Investigation." His eyes moved from Michael to the body lying across the center of the trail. "Looks like you've had yourself one hell of a day."

Yazzi was clearly a Native, likely from the Inuit tribe based in the area. He was built like an NFL lineman with a stomach that protruded just a bit over his belt. Yazzi was big everywhere and, as he drew closer, Michael saw he was all of six-foot-three or -four, carrying nearly three hundred pounds on his big-boned frame.

Yazzi knelt over the body, the other ABI officers hovering near him. "We already have a decent notion of what went down back at the museum. But I need you to take me through everything from the point this guy shot the tour guide and you gave chase."

"What about the kids?" Michael asked him.

"I'm not following."

"The murdered couple, the suspects I was following, had twin teenage boys, thirteen years old. I told the ranger back there to look after them."

"Oh," Yazzi said, nodding, "I left the kids in the care of your ranger. No book to follow when it comes to such things, is there?"

"Not that I've read," Michael agreed. "We need to find out who their closest relatives are and make that call."

Yazzi swung from the killer's body toward Michael, looking a bit perturbed. "What *we* need to do is get straight the chronology of you pursuing this man and gunning him down. The rest can be dealt with later."

Michael nodded because Yazzi was the one in charge here, calling the shots, even if he didn't share the man's priorities.

"You're right, Captain, it's been a hell of a day," he said, as Yazzi stood back up.

Michael provided the blow-by-blow of all that had transpired from the moment of the shooting inside the Sheldon Jackson Museum and then chasing the man he'd killed through the woods. He was as detailed as he thought was necessary, so as not to burden Yazzi and the other ABI officers with more facts than they needed. Yazzi nodded through most of the story, then cringed when Michael got to the actual shooting.

"Why do I get the feeling this wasn't the first time things went to guns for you?"

"Because it's not," Michael said.

Yazzi seemed to be looking at him differently. "And the stolen artifact, this urn, it's still in the leather shoulder bag on the ground there?"

"It is. The FBI is already en route. You need to tell them to get its contents analyzed at their nearest lab."

"Contents? First I've heard of any contents."

Michael nodded. "Approximately two pounds of black, powdery crystals."

Yazzi's eyes flashed concern. "You opened the urn."

"The lid came free," Michael said.

He'd broken protocol, especially lacking evidence gloves, but his actions would now assure the artifact wouldn't linger on some evidence shelf through the course of the investigation. And identifying that black powder had now become priority one, since all indications were that it was behind all the smuggling and, likely, the killing of the couriers.

"Here's our quandary," Yazzi said, instead of criticizing his actions. "Who sends someone like this guy to kill a pair of smugglers?"

"That's why we need to identify that black powder, crystals actually. I think the Park Service had this wrong from the start. It was never about smuggling artifacts for curiosity collectors. It was about what was being smuggled inside them. It will be up to the nearest FBI crime lab to determine exactly what that is."

Captain Yazzi's phone buzzed, and he answered it. "FBI just got here,"

Captain Yazzi reported to Michael. "They're holding back at the museum and are leaving the crime scene to us for now. I'm supposed to tell you that the chopper they arrived in is your taxi to Glacier Bay."

Michael set out with Yazzi back to the museum, leaving two lead investigators at the scene along with the uniformed officer handling the forensics. He didn't even recognize the trail, except for a few landmarks. It had passed in a blur as he rushed down it with pistol held at the ready, more concerned with getting shot at than the scenery.

His cell phone vibrated, startling him for a moment, and he eased it from his pocket.

"I need to take this," he said, when he saw **GINA DELGADO** on the caller ID.

CHAPTER 13

⊢•◦•⊣

DANIEL BEARD CENTER, EVERGLADES NATIONAL PARK

The USGS works with the Department of the Interior
on many scientific research studies that include natural
hazards, energy, minerals, and water resources.

"Cold Burn," Gina repeated.

"I'm going to assume you've never heard of the Atlantic Meridional Overturning Circulation, or the AMOC," Rosalee Perry continued.

Gina felt her phone vibrating with an incoming call in her pocket and wished she'd turned it off altogether. "Your assumption is correct."

"Okay," Perry said, leaning forward across her desk. "This AMOC works like a giant global conveyor belt, taking warm water from the tropics toward the far North Atlantic where the water cools, becomes saltier, and sinks deep into the ocean, before spreading southward."

Gina was totally lost, but didn't want to show it. "Okay."

"The Gulf Stream, the object of our particular project, is part of the AMOC. That project started out as just a routine monitoring study. Our initial findings six months ago changed that in a hurry."

"So Bidwell joined things late."

"It's not unusual at all for a USGS intern to join a project that's already underway. Another of the junior members on the team suffered an accident, so the timing of his application was perfect. He had just the knowledge and field experience we needed."

Gina's phone buzzed again, and this time she reached into her pocket to send the call straight to voicemail. "Let's get back to this study, ma'am, or what started out as a study."

Perry fidgeted briefly before settling herself again. She sniffled and dabbed at her eyes with her shirtsleeve, which came away darkened with moisture.

"Sorry," she said, clearing her throat and hardening herself to the task at hand. "This has been ongoing in a broader sense for years," she resumed. "The Everglades is at the heart of the nation's ecosystem. If this area succumbs, well, let's just say we're looking at an environmental catastrophe that can't be reversed or prevented."

"Succumbs to what?" Gina wondered.

"The collapse of a series of subsystems of ocean currents."

"How can ocean currents collapse?"

"It's not like a structure collapsing, but it's the same idea. Basically, it refers to the shocking trend we uncovered in the Gulf Stream of the currents slowing. A collapse would be the currents stopping their flow, which would halt the respective movements of warm and cold water, basically the glue that holds the planet together."

That metaphor helped Gina grasp the stakes of whatever it was that the USGS team working out of the Daniel Beard Center had uncovered in their work. "And this involves—what did you call it?—that AMOC."

Perry nodded again. "A large system of ocean currents that transfers warm salty water northward. The water cools on its journey north, making it denser. As the cold water sinks, water from other oceans is pulled in to fill the surface, driving the circulatory system back down south again."

"And if this set of ocean currents collapses in the Gulf Stream and elsewhere . . ."

"Okay, bear with me here and I'll try not to sound too much like the science geek that I am. Ocean currents are driven by winds, tides, and water density differences. In the Atlantic Ocean circulation, the relatively warm and salty surface water near the equator flows toward Greenland. During its journey it crosses the Caribbean Sea, loops up into the Gulf of Mexico, and then flows along the U.S. East Coast before crossing the Atlantic. This current, commonly known in these parts as the Gulf Stream, brings heat to Europe. As it flows northward and cools, the water mass becomes heavier. By the time it reaches Greenland, it starts to sink and flow southward. The sinking of water near Greenland pulls water from elsewhere in the Atlantic Ocean, triggering a repeat of the same cycle, kind of like a conveyor belt churning. Are you with me so far?"

"I am." Gina nodded.

"Too much fresh water from melting glaciers and the Greenland ice sheet can dilute the saltiness of the water, preventing it from sinking and weakening that conveyor belt which, as a result, transports less heat northward and enables less heavy water to reach Greenland, exacerbating the problem by further weakening the conveyor belt's strength. The inevitable result is a tipping point."

"Meaning?"

"The geo-physical composition of this planet has changed radically before and, if the conveyor belt stops churning, it will do so again. The end result? The kind of globe I had on my desk as a kid would be obsolete and its replacement will bear little resemblance."

Perry paused to let her point sink in.

‡‡‡

"The ecology of the ocean would be severely compromised. The world's population would see vastly warmer temperatures in some places and vastly colder ones in others. Parts of North America, for example, could end up like the Arctic, while rising temperatures in the Arctic lead to a vast flow of melting ice spreading southward."

"We're not talking about global warming, then."

"Global warming and climate change, Agent, are not interchangeable, and global warming paints a false picture. Because as some areas warm, others will cool in kind to preserve whatever balance nature can still manage. The problem is people in New York or Los Angeles aren't ready for temperatures approaching thirty degrees below zero on the one hand and, maybe, a hundred and thirty degrees on the other. Those kinds of swings are well within the range of possibility if the collapse of the ocean currents reaches that point."

Gina stopped to assess the impact of what Rosalee Perry was explaining to her. She couldn't grasp the science behind it, but realized all too well the ultimate ramifications, which brought her back to the research the USGS team was doing here.

"Get back to Cold Burn," she told Perry. "What exactly the project, and your efforts, consist of."

"We aren't just monitoring the effects of AMOC and the collapse of

Gulf Stream currents. Project Cold Burn is comprised of any number of strategies we're pursuing to reverse the process."

"You just said it was irreversible."

Perry sighed. Gina could understand now why the head of this particular United States Geological Survey team hadn't wanted to share this information with Law Enforcement Park Ranger Clark Gifford. Perry had just passed on information very few understood and a like number dismissed as the mad rantings of obsessive environmentalists. The fastest way to cause a panic would be to release the same information unfiltered and unencumbered, potentially detailing the end of life on Earth as we know it.

"I'm a scientist," Perry said finally. "Which means I can't accept that something is inevitable, any more than I can that something else is irreversible. The USGS is in the business of problem solving, not just problem spotting."

"Would make a nice motto," said Gina. "But Jamie Bidwell wasn't murdered over a motto." She collected her thoughts again. "He was murdered likely because of the work he was involved in down here."

"How can you be so sure of that, Agent? Why couldn't Jamie have just been the latest victim to be claimed by Florida's current crime wave?"

"You know your way around ocean currents, Rosalee. I know my way around crime scenes and corpses. I'd rather I didn't, believe me, because it's a skill set that invites pain and heartache."

"But why him? He was just an intern, one of two on the team, replacing that climate scientist who was injured. If you're right about his work being the reason he was killed, it could have been any of us, right?"

"That's one of the questions the investigation we're conducting needs to answer. You just told me, Rosalee, that you weren't just studying the pending collapse of these ocean currents in the Gulf Stream, your team was also looking into how to reverse it. Did Jamie Bidwell have a specialty or particular area of expertise in that realm?"

Perry sniffled, her eyes moistening with tears. Gina realized in that moment what had put Perry so on edge upon learning of, and then discussing, Jamie Bidwell's death: they had been romantically involved. Gina would have bet anything on it, but saw no reason to question the woman on that now. Her pain was palpable and there was no need to press her further on something that may have nothing to do with the young man's murder. And what Perry had said was true, that at this point there was no concrete evidence linking Bidwell's murder to the work of the USGS team.

Gina felt her phone vibrating yet again and this time yanked it out of her pocket to see who was calling. It was a dummy number, but Gina recognized it all too well as the exchange used by the president's chief of staff whenever he needed to reach her. He must be calling for the update she was still trying to compile. And she didn't dare interrupt Perry's train of thought or the flow of the interview.

"As an intern, how much was Jamie Bidwell privy to about your team's work, Rosalee?"

"Everything, pretty much. He worked primarily in the field and recent tests we conducted on the currents here in the Everglades showed we may have struck scientific gold."

"By which you mean . . ."

"We were able to lower the temperature of the ocean—not by a lot or in an area beyond the sample size. I mean we're talking no more than half a degree in an area not much bigger than an Olympic-size swimming pool, but that's compared to a rise in water temperatures by nearly a degree and a half outside the sample. Enough to be deemed statistically significant."

From her work with explosives, Gina knew the slightest variation in the chemical makeup or detonation system could be the difference between success, failure, and disaster. That was enough to tell her lowering the ocean's temperature by even the slightest amount was a big deal.

"Of course, the sampling was too small to be definitive," Perry continued, "and easily passed off as an anomaly due to other conditions or even a natural phenomenon in this particular sample section. That's why we've only reported our findings up the chain to USGS headquarters."

"Not to the Park Service?"

"There was no need. The Park Service's only involvement is that they maintain the waters in Everglades National Park where we've been doing our testing and experimentation."

"Until Jamie Bidwell's body washed up, which made it their business." Gina leaned forward, shrinking the distance between the two of them. "I need to ask you a difficult question, Rosalee. Was your relationship with Jamie strictly professional?"

Perry grabbed some tissues from a pop-up box of them on her desk and dabbed at her eyes, sniffing again. "What do you mean?"

"I think you know," Gina said, holding her gaze sympathetically.

"It had nothing to do with me taking advantage of Jamie as his superior. He made the first move. I don't think anything we did violated any workplace rules."

Gina didn't press the point; it was clear Rosalee Perry was in enough pain already and the details of their relationship were outside the purview of her investigation for now. "So you developed an intimate relationship with the young man."

Perry nodded, almost imperceptibly. "Yes."

It was easy to picture an attractive, younger man like Bidwell seducing her to obtain information he otherwise couldn't. The fact that he was a team member, and thus privy to the operational details of Cold Burn, suggested that might well have been the case. And in Gina's mind, absent any other potential explanation, what he'd been working on here remained the most likely motive for his murder.

And that's where things got tricky. The circumstances certainly suggested someone with the resources to hire professionals capable of leaving no sign behind in their search of his hotel room and, somehow, not show up on hotel security camera footage. Corporate espionage maybe, or some powerful force or individual looking to exploit the USGS's work down here. Gina wasn't about to dismiss the possibility of involvement by a foreign, potentially hostile country either.

"Can you enlighten me on more of the specifics about how your team managed to lower the water temperature by half a degree?"

"You realize the unprecedented nature of that, of course?"

"Enough to figure science has never managed it before."

"Then you also realize that it's something I'm not at liberty to share, even with the FBI."

"Did you share it with Jamie, Rosalee?"

Perry's suddenly evasive gaze and fidgeting in her chair gave Gina the answer. She swallowed hard, but didn't speak.

"Rosalee?" Gina prompted.

"We were both climate scientists. We discussed a lot of things."

"I'm talking about one in particular."

"Some things may have come up in our conversations."

"You cared about Jamie."

Perry's eyes moistened again. "Yes."

"A lot."

Perry nodded.

"So you want his killers to be caught, to face justice for what they did. That means telling me anything that can help me do that."

Perry dabbed at some tears, her lips trembling. "I may have told him some things."

"Things you shouldn't have told him? Things you can't even tell the FBI?"

"Maybe."

That was enough for Gina to be sure that Jamie Bidwell had been made privy to classified information he never should have. Again, she began to consider whether that explained the seduction. Had the young man been planted here? Was he some sort of spy? And, if so, how did that lead to his death at the hands of clearly professional killers? Gina was convinced she had locked in on the motive for Bidwell's murder. And the fact that his room had been thoroughly searched in the wake of it indicated either his killers hadn't gotten out of him what they wanted or wanted to be certain he hadn't left anything behind for someone else to find. Either way, the key had to be the means by which the USGS team operating in the Everglades had managed to lower ocean temperatures by even a minute amount in a small area.

"I need to ask you something," Perry said suddenly.

"If I can answer it, I will."

"It's about Jamie. You didn't mention how he was killed and, don't worry, I'm not going to ask for the specifics. I just need to know if he suffered. Can you tell me that much?"

"No," Gina lied, "he didn't."

‡‡‡

There would be time to set the record straight on that and Perry's revealing classified information to Jamie Bidwell later. For now, Gina saw no need to cause Rosalee Perry any further heartache, especially since she knew there would be more interviews to follow with her. Gina needed her trust, needed to be seen as the person who could find justice for someone she'd fallen in love with, instead of the person out to get her for committing a gross breach of security.

Outside Perry's office, Clark Gifford had just risen from a chair in a small reception area to join her, when Gina's phone rang from the same dummy number as before. She answered the call standing against the nearest wall, out of earshot of anyone walking or inside one of the nearby offices.

"Captain Delgado," said a familiar voice she hadn't heard in a while.

"It's been too long, Colonel Beeman."

"Not really, because if I'm talking to you it means the shit's hit the fan again. Pardon my French."

"No need."

"I was talking to the president. She's standing right here and I'm handing her the phone."

"Hello, Gina," President Jillian Cantwell greeted.

"Madam President . . ."

"How many times do I have to tell you to call me Jillian?"

"At least one more, apparently. And I wasn't expecting to hear your voice or Colonel Beeman's."

"That's because what I'm about to share with you involves a top-secret military matter of the highest sensitivity, and I need you in Alaska."

"I think I'm onto something down here. The murder your office sent me to investigate is connected to—"

"Never mind that now. You're heading to Alaska. Colonel Beeman will brief you on the details. What I want you to hear from me is that the entire crew of a Virginia-class submarine was found dead and I need you to be my eyes and ears on the investigation into what killed them."

‡‡‡

The president turned the phone back over to Colonel Beeman, who informed Gina that a private jet would be landing in Miami in two hours to fly her to Alaska. He provided no details as to where it would be landing or what her instructions would be upon arrival. That meant either a strict security protocol was being followed or this was all unfolding on the fly with those final details yet to be finalized.

Either way, the flight schedule left Gina little time to both collect her belongings and make sure Clark Gifford was ready to take full control of the investigation. She needed to brief him on at least the broad strokes of what Rosalee Perry had broached about Operation Cold Burn.

After Beeman ended the call without putting the president back on, Gina returned her attention to the murder of Jamie Bidwell, something that had been bothering her about the relatively pristine condition—for the Everglades anyway—that his body had been found in. She had questions and knew just who to call to get answers.

"Hey, Michael," she said, after he answered.

CHAPTER 14

SITKA NATIONAL HISTORICAL
PARK, ALASKA

Sitka was the Russian colonial capital in the 1800s and
was known as New Archangel.

"I'm guessing this isn't a social call, Gina," Michael greeted, still trying to keep pace with Captain Yazzi from the Alaska Bureau of Investigation.

"Nothing social about murder, Michael. What are you up to these days?"

"Investigating what started out as a smuggling ring specializing in Native artifacts up here in Alaska. But I'm headed to Glacier Bay National Park on something else. So how is my favorite secret agent?"

Gina fanned herself with a brochure. "Steaming hot."

"Where are you? Are you allowed to tell me that?"

"I am, because I need your help. That's why I'm calling. I'm in Everglades National Park."

"Want to trade places?"

Another pause. This time Michael let it go and waited for Gina to continue on her own.

"I'm working a case where a murder victim washed up in the Everglades."

"You mean, what's left of them."

"No, we got lucky. The victim's body was largely intact."

"An oddity in itself for sure. Bodies dumped in the Everglades often never turn up, outside of a few stray pieces. The gators and crocs don't leave much behind and the Burmese pythons can swallow a body, dead or alive, whole."

"What does that tell you, Michael?"

"Well, whoever did the dumping doesn't know the area," he explained.

"They dumped the body upstream instead of downstream. Downstream would have meant there wouldn't have been much left of a body to recover. Upstream means it would wash toward shore, get snared in the mangroves and overgrowth."

"That's exactly what happened."

"Then you're looking for killers who aren't familiar with the Everglades. Have you checked boat rental places?"

"That was my next stop," Gina said.

"Because the way you're describing it, they dumped the body in the water, just in the wrong place. They'd need a boat to do that."

"This is just why I called you, Michael."

"Nice to know I'm good for something, though not good enough to be told what you're really up to."

"Is it that obvious?"

"It is to me."

"Hopefully, we get the chance to get to work together again," she told him.

"Hopefully, we won't have to save the country again," Michael said, his thoughts turning back to the mysterious black powder.

‡‡‡

Ed Trapscott, a seasonal park ranger currently stationed at Glacier Bay National Park, was waiting back at the museum for him, when Michael returned alongside Captain Yazzi. Angela Pierce had arranged for the same helicopter that had ferried the FBI agents here to take Michael and Ed Trapscott to the town of Gustavus's landing strip.

Michael hated leaving a case like this, especially one where his involvement was this deep, but orders were orders. And, between the Alaska Bureau of Investigation and the FBI, the investigation was in good hands. Most importantly in his mind, the urn containing the black powder would be transferred to the FBI crime lab, likely in Anchorage, for analysis. If the science techs couldn't identify it or explain its significance, the Bureau would find someone who could.

At this point, Michael's concern rested primarily in how the powder fit into the contours of the smuggling operation that had been going on for at least three years. If it was truly at the root of that operation, vast resources had been brought to bear to stockpile as much of the substance as possible.

He'd keep tabs on the case as best he could, but for now Glacier Bay and that missing United States Geological Survey team beckoned.

"I've got your clothes from the ship in my truck," Trapscott informed him, as they walked toward the white Ford Expedition that was standard Park Service–issue detailed in green striping and lettering. "Didn't have time to pick up the kind of gear you're going to need in Glacier Bay, though. Do you have an expense account?"

Michael almost laughed. "Enough to buy a pack of gum, maybe just a few sticks thanks to inflation."

"Anyway, we should reach the town of Gustavus before the stores close, so we can get your wardrobe taken care of."

"We're not heading into Glacier Bay right now?"

Trapscott looked up at the sky. "Not enough light left and, believe me, you don't want to be anywhere near a Native village on Lester Island at night. Too easy for somebody to take a shot at you."

"You're kidding."

"Nope. The good thing is the Tlingits are great shots, so when they aim to miss, they miss. The point is to scare and intimidate us, not kill us."

"What you're saying," Michael continued, "is that we shouldn't expect a lot of cooperation."

"Any would be a surprise. You ever hear of the *Kiks.ádi*?"

"They were Tlingit warriors, right?"

"Not were, *are*. They had already fought and died for this land once in the early 1800s, particularly in the Battle of Old Sitka in 1802, which they won, and then that final battle in 1804, which they lost. I assume you're familiar with that."

"Both actually," Michael said, nodding. "I was at the site earlier today where experts believe the fort the tribe built to withstand a Russian invasion was located."

The trouble with the Russians hit a boiling point when the Tlingits settled near the mouth of the Indian River, following their victory over the Russians at the Battle of Old Sitka in 1802. They chose the site because the river mouth was too shallow for Russian ships. A sapling fort housed the Tlingits for two years before the Russians returned in 1804, accompanied by the man-of-war ship, the *Neva*. Even though the fort was built with slanted sides designed to withstand cannon fire, and the Tlingit warriors wore body armor strong enough to stop musket fire, the Russians overwhelmed the Tlingits. After six days of battle, five hundred Tlingits escaped in the middle of the night. They walked all the way to Chichagof Island in the depths of winter where they lived until they returned to Sitka in 1816, before finally settling on Lester Island.

"So these Tlingit warriors," Michael continued, "the *Kiks.ádi* . . ."

"They maintain a significant voice in all tribal decisions and have de facto veto power over any initiative involving relations with the Park Service and state government. To call them militant in their views regarding land would be an understatement."

"What about violence?"

"They steer clear of that, at least off their land. But they do a lot of training and have amassed quite an arsenal of weapons, by all accounts."

"What are they training for exactly, Ed?"

"It was their land before the Russians took it. Then the Russians left, and America took it when Alaska became a state in 1959, and then the Park Service took control in 1980—at least that's their perspective."

"They're not wrong, given all the fishing bans. It wasn't just their land they think we stole, it was their lifestyle."

"And 'we' is an accurate way to put it, because the National Park Service has drawn the bulk of the Tlingit people's ire, becoming a symbol for their way of life being demolished. All the efforts the NPS has launched toward reconciliation and accommodation have been mostly effective, even game-changing, but not with this particular tribe who control the land where that USGS team went missing. Maybe you'll have better luck than I've had."

"To get them to help or to stay alive?" Michael asked him.

Trapscott shrugged. "Guess that's something we'll find out tomorrow."

CHAPTER 15

·▸◂·◦·▸◂·

EVERGLADES NATIONAL PARK,
FLORIDA

The Everglades is the only place in the world where
American alligators and American crocodiles coexist in
nature.

Gina's plane wouldn't be arriving for two hours, giving her time to follow
up on one more lead down here in the Everglades before heading to the
private departure terminal at Miami International. The death of an entire
submarine crew, from circumstances that remained unexplained, definitely qualified as an emergency. But so did what she'd just learned about
a murder very likely connected to a secret project.

Rosalee Perry had sought to downplay the significance of her team's
work in the Everglades, but Gina knew full well that finding a mechanism
to lower ocean temperatures by any amount, even that half of a degree
Perry had mentioned, qualified as a major scientific achievement. Whatever Operation Cold Burn consisted of had, in all likelihood, flown purposefully under the radar until more definitive data could be collected and
collated.

Which hadn't stopped someone very professional and very good at
what they did from killing an intern. The only mistake the young man's
killer or killers made was to dump his body in the wrong place. Fortune
had further worked in the investigation's favor when the body had gotten snared close enough to shore to be spotted and recovered before the
smaller game could have their way with it. Another few days and there
wouldn't have been anything recognizable left of Jamie Bidwell and, almost surely, no hotel key card recovered from his shoe.

"What are you thinking?" Clark Gifford asked Gina, as soon as she was
off her call with Michael Walker.

"How many boat rental places service the Everglades?" she said, thinking of what Michael had just told her.

"It would take a whole lot of fingers to count them all."

"I want to call as many of them as I can before I catch that plane."

‡‡‡

While Gifford drove in the direction of Miami International, she started with the biggest boat rental outlets that serviced the Everglades. Her thinking was that the killers would want the cover of the busiest operations where the clerks and operators would have less ability to remember them. Of course, there would also be security camera footage but, based on her experience at the Tru hotel, Gina wasn't expecting that to be very helpful.

She struck out on the first five calls and noticed Gifford snickering as she pressed out the numbers for the sixth.

"What's wrong?"

"Your last call was to Everglades City Marina, which is about a two-hour drive from where the body was found, even slower by boat."

Gina realized she hadn't been paying attention to distance. "Oh, jeez . . ."

"There's a map in the glove compartment. Let's see if we can find some rental outlets closer to where the body turned up."

That gave Gina an idea. Since the killers never intended to increase their exposure by returning the boat, they would very likely have rented from an outlet that normally didn't service the Everglades. Off the beaten path, as they say, to maximize the likelihood that this particular lead would end up going nowhere.

Gina pulled the map from the Expedition's glove compartment, folded it up so the area in question was highlighted, and notated the locations of ten marinas offering rentals in the general Miami area. She hit pay dirt with the fourth, just as they were passing a sign that said MIAMI INTERNATIONAL AIRPORT—20 MILES.

"Have you had any craft go unreturned in the past week?" she asked the perky woman who answered the phone at Bruschi Boat Rental located at 2510 Northwest North River Drive in Miami.

"Did you find it?"

Gina put the call on speaker so Gifford could hear. "When did you report it missing?"

"Not missing—rented and never returned. They stole it and when we went to bill the credit card they gave us for the insurance deductible, it was declined. I made the calls myself. Called everybody: Fish and Game, Park Service, Highway Patrol, Homestead Police. Which one are you with?"

"FBI. Special Agent Gina Delgado."

"I never called the FBI," the perky woman said, sounding wary.

"Report got passed to us."

"The FBI?"

"I'll explain when I get there."

‡‡‡

Fortunately, Bruschi Boat Rental was just past Miami International, meaning Gina would likely get there around the same time as the private jet coming for her landed. It was housed in a single-story white, standalone building with paint peeling on the south side that got the most sun.

"You want me with you?" Gifford asked deferentially after swinging into the parking lot.

"It's your case as soon as I board that plane, so absolutely."

He nodded and pulled into a space amid a smattering of other vehicles.

Gina entered with Gifford right behind her. The young woman behind the counter gave him a longer look.

"I thought you were from the FBI," she said, in the familiar perky voice.

"I am," Gina said, removing her ID wallet and badge from her pocket as she approached the counter. "Special Agent Gina Delgado. This is Law Enforcement Park Ranger Clark Gifford from the National Park Service. We're working the case together."

The young woman's name tag read AMY. "Two heads are better than one," she said with a smile, perky as ever. "Right?"

"We can hope so."

"So has our Element 16 been recovered? Did you find it?"

Gina looked toward Gifford for elaboration. "Seats four. Seventy-five horsepower engine is the norm."

"Features car-like handling and class-leading safety features," Amy picked up. "Top speed of thirty miles per hour depending on weight and our most popular rental. It's off-season so the price is only a hundred and twenty dollars per hour."

"We're not here to rent a boat, Amy," Gina reminded her.

"Right. Sorry. I got carried away. Happens a lot. So has the boat been recovered?"

"I'm afraid not. That's why I'm here. See if I can latch on to some clues the other law enforcement bodies you called might have missed."

"Missed? They didn't even try. The only one who even showed up was the local police. They gave me a form to fill out and left."

Gina wasn't surprised. Boat theft in these parts, particularly from a rental outlet, wasn't something any law enforcement body was going to invest a lot of resources in, not with so many other crimes demanding their attention.

"That's why I'm here," she said simply. "I need you to pull the rental agreement."

"Already did as soon as I got off the phone with you, when you said you were on your way over." Amy handed it across the counter to Gina. "For all the good it will do . . . The one thing the local cops told me was that the address on the driver's license the guy who rented the boat used was a fake and so was the license. They told me they ran it through some system and drew a blank. Then they sent a report to forward to our insurance company. Case closed."

Gina regarded the rental agreement and saw exactly what the locals had seen, but the boat had been rented on Saturday, the day after Jamie Bidwell hadn't shown up at the Daniel Beard Center, in keeping with the timeline she had developed.

"Not anymore, Amy. Were you working the day the missing boat was rented?"

"Yup. It was Saturday. I'm assistant manager, so I can't miss any Saturdays."

"And do you recall the transaction?"

Amy nodded. "Uh-huh. He was a white guy, had sunglasses on, expensive ones. He never took them off. Everybody takes them off inside, except for the prescription ones that get lighter."

"Can you describe him beyond that?"

She frowned, looking unhappy for the first time. "I wasn't paying a lot of attention. He was just another customer. But his hair was dark for sure."

"Was he tall or short?"

"I had to look up at him."

"How would you describe his build?"

"Hard to say. He was wearing a baggy tropical shirt with impressions of the sun all over it. He had big forearms. And now that I think about it, when we get bodybuilders in here that's the kind of shirt they wear. Oh, and there was something else."

"What?"

"He was wearing shoes. Who wears shorts and shoes? Almost everybody who comes in here is wearing sandals or sneakers."

"Was he alone?"

"Yes," Amy nodded, "and he boarded and drove off in the boat he rented alone, too. I'm sure of it."

That was just as Gina had expected. It had taken at least a two-man team to kill Jamie Bidwell and dispose of his body. Under that scenario, she pictured the man who'd rented the boat piloting it to some out-of-the-way dock where one or more accomplices would have been waiting with the body in tow.

"What about security cameras?" Gifford asked the young woman behind the counter, just as Gina had been about to.

"I keyed up and copied both the footage from that one," Amy said, twisting to indicate the camera mounted on a wall just behind the reception counter, "and the one outside on the dock. I can show them to you if you like."

A second salesclerk, probably returning from lunch, slid through the door and fixed her gaze immediately on Gina and Gifford.

"You guys finally going to do something about our missing boat?"

Gina didn't bother to tell either one of them it had almost surely been sunk to erase any forensic evidence either Jamie Bidwell's body or his killers left behind.

"Can you watch the desk, Tara?" Amy requested, anticipating Gina's next request.

She led Gina and Gifford into a back office cluttered with boxes, filing cabinets, and a single metal desk that had an institutional look to it. They both watched as the young woman sat down at the desk before a twenty-four-inch computer monitor and pressed a key to rouse it from sleep mode. Amy angled the screen so both of them could see and then keyed up the security footage from the reception room.

According to the clock counter ticking upward in the video's corner, it took seven minutes to complete the transaction and hand the man his keys on Saturday. The sunglasses he never removed would have made identifying him hard enough on its own, but the man made it doubly hard by canting his body sideways to avoid giving the camera a good look. The same was true of the outside camera mounted on a telephone pole that overlooked the dock. Every motion suggested he was keenly aware of the camera's placement. The last thing she saw before the footage ran out was the man driving the Element 16 toward wherever his fellow killers were waiting.

"Can you make use of it?"

"We'll certainly try," Gina said. "Ranger Gifford, why don't you give one of your cards to Amy here so she can email you the footage she pulled?"

He fished one from his ID wallet that featured the distinct logo of the National Park Service.

"Phone numbers are on there, too," he said, as he handed it to Amy.

"Did anyone else ask to see the footage?"

Amy rose from a desk chair with green faux-leather upholstery that looked just as institutional as the desk itself. "The sheriff's department was the only one. I sent it to them, and unprompted, to all the other agencies I'd already contacted. The others still haven't gotten back to me. And I've called the sheriff's department maybe three times since the boat went missing. All they do is ask me to send the footage again. Tells you how seriously they're taking it."

Gina wasn't really paying attention at that point. Since he was snatched on Friday and the boat rented on Saturday, she figured Bidwell was already dead at the time her mystery man had walked into Bruschi Boat Rental. Similarly, this confirmed in her mind that the body had been dumped on Saturday, since the killers wouldn't have wanted to hold on to the boat any longer than necessary. There had been no signs of a struggle in the young man's hotel room, including the subtle ones, which told her his eventual killers had snatched him up somewhere else. Rosalee Perry had told her that Bidwell had no car and Ubered or cabbed it everywhere. She found herself wondering whether that proclivity explained how his eventual killers had gotten him.

Gina's Army training included parachuting. The free-fall portion started the moment you exited the plane and stopped when the parachute was released. During free-fall, you were literally falling freely with belly to the ground, wind in your face, your mind wide open.

She was now in the free-fall portion of this case, not just assembling a puzzle with existing pieces, but also finding new pieces to fit into place. She couldn't separate the notion of the potentially groundbreaking discovery the USGS team had made, wholeheartedly believing that there was a connection between that scientific breakthrough and Jamie Bidwell's murder.

"Could you bring up the dock footage again, please?" Gina said to Amy, clearing her throat.

She only needed to watch it once to see it pictured the suspect from the rear and, for a few seconds, from the side. No front-facing shots, which left them with just the footage from the counter camera in that regard.

"Play it again," she said anyway.

And this time she spotted something on the man's tropical shirt.

"One more time," Gina told Amy. "Stop when I tell you to."

The footage began to unspool, reaching the moment that had grabbed her eye.

"Stop!"

Amy smacked a key. The screen froze. Both Gina and Clark Gifford leaned in closer.

Gifford squinted so tightly his eyes seemed to disappear. "Is that a . . ."

"Yes," Gina said, when his voice trailed off. "You bet it is."

"Holy shit."

CHAPTER 16

MICHOUD ASSEMBLY FACILITY, NEW ORLEANS, LOUISIANA

The complex was constructed in 1940 for building cargo planes and landing craft.

"Looking at your rocket ship from different angles isn't going to change the fact that it doesn't work," Dr. Elizabeth Fields said, as Axel Cole passed her for the second time. "At least not as your original designers envisioned in trying to build a craft capable of reaching Mars and coming back to talk about it."

"Well," he said, forcing a smile, "it is called the *Death Star*."

"Musk named his craft *Starship*."

"That's why I named mine for something bigger and more powerful."

"Oh, it's both of those things, Axel, but it doesn't work any better."

Cole realized their voices were echoing in the sprawling display area. The room held prototypes of the various craft he envisioned making up a space fleet under his direction and control in a near future. This vision grew further and further away with each failed experiment. The few modest successes Cole Industries had achieved did little to move the needle. Yes, they would be able to reach the moon and be the first craft to carry civilians there for a hefty price. At this point, though, not a single simulation or analysis gave the *Death Star* any chance to reach Mars.

"Maybe you should focus more on that flying car you showed me."

"Not unless you and your team can figure out how to drive it to Mars, Elizabeth."

She ran a hand through her gray hair. "The odds of that are the same as me waking up a blonde again tomorrow morning, Axel."

Dr. Elizabeth Fields, the twelfth or thirteenth head of his Design and Technology team, was the only person Cole let talk to him that way, because she talked to everyone that way. It was the price men like him paid to hire her, along with more money than any scientist had ever made in this case, not to mention the promise of a $1 billion bonus when the first *Death Star* set down on Mars.

For more than sixty years, NASA's Michoud Assembly Facility in New Orleans, Louisiana, has been "America's rocket factory," the nation's premiere site for manufacturing and assembly of large-scale space structures and systems. The government-owned manufacturing facility was one of the largest in the world, with forty-three acres of manufacturing space, an area large enough to contain more than thirty-one professional football fields. Michoud was managed by NASA's Marshall Space Flight Center in Huntsville, Alabama, with several areas of the facility used by commercial firms or NASA contractors.

This was where Cole's massive engines, solid rocket boosters, and the *Death Star* had been built. It was adjacent to where Elon Musk's multiple *Starships* had been constructed—multiple, because they kept burning up upon reentering the Earth's atmosphere. The cylindrical *Death Star* was the size of a whale and resembled a flying one in more than one respect, including the two fins that jutted out from each side at the rear and a thicker, squatter fin centered directly above them.

Cole and Fields stood in the shadow of the prototype that sat upon six-foot steel pedestals. It had taken two cranes to lower the ship onto the pedestals to ensure a perfect weight balance so it didn't crash before making its first flight. It was more than twice the size of NASA's space shuttle, stretching over eighty yards in length and standing nearly half that in height with a weight of over seven million pounds before passengers and crew were added to the mix. None of the nine vehicles in this cavernous space allotted to Cole had ever gone beyond the prototype stage or had been tested in anything other than simulations. The *Death Star* looked to be the exception, a sleek, elegant vehicle that next month would make its maiden test flight. With the likelihood being that it would burn up on reentry, a second model's manufacture was just about completed.

So far, the technological challenges Cole's space program had faced had proved just too much to overcome in this lifetime. Foremost among those was the weight and composition of both the fuel and the reusable rocket boosters. Every designer he'd brought in had assured him they knew how to build one that would actually work on a basis deemed secure enough to actually allow flights into deep space to Mars. Every one of them had failed to even come close, despite initial promise and great expectations. Fields was the latest project manager he'd brought on and the first he was about to entrust with what he'd been smuggling out of Alaska for the past three years.

"There's a reason why I asked to meet you alone, Elizabeth."

"Are you going to fire me, Axel?" she asked, sounding like it wouldn't have bothered her at all if he did.

"On the contrary, I'm going to give you the means to make both our dreams come true."

"That billion-dollar bonus?"

"Make it ten billion, if you can figure out how to make what I give you work."

"Give me? What are we talking about here?"

Cole didn't hold back. "What if a gallon of gas could be concentrated into a single drop?"

"You'd need a lot less gas to fill your tank, Axel, seventeen drops on average. Is this a quiz?"

"No, Elizabeth, it's an opportunity, maybe the greatest, most world-changing opportunity of all time."

‡‡‡

He laid it all out for her as he had never done with anyone before.

How he had spent billions scouring the planet for some magical fuel source he was certain existed but no one had ever found . . .

How just over three years ago, thanks to reliable information obtained from a corrupt government official at significant cost, his exploration crews had been directed to what appeared to be a new element within Alaska's permafrost worthy of joining the periodic table . . .

How he'd been systematically smuggling it out inside Native artifacts with couriers traveling the Alaskan coast on cruise ships . . .

Fields listened wide-eyed to the entire story, mesmerized by his words but not at all convinced by them, growing more and more cynical the deeper he got into the story of the substance destined to make him the world's first trillionaire.

"You boasted in your biography that you've never done drugs."

"I appreciate you reading it."

"So what are you on, Axel? Only someone taking serious drugs could concoct a story like that."

"It's all true, I assure you."

"And what exactly do the scientists who've managed to remain in your employ tell you this substance is?"

"Oil—at least that's what it started out as millions of years ago deep in the Alaskan tundra."

"And what is it now?" Fields asked him, sounding like she was playing along or maybe waiting to be offered whatever he was taking.

"Still oil, but radically transformed on the molecular level."

"I'll say, if a gallon has become a drop. And how did this transformation happen, according to your scientists, Axel?"

"Exposure to a foreign organism."

"Foreign, as in outer space?"

"Foreign, as in never encountered on this planet before, Elizabeth."

Her expression changed, clearly not just playing along anymore. "I'm still listening."

"It's oil, but not as we know it. Oh, it started as oil, no doubt about that, oil buried deep in Alaska's permafrost."

"So not crude, then," Fields surmised. "Not something you can suck out of the ground with a giant straw, right, Axel?"

"You're stealing my thunder, Elizabeth."

"The lightning next: this is the point you tell me that we're talking about shale oil that can only be reached by drilling horizontally instead of vertically. Fracking, in other words. Right or wrong?"

Cole remained impassive. "Right in the sense that our working theory is what we're extracting started out as shale oil."

"Extracted illegally, of course."

"Progress waits for no man. Or woman. But what we found was a solid, not a liquid."

Fields tried to pretend she wasn't impressed, but the act wasn't fooling Cole one bit. "We finally come to that one drop that could replace an entire tank of gasoline."

"That estimate is likely conservative, Elizabeth," Cole said.

With that, he extracted a small tube made of an experimental polymer another of his companies had developed to assure an airless, impenetrable environment. The polymer couldn't shatter, melt, freeze, crack, or be crushed. Contained inside were powdery black crystals that sparkled slightly in the overly bright light of the museum-like space.

"This could power all of New York City for an entire month. Every building, every vehicle, the subway system, the power grid—all running on the concentrated power my discovery contains."

Fields spoke with her eyes glued to the black crystalline powder encased within the polymer. "How much of it have you managed to harvest from the permafrost, Axel?"

Cole turned his gaze on the *Death Star,* backing up a bit in order to take it all in. Fields followed in step, as if not wanting to drift too far from the vial he was holding.

"How much do I need to get my rocket ship to Mars and back?"

"A hell of a lot more than what I'm looking at now."

"You understand what this means, Elizabeth. No more solid rocket boosters. Musk's so-called Super Heavy booster requires thirty-three engines to lift his ship into space, only to keep burning up on reentry. It's two hundred feet tall and stores the three-quarters-of-a-million gallons of super-cooled liquid oxygen his *Starship* needs."

"That's why it will never work, not as he envisions anyway."

Cole let her gaze linger some more on the alternative contained within his experimental polymer. "I'm offering you the opportunity to lead a project aimed at doing away with solid rocket boosters altogether once orbit is achieved, and shepherd the first fully autonomous space vehicle all the way from prototype."

Fields finally lifted her gaze from the powdery crystals. "You haven't answered my question yet, Axel: How much of this do you have in your possession?"

"And you haven't answered mine, Elizabeth: How much do I need?"

She thought for a few moments, holding her stare on the *Death Star* as she replied. "I'll need to run tests, lots of them. Actual simulations, in addition to computer ones. I'll need to run diagnostics, as well as chemical and molecular analyses, on your discovery to learn everything I need to know before giving you an educated answer."

"Rome wasn't built in a day, as the saying goes, so I guess I can wait more than that to change the world forever."

"An understatement, Axel, if you're right about what you're holding in your hand there. You would need at least two hundred and fifty thousand barrels of crude oil to power New York for a month. I don't think you could hold that in your grasp."

Cole smiled thinly. "I wouldn't be so sure of that. The bankruptcy courts are filled with those who've underestimated me before, Elizabeth."

Fields smiled back. "Such bravado didn't work out too well for Prometheus when he stole fire from Olympus and gave it to man, did it? He was chained to a rock for eternity so an eagle would be free to eat his liver, which regrew every night to give the eagle a fresh meal the next day."

Cole pulled the vial back, just far enough to be out of Fields's reach. "You've just performed your first task as head of my Special Projects Division, which is already fully staffed and equipped right here at Michoud: you've given my discovery a name. Prometheus, Elizabeth," he finished. "How soon can you start?"

CHAPTER 17

ICY STRAIT, ALASKA

Icy Strait Point has cabins to rent, managed by the
Forest Service. Though they lack electricity and
running water, they offer a great opportunity to enjoy
the surrounding wilderness.

"Change of plans, Admiral," Admiral Jock Wendall told Ben Mosely over the
secure video channel, "since this is obviously no longer a rescue mission."

In his quarters aboard the Coast Guard cutter *Reef Shark*, Mosely
waited for Wendall to continue.

"The SRDRS is approaching your station now, but will only be utilized
to bring the bodies back to the surface in its decompression chamber.
We'll be handling the retrieval process remotely through an ROV and her
robot crew."

Mosely offered no input, other than to nod. He knew his role here was
to continue acting as Wendall's eyes and ears with no command discretion
to be utilized.

"The crew of the *Reef Shark* and I are standing by to help in any way
we can."

"What's the weather looking like?"

"Threat of storms right now, but we've got an extended clear window
coming up in two hours. So long as your crew can handle the cover of
darkness."

"It's always dark where those vehicles are headed," Wendall noted.

‡‡‡

The transport carrying the SRDRS vehicle and its companion ROV arrived
at the nearest airport. Both were lifted onto a waiting flatbed truck and

then driven to a nearby pier where a crane-equipped barge was waiting to facilitate a rendezvous for the vehicles and their respective crews with the *Reef Shark*.

Of course, Mosely knew that the crew manning the ROV would perform all their work aboard the cutter in a space Mosely had cleared for that purpose. That ROV would be tethered to the *Reef Shark* and would dive to the *Providence*, at which point it would maneuver into position to mate with the sub via an articulated skirt. Normally, that would provide access for the stranded sailors to exit their ship into the SRDRS. Today, though, the remote operators were entirely calling the shots and the sole purpose of the attached SRDRS was to deliver the bodies recovered by the robots back to the surface.

Mosely didn't like surrendering any part of his ship to an outside party, but understood the role he was expected to play both in Admiral Wendall's stead and at his behest. He met the six-man crew who'd accompanied the ROV and SRDRS on the barge. Two of them would be piloting the SRDRS vehicle, two more facilitating the placement of the bodies within the decompression chamber, and the final pair would be piloting the ROV and the robots on board from this command center once it had docked with the *Providence*. Pretty much all they needed were outlets to plug in their laptops outfitted with the software required and a larger console that contained the joystick controls for the robots that would be retrieving the bodies.

Setting up and testing the equipment took two hours, during which a secure channel was established with Admiral Wendall so he'd be able to follow everything in real time, as well as have a bird's-eye view of the makeshift command center via a *Reef Shark* security camera. It was a laborious process, but everything went smoothly right up to the ROV and SRDRS being lowered into the water by a crane the barge was equipped with. All the com lights were flashing green and the tests to make sure all was aligned properly went off without a hitch. An hour short of dawn, the submersible vehicles dropped under the surface of the sea and began their descent for the *Providence*.

Mosely had never witnessed the actual docking process before and found it fascinating. He couldn't even contemplate the skill level of the remote operator, Ensign Sam Willis, in managing a perfect seal, after which his tech partner, Ensign Janice Caraberis, ran a scan of the conditions on board the *Providence*.

"Oxygen levels still strong," she pronounced. "Temperature holding at sixty-two degrees. No hull damage and structural integrity sound. Our bots will have free rein of the ship. I've confirmed placement of one hundred and twenty bodies and am sending the locations to the bots for retrieval."

Mosely had no idea how the order of such retrieval was determined or how long it would take. The robots themselves were fire hydrant–sized drones with fully articulated arm assemblies capable of lifting and toting three hundred pounds at once. Their operation was similar to that of an advanced flying drone, only with the added challenge of manipulating the arm assemblies that finished in handlike pincer attachments. The robots would lift and secure one crewmember's body at a time, and ferry them into the decompression chamber on board the SRDRS for transport back to the surface. Had the crew been alive, one hundred and twenty of them could never be squeezed into that chamber, necessitating multiple trips back and forth to the surface. The fact that this was now a recovery mission meant there was ample room inside the chamber for the bots to stack the bodies, keeping the *Reef Shark*'s crew members from coming into any contact with the remains at all. The bodies would then be offloaded onto a Navy ship properly equipped to handle a potential biohazard situation soon to be on station. What struck Mosely the most about all this was how many resources had been devoted to a program and procedure that was seldom, if ever, used. But being prepared for such an eventuality was proving its worth today. Had the crew of the sub fallen to some pathogen, then the robots performing the extraction process meant no humans need be exposed to whatever in the environment had killed them.

"Opening hatch and deploying Robbie," Ensign Willis said. "Retrieval is underway."

On-screen, Mosely watched as the emergency hatch of the *Providence* opened and the drone bot named Robbie seemed to float inside a corridor of the submarine large enough to accommodate its size and flight. To him, the scene looked like something out of a science-fiction movie, but it was anything but that. Robbie's articulated arms were curled upward and pressed tightly against the robot's cylindrical body to make the bot as maneuverable as possible.

Mosely wasn't sure exactly where on the sub the bot was when it reached the first body—the engine room, it looked like—as Ensign Willis continued to deftly maneuver Robbie through the tight, twisting turns and the narrower spaces, barely slowing the bot's speed.

"Retrieval process commencing," he announced, as Robbie settled over the first crewmember's body.

"Sending in Tommy," Ensign Caraberis said, as the second bot on board the ROV passed into the *Providence*, following Robbie's path at the outset before diverging toward another part of the sub.

Mosely kept his attention trained on the bot named Robbie, who was extending his mechanical arms downward and maneuvering them beneath the corpse. He was impressed to no end with the incredible dexterity Willis employed to manipulate the joysticks controlling those arms. Mosely could only imagine the potential strength Robbie wielded, even as Willis worked the controls to make the robot squeeze the lower extremities of its arm assemblies gently into place.

"Lifting now," Willis announced.

On his screen, the body didn't budge.

"Increasing pressure," Willis said, an edge to his voice.

The body still didn't move.

Willis didn't narrate his actions this time, just pulled farther inward on the toggle controlling Robbie's pressure.

Still nothing.

"Sir"—he looked at the small picture of Admiral Wendall in the left corner of his screen—"the body appears stuck to the floor."

"Extract at all costs," Wendall ordered.

"Aye-aye, sir."

Willis increased the pressure more. Mosely heard a tearing sound through the speaker, the body separated from the floor and rising slowly until . . .

His breath caught in his throat at the sight on the screen.

. . . an arm broke off, falling out of the frame. A hand on the other side followed and then a leg, followed by a foot.

"Cease operations!" Admiral Wendall ordered. "Cease all operations!"

The makeshift command center fell into a collective silence as Willis and Caraberis froze the robots they were controlling in place, awaiting further orders.

"What the hell happened to them?" Wendall said, his voice barely audible. "What the hell did this?"

CHAPTER 18

━━━◆━━━

GUSTAVUS, ALASKA

Formerly known as Strawberry Point, the United States
Postal Service forced the name change to Gustavus in
1925.

"Morning, Ed," Michael greeted early the following morning, as he climbed into his standard ranger-issued Ford Expedition with the green markings over the shimmering white paint. "And thanks for this."

Michael tugged at the folds of a park ranger uniform that he'd found in his closet at the Bear Track Inn in Gustavus upon checking in. At this point, the USGS team had been missing for almost twenty-four hours, still with no contact or any indication they were still alive.

Behind the wheel, Trapscott's expression remained utterly flat. "Don't thank me, Michael. It's the last thing you want to be seen wearing on Tlingit land."

Having his luggage from the cruise ship proved a godsend for any number of reasons, most prominently that he was able to properly care for his prosthetic instead of cleaning it with whatever he could find in Gustavus. And he had the proper medications to treat the stump at the edge of what remained of his ankle to avoid infection and keep the skin from drying out and cracking. Those who didn't know Michael wore a prosthetic likely never would have suspected he was missing his foot. That, though, didn't change the level of proper maintenance to keep the prosthetic, and the leg it was attached to, in optimal condition. Even with that, specialists recommended the kind of advanced prosthetic with which Michael had been fitted be replaced every year. The National Park Service picked up the tab for that, including the excess that insurance didn't cover. But that didn't include a spare, which meant damage to his prosthetic, depending on the severity, could result in a two- to four-week wait for a replacement. The thought of spending that long on crutches was reason enough to never miss a beat in terms of care and maintenance.

Despite being exhausted, Michael had slept fitfully, his slumber roiled by dreams that felt more like reenactments of the chase through the woods and ultimate shootout with the man who had murdered Steve and Olivia Morgan.

"How long have you been posted up here?" Michael asked Trapscott as their Ford Expedition cruised toward the town's small marina.

That's where another ranger was waiting in a boat to take them across Cross Sound to Lester Island where the Hoonah Tlingit village they needed to reach was located. Trapscott had called ahead to alert the village elders they were coming and had managed a frown when Michael asked him how long he'd been posted in the region.

"Going on twenty years. I'm Alaskan born and bred," he said. "I can't imagine being up here for even a fraction of that continuously otherwise."

"So if you had to guess what happened to this USGS team . . ."

"I wouldn't. Too many possibilities to speculate in the wake of the kind of avalanche they found themselves trapped in. My first guess would be they were buried alive. But we can't be sure of that until we've completed an adequate search of the area in question."

"On lands in Glacier Bay National Park that the Park Service returned to Tlingit control . . . Why do they blame us for creating policies we had nothing to do with?"

"Because we're charged with enforcing the fishing and hunting bans, along with formerly keeping them off park and preserve lands that belonged to them." Trapscott cocked a brief gaze his way again, turning back to the road when a rut nearly swallowed the front left tire. "Look, Michael, I know you're aware of some of what happened, but the truth is it all goes back so long nobody really has a grasp of the total picture. First it was the Russians, then the United States, then the environmentalists, and finally the National Park Service. That may not be totally fair or totally accurate, but it's the truth we have to live with."

"This is about six innocent people who no one's heard from in a day now."

Trapscott nodded, looking like a patient teacher trying to make a point to his class. "Archaeologists have found Hoonah Tlingit artifacts in the Glacier Bay area from as early as 1250, and according to the tribe's lore, their people have inhabited the region much longer than that. For early inhabitants, the bay was a land of abundance that provided good lives: forests offered berries and an array of medicinal plants. Salmon clogged the rivers, and the ocean teemed with seals, fish, and kelp."

"Until we came along . . ."

"'We' in the collective sense, yes. I may have exaggerated how far they'll go, but I didn't exaggerate about the commitment or skill level of the *Kiks.ádi* warriors. How much do you know about all this?"

"Quite a bit, it turns out," Michael told him.

His fascination with the battles between the Tlingits and the Russians in the early nineteenth century had given way to a fascination with the circumstances forced upon the Natives by the United States government that imperiled their way of life dating back centuries. The government's intentions, along with the State of Alaska's, may have been well-founded and undertaken out of concern for the environment. But that didn't change the fact that the laws, policies, and edicts enacted threatened the tribe's food supply, ability to work their own ancestral lands, and long-established traditions that defined them as a people.

Severe restrictions, for example, had been placed on fishing in waters that had supplied the tribe with the bulk of its food supply. Some areas were subject to outright bans and others required fishing licenses that limited the catch to well below what the tribe needed to survive, especially considering the need to stockpile food for the always cold and often brutal winters. Again, the state and national government's intentions to protect the environment and avoid areas being overfished were fine, but they failed to consider the reality that tribes like the Tlingit resided nowhere near a supermarket or anywhere else they could conveniently purchase even the bare minimum they required. They had lived in cooperation with the land, and the environment, for more centuries than were documented and, suddenly, they were told they had to make do when there was no way to do so.

Michael put himself in the position of the tribe, wondering how he would react to his very way of life being managed and overseen from afar. It was something he could not relate to, even with his experience losing a foot, since his life had hit restart from that point forward. Nothing was as it had been before. So much he had always taken for granted became a struggle as he was forced to relearn how to walk, run, and climb stairs, to the point where previously simple things became a challenge, if not an ordeal. However, he eventually got used to the titanium and plastic replacement for the foot he had lost. There was no prosthetic for what the Tlingits had lost.

Trapscott slid the vehicle to a halt in one of six parking slots perched before a marina with six berths, one of which was occupied by a twenty-eight-foot catamaran pilot and escort boat that lacked the typical National Park Service markings that highlighted the NPS's fleet of Ford Expeditions. Christened *Serac,* the boat was constructed entirely out of aluminum and featured a semi-displacement hull which made it as efficient as it was environmentally friendly. The term "serac," after all, was indicative of a desire for leaving a mark on the world—or in this case, as little a mark as possible.

"Sooner or later the *Kiks.ádi* are going to be looking to make an example, Special Agent Walker," Trapscott resumed. "Let's hope today isn't that day."

CHAPTER 19

GLACIER BAY NATIONAL PARK
AND PRESERVE,
LESTER ISLAND, ALASKA

Coast Guard and Geodetic Survey named the island
after Rear Admiral Lester Beardslee in 1942.

The three shots kicked up mud ten feet away with enough force to splatter the lower reaches of Michael's standard-issue green ranger slacks in an impressionistic pattern.

"Hold your ground," Trapscott advised, standing stiffly by his side with flecks of wet dirt dotting his face.

After a fifteen-minute ride, the *Serac* had pulled up to a dock amid a trio of piers with slips accommodating dozens of the Natives' fishing boats where the contours of Lester Island swung to the north. The pilot remained behind, while Michael and Trapscott walked along muddy grounds through a tightly packed grove of spruce trees into the center of what passed for a main drag in the center of the Hoonah Tlingit village of Xunaa, which translated as "protected from the north wind." Structures mostly uniform in design and similar in footprint lay on both sides of a flattened stone and gravel road currently laden with muck that the new pair of boots Trapscott had provided sank into and oozed gritty streams out from the treads. They were designed to handle all the varied elements nature could serve up, a perfect fit except for the fact the height of the left heel failed to account for Michael's prosthetic.

He noticed a central square where a ceremonial totem pole had been wedged into a circular rock garden surrounded by ornate wooden framing. The buildings that looked out upon the makeshift rotary the totem created appeared entirely commercial, with the residences climbing up a graded hillside shrouded in clouds of gray mist that swallowed the treetops of even thicker trees forming natural groves in which the majority of the homes for the nearly thousand residents were clustered. Smaller clusters nestled closer to the shoreline on either side of the trees that cast shadows onto the waters beyond, the homes to the east stretching farther along the water than those to the west. The newer structures, both commercial and residential, had been constructed of fresh logs, helping to account for the scents of spruce, maple, and pine that filled the air, clashing with the smell of standing mud. The rest of both single- and two-story structures looked more like clapboard and Michael guessed the bulk of those structures had been built long before, potentially by whatever government body was responsible for the tribe at the time. They were small and tightly packed within shared green space instead of individual yards, and looked extremely well maintained.

A single sweep of his gaze along both sides was enough for Michael to spot a one-story building with a peaked roof and bold letters pronouncing it XUNAA SCHOOL. A familiar red cross designated a nearby building as what must have been the village's medical center. Michael also spotted a combination hair and nail salon, a municipal building, and a smaller structure with the United States Post Office sign posted on its front with PRINTING AND FAXING SERVICES AVAILABLE stenciled beneath it. He took the largest building as some sort of village center that doubled as a meeting hall, a gray structure longer than it was wide, but still the widest in sight. It bore the paint color distinctions in patches, denoting several additions made over time. Michael couldn't see a graveyard anywhere in his line of vision, but he was certain it was somewhere about, likely perched on one of the gently sloping hillsides on which many of the village's residences rested today. Besides the satellite dishes adorning many of the buildings and residences, and cars rimming the street, Xunaa looked unchanged from its founding more than a century before.

Michael couldn't spot the shooter from this vantage point, but the force of the trio of ground bursts told him the bullets had likely been fired from a 30.06 hunting rifle. Meanwhile, he realized Trapscott hadn't moved an inch.

"You get used to it," he told Michael. "Call it the Tlingit way of welcoming us to their land."

"Nice to know, Ed," Michael said, "though a warning might have been nice."

Trapscott choked back the grin that was forming. "I wanted you to experience the tribe's hospitality for yourself."

"Oh, is that what you call it?"

"They've also got a helicopter, Michael."

"You forget to mention that earlier?"

Approaching the village along a rut-strewn road, Michael recognized the scent as that of fir and balsam trees as well as the evergreens, and even when harvesting the forest for wood, the Tlingits were careful to only choose mature or aging trees to help them survive the chill that descended on the area for nine months every year. Since it was early spring, the weather could change violently in a hurry. The wet muck puddled here could be feet of snow elsewhere in Glacier Bay National Park, and this central artery was likely a sheet of shiny ice in the depths of winter.

In addition to not further violating the rules regarding tribal lands within the park, which included the Lamplugh Glacier, Michael not only needed the tribe's approval, but also their help. He had to proceed on the chance, at least hope, that at least part of the missing United States Geological Survey team was still alive. Even optimistically, though, they wouldn't be for much longer.

Suddenly, a woman appeared, trudging through the churning mud that made a squishing sound under her boots and those of the three men who shadowed in a protective ring. Each carried a 30.06 hunting rifle, any one of which could have supplied that greeting to the just-arrived rangers, and all were as big and broad as offensive lineman in the NFL.

They were *Kiks.ádi* warriors, Michael thought, and, if nothing else, they certainly knew how to make an entrance.

The woman leading them had the same confident, athletic stride as his late wife, Allie. Same sinewy build, too, the development of her muscles obvious even through her thick turtleneck sweater and riding her five-foot-nine-inch frame well.

Also just like Allie.

The resemblance stopped at the neck, the woman's narrow and knobby, lengthening out of the high-collared sweater. She wore no gloves and if her boots weren't visible thrashing through the mud, Michael imagined they would show the wear of many seasons with each scratch and ding telling its own story. She had long, straight, raven-colored hair to go with peaked cheekbones, black eyes full of soul, and a strong, narrow face unmarred by too many smiles.

She stopped four feet from Michael, regarding only him, as if someone had erased Trapscott from the scene.

"I'm Amka Reynolds," she greeted, too far away to bother extending a hand.

"Michael Walker, special agent with the Investigative Services Branch of the National Park Service," he said, pulling back his jacket to display his badge. "And this is—"

"I know who he is. And who he is doesn't matter because he's not welcome on our land. Since you accompanied him past the area of your patrol, you're not welcome either."

Michael could feel Trapscott looking his way but kept his gaze trained on Amka. "I'm going to assume you're the one in charge here."

"As much as anyone. My grandfather is the tribal chief."

"We need his help. Yours, too."

"Then you came to the wrong place. You come here for our help, but when we call you for it, there's no response and no one comes."

Michael looked toward Trapscott, who had visibly stiffened, his brow furrowing, further giving Michael the clear impression there was something his fellow ranger hadn't shared with him.

"You only come here when it suits your purposes," Amka continued. "You don't come here when it suits ours."

"I'm here now," he said, the words sounding lame in spite of the forceful intent he had hoped to instill behind them.

"Not for long," the woman said, the three figures behind her stiffening and seeming to grow even bigger.

"You haven't asked what we're doing here."

"I don't have to. Word was passed on to me. Missing scientists on our land potentially stranded on the glacier. They're dead for sure. It was the worst avalanche anyone up here has seen for years. If you haven't heard from them, they didn't survive."

"Some of your people were there?"

"No," Amka told him. "We heard."

Michael waited for her to continue, wondering how the effects of even a powerful avalanche could be noted from somewhere around two hundred miles away.

"The ground spoke to us," she resumed. "The ground told us of the severity of the avalanche."

Michael had heard how elephants know when an earthquake or tsunami is coming because they can feel the vibrations of the ground beneath their feet. If that were true, he supposed it was possible a people living off the land for thousands of years could manage the same feat.

"And it's your fault, your people's, for what you've done to the world," Amka snapped before he could comment. "You make laws that changed our way of life, killed our way of life, you claim out of concern for the environment. You say that while your actions speak otherwise."

"Not mine, not personally anyway."

"This isn't your world?"

"Not this part of it. I was sent here to look for that missing USGS team, because I was already in the area. I don't work the parks, I investigate the crimes that take place within them."

"Including Glacier Bay, *dleit káa*?"

"Means 'white man,'" Trapscott whispered.

"I figured that out all on my own, Ed."

Which drew the slightest of smiles from Amka Reynolds, something positive anyway.

"The answer's yes," Michael told her. "Including Glacier Bay."

"Then you need to investigate a crime here that has claimed many victims, taken their lives. Call it murder."

Michael felt the hairs on the back of his neck stand up. What had he stumbled upon here?

"How many victims?" he asked Amka.

"Hundreds, thousands even. They're waiting for you as we speak." She turned sideways, as if to beckon Michael to follow wherever she was going. "Come, I will show you, so you can investigate." Her stare hardened on Trapscott. "But not him. We called and he never came."

"I'm happy to stay behind," Trapscott said, hands held in the air as if he were surrendering.

"No, *dleit káa,* you go. I want you gone. The elders reached out to you about our education issues, and you didn't reach back. I reached out to you about health care issues and you didn't reach back, just like we received no response on the latest report I made."

"About that, I was just going to—"

"You had your chance," Amka interrupted. "Since you didn't take it, you're not welcome."

Trapscott looked at Michael, indignant and helpless at the same time.

"Take the boat back, Ed. I'll be in touch."

Trapscott could only shrug. He looked like he was about to say something, then just shook his head, turned around, and headed back toward the dock, his boots kicking up a fresh fountain of mud.

┈┈•┈┈

CHAPTER 20

JOINT BASE
ELMENDORF-RICHARDSON,
ANCHORAGE, ALASKA

Elmendorf Air Force Base and the U.S. Army's Fort
Richardson merged in 2010.

Gina fretted, stewed. Being placed in a room where she had waited for three hours for someone to let her do the job the White House had sent her up here to do was not acceptable, and if she had access to a phone or a signal, she would have already informed Chief of Staff Daniel Grant of that fact.

It was times like these that made Gina regret leaving her post as Assistant Special Agent in Charge of the FBI's New York field office and abandoning the traditional track for climbing the Bureau's ranks.

Joint Base Elmendorf-Richardson was a massive facility, covering over sixty thousand acres outside of Anchorage on coastal lowlands surrounded by high mountain chains. More than thirty-two thousand service members and civilians and their respective families live and work there. The Air Force and Army bases had been combined in 2005, one of twelve joint bases to be so merged.

Not that Gina had seen any of those sixty thousand–plus acres, beyond the front gate and this building where she'd been instructed to check in. That had been three hours ago with nothing to read or watch and no cell phone signal. That frustrated her as much as anything. She'd left the Everglades murder investigation of Jamie Bidwell after a potentially major breakthrough, and she wanted to call Ranger Clark Gifford to see if it had led anywhere. They had been watching the marina's dock security footage of a man she was convinced was closely involved with the murder, when she spotted something that seemed out of place in a shot of the suspect from the rear in his tropical shirt. She had noticed it first, Gifford just a moment later.

"Is that a . . ."

"Yes," Gina had told him. "You bet it is."

It was a clothing tag from a nearby department store. Since Gina had to get to Miami International to catch her flight, Gifford would be following that lead on his own as soon as he dropped her off at the airport. She still had no idea why the murder of a United States Geological Survey intern had reached the radar of the White House. The murder hadn't been random and it hadn't been a crime of passion or anything like that. Someone had dispatched professional killers and the reason for the White House's interest in the case must have been directly related to the reason why.

Gina stepped out into the hallway, holding the door open so it wouldn't close and lock on its own.

"Excuse me?" she called out. "Anyone there? Anyone?"

She heard the clack of footsteps echoing slightly and saw a figure round the top of the hallway that seemed a mile away.

"Can I help you?" a male officer in camo fatigues asked, suspiciously.

Out of habit, Gina flashed her FBI creds even though he'd barely be able to make out even the badge from thirty feet away.

"Gina Delgado, special envoy from the White House," she said, leaving it there since she had no idea how much the officer knew or the level of his security clearance. "I'm here on an assignment and was wondering if there's a phone I can use while I'm waiting."

Recognition flashed in the officer's eyes. "You've been here for hours."

"That's right."

"I can let you use a phone, but it will have to be on speaker with me listening to both sides of the call. Is that acceptable, ma'am?"

"So long as you don't mind being bored. I need to talk to a fellow investigator on a case I left to come up here."

"In that case," the officer said, waving her forward, "right this way."

He led Gina past a bank of offices, all with their doors closed, to a single desk that sat in what looked like a reception area. Except it wasn't a reception area, because there were no chairs to sit on.

"I have to dial the number, too, ma'am."

Gina recited Gifford's cell number from memory. The officer pressed it out and hit the speaker button.

"Gifford," the law enforcement park ranger greeted, so loudly that the officer turned down the phone's volume.

"It's Special Agent Gina Delgado, Clark," she said, formally because of her audience.

"What's this number? Where are you calling from?"

"It doesn't matter and I can't tell you anyway, any more than I could tell you where that plane I boarded was headed."

"Well, I called and texted you a bunch of times."

Gina felt the prick of excitement before he continued. "A bunch of times" implied he'd found something.

"I don't have any coverage here," she said, not bothering to elaborate further.

"Then let me catch you up," Gifford continued.

"The store tag?"

"Paid off in a big way, Agent. Our suspect was careful about the security cameras in the marina but not so much at the department store. We got a clear frontal shot of him at the cash register buying that tropical shirt. Not wearing his sunglasses."

Gina felt another twinge of excitement. "What about prints?"

"I shut the counter down and called the local PD to send a tech. The footage does show our suspect touching the counter, but there were an awful lot of customers before and after him."

"Can't hurt to try."

"That's what he's doing," Gifford affirmed. "But it's going to take some time to sort through all of them, and that's assuming we get lucky."

"Really lucky," Gina elaborated, having been down this road before. "Hey, whatever we get might not be good enough to help make our case in court, but it still could help us ID him."

"Speaking of which, I ran the best shot I could find on the security footage through facial rec at the same sheriff's station that sent the fingerprint tech. No match yet."

Gina didn't expect there would be. Professional killers had a way of keeping themselves out of standard criminal databases. Since this case had come to her from the White House, they could run the picture through databases operated by the military and intelligence communities. The kind ordinary police departments can't access.

"Can you text the picture to my cell?"

"You just said you don't have coverage."

"I can forward it on as soon as I get it back."

"Why not just let me forward it to the Bureau?"

Gina hoped her silence would speak for her and it did. Gifford was professional enough to realize that no answer was all the answer he needed. The FBI's database went well beyond that of local law enforcement officials, but the ones at the Defense Intelligence Agency, Homeland Security, and the National Security Agency went well beyond what the Bureau had.

"Just texted it to you, Agent," Gifford said finally.

"Thanks, Clark."

"Got something else that's sure to interest you from this end regarding Jamie Bidwell."

"I'm listening."

"He's not Jamie Bidwell. The Florida DMV has no record of him. His driver's license was a fake."

Gina let that process for a moment. "We dusted his hotel room for prints, right?"

"And came up with a ton of them, virtually all belonging to whoever he really is. But no match through AFIS," Gifford said, referring to the Automated Fingerprint Identity System used by local and federal law enforcement officials alike. "No hits on facial recognition software either. So at this point we don't even know who our murder victim really is."

Again, Gina paused to consider the ramifications of that. The fact that Jamie Bidwell was actually someone else definitely widened the approach they needed to take with the investigation, since it added another layer to the mystery. Given the magnitude of the work being conducted under Operation Cold Burn in Everglades National Park, that opened up any number of new avenues, including espionage. And the fact that Bidwell might have infiltrated the team, more than just joined it, raised the stakes considerably.

"Anything else you want me to do on this end?" Gifford posed.

The more she worked with the ranger, the more she liked him. He knew his role and clearly suspected the young man's murder involved something beyond his pay grade.

"One guy rents the boat," Gina started, "which leaves the other, or others, with the body to load someplace. How well do you know the Everglades, Clark?"

"I've been down here for ten years, so I'd say better than anyone you've ever met in your life. And I know what you're going to say."

"What am I going to say?"

"Do a rough mapping of the body's drift upstream and check out all the potential docks in the area. How'd I do?"

"Spot-on."

"I pulled three other law enforcement rangers to help check each and every one of them, along with the surrounding areas. It's a pretty big space."

"Huge," Gina agreed.

"I've got two more joining the team tomorrow."

The phone she was on buzzed and she could feel the officer getting anxious.

"I've got to go, Clark. I'll call you again as soon as I can."

The officer ended the call before Gifford could respond and picked up the receiver.

"Yes, sir," he said. "Of course, sir." He hung up the phone and looked toward Gina. "Someone's on their way up now, ma'am. They're ready for you."

CHAPTER 21

GLACIER BAY NATIONAL PARK
AND PRESERVE, LESTER ISLAND,
ALASKA

An infestation of spruce beetles hit Lester Island and
Eastern Alaska in 1977.

Michael watched Trapscott disappear into the tree line. He didn't blame the Tlingits for their hostility toward the National Park Service, though that fraught relationship threatened to lower the odds of mounting a successful rescue of any USGS team members who'd survived the avalanche.

"I need to get to the Lamplugh Glacier, Amka."

"I already told you that—"

"I know what you told me," Michael interrupted. "But I've got to see for myself. And as long as there is any chance at all that there might be survivors . . ."

Michael let his voice trail off there, having said enough. He was in her world now and needed to show deference if he expected her help, walking alongside Amka toward what looked like a barn on the outskirts of a village.

"Where are you from, Special Agent Walker?" she asked through the sloshing of their boots through the mud.

"Virginia originally and I'm actually based out of there right now, though I'm not home very much."

"If that's your territory, what brings you all the way up here?"

"I was already working another case in these parts when word of the USGS team's disappearance reached the Park Service. And I don't really have an assigned territory anymore."

Amka nodded as if she understood, her black hair tossed about by the whims of the wind, as their boots continued to kick up mud. "The guy they send on jobs nobody else wants, like this one."

"As I said, I happened to be in the area and time is of the essence."

Almost to the barn, Amka stopped. "The members of this team are all dead."

"Maybe. But we can't be sure of that."

"The land is sure. It speaks to whoever can listen."

Michael held her dark eyes. "Will you help me, Amka?"

"First, you have to help me."

Two of the *Kiks.ádi* warriors accompanying them yanked open the barn door to reveal what looked to be more of a garage, with both large vehicles and smaller ones. The biggest trucks were outfitted with snowplows for clearing the roads, a service the state or local municipality provided anywhere outside of sovereign land. The smaller vehicles were an assortment of ATVs the tribe's members used to avoid getting stuck in snow or mud. He noticed a neat row of Polaris Ranger XD 1500 premium models, absolute top-of-the-line. The Park Service had begun transitioning to these because of this particular line's power and versatility.

These Rangers put out 110 horsepower via a 1500cc engine. They could tow 3,500 pounds and haul up to 1,500 in the rear section, which was also outfitted to take a third passenger. There was a roof and tires as big as that of a car, but no windows or windshield, exposing riders to the elements. Equipped with full-time all-wheel drive, these Rangers were the best ATVs for unforgiving landscapes, as opposed to recreational off-roading. In these parts, they helped you survive, not play.

"You'll ride with me," Amka told him.

Michael offered no argument and climbed into the passenger seat. He watched Amka fire up the engine and drive off in the lead, the *Kiks.ádi* each climbing into their own ATVs. He pictured men like these defending their way of life against the Russians in the Battle of Sitka in 1804. They would have made for an exceptionally formidable force, especially making their stand from the fort. But the *Kiks.ádi* lost their gunpowder supply in an explosion while transporting it to the Fort of the Young Saplings, located at what is now the tip of Sitka National Historical Park. They were forced to retreat and cede the land to the Russians.

"These vehicles don't come cheap," Michael said to Amka, raising his voice above the engine noise. "Government grant?"

She snickered. "What government would that be? No, we obtained these through another source."

"What's that?"

"Me. I lived off-site for seventeen years, returning only to visit. After I returned, I needed to contribute, do my part."

Michael did the math. Based on what he'd already surmised, that would likely take her back to freshman year in college, making Amka right around thirty-five years old. He did more math, multiplying the number of Rangers he'd spotted in the barn garage by their $30,000 price tag to arrive at a substantial total.

Michael caught Amka looking down at his legs scrunched up a bit in the passenger seat. "How'd you lose your foot?" she asked him, as she looped around the outskirts of the village onto a trail naturally worn to accommodate these ATVs.

"How'd you know?"

"Educated guess. The way you walk, a slight list to your dominant side. Also, I almost became a doctor, with the intention of coming back here to give back and do some good."

"What changed?"

"I fell in love with microbiology, and earned a dual PhD in that and pharmacology. Made more than I deserved doing research and development on cutting-edge drugs, particularly ones to treat the myriad diseases indigenous peoples are afflicted by."

"Giving back, doing some good . . ."

Amka nodded. "To do some real good, thanks to something else I was responsible for engineering in my lab. I won't bore you with the details."

"Speaking of details, the yellowing of your nail beds and pale skin color tell me you endure long stretches without being exposed to much sun. And your boots are worn down. That tells me you've settled back in with no plans to leave."

"My fourth pair of boots since I returned," Amka acknowledged, as the ATV sent a curtain of brown water and thin muck showering into the air around them. "My ancestors' blood is soaked into this land, Special Agent Walker. We've had so much taken from us, even need fishing permits from your Park Service to fish our own waters. We have lost a lot, but we haven't lost our pride and being back here allows me to lead the charge to never lose it, no matter what it takes."

"That sounds more like something one of your *Kiks.ádi* warriors would say," Michael said, noting her voice's suddenly ominous, foreboding tone.

"The government and the Park Service are always looking for ways to categorize us." She glanced at him briefly, before turning back to the trail. "So, again, how'd you lose your foot, Special Agent Walker?"

"Gunfight on Mount Rainier when I was still a law enforcement ranger," Michael said.

"Then you became ISB afterward."

"They wanted to put me behind a desk. This was the only way to avoid that."

"Wise choice."

"Like the one you made?"

"I came home to take care of my brother—well, half brother. I came back so the state of Alaska wouldn't make Yehl a ward of the state and place him in the foster system."

"Was that the only thing that brought you back?"

Amka ignored his question and fixed her gaze straight ahead.

"I need to get to the Lamplugh Glacier. Any surviving members of that USGS team need to be rescued, Amka."

"And we will take you there, *dleit káa*. Consider what I'm about to show you as the price for that. You'll be able to smell it any moment now."

‡‡‡

Amka was right; it was the smell that alerted Michael, a half-mile or so down the curving track cut naturally to avoid boulders, tree stumps, and thick areas of overgrowth amid the rockiest sections of terrain along the Lester Island shoreline well beyond the group of homes to the east. A rancid stench thickened in the air as they drew closer to the coastline. Tlingit villages like Xunaa were always erected near water since their primary food source was fish. Now, though, the tribe needed a permit every time they wanted to go out and Michael knew obtaining them could be subject to delays depending on the backlog or even draw an outright rejection with no reason provided. In these parts, that had led Tlingit fisherman to defy the law and fish absent a permit. Fines, the issuing of summonses, and even arrests had followed. Some of those arrests, Michael knew, had turned violent with rangers ill-equipped to deal with such determination and rancor, often getting the worst of things.

The stench that started to actually sicken him reminded Michael of coming home from a long trip to find the refrigerator had failed. You open the door and the pent-up smell flooded out with enough force to knock a person off their feet. While this scent wasn't enough to knock him from the ATV, he had to steady himself with several deep breaths to avoid getting nauseous. He tried to focus on the sound of the currents softly breaking on the nearby shore to which they were headed to calm himself and his stomach, but that did nothing to cushion the blow when they rounded the bend:

Fish, thousands and thousands of them, washed up on shore, dead.

CHAPTER 22

GLACIER BAY NATIONAL PARK AND PRESERVE, LESTER ISLAND, ALASKA

The Bartlett Cove Cannery was established
on Lester Island in 1883.

Amka ground the ATV to a halt on the rock-strewn shoreline, a jagged cut-off coastline jutting out into the sea, apart from the tribe's primary fishing grounds.

Michael cast his gaze over the literal piles of fish the currents had stacked in clumps atop the rocks and stones. "Why didn't you report this?"

"We did," Amka told him, "to everyone in authority. When I called back to ask what action they were taking, each told me to call another agency. I was stuck in an endless loop, including with Ranger Trapscott."

"Bureaucracy." Michael nodded.

"Or apathy. Incompetence comes to mind, too."

"You have every reason to be upset, Amka."

"Don't patronize me, Special Agent Walker."

"I'm not. I'll include all this in a report I'm going to file. I can't promise how effective that will be, but I can promise to shake some sense into people."

"You mean, you promise to do your best. You can't promise they'll actually take action."

"Yes, I can," Michael insisted, "even if it means driving them here myself."

"You're a determined man." Amka glanced down at his prosthetic foot. "You pushed yourself so you could come back to the Park Service and I'm guessing you've had to continue to push yourself to stay there."

"True enough," he said. "I've been around fish blights, caused by algae blooms or oil spills, but never anything like this."

Amka started walking toward the largest concentration of the collected fish and Michael fell into step behind her. The two *Kiks.ádi* warriors remained in place, hovering over their ATVs while never seeming to blink as their eyes trailed them. As they drew closer to the rock bed forming the shoreline, Michael spotted an old Tlingit man kneeling on the stones. His eyes were closed and he seemed to be speaking, or chanting, to himself.

"That is Chief Xetsuwu, our oldest remaining elder," Amka said, following his stare. "He has led the Hoonah Tlingit nation for many years and was descended from the elders who manned the fort at the Battle of Sitka. He is also my grandfather."

"Grandfather? How old is he?"

"Nobody knows."

"What's he doing?"

"Why don't we ask him?"

Amka signaled Michael to hold his ground twelve feet from the old man and approached the rest of the way on her own. The chief's eyes were glazed over with untreated cataracts, which didn't stop him from following her every move. Michael listened to Amka greet her grandfather and then open a conversation in the Tlingit language. She nodded through whatever Chief Xetsuwu said in response, turning toward Michael when he stopped.

"He says the gods of the sea are angry."

The old man began speaking in his native tongue again.

"He said this is punishment."

Michael couldn't find any sense in that. "Punishment for your people?"

Amka shook her head. "For the world. My grandfather says it is beginning."

"What's beginning?" Michael asked, and then listened to Amka pose a question which her grandfather answered not only with his voice, but also with a series of hand gestures to better make his point.

Amka finally turned back his way. "There is a story my people tell about the end of the world. The world is constantly spinning, balanced on a stick held by a giant named Amala. But Amala's muscles get tired, and so once a year a servant of his rubs his muscles with duck oil to ease the pain. But one day the ducks go extinct, and there is no more duck oil for the giant's muscles. So he drops his stick and the world will end. That's the story my grandfather just told me. He finished by saying the ducks are gone now, so the world is going to die, beginning here."

Michael retrained his gaze on the endless piles of fish collected on the shoreline. He had heard any number of rangers speak of similar situations they had encountered in national parks. But it had always been dozens of fish, a few hundred at times. Never anything like this. The only thing that came even remotely close in his experience had been relayed to him by an Irish counterpart to a park ranger, known as a warden, who was spending a summer in Zion as part of an exchange agreement.

The warden had told him of a massive fish kill in the Callan River, a tributary of the Blackwater, one of the main rivers flowing into Lough Neagh. Pollution was the cause in that case, specifically a coal sludge, or slurry, spill that devasted an area that included nursery grounds for juvenile salmon. The warden had shown Michael pictures that didn't even approach what he was looking at here. From an environmental standpoint, the only thing that could have caused a fish kill of this magnitude was a massive oil spill, but that would have left considerable telltale signs that were nowhere to be found in this case and would have been of a magnitude that made it a lead story in the news. Something else then.

But what could possibly account for a kill of this magnitude?

Michael was pondering that when Chief Xetsuwu began speaking in the Tlingit native language again.

"My grandfather says you are asking the wrong question."

Even though Michael hadn't posed his question out loud, it jarred him a bit. "Ask him if he has any idea what caused this."

"I already have, several times. He doesn't."

But the old man resumed speaking anyway, as if he'd heard Michael's question.

"He says there is an evil here," Amka translated.

"Can he be more specific?"

But Chief Xetsuwu had already resumed speaking, Amka ready to translate instead of posing Michael's question to him.

"He says this is only the first wave, that the death will multiply." Amka spoke faster, trying to keep up with her grandfather. "And that the death will move from the water onto the land and man will die on the ground he has despoiled. He says that nature has grown angry because all of her previous warnings have gone unheeded. He says there will be no more warnings. Nothing can change what is to come."

Michael turned his gaze back on the fish still collecting on the rocky shoreline. "What did your grandfather mean about the death moving from the water onto the land?"

Amka repeated the question to her grandfather in the Tlingit native language, then followed up with something else when his answer seemed to confuse her.

"My grandfather speaks in an old tongue not spoken any longer. I didn't translate his words accurately in this case or the point he was making. He says this is *yadujeeyí,* punishment for man's sins committed against the land. He says that man has angered the spirit of the forest and the trees. He speaks of our people's legend of *Kóoshdaa Káa,* a furry monster that could shape-shift into the form of a loved one, or play tricks like mimicking the sound of a crying baby to lure you into the woods or out to sea. Once captured, its victim would turn into a *Kóoshdaa Káa* as well. The Tlingit people used to believe anyone who went missing at sea or in the forest likely became a *Kóoshdaa Káa.* There's an unverifiable account of a landslide in Thomas Bay wiping out a Tlingit village and killing hundreds, whose bodies were never recovered—all turned into *Kóoshdaa Káa.* He says when the ground grows angry, the monster comes."

Amka stopped only because her grandfather had. He was nodding now, as if his point had been made.

"What does this monster have to do with dead fish?"

Again, the old chief seemed to understand the question posed in English and began speaking before Amka could translate.

"He says the *Kóoshdaa Káa* caused the avalanche to punish those who would spoil our land." She continued translating in quick bursts that trailed her grandfather's words by mere seconds. "He says the *Kóoshdaa Káa* grow angrier than ever before and that their anger poisoned the sea and killed the fish."

Amka stopped there, thrown off by something her grandfather said before falling silent.

"He says the *Kóoshdaa Káa* caused the avalanche that swallowed the people you came here to find, but you'll never find them because they're gone, turned into *Kóoshdaa Káa* as well."

"How could he know about the missing USGS team? How could he know I came here to find them?"

"I didn't tell him, if that's what you're getting at. And I can't tell you how my grandfather knows such things, because I don't know myself."

Michael met the old man's milky gaze and thought he detected the slightest of smiles. "So am I looking for a monster?"

"The monsters are everywhere, Special Agent Walker," the old man said in English.

CHAPTER 23

FISHERS ISLAND, NEW YORK

The island was called Munnawtawkit by the Pequot Indians.

Axel Cole's three-year-old son, Basil, crawled up into his lap, lugging a book he'd grabbed from his bookshelf.

"Let's read this one, Daddy. It's my favorite!"

Cole took the book entitled *The Safe Place* from his grasp and smiled. "We read this one yesterday."

"Again, Daddy, again! Please!"

"Sure," Cole agreed, opening to page one.

He couldn't have been happier with his son's choice. *The Safe Place* was a children's survivalist book, detailing the exploits of a family that moved into a fortified bunker constructed beneath their home. Cole figured Basil enjoyed it as much as he did because a comparable bunker, though far bigger and much better stocked, lay beneath the home he had rebuilt on Fisher Island's Isabella Beach Road.

"Who was that man you were talking to before with the big eyes?"

The man Basil was referring to wore thick glasses that made his eyes look extra large. "Nobody."

"What's that mean?"

"Nobody important."

"Why don't you like him? Why, Daddy?"

"Because he told me a story I didn't like."

‡‡‡

"Wonderful view, Mr. Cole," Phillip Farnsworth said that morning, admiring the ocean through the wall-length, floor-to-ceiling glass that dominated his Fisher Island home's vast family room.

It was Cole's favorite room in the house, in large part because of the view Farnsworth had taken note of. Though his name was Phillip, he went by PT, no periods, on the blog he claimed had five million readers. Maybe so, but it hadn't attracted anywhere near that many until Farnsworth took to focusing on Cole and his businesses. And the audience he boasted came courtesy of the following he'd built on Cole's own social media site.

"I can see why you call this the favorite of all your homes," Farnsworth continued, turning from the view to face Cole, who was seated on a couch that cost more money than Farnsworth's *In Your Face* blog would reap in a year.

Right now, he was spoiling Cole's view. Cole couldn't stand the sight of his overweight frame dressed in rumpled clothing that looked pulled from a clothes hamper. His hair was a windblown mess, worn long to hide his premature balding state. Clumps of it dropped toward the glasses he wore, with lenses looking as thick as the glass he'd just been peering out of.

"Was that your first trip on a private jet, Phillip?" Cole asked, hiding his scowl behind his words.

"I go by PT now, Mr. Cole, and yes, it was my first time. But not my last, now that *In Your Face* is taking off."

"Yes, thanks to me in large part. I don't enjoy your coverage, PT, but you know how much I believe in the First Amendment and that includes on the site I own."

"Practice what you preach, in other words."

"Have a seat, PT."

Farnsworth waddled over to a pair of armchairs located in front of the couch and seemed to carefully consider which one to take. "This is some place you've got here, Mr. Cole," he said, after finally making his choice.

Axel Cole had eleven homes scattered across the world, four in the United States, of which this one, on Fishers Island off the New York coastline, was the most recent and renovated to be the family's safe house. Except for the unseen bunker added during the renovation, though, it didn't look all that different from the homes closest to it a half mile away. The fifteen-thousand-square-foot house boasted a lot of attractive features, but its isolation on an island setting had been the reason why Cole had made it his eleventh home. As always, he had made a handwritten list of everything he was looking for and this location checked every one of those boxes. While extensive renovations had cost more than double the original $6 million purchase price, the house's placement and structure allowed Cole to realize all the components of his vision, starting with that four-thousand-square-foot safe house. A construction crew that specialized in catering to that particular task for the few that could afford it had burrowed beneath the home's north-facing rear and both sides.

Built originally on a man-made hill shored up by rocks, loom, and bushes, the sprawling home backed up against woodlands that Cole had fortified with motion detectors and booby-traps. His wife complained mightily when his older son and daughter came upon what was left of a fox that triggered one of those traps that were activated only at night, but she wasn't complaining now, given the constant threats the family had been receiving thanks to Cole's outspoken, unpopular stances on pretty much every issue. With that in mind, Cole opted to be proactive rather than reactive. He might never once have played it safe in business, but when it came to his family's and his own survival, all bets were off.

"Well," Cole said to Farnsworth, "I'm sure once your blog blows up, you'll be able to afford your own private jet. And that's what I brought you here to discuss: your future."

Farnsworth leaned forward expectantly.

"I've gotten word about the next piece you're planning to drop. That's what I mean about the future, PT, because yours can go one of two ways depending on what you decide in the next five minutes."

‡‡‡

His son tugging at his hair snapped Axel Cole back to the present.

"Read it, Daddy, read it!" he said, slapping at the children's book.

Cole's favorite parts of the house were the bulletproof windows and blast-proof titanium hurricane shutters that could be lowered over them in the event of an attack. The third-floor tower room, meanwhile, offered 360-degree views of the property. His wife loved it because it was the perfect setting for her to paint, drawing inspiration from the view, while Cole loved it because it offered his security team an expansive view all the way to the sea beyond the woods abutting the rear of the property. With guards stationed there twenty-four hours a day, there was no way anyone could approach the house without being spotted.

"Once upon a time," Cole started, feeling his son pat his thick, curly locks like he was a dog, "there was a family named Good that lived alone far away from anyone else. The Good family wanted to protect itself from the terrible, bad things that happened to other people. There were bad people out there who wanted to hurt people like the Goods. Robin and Chris Good decided to build a safe place to go to when really bad people came or really bad things happened. The threats were everywhere and, sooner or later, the Goods knew they would have to face those threats."

Like the threat Cole had faced earlier in the day.

✝✝✝

Farnsworth's round face puckered, his cheeks looking like they were pumped full of air. "Whatever you've heard—"

"Not just heard, PT, seen with my own two eyes. Just a rough cut, but unflattering to say the least. You accused me of murdering my older brother so I could inherit all of our father's money, without producing a shred of evidence. This witness you claim to have doesn't exist. You made him up."

Farnsworth was smacking his lips together. "I don't know what you think you saw, but—"

"I know what I saw was defaming. Not just the accusation about my brother's death, this absurd allegation that I killed him to claim all of my father's inheritance, but the allegations you lodged against my father and grandfather, also while providing no evidence. I considered suing you, until my people told me you've got no assets for me to take. So I decided to offer you this opportunity to stop posting about me, starting with this new story composed of nothing but lies."

The rolls of fat lining his jowls shook as Farnsworth shook his head. "I have principles, Mr. Cole. I can't do that."

"Principles . . . That's your decision?"

Farnsworth's big, round eyes glistened. "Unless you want to pay me to change my mind. You know, catch and kill."

"My offer is nothing. Take it or leave it."

Farnsworth managed a nod. "Maybe I shouldn't have come here."

Cole flashed his trademark smile. "And miss your first ride on a private jet? Then I would have lost the opportunity to see your reaction to what you've done to yourself. At least I gave you a chance."

✝✝✝

Cole kept reading, but without the usual enthusiasm or invective he used to get his son to smile.

More than a day had passed since he had flown here from New Orleans at the conclusion of his initial meeting with Elizabeth Fields, his jet landing at the field on the western end of the island where he had relocated his family. The murder of his couriers in Alaska, and theft of the latest shipment, could only mean someone was onto him, someone as ruthless as he was. Worse, the Alaskan authorities were now in possession of that final shipment. Sooner or later, they'd figure out what it was. They wouldn't believe it, of course; even Cole himself didn't believe it when the discovery was first made deep in the Alaskan ice. The whole artifacts smuggling ring had been conceived by him personally to minimize the chances of detection. So, too, the crews he had scattered throughout Alaska, probing and digging in the ice, were kept small. Bribes were paid in place of official permits, and the officials pocketing the money knew better than to ask what he was pulling out of the tundra.

If Cole had told them, they would have dismissed him as an eccentric multibillionaire who had nothing better to do with his time. But thanks to what his teams had found hidden within the permafrost of Alaska for thousands, if not millions, of years, multibillionaire was nothing compared to what was to come.

Cole flipped to the next page of *The Safe Place,* his son hanging on every word.

"Then one day, the bad people came."

‡‡‡

Cole worked his phone, typing something, as Farnsworth watched. "Check your website."

Farnsworth took a tablet-sized phone from his pocket and clicked, eyes widening at what he saw.

"It's gone. Something's wrong."

"Yes, there is."

"You did this."

Cole nodded. "Your data's gone, irretrievably I'm told, from my social media site as well." He typed some more. "Oh, and you won't be able to take the ferry home because your bank account has been wiped and your credit cards canceled."

Click, click, click . . .

"And the contents of your server are now in the hands of the FBI. You know what the penalty is for distributing child pornography these days?"

Farnsworth's lips moved, but no words emerged, only gushes of hot air. "I don't know what you're talking about," he said finally. "This is crazy. I've never looked at child porn in my life!"

"Then the fact that my tech people fabricated the evidence will remain our little secret, PT. You're looking at a five-year sentence if you plead out. That would be my recommendation."

"I'll do what you say!" Farnsworth pleaded. "The story about your background will never see the light of day!"

"Of course it won't, because it's been deleted. Time's up, PT. I think you should be on your way."

‡‡‡

"For Robin and Chris Good, defending their family against people who wanted to hurt them was the most important thing in the world," Cole read, nearing the end of *The Safe Place*.

Basil had slipped off to sleep, and Cole cradled the boy against his chest. The cell phone he'd stowed on the chair's side table buzzed, **ELIZABETH FIELDS** in the caller ID. He answered it with his son still napping on his lap.

"Progress already, Elizabeth?" he said softly.

"Why are you whispering? I can barely hear you."

"Tell me why you called."

"Not over the phone, Axel," she told him. Cole was unable to discern whether her tone was excitement or panic. "I need to see you at Michoud. How soon can you get back here?"

CHAPTER 24

JOINT BASE ELMENDORF-RICHARDSON, ANCHORAGE, ALASKA

Soldiers and troops use rail to travel over the often-treacherous four hundred miles to Fort Wainwright.

The officer had said someone was coming *up* to get Gina. Since they were on the first floor, that meant more than just a basement was contained beneath them.

"Please join me, Special Agent Delgado," another officer said, emerging from an elevator set off from the rest of the bank.

He had coarse black hair trimmed military short, and bushy eyebrows thick enough to cast shadows over his hooded eyes. This officer, too, wore no rank or lapel patch identifying him by name. Such practice was reserved for personnel assigned to the most secretive of operations where the term "classified" didn't even begin to describe their work.

She joined him inside the elevator, the door sliding closed as soon as she was inside. The cab slid into a smooth descent through the frozen tundra of the area, necessitating a construction job of nearly unprecedented scope, accounting for the ultra-classified operations that must be taking place in this particular section of the base.

"You are about to enter one of only ten operational facilities like this in the country, ma'am," the man said, as if reading her thoughts. "I apologize for the delay, but we don't have a lot of experience with visitors here."

"I understand, sir."

"I don't think you do, ma'am, and I don't mean any disrespect by that."

"None taken, but as one of only ten operational facilities like this in the country, what is it exactly that you do here?"

The officer's brow furrowed, his bushy eyebrows for an instant looking like one long unbroken patch. "The White House didn't provide those details?"

"They sent me down here to report directly to them on what killed the crew of a Virginia-class submarine."

"We haven't determined the what yet, ma'am, only the how and it makes no sense."

‡‡‡

The descent continued for ten seconds. Gina had no idea how many floors they were passing or how deep into the tundra this facility went. She couldn't imagine the scope of the efforts to construct such a facility, much less the additional nine she assumed were scattered strategically across the country.

The cab eased to a gentle stop and the single door whooshed open, revealing a hallway that might have been a twin of the one back on the surface.

"I reviewed the secure file the White House forwarded on you," the officer said, as they stepped out. He planted himself before her, blocking her way down the hall. "You served with a Special Forces A Team in Iraq."

"Yes, sir, I did."

"Demolitions. Impressive work. If they gave medals for that kind of covert ops, you'd have earned a chest full."

"Thank you, sir."

"What are your orders from the White House exactly, Captain Delgado?"

It had been a long time since Gina had been addressed by her military rank. "Observe and report."

"And how much background did they provide you?"

"Just what I told you. The crew of a Virginia-class submarine was found dead."

The officer nodded stiffly. "The sub was on a training mission when it was struck by a World War Two mine being raised from the sea floor by a salvage vessel unaware she was in the area. The explosion caused a reactor SCRAM that knocked out her engines and she sank to the bottom, more than thirteen hundred feet down." The officer stopped there. "This way, ma'am."

He continued as he led Gina down the long hall with no visible door-ways on either side. They reached the end of the hall and swung the only way they could, left, down what looked like another matching hallway, without breaking stride.

"Once the rescue team became aware the entire crew had perished, the rescue operation became one of recovery instead," the officer continued. "And the one hundred and twenty bodies were brought here, observing all safety protocols consistent with the possibility of a biological attack, after an extremely challenging extraction process from the submarine."

Gina let that remark go. "The Russians?" she posed, aware that their subs were known to frequent the waters off the Alaskan coast.

"That has pretty much been ruled out. There's nothing in the ship's recorded log about any Russian sub in the area. And even if there was, we don't believe any adversarial action it might have taken could possibly explain the circumstances of the crew's deaths."

They reached a single door. The officer laid his palm against the face of a wall-mounted scanner. A beep sounded and the door slid open to reveal what appeared to be an anteroom offering access to one of a half-dozen steel doors, some kind of lab almost surely located behind each one.

A soldier rose before a console that curved around a hefty portion of the floor and saluted. The officer saluted back and led Gina to the console, while the soldier remained at attention.

"At ease, son. And bring up the Tomb on your screen."

The soldier retook his seat and worked his keyboard. The central screen on the state-of-the-art curved console came to life, displaying what looked like a massive morgue outfitted with what appeared to be an endless array of steel tables, one for each of the crew members of the submarine now lying naked atop them.

"What you're looking at is an airtight, impregnable facility directly below us," the officer explained. "The lights you see flashing across the console represent individual sensors monitoring each and every body for any potential discharge into the air."

"You suspect something biological was to blame for this?"

The officer didn't answer her question directly. "A hundred and twenty people died of the identical cause in the four hours that passed between the time of the distress signal being sent via SLOT buoy and the deaths being visually confirmed via onboard cameras."

As he continued, the soldier manning the controls worked a track ball that rotated the room's cameras in a slow pan over all the bodies. The skin tone of all of them was a frosty white with a bluish tint. The rest of the console was taken up, she realized, by flashing grids and diodes that were actually real-time data supplied by drones, one for each row, that were making continuous passes with remote scanning devices responsible for the readouts flashing on the LED screens.

"Each of those bodies, Captain Delgado, has been subjected to every imaginable scan and test with the most sophisticated diagnostic equipment on the planet," her nameless escort resumed. "The blood, tissue, and bones of every one of them has been tested, and not a single clue as to what caused their deaths has been found. Nothing out of place. No biological or chemical anomalies that, by all rights, should have been there. I can also tell you that the sub itself has been thoroughly examined for anything and everything that might explain this, and nothing was found. The emergency systems were functioning perfectly, the temperature kept stable at sixty-six degrees and absolutely no sign of any anomalies in the air recirculation or filtration systems. They should have been perfectly able to survive on the bottom for four days, and the crew would have been rescued well before that. Damage from the mine was limited to the propulsion system. Everything else was running in the green, and there was plenty of emergency power left in the tank. Because an extremely virulent pathogen was considered as a likely cause, we analyzed samples of the air from every section of the ship, and I can tell you in all certainty that if a pathogen was behind all those deaths, it must have died with them, since the air tested one hundred percent clean. The White House has been apprised of all that with hourly updates, with one exception because we only arrived at a firm conclusion while you were waiting upstairs, which explains the delay in bringing you down here. We wanted to be absolutely sure and now we are."

Gina spoke while the drones continued their work on each of the rows, moving from one body to the next and then repeating the process. "You're talking about how exactly the crew died, aren't you?"

"Yes, I am, ma'am, and it makes absolutely no sense yet to the best scientific minds this country has to offer. Remember what I just told you about the onboard temperature?"

"Steady at sixty-six degrees. Is that important?"

"Vital," the officer told her. "Because the crew froze to death, each and every one of them."

⊢•⊙•⊣

CHAPTER 25

GLACIER BAY NATIONAL PARK AND PRESERVE, LAMPLUGH GLACIER

An eight-mile glacier located 43.6 miles northwest of Xunaa.

"Fasten your seat belt," Amka told Michael. "And your headset's in front of you."

Michael reached for the frayed shoulder harness of the 1966 Bell UH-1H Huey helicopter she had explained had been rebuilt from scratch by *Kiks.ádi* warrior mechanics after it was plucked off the salvage heap years before. Choppers like this had racked up thousands of hours of service in Vietnam, ferrying troops in and out of harm's way and also served as the primary platform for emergency medical evacuations from the field. As far as he knew, none of these Hueys had seen action in decades, but plenty had been sold off to the militaries of other countries where they remained in service until spare parts that were difficult to obtain became impossible, once there were no more junked ones to harvest from.

"Why aren't we taking off?" he asked, the *Kiks.ádi* pilot having gotten the rebuilt engine all warmed up.

"Waiting for one more," Amka said.

In that moment, a teenage boy hoisted himself on board, his long black hair bouncing about his shoulders.

"Special Agent Walker, this is my brother, Yehl."

"Did my sister lay the guilt trip on you about having to come home to keep me out of jail?"

"She mentioned foster care."

Yehl glanced toward Amka. "Oh, so she didn't tell you . . ."

Amka spoke with her gaze fastened on Yehl. "My brother has friends on the mainland—"

"White friends," the boy interrupted, "which she doesn't want me to have."

"I don't care that they were white. I care that they were criminals." She looked back toward Michael. "He was arrested twice, once for vandalism and once for possession of marijuana."

"Like an eighth, that's all. And it was lousy shit anyway."

"It's still illegal," Amka picked up, still addressing Michael. "And with our father hospitalized at the time, if I didn't come home, it would have been jail or foster care—maybe both."

"She'd been gone so long, she didn't even recognize me at first, right, *sis*?"

Amka returned his remark with a glare. "I told him if I caught him smoking weed or sneaking off the island to meet up with his friends, I was done."

"She left here before I was born. Girl doesn't even know me." Yehl pulled a lighter from his pocket. "I still carry this to piss her off. She caught me eating gummy bears one day and thought they were edibles. Even tested them in her lab. I'm still waiting for an apology."

"I said I was sorry."

The boy grinned. "But I wanted your new boyfriend to hear it."

Amka shook her head. Michael tried not to laugh.

"My brother was named for a Tlingit trickster of lore," Amka told Michael. "He's definitely living up to his name."

Michael pegged Yehl as right around sixteen years old, give or take a few months. He had the same black hair as his sister, dangling past his jacket's collar, and boasted the same strong features. He was of average size and build, nothing that stood out at all, besides the perpetual smirk that rode his expression, as it did for all teenagers.

"My brother is a tracker," Amka told him. "It's a skill one is born with, not taught. And my brother's birthright is to be the next chief of our tribe when our grandfather passes."

"Yeah, lucky me," Yehl said, rolling his eyes.

"Do we really need a tracker?" Michael asked Amka.

"Do you know where to look for your missing scientists once we reach the glacier?"

Aerial searches by satellite, plane, and helicopter had failed to turn up any trace of the USGS team, which meant traversing the glacier was the only way to find them.

"No," Michael conceded.

"Then it will be left to my brother to find them."

Even with the three of them, the pilot, and two additional warriors, there was plenty of room on board the Huey to evacuate all members of the United States Geological Survey team, if they were lucky enough to find any left alive.

"Normally, we use this only for trips to the mainland for supplies and emergency situations," she said.

The *Kiks.ádi* pilot threw some more switches on the ancient warhorse and the rotor lurched into a lumbering spin that quickly turned to a blur. Amka reached for her headset and signaled Michael to do the same, as the chopper lifted off from the makeshift helipad on the outskirts of town.

He wasn't sure why two *Kiks.ádi* in addition to the pilot had joined them on the trip. Was there reason for Amka to fear for her safety? Did she think the Park Service would hire gunmen to come after her because of the trouble she continued to stir up? Or maybe it was for protection against the *Kóoshdaa Káa*, the legendary monster her grandfather claimed was lurking about.

"You haven't spoken your thoughts about what you saw on the shoreline, *wáachwaan*."

"I'm not a policeman," Michael corrected tersely, translating the word she'd just spoken.

"You didn't tell me you spoke our language," Amka noted into her headset.

He smiled. "I'm full of surprises."

Twenty minutes into the flight, the Huey slowed to a hover over a large, mostly flat plain that abutted the sprawling Lamplugh Glacier itself. As it turned out, there was little ice and snow over these lower reaches that was the USGS team's last reported position. That made for an easy landing for the chopper, which set down into the wind, enough to tell Michael the warrior pilot was no stranger to the Alaskan conditions and had likely piloted more modern crafts in war zones. Only military pilots, in his experience, had the steely-eyed, fearless demeanor the man behind the chopper's controls had exhibited.

Michael swung open the door on his side, which offered a majestic view of their surroundings. He saw that the icy landscape grew thicker and thicker the farther up the glacier his eyes went. The residue of the avalanche had deposited several boulder-sized rocks wrapped in ice down here in the plain and had generally left what should have been reasonably flat land difficult and even precarious to negotiate. The conditions would be quite a test for his prosthetic, something Amka seemed to acknowledge when the pilot cut the Huey's engine.

"My brother and I can go ahead and scout the area. You don't need to accompany us," she said, as they waited for the rotor to slow before exiting the craft. "We can call you on a walkie-talkie I can give you."

"I'll tag along, if it's all the same to you . . . and them," Michael added, eyes tilted toward the pair of *Kiks.ádi* unstrapping themselves farther back in the cabin.

Amka cracked a slight smile. "Unless you plan on doing me harm, you have nothing to fear. They're here to protect all of us."

"From what? I can safely say the Park Service doesn't hire hitmen to deal with tribal leaders."

"The Park Service is far from our only enemies up here. The *Kiks.ádi* accompanying me are out of an abundance of caution. It is their way."

"Shouldn't that make you the next chief of the tribe, following your grandfather?"

Amka dropped down out of the cabin to the ground, while Michael used the ladder extension to minimize the stress on his prosthetic. Yehl emerged next, touching down gracefully on the ground and immediately setting off to locate the trail, first with his eyes before kicking at the ground and then crouching down to run his hand across it in a smoothing motion until, ten feet later, he stopped at a spot that had drawn his interest. He seemed to follow something that had caught his attention another ten feet along the same line.

Amka looked toward Michael. "Our father, the rightful heir, is in the local hospital being treated for acute liver failure. Absent a donor, he doesn't have long to live. And our tradition insists the position must be passed down to a male in the bloodline."

"Not very modern, is it?"

"Neither are we, Agent Walker."

"What happened to your mother?"

"Over here!" Yehl called out to them.

‡‡‡

He was crouching, smoothing the ground with his hand and sifting through dirt, pebbles, and small rocks before letting them settle again. The debris field left behind by the avalanche covered the whole of the jagged surface. Anyone familiar with this area was aware that that was nothing new. In June of 2016, an entire mountain collapsed onto the Lamplugh Glacier, causing a massive landside that dropped an estimated one hundred and twenty million tons of rock. In that case, the debris field had been over five and a half miles long.

"There were six of them," the boy said, when Michael and Amka reached him. "They were standing here in a tight grouping." He rose and started walking, not seeming to care whether Michael and Amka followed or not. "Then the avalanche made them rush toward the glacier. Their spacing widened. At least two of the six, both women based on the size and shape of their shoes, lagged behind. They headed that way," he finished, pointing to a rise in the glacier that was stark white, encrusted in ice and snow. "Going in this direction and angle was the only way to escape the avalanche."

Michael cast his gaze up the sides of a narrow, imposing trail that wound its way up the glacier, as Yehl moved on.

"You should stay behind," Amka said, sounding compassionate this time. "We don't want the glacier to claim another victim."

"We haven't confirmed it's claimed any yet."

"You heard what my grandfather said. He is never wrong about such things."

Yehl's voice called to them from another dozen feet ahead on the plain. "I found something else."

CHAPTER 26

GLACIER BAY NATIONAL PARK AND PRESERVE, LAMPLUGH GLACIER

The glacier was named after George William Lamplugh, a celebrated British geologist, in 1912.

"Another set of tracks begins here," the boy said, still smoothing the ground from a crouched position. "No trace of them anywhere before here."

"How many men?" Michael asked him.

"A dozen. And these tracks are fresher, which means the men came in hours after your scientists. Maybe a half day later, something like that."

Amka drew even with Michael. "Any word of another rescue party?"

"No, which tells me maybe this wasn't a rescue party. They must have come in by helicopter. That's the only explanation for why their tracks only begin here."

She managed a nod. "That long after your USGS team went missing, the wind would have died down enough for a chopper to approach. It couldn't have landed, but the dozen men those tracks belong to could have winched down."

Michael and Amka watched Yehl stand all the way back up again and sweep his gaze toward the base of the glacier.

"This way," he beckoned, moving along the trail only he could see, while his eyes remained fixed upward.

‡‡‡

At first, Michael thought the boy had chosen the most walkable parts of whatever remained of the icy trail leading up the glacier because they were the easiest to navigate. Then he realized from Yehl's mannerisms, the way he kept stopping and sifting through the land's surface, that he was following the trail the missing USGS team members had left. For his part, Michael couldn't see any indication at all of anything resembling footprints, no telltale depressions on icy land the avalanche had rolled over in its path.

Amka was content to let the boy practice the ancient skill Michael had never realized was a genetic birthright until today. She let him climb on ahead of them, going off in one direction at times, only to double back and start again.

"There is more to tracking than footprints, *wáachwaan*."

"I told you not to call me that," Michael said lightly.

"We have no word in our language for special agent."

"What about ranger?"

"Yes, it's pronounced ass-hole."

Then, she actually smiled, the two them looking at each other when her brother called out, "Up here!"

He had climbed more than thirty feet ahead, waving his arms to make sure he had their attention.

"I think I found where they went!"

Then he pointed at what looked like the mouth of a cave.

‡‡‡

Amka was right, Michael realized halfway up the trail that stretched over a hundred feet up the side of the glacier: he should have stayed behind, based on the strain the climb was taking on his prosthetic. Several times his balance betrayed him and he was afraid its housing was about to crack or snap. Once the foot snared in a narrow gap between two jagged ice formations. Before he could call out for help, Amka slid back to work with him to extract the prosthetic from its snare.

"You good to go?" she asked him.

Michael tested the foot. "I'm tougher than I look."

"The flesh and blood part of you, you mean."

He cast his gaze back down the trail. The *Kiks.ádi* were hanging back by the spot where Yehl had first picked up the presence of those dozen men who came in by helicopter.

"They didn't follow us," he said to Amka.

"They can't save me from the dangers of climbing a glacier, *dleit ñáa*," she told him, using the word for white man again.

"We back to that?"

"You don't like me using *wáachwaan* and I've got to call you something."

"What's wrong with Michael?"

"Not sure I trust you enough yet."

The trek up the glacier's winding, ice-laden path was even more arduous than it had looked from ground level. The Lamplugh Glacier in total was over twenty-one miles long and almost a mile wide, and nearly one hundred and seventy-five feet at its highest point—all of it located within the grounds of Glacier Bay National Park. From the plain below, it extended for as far as the eye could see and at this point Michael had no idea what had brought the missing United States Geological Survey team here in the moments before the avalanche roared downward off Mount Cooper, which loomed ominously above. He tried to picture what it must have been like, running into the path of that avalanche to find safe harbor from the rolling debris packing thousands of tons coming straight for them.

Barely seventy feet up from ground level, the world seemed to have changed entirely. The wind grew stiffer and the air distinctly colder with the glacial ice all around them, seeming to take on a bluish tint when the angle of the light was right. Michael realized they must have been actually climbing atop what the debris field had left here in its path.

Yehl was scrutinizing a particular patch and seemed to be waiting for Amka and Michael to catch up. When they finally did, the boy kept his gaze downward at a patch of icy snow he had cleared. Michael had no idea what that process had revealed to him, but Yehl continued to work his hands through the ice and snow he continued to peel away.

"Two of them were injured here," the boy explained, gaze still locked on the ground. "Something broken or sprained in both cases. Two other team members helped the two who were injured. They fell behind the others but followed the same trail."

Yehl traced the air with a hand, pointing with his finger when he spotted something another fifty or sixty feet up the trail.

"To that," he said, aiming toward the same cave mouth as before.

Michael was aware that warming temperatures had substantially reduced normal snowfall totals. As a result, the same subglacial stream responsible for the muddy conditions below just short of the glacier's base flowed in a way that created large caves in its face. With Yehl having followed the USGS team's trail up the glacier, it stood to reason that the team had sought refuge in one of them.

"What about the second set of tracks you found below?" Amka wondered.

"Same thing here. Whoever came in that helicopter followed them up this trail hours later. And . . ."

"And what?" Michael prodded, when the boy's voice trailed off, as if he were unsure about something.

"There's a second trail indicating the men who followed came back down."

"But not the USGS team members."

Yehl shook his head. "No."

The point the boy was getting at was obvious. Michael looked toward Amka.

"Just like my grandfather said," she told him.

They climbed the rest of the way up the icy trail together, the boy performing only cursory checks at his feet to make sure he hadn't missed anything. When they neared the entrance to the cave, Michael slid in front of them and stopped at the mouth, which was formed entirely of ice. It looked to be between fifteen and eighteen feet wide and just as deep. He couldn't see much through the darkness beyond, but it was enough to tell him no one was inside, dead or alive.

He was about to enter the cave, when Amka clamped a hand on his jacket.

"We must remain here, not risk disturbing what Yehl needs to see and feel."

The boy moved past them wordlessly, his long black hair swimming past the fur neck of his parka, concentrating on the cave floor.

"Do you have a flashlight?"

Michael unclipped a Maglite from his belt and handed it to the boy, careful not to go beyond the entrance. Yehl switched it on and began sweeping it across the cave floor in widening concentric circles. Michael had no idea what he was looking for, or sensing; very likely, the boy didn't know himself. In his years of experience with the Park Service, this was the first time Michael had seen a Native tracker in motion, and it was nothing like he'd expected or seen depicted in films.

"All six in the original party I followed made it this far," Yehl said suddenly, the flashlight beam looking like a strobe as he continued to sweep it about the cave. "This is where they collapsed and their spirits left their bodies."

"You're saying they died here."

The boy just looked at him. "It's what the land says. I'm just relaying the message. The men who came in the helicopter got here hours after the spirits left the bodies of those who died. The disturbances in the ice makes their presence clearer. They arrived a half day later for sure."

That meant they'd come at night, when chances of their presence being detected were substantially lower.

"This explains what I couldn't figure out about the second set of tracks leading downward instead of upward," Yehl resumed. "The excess weight left deeper depressions in the snow and ice."

"You didn't mention that before."

"I wanted to be able to explain the reason first. It's what trackers do," Yehl told him.

"The second group who came up the trail must have carried them down," Michael concluded.

He had located the spot where the USGS team had fled to avoid the avalanche, but another group had clearly gotten here ahead of this de facto rescue party. Who? And why take the bodies with them?

"There was something else in the cave," Yehl said suddenly.

Michael watched him move to the farthest reaches of the cave and resume the process of sweeping the icy floor, first with the flashlight beam and then with his hands. The snow and ice the boy was inspecting appeared sunken.

"It was right in this spot, where it had been for a very long time," Yehl said in a droll monotone, the product of the tracker daze that had consumed him, as Michael and Amka crouched alongside him. "Very old, frozen for thousands of years. Some kind of animal, I think."

"The *Kóoshdaa Káa*," Amka muttered.

Michael recalled the story of the vengeful monster her grandfather had told them. "This coming from a scientist?"

"My grandfather is known to speak in figurative terms. It may not have been the *Kóoshdaa Káa*, but a monster is behind what happened here all the same."

"What's that?" he asked her, spotting something.

Amka shined her flashlight toward what he was pointing at. Sure enough, what looked to be long strands of matted-together hair were protruding from the cave floor in a clump. Michael removed the glove on his right hand so he could put an evidence glove in its place. Readying a sealable evidence pouch, he reached down to pluck the matted hair loose from the ice that had snared it.

"Be careful," Amka warned.

"I am being careful."

"I mean be careful how you treat the land. The Tlingit way is to leave everything as we found it."

"This is a crime scene," Michael reminded her, "murder potentially, and this is the only evidence we've got."

"The members of the team, the first ones in here," Yehl said to them, having shifted back to the area he believed all the bodies had fallen nearer the front of the cave. "They died within moments of each other, no time for any of them to help another. Whoever took the bodies, took whatever was inside waiting for them, too. Did their best to hide their presence but didn't do a very good job."

"Can I see for myself?" Michael asked Yehl.

The boy beckoned him forward, while Amka continued to inspect the cave's rear, searching for more evidence of what the USGS team had found when they entered the cave. But Yehl's gaze remained locked on her as she searched for more evidence around where Michael had plucked the animal hairs from the floor.

"She doesn't think I'm ready if time finally takes our grandfather," the boy said softly, looking up from the ground he'd been smoothing and sifting through.

"You're only, what, sixteen?"

"Almost. She thinks it should be her. She came back when our father got sick, expecting Grandfather to name her as his heir."

"As opposed to sticking with tradition?"

"By not naming her, Grandfather left that tradition in place." Yehl looked toward Amka and lowered his voice to a whisper. "My sister thinks I'm worthless, wandering through the years without purpose or direction. She doesn't think me fit to be chief, but Grandfather isn't going to live forever." His eyes widened. "I'm going to embark on my spirit walk soon and prove her wrong."

"Spirit walk?"

"What other Native American tribes call a vision quest. The Hoonah Tlingit tradition requires passing an ultimate test with nature and the elements in order for a boy to become a man."

And that's when Michael heard the crackle of gunfire erupt from outside the cave.

PART THREE

——⟫·⟪——

If future generations are to remember us with gratitude rather than contempt, we must leave them something more than the miracles of technology. We must leave them a glimpse of the world as it was in the beginning, not just after we got through with it.

—President Lyndon B. Johnson

——⟫·⟪——

CHAPTER 27

GLACIER BAY NATIONAL PARK AND PRESERVE, LAMPLUGH GLACIER

Lamplugh Glacier is losing fifty to one hundred feet a
year due to calving sections of its ice face.

The shots were coming from the rocky plain below, where Yehl had first
picked up the trail. Michael recognized the staccato bursts of assault rifles
wielded by *Kiks.ádi* warriors, but those hadn't been the first shots fired.
And, based on the flurries of fire, it was clear the *Kiks.ádi* were confronting
a superior force, vastly superior.

"Did you expect this, Walker?" Amka challenged. "Was there something you held back from us?"

"No and nothing. Whoever it is must be part of the same party that
removed the bodies from here."

"Are you saying they've been lying in wait for someone else to come?"

"No, they came because they knew we were here. That means they must
be staging from someplace close, a ship in all likelihood."

Michael drew his pistol, removed the magazine, and snapped it back
home.

"Do you have another gun?" Yehl asked him.

"No."

"Because I'm a pretty damn good shot. I practice a lot."

Michael didn't press the boy further on that. "I don't carry a backup."

"Too bad."

The boy didn't appear scared at all, at least not yet.

Michael looked toward his sister. "These caves sometimes have openings on the other side. You might be able to find a passageway all the way through."

"Or get lost or stuck trying. We're staying here," Amka insisted, stiffening. "With you."

"My sister's really stubborn," Yehl told him.

He could still hear the ratcheting fire of the *Kiks.ádi,* returned in near constant flurries by the force they had confronted. If the enemy got past them and headed up the glacier on the same trail they had used to get here, the three of them would be sitting ducks. Trapped in the dark and cold with only two magazines, twenty-eight bullets, with which to defend themselves.

Michael moved to the mouth of the cave to check the trail for anyone coming up it and saw that a thick fog bank had sprung up out of nowhere, the cloudy temperate conditions just right for this mist as thick as soup to roll in, seeming to rise out of the ice. At this point, it didn't matter what had brought these gunmen here; all that mattered was getting out of this alive.

Michael didn't know the Lamplugh Glacier's contours well enough to negotiate them blindly, but he had been involved in enough rescues in national parks under comparable conditions to know how to gauge movement and follow a path where only the next foot, or yard maybe, was visible.

"I'm going out there," Michael announced simply to Amka and her brother. "You need to find a passage to the other side of the glacier."

Amka looked up from one of the emergency propane heaters lying on the cave floor. "I've got a better idea."

‡‡‡

Michael took a single step through the cave mouth and was immediately hit by a blast of wind strong enough to threaten his balance. It seemed to swirl in all directions at once, further shutting out the world before him. While he was no stranger to these conditions, he hadn't encountered them in his capacity as an ISB agent, forced to negotiate unfamiliar terrain blindly with a prosthetic foot.

He had to figure, at least hope, that whatever these forces were, they had never found themselves swallowed by a fog bank of this nature. The fog may have extended all the way to the rock-strewn, snow-mottled plain below, but in a fashion not nearly as intense or blinding. Fog banks like this tended to be whipped up by dramatic deviations in weather fronts and temperature, like the one he, Amka, and Yehl had encountered in a climb that had seen the temperature drop ten degrees or even more.

Michael listened to the *rat-tat-tat* of the *Kiks.ádi*'s diminishing fire as their ammo waned. He assumed some number of the attacking force had made their way to the trail, while the bulk of the invaders provided cover. The trio of *Kiks.ádi* warriors might have been able to stop the rest of them in their tracks. But such a defensive posture effectively rendered them stuck in place, and with dwindling ammunition to boot, as evidenced by the decrease in the fire he recognized as theirs echoing from below.

Michael steadied himself within the blinding blanket of fog. The enemy's approach left him with the high ground. That gave him a distinct advantage, so long as he didn't slip on the icy grade of the trail his boots fought for purchase on. If any of the enemy force followed the trail up to the cave, they'd be exposed, which would give him time to measure off his shots before they spotted him through the fog.

There was a slight depression in the icy contours of the trail off to the right of the cave and Michael tucked himself into it to steady his balance and make his frame even harder to distinguish. The fog wrapped around him in layers so thick he could barely see anything in front of him at all, not even the hand in front of his face. His left hand was still garbed in a glove, but he didn't trust shooting with his right, so he kept it tucked into the pocket of his ranger-issue parka, holding fast to his SIG Sauer, under the assumption he'd have time to ready it if he spotted any of the enemy force ascending the trail.

The *Kiks.ádi*'s fire from below had become even more sporadic, just single shots now, indicative of fewer targets, diminished ammo, or some combination of the two. That's when Michael gleaned a dark silhouette moving through the opaque, ice-encrusted world before him. He spotted a second flash of movement a few yards back, and a third just a few feet behind that one. That made three in all, clinging to a trail they could barely see en route to the cave where Amka and Yehl were defenseless.

Michael weighed his options. The best thing he had going for him was the element of surprise, and he had to take full advantage of that. Right now, the three gunmen would be focused entirely on managing the climb over ice in blind conditions, almost surely more concerned with clinging to the trail than a surprise attack.

A series of more rapid bursts echoed from below, that fire returned in kind by the enemy still making its stand down there. Michael knew the climbers must have heard it, too, and would almost surely be distracted enough to squander more of their advantage in numbers.

The exchange of gunfire below had become rapid and intense once more, one side or the other mounting a determined attack. At that point, instinct drove Michael to lurch upward and twist himself into the middle of the path, finger curled around the trigger as the treads of his boots struggled for purchase on the ice. Having followed the progress of the silhouettes ascending through the soup, he fired at targets impossible to lock down, rotating his fire in a neat arc to down all three of them in the same sweep.

He thought he detected cries and grunts of pain, though the wind stole all other sounds, like that of bodies falling and tumbling, as he snapped home his second and final magazine. Michael brought the pistol back up to firing position, aimed downward again in search of more dark flecks of motion superimposed through the soup, and that's when a blur of darkness burst out of the blanket of fog and slammed into him.

He smelled sweat, blood, and body odor as he lost his wind and felt his head crack against something cushiony at first with what felt like a hard shell beneath it. Only then did Michael realize he'd hit the ground with the figure atop him, barely visible through the fog. He felt for his SIG, only to find it lost from his grasp upon impact. The man's hands dug into his throat as they slid downward together, stopped by a ridge in the ice. The man's fingers struggled to find firm purchase through his thick gloves. Already dazed from the fall and having the wind knocked out of him, Michael fought for any breath he could grab.

When that failed, he tried to pry the hands free and flailed at the face above him which proved too distant to reach. Feeling consciousness beginning to ebb, Michael groped about the ground for some potential weapon, a rock or chunk of ice, to take in his grasp. But his outstretched hands began to feel tingly, before going numb. He tried to move them but couldn't, tried to suck in some air but there was none to be had.

Suddenly, the world erupted in a blinding, hot flash. Just a burst at first that settled into a hot curtain of flame that swallowed his would-be killer's head, bright enough to break through the fog. The screams that followed were the most awful, ear-splitting sound Michael had ever heard, the attacker's hands instinctively clutching for his face as he rolled away and tried to douse the flames in the snow and ice.

Freed, Michael had enough presence of mind remaining to scrabble back up the ice, pushing with his arms and legs to stay clear of the flames that now spread down the man's entire body. The bright glow sliced through the soupy air like a beacon, illuminating Amka standing there and Yehl emerging from the cave.

"Stay inside!" she ordered the boy and crouched over Michael. "Are you okay? Can you move?"

He was still gasping for breath. "Yes, and yes," he managed.

His sharpening vision focused on the attacker's now still frame belching the stench of burned flesh, hair, and fabric.

"What did you do?" he asked Amka.

Michael thought he detected the slightest of smiles. "I soaked my sweater in what was left of the liquid fuel in those emergency heaters," she explained.

"But how did you light it?"

Amka cocked her gaze back toward Yehl standing in the cave mouth. "He gave me his lighter. Sometimes it pays to have a brother who used to smoke weed."

‡‡‡

The fog passed minutes later, with them back inside the cave. Michael's bullets had left two bodies sprawled on the ice where they'd slid farther down the trail, the remnants of the third still smoldering and smelling of burnt flesh mixed with the pungent odor of propane. Amka's homemade firebomb had cleared the top layer of ice from just before the cave mouth in an odd impressionistic design with the charred corpse smoldering at its outer reaches.

The retreating fog had left an icy sheen to the winding path, making the trek down far more precarious than the one up had been, further complicated by the fact Michael still felt awkward on his feet from the struggle that had nearly cost him his life. The treads of his boots were the only thing that saved him from slipping and falling several times, Amka and Yehl supporting him on either side through the steepest stretches.

The air cleared more and more the closer they drew to the bottom, barely touched by the fog, where the three *Kiks.ádi* warriors stood waiting.

They looked grizzled, their expressions twisted into matching snarls bent in resolve as much as anger. They carried their assault rifles at the ready, even though Michael wondered if they could possibly have any rounds left. All told, he had never seen men any tougher or more imposing than these.

One of the *Kiks.ádi* held up seven fingers.

"Seven others came. All dead," Amka said.

"I figured that out for myself."

The same *Kiks.ádi* then spoke in the native language, which was all they ever conversed in, having shunned the use of English. Michael could tell from the look on Amka's face that part of his words had unsettled her.

"He says they were Russian," she told Michael, eyes widening in concern.

» — • — « —

CHAPTER 28

JOINT BASE ELMENDORF-RICHARDSON, ANCHORAGE, ALASKA

The population of service members, family members, and civilians on the base is over thirty-two thousand.

"*Because the crew froze to death,*" Gina heard repeated in her head, "*each and every one of them.*"

Gina was still trying to make sense of that. She didn't comment, opting to let the unnamed officer behind the console explain the circumstances in his own way, as the pictures continued to shift on the monitors before them.

"The indications of the cause of death are clear, even though we haven't performed detailed autopsies. I'm sure you understand why."

The officer, clearly a medical professional, must have assumed Gina was here because she had expertise in the field. She didn't, of course, but the more she appeared to, the more likely he was to confide in her as a colleague instead of just an investigative liaison.

"You don't want to risk releasing a potential biological or chemical agent that may have killed them," Gina speculated.

To her relief, the officer nodded. "It's possible that whatever that agent is, if it's even still present at all, can no longer spread while confined to a body postmortem and thus is no longer subject to cellular division. In layman's terms, such an agent could be waiting to break free to resume its spread."

"Of course," she agreed. "Absent autopsies, do you have any theories as to how they could have frozen to death when the temperature of the sub was sixty-six degrees?"

"Have you viewed any of the footage recorded by the sub's onboard cameras?"

"It wasn't provided to me," Gina answered simply.

"There were twenty-seven cameras, not enough to chart everything in real time, but plenty to determine the general timeline. A scrutiny of that footage led us to conclude that the first indications of something going seriously awry came less than one hour after the *Providence* hit the bottom."

"Do you believe there to be a connection?"

Gina realized the room's bright lighting was canted in a way that left murky patches. The officer was seated in one of them, blurring and rendering him even more of a mystery.

"It's possible," he said, "but we're still in the process of reviewing all the footage starting with the past week to see if anything stands out with regards to causation. Something we can spot about the food, for example, or an environmental contaminant or an incident in which whatever this agent managed to get on board."

"Onto a submarine operating at sea?"

The officer shrugged. "I know. That one's a long shot, but we have to consider all possibilities, and so far the vast bulk of our focus has been directed at the timeline of the deaths."

"Sorry I interrupted."

"Don't be sorry, Captain Delgado. That's why you're here, isn't it?"

Again, Gina said nothing, waiting for him to continue.

"I can provide you with a detailed schematic of the timeline. In the meantime, between the first hint of something going physically awry, and the first death, exactly thirty-nine minutes passed. Slightly over two hours later, the entire crew was dead. It was approximately three hours after that, the camera footage revealed the crew's fate to naval command and this facility was scrambled into action."

"Can you tell where the crew members to first show symptoms were at the time?"

"Good question, Captain, but the better question is where were they when they were exposed to whatever killed them. We're in the process of backtracking through the footage toward that end. We don't expect it to be obvious so we have to review the footage from all twenty-seven cameras in painstaking fashion, certain we don't miss anything because it could literally be anything that we're looking for. I've got personnel working on that right now. If they find something, you'll be the second to know."

The officer managed an uneasy smile.

"Now, getting to the specifics you'll want to report to the White House, the crew didn't actually freeze to death the way most understand the term."

Gina simply nodded.

"Their lungs and esophagi froze first and they actually suffocated to death. The body, as you're aware, has a bit of a resistance to it, but not so much the lungs and esophagus. Imagine how your throat feels when you swallow something really cold. Now imagine that maybe a hundred, even a thousand, times worse. You wouldn't die from freezing, you would die from suffocation.

"A healthy body, Captain, functions best at an internal temperature of about thirty-seven degrees Celsius or ninety-eight-point-six degrees Fahrenheit. But everyone has their own individual 'normal' body temperature, which may be slightly higher or lower. Our bodies also constantly adapt their temperature to environmental conditions. It goes up when we exercise, for instance. It's lower at night and higher in the afternoon than in the morning. Our internal body temperature is regulated by a part of our brain called the hypothalamus. The hypothalamus checks our current temperature and compares it with those mean temperatures. If our temperature is too low, the hypothalamus makes sure that the body generates and maintains heat. If our current body temperature is too high, heat is given off or sweat is produced to cool the skin."

Gina knew the officer was getting close to whatever point he was trying to make.

"Strictly speaking, body temperature refers to the temperature in the hypothalamus and in the vital internal organs. Because we cannot measure the temperature inside these organs, temperature is taken on parts of the body that are more accessible. But these measurements are always slightly inaccurate. You can lose consciousness, for example, at any point after your body temp dips below eighty-two degrees Fahrenheit and suffer potentially fatal hypothermia at any point below seventy degrees Fahrenheit. The average temperature of the bodies displayed on those monitors is forty-five degrees Fahrenheit. By all accounts, they froze from the inside out, Captain."

This time when the officer stopped, he didn't resume, inviting Gina's questions or comments.

"And this all unfolded in the space of two hours and forty minutes. I'm guessing your working theory is that we're looking at an agent that attacks the hypothalamus."

The officer nodded, pleased that she had grasped that much. "Or the mitochondrial system as a whole, Captain, causing catastrophic bodily systems failure. We've performed high-resolution scans on all the bodies in search of the definable origins of the spread. Because there was so much damage done at the cellular level, the results of those tests have been inconclusive and we're rerunning them with different parameters in the hope we can find something definitive."

The officer stopped again, giving Gina time to consider the ramifications of what she needed to report to the White House. He was describing some kind of biological or chemical agent of unprecedented virulence that could kill faster than any pathogen she'd studied as a potential bioweapon in her former position on the Joint Terrorism Task Force. The biggest remaining question, of course, was whether it was some aberration of nature or the product of a hostile action, which was even scarier.

The officer seemed to read her mind. "In your report to the White House, you need to include something just confirmed by naval intelligence via satellite telemetry. We were in the midst of reviewing the findings with them when you arrived, another reason for the delay in bringing you down here."

"What findings would those be, sir?"

"There was a Russian Typhoon-class submarine in the area when the *Providence* fell to the bottom."

CHAPTER 29

HROZA, UKRAINE

Hroza translates as "thunderstorm" in Ukrainian.

"Killing humans in war time is no different than killing animals, except in this case animals are worthy of sympathy and compassion. Not our enemy, though."

General Viktor Adamovitch, supreme commander of the Russian armed forces, spoke from the shadows of a bombed-out building that still had three walls and a jagged section of its roof attached, addressing four boys dressed as soldiers who'd yet to reach their twentieth birthdays. His presence clearly intimidated them and when Adamovitch asked them to follow him into what remained of the structure, they visibly trembled, afraid some transgression they had committed was about to end their lives. The young conscripts undoubtedly knew him by reputation, although rumors had been spreading that he wasn't real, just a made-up myth given credit for brutal behavior in the war that should have been attributed to others. After all, no man could be responsible for all of them, the thinking went.

But the thinking was wrong.

Adamovitch had ascended to this position while the war against Ukraine was going miserably for Russia, replacing another general who'd taken over for the original battlefield commander who had reportedly vanished after being pinned with the blame for the abysmal failure of the war's opening days. President Putin had personally given him the job and ever since, almost to the very day, the tide of the war had changed. In part, this was due to improved tactics and strategy, but mostly it was due to the psychological elements Adamovitch brought to the conflict, aimed at breaking the back of the Ukrainian resistance.

The truth was Adamovitch found himself admiring the Ukrainian soldiers far more than the ones in his charge, pups like the boys standing before him with more fear than respect. Boys who had no business holding weapons they were ill-trained and ill-prepared to use. Adamovitch had not come to this part of the Russian advance's front to improve those skills, he came to instill in his soldiers an understanding of what it takes to win.

"Our enemy is below an animal," he continued, moving his eyes from one boy to another down the line and back again. "Our enemy deserves to die for not pledging their loyalty when they had the chance."

As he finished, a single shot echoed from beyond. A brief pause followed, then another shot came.

"There are few men to kill in this village, because they have taken their fight elsewhere in the country. Chances are most of them are dead. You need to know," Adamovitch said, forming his lie as he spoke, "that far more of their number have died than is being reported, just as far fewer of our troops have perished than the world believes. Let the world believe whatever it wants. What matters is what you believe. You fight for the noblest of causes, that of your country, but I do not want you to lay down your life for Mother Russia—I want you, instead, to take many other lives."

Another series of shots rang out from beyond, echoing through the stale, gray air. Adamovitch walked along the row of boys, glaring at each of them. One was wearing eyeglasses, which made the reflection of the general's round face look absurdly large, his jowls taking on the shape of meat slabs hanging from his jaws. His eyes were ice blue and he had been shaving his head since he'd been about the age of the boys who'd accompanied him in here. It had rained torrentially for three consecutive days, turning the bomb-riddled, mud-strewn streets to pure muck that squished beneath his boots. A sliver of sunlight found his face and he quickly moved out of it, much preferring to be regarded in the shadows.

"Wars are not won by bombs or bullets," he told the boys, "and they are not won by love or loyalty either. They are won by fear, terror struck into the hearts of the vanquished to steal their hope. Hope, you see, is the greatest weapon of all. Take that away, and your enemy is left with nothing. Pursuing that strategy had been the biggest change I've made since taking over the war effort, and today I will see you become a part of that. I will see you become true men, true Russians, far from your mother's bosom so you can reap the glory of victory and revel in the deaths of the enemy at your feet."

The next series of shots came, and Adamovitch waited for them to subside before continuing to address his charges.

"When we arrived in this town, we found nearly two hundred women, children, and the feeble old still trying to live their lives, indignant in the face of defeat, still with a hope we must take from them. Taking hope is more productive than taking the lives, because what do the lives of women, children, and the elderly mean anyway? Nothing. They offer no resistance beyond their stubbornness in remaining, and that is enough to warrant punishment. We must dispense it in a way that our point will be made and such behavior discouraged in those who will cower before us and cry as they beg for their lives and the lives of their children. You understand what is happening out there in the street?"

Before any of the boys could answer, as if to enunciate the general's point, more shots echoed, wisps of gun smoke rising toward the gray sky faintly visible through the missing chunks of the ceiling.

"We will not kill them all," Adamovitch continued. "We will kill exactly half while the others watch and weep, fearing they are to be next. The ones we don't kill we leave alive to spread the tale, to strike terror in the hearts of the people who will no longer have the stomach for this war. Support will drop among the populace. They will begin to wonder what this was for, what it was all about, why they had bothered to fight back in the first place, now that they have paid such a high price for their misjudgment. When the hearts and minds of the people are lost, the war is lost."

Adamovitch held the gaze of each of the boys for a long moment. None of them broke his stare, a good sign. He noticed for the first time that their uniforms were too big for their frames and not fashioned of winter wool. The preparation for this war had been atrocious, the enemy underestimated at every turn. And the failure was exacerbated by the leadership's refusal to fight to win at all costs.

That all changed when he was placed in command. Viktor Adamovitch knew that move had been as necessary as it was inevitable. He knew it was coming and was prepared when it did, just as he was prepared for what would come after, how he would use the victory anyone who mattered in Russia would know came at his direction. The one man he reported to now, the president, was too busy counting his billions and buying new villas on islands the world over to realize he'd gone soft and weak. A man must be both soldier and politician, but the president he served had long forgotten what it meant to be a soldier and how a war was won. By the time this war was over, he had heard the president say over and over again, Ukraine's spirit would be broken. He did not understand that breaking the spirit was the best way to win the war in the first place.

"Come with me," Adamovitch said to the four boy soldiers in his charge, when the firing did not resume after a pause. "It's your turn now."

‡‡‡

It was freezing in the square, a central gathering point on what had once been the town's main drag transformed into a storage dump for the refuse of blown-out buildings. Drawing closer, Adamovitch heard the pleasant sound of people crying and screeching, accompanied by the sight of two dozen bodies lying dead on the ground. The residue of what he left here today would resonate in especially strong fashion when word began to spread to nearby villages and, from there, to others farther away.

"Now," he said, backpedaling after turning to face the boys, "who wants to go first?"

All four raised their hands without hesitation. Good. He pointed to one at random.

"You. Choose your victims from those assembled, a mother and a child. Choose a mother who has more than one, so her other children will carry the scars of this day for the rest of their lives under Russian rule."

Adamovitch ground his boots to a halt amid the muck-strewn rubble, focusing on the boy soldier he'd chosen. "Go."

The boy walked forward stiffly, but again without hesitation. He never looked back, flashed no doubt over the task before him. Also good.

He yanked a woman and a girl who must have been her oldest daughter from the tight grouping of residents. His motions suggested a young man learning to love power, that being feared was the greatest feeling in the world, because instilling terror in others was the basis for strength. Not how much a man could lift or how big or brave he was, but how people cowered before him. You didn't need to be a great shot, because the ability to instill fear meant never having to use your gun.

As ordered, the boy soldier pushed the child into a kneeling position first, so the mother's final act would be to watch her die. It was almost too glorious to bear.

The boy soldier readied his Tokarev semi-automatic pistol, the latest TT-33 model the general had insisted be provided to even the youngest and rawest of conscripts. While he jammed back the slide and aimed the barrel downward toward the child, Viktor Adamovitch considered his own next steps that were destined to bring him to power in Russia, supplanting the president and taking his rightful place as the head of the new Russian empire.

Bang!

The screams of the child's mother curdled his ears but the sight made the discomfort worth it. The boy soldier yanked the mother down to a kneeling position next and steadied his gun on her. It trembled briefly in his grasp, then stilled. To be expected from those unused to killing who needed to have the process of it ingrained onto their psyche.

Bang!

Soon America would fall, just as this village already had amid the dingy air, thin clouds of gun smoke dissipating as they wafted over the scene. The wheels of that inevitability were already in motion, and the weapon at its root would soon be in his possession. A soldier knew bullets and bombs, but a president needed to be well versed in greater weapons that rendered those obsolete. The fear that could be stoked in an entire country, mirroring the fear that would command this village and others when the troops at his disposal departed.

All was going according to plan. The first reserves of a weapon that would change Russia's future were soon to be in hand, his country cast in a position to command the world or destroy it.

"Who's next?" he said, turning back toward the boy soldiers.

Three hands rose into the air, and the general made his selection. As the second boy soldier advanced toward the cowering crowd, Adamovitch pulled his satellite phone from a pouch holstered through his belt. He switched it on, ready to make a call when it rang.

"Yes," he greeted.

"General, it's—"

"I know who it is. Names aren't necessary."

"I understand, sir."

The man, a trusted associate in charge of his American operation, sounded anxious, even out of breath. Maybe both.

"You are not supposed to call. You know that."

"Yes, General. But you haven't checked in and I needed to—"

"I've been busy winning a war. That was commanding my attention, but you have it now, so speak."

"Our operative in Sitka never made his rendezvous."

Adamovitch gnashed his teeth.

"We believe he was shot and killed after completing his mission."

"By who?"

"Undetermined at this time. Details are, how should I say, sketchy. But we are proceeding on the assumption that the reserves he recovered after eliminating the couriers we identified are now in the possession of the American authorities. And there's something else."

"Go on."

"We've lost contact with a team dispatched to the glacier to deal with an American rescue party."

Adamovitch felt the grip of uncertainty, a grasp he was utterly unfamiliar with. Being so far away from the work that would determine his future left him with the sense of being helpless and ineffectual. The timetable for the next stage would have to be advanced. He could no longer tolerate being held hostage to the actions of others who had been dispatched in his stead to do his bidding.

"Sir," the voice on the other end of the line resumed tentatively, "what are your orders?"

"The next time your phone rings, I want you to be able to tell me what happened to this team dispatched to the glacier. If you can't do that, don't bother answering."

Adamovitch stopped there to let his point sink in. The remaining boy soldiers were looking toward him, awaiting his selection of which would go next. Instead, he drew his own pistol, a trusty Makarov PM, from its holster.

"You will do this, and you will find out who killed our agent," he said, squeezing his satellite phone so hard he thought he heard something crack, "while I pay a visit to the man who will be our partner."

CHAPTER 30

GLACIER BAY NATIONAL PARK AND PRESERVE, LAMPLUGH GLACIER

George William Lamplugh was a world-renowned
British geologist who passed away in 1926.

"The village! We have to get back to the village!"

They piled back into the Huey, taking the same seats they had during their flight here, except for Amka, who took the co-pilot's seat. Michael looked at the space remaining in the cabin and couldn't help but think of the members of the USGS team that wouldn't be making the return trip with them, as he had hoped. Michael watched Amka lift a microphone from an old-school radio and bring it up to her mouth, as the pilot fired up the Huey's engine.

"Mama Bear to Xunaa watch, Mama Bear to Xunaa watch, do you copy?"

"We copy, Mama Bear," Michael heard a male voice crackle over the speaker.

Amka looked visibly relieved. "Report status."

"All copacetic here. Nothing to report."

"Good. Erect security perimeter and watch stations to make sure it stays that way."

"Roger that, Mama Bear."

"We're twenty-five minutes out. No one from outside the village enters until we're back. No exceptions. Get boats out on the water to cover that route, too."

"That's a roger, too, Mama Bear."

Looking relieved, Amka returned the mic to its stand and retook her seat next to Michael in the cabin.

"You didn't mention anything about Russians, Agent Walker."

"Because there was nothing to mention," Michael said, raising his voice above the din of the engine noise. "The first I knew of their involvement was back there on the glacier."

Silence settled between them, broken by Michael.

"You saved my life," he said suddenly. "I want to thank you for that."

"We share the same enemy, Agent Walker."

"Pretty ingenious method, I've got to say."

Amka took a deep breath. Her eyes, fixed on the sky beyond, lost a measure of their steely focus, making her look uncertain. "I've never killed anyone before."

"I have."

"I know. My grandfather told me. He said you are no stranger to great battles."

Michael didn't bother pressing her on how the old man might have known that. "An accurate description."

"Of you or the battle, Agent Walker?"

"Both."

Amka held his gaze. "My grandfather says you are troubled. He says you are letting loss define you, but he wasn't talking about your foot, was he?"

"No," Michael conceded from the passenger seat, "he wasn't. I lost my wife on Mount Rainier. She was a park ranger at the time, trailing what she thought was a poacher. I was a law enforcement ranger trying to help her."

"What happened?"

"A gunfight," Michael said, leaving out the details. "The same gunfight that cost me my foot cost Allie her life."

Amka nodded. "I understand now. . . ."

"Understand what?"

"What my grandfather told me about you, what makes you a troubled soul."

Michael had no idea how to respond to that.

"You must stop reliving that day, Agent Walker," Amka resumed, saving him from the need to.

"There are some things you can't get past."

The Huey lifted off, battling the buttressing winds before leveling out and streaming back for Xunaa.

Amka cocked her gaze toward Michael. "When we get back to the village, there's something I need to show you."

CHAPTER 31

JOINT BASE ELMENDORF-RICHARDSON, ANCHORAGE, ALASKA

Headquarters to many units of the Armed Forces including Alaskan Command (ALCOM) and the Joint Task Force-Alaska (JTF-AK).

"A high probability anyway," the officer continued, not wanting to commit to a finding he couldn't definitively prove.

Gina was still trying to make sense of what he had just told her. "Do we have any idea how close the Russian sub came to the *Providence*?"

"The Typhoon-class, I'm told, is notoriously difficult to track, so naval intelligence is still working to ascertain that, in conjunction with North American Aerospace Defense Command and U.S. Northern Command. That's why a report hasn't been issued to the White House yet."

Gina had enough of a national security profile to know the presence of Russian submarines in Alaskan waters wasn't all that unusual or unprecedented since, technically, the bulk of those waters were international in nature. Based on what she knew about the positioning of the *Providence*, though, she was in U.S. territorial waters in Icy Strait at the time she'd inadvertently been struck by a salvaged World War II mine. That implied a dangerous provocation on the part of the Russians in the form of their Typhoon-class sub straying into the territory of the United States in what could be considered an act of war.

Beyond that, the sub's presence suggested the very real possibility that the Russians had been involved in the fate of the *Providence*'s crew. How, though, could the Russian sub have possibly introduced a pathogen, or a biological or chemical agent onto the *Providence* in the immediate aftermath of her being stranded on the bottom of Icy Strait? Under that scenario, it was impossible not to consider whether this was some sort of beta test to evaluate a bioweapon that could render the entire submarine fleet of the U.S. Navy obsolete. Was that why the White House was being so coy, leaving her to figure so much out on her own without voicing any of the suspicions that officials may have feared themselves?

"You should ask yourself, Captain Delgado," the officer said, seeming to follow her thoughts, "if the presence of that World War Two mine that struck the *Providence* was a coincidence or whether it was planted."

"Is there any evidence that the Russian sub approached the *Providence* at any point?"

The officer shook his head. "None at all. We're currently scanning satellite imagery in the general time period to make sure we can identify every single ship above the surface as well. Sometimes, Captain, the sea feels as big as the sky."

Gina's gaze drifted to the monitors displaying a constant rotation of the corpses laid out in the airless chamber one level beneath them.

"What else can you tell me about the bodies, the cause of death?"

"I've told you everything pertinent that we can currently attest to with a reasonable degree of certainty."

"Go beyond the pertinent and forget about a reasonable degree of certainty. We're not dealing with certainty here because it's unprecedented. Nothing's certain at this point, except that the entire crew died of the same cause within just over two hours of the sub's stranding at the bottom."

"Well, with the air recirculation systems disabled, Captain Delgado, they'd be burning oxygen candles to breathe."

That caught Gina's attention. "What are oxygen candles, sir?"

The officer studied her briefly, as if she were an unruly child posing an obvious question, before responding. "They're made of iron and sodium chlorate. A firing pin sets off a reaction between iron filings and sodium chlorate, which in turn releases oxygen. These candles are a very efficient form of oxygen storage; the mass of oxygen per unit volume is greater than the mass of compressed oxygen. The candles release up to ninety-four percent of the oxygen bound in the chlorate. The *Providence* would have maintained a sufficient supply to provide breathable air for a minimum of four days."

"And these candles wouldn't be activated until the ship's main power systems failed after being struck by the mine. Do I have that right?"

"You do. According to the ship's log, it was actually once the sub reached the bottom."

"Ship's log," Gina repeated. "How detailed is it?"

"Under normal circumstances, very. These, of course, weren't normal circumstances. And this isn't a ship's log in the traditional sense, kind of a diary at sea. It's more like the sub's black box, automatically recording all issues encountered at sea and how they were dealt with."

Gina knew she had something here, but wasn't sure what it was yet. "And you reviewed this computerized log?"

"Not me personally—other officers, but they've only done so in cursory fashion, ma'am. We only obtained the log a few hours before you arrived and this is the first time this facility has actually been fully operational."

"You mentioned those twenty-seven cameras don't cover the entire sub."

"They don't, Captain. Broken down, I'd estimate they cover around fifty percent. The crew's quarters and all washroom facilities are left out for obvious reasons. There are cameras covering the engine room, of course, but not ancillary maintenance and storage areas where there isn't much to see."

A picture continued to form in Gina's head. "So the ship's log could potentially cover something the cameras missed."

"I suppose. It's certainly possible."

"Mind if I take a crack at it?"

‡‡‡

Prior to beginning her scrutiny of the ship's computerized log, Gina asked the officer to take her to a secure area with a secure phone so she could call the White House and report.

"How about my office?"

He escorted her to a small, obviously windowless space with only an institutional-style desk and chair inside, besides some shelves that contained virtually nothing. There was a phone and computer atop the desk and nothing else. No pen and paper clip caddy, no family photos, no calendar, and the walls were utterly stark.

"I'll need to dial the number for you, Captain, but will leave as soon as the call goes through."

The man upstairs had done the very same thing to enable her to speak to Law Enforcement Ranger Clark Gifford down in the Everglades. She figured this was just procedure, another layer of redundant security measures that made no sense when considered individually. Except on this call, she'd be speaking to the White House in private.

"Captain," the officer said, handing her the phone and taking his leave.

"Grant," the voice of the president's chief of staff answered.

Gina waited until the office door closed before speaking. "Did you know about potential Russian involvement in this, Grant?"

"*What?* No. What are you talking about?"

"A Russian Typhoon-class submarine that a review of our satellites found in the general vicinity of the *Providence* around the time she went down."

"Shit . . ."

"That was my thought, too."

"Why hasn't the White House been made aware of this already?"

"This . . . station at Elmendorf only just received it, and it's not a positive ID. They're working to confirm it, but this is the kind of news I didn't think could wait. That's why you sent me up here, isn't it? To make sure you got the total picture, nothing left out or glossed over."

"And, apparently, it's a good thing we did."

"The total picture includes something else, Grant. Like planes, all commercial, and even large recreational ships, at sea have transponder codes similar to airlines. The station here is checking to see if any other anomalies show up on that end in the form of a ship with no transponder or one that doesn't check out, to see if any potentially enemy vessels were in the area."

A pause followed, as Chief of Staff Grant considered her words. "What do you need from us?"

"The station is fully operational for the first time, so they could use some help. You think the White House can run a satellite check going back a week or so to see if there've been any ships in the area of Icy Strait that stand out for all the wrong reasons?"

"I'll start the search in the area of Icy Strait and expand from there. Jesus, the goddamn Russians . . . I better put away the breakables before I tell the president."

"I didn't think she had a temper."

"She doesn't, but this seems to be the day for exceptions."

Grant paused again. Gina heard a scratching sound and pictured him jotting notes down on a pad he was either holding or had laid down before him.

"What else can you tell me, Special Agent Delgado? We've seen the preliminary report that the crew impossibly froze to death, and now you're suggesting at least the possibility that it was the result of hostile activity on the part of this Russian sub in American territorial waters. If that's the case, it's an act of war."

"Precisely why I don't believe it is. If there was a Russian sub in the same general area as the *Providence* at the time, I think it was there for another reason altogether. That's why we need to find out if it was alone or shadowing one or more Russian surface ships."

"Get back to the cause of death. What's the latest there?"

"There is no latest, just a hundred and twenty corpses who couldn't have died the way they did. I'm about to begin a detailed review of the computerized ship's log to see if I can find some indication."

"Indication of what?"

"How whatever killed the crew of the *Providence* got on board."

CHAPTER 32

GLACIER BAY NATIONAL PARK AND PRESERVE, LESTER ISLAND, ALASKA

The island is covered with 150-year-old Sitka spruce,
alder, and hemlock.

Kiks.ádi warriors had set up checkpoints at all the primary access points to the village, visible from both the air and then on land once the Huey set down atop the makeshift heliport.

"No hostile activity or any signs of a hostile presence anywhere in the area," Amka told Michael, after receiving the report from one of the *Kiks.ádi* on the inner perimeter they'd erected.

"I thought I knew the Tlingit language a bit, but not that dialect," Michael said, after listening to the exchange.

From the makeshift helipad, Yehl trailed Michael and Amka toward a small group of homes built into the sloped hillside that looked down on the center of the village, overlooking the sea. "They speak the dialect of the ancient Hoonah Tlingit tribe, the oldest of our people. The *Kiks.ádi* are traditionalists. They don't believe any of the changes forced upon us are for the better and prefer to speak in the language of a time before the Park Service regulated our land."

"You mean, back to a time when the Russians stole it outright."

Michael and Amka, with Yehl trailing them as if lost in his own thoughts, walked from the helipad to a smaller grove of evergreen trees where two matching, cream-colored one-story homes sat side by side.

"My grandfather lives in one," Amka explained, "my brother and I in the other."

Michael noticed the paint of both had been chipped by ice storms and discolored in spots by bird droppings. Otherwise, the homes looked extremely well-maintained and featured a simple, modular design comparable to the others located on the land around it. Michael wondered if these modular-style structures had been provided by the government as a small gesture to compensate for all the injustices perpetrated on the tribe.

"The *Kiks.ádi* believe the *dleit káa,* the white man, caused the fish to die because you're trying to starve us to force us off our land," Amka explained, just short of the door to the home she and her brother shared. "You saw the rotting piles with your own two eyes, Agent Walker. The question is can you see the truth? Somebody wants this land. Somebody has always wanted our land. It's no mystery why non-Natives aren't welcome here. Natives are the only people we can trust."

"It's not the truth, Amka. It barely passes as a theory. Fish blights of this scope are unusual, but not unprecedented. There was one in Texas in 2023. Tens of thousands of dead fish washed up on the beaches of the state's Gulf Coast over a single weekend, prompting beach closures and a stench that spread for miles. The cause, according to wildlife officials, was low levels of oxygen in the water."

She nodded. "I'm familiar with the story. It happened during the summer and as the weather heats up, the shallow water near the beach also gets hotter. When temperatures increase, the water cannot hold as much oxygen. The water temperatures in our seas hover in the low fifties."

"All the same, I'm sure there's a comparable scientific explanation for what's happening here."

"Like what?"

"A long series of overcast days. With clouds blocking the sun, microscopic phytoplankton and macroalgae cannot photosynthesize as much, and as a result, they produce less oxygen. Meanwhile, though, fish continue to consume the same amount of oxygen as they normally do, leading to a rapid, even deadly, decrease in overall levels."

"Except under that scenario, before a kill event occurs, fish can be seen trying to get oxygen by gulping at the surface of the water early in the morning because they're starving for oxygen."

"Fair point, Amka. But there has to be an explanation other than the one the *Kiks.ádi* have convinced themselves is true."

"There is," she told him. "And I think I've found it. That's what I wanted to show you."

‡‡‡

Amka led Michael inside the well-kept and well-furnished home. The interior boasted a cookie-cutter design featuring a combination kitchen and living room and what appeared to be three relatively small bedrooms. Yehl slipped past them and entered the bedroom farthest down the hall, the door closing behind him.

Michael followed Amka to another of the three bedrooms. He noted a key lock that looked like it had been added in the relatively recent past and then watched as she fit a key in and pushed.

The door swung open to reveal what appeared to be a fully stocked bio-lab. A trio of computers and a hard drive dominated one long table set against a sidewall. In the middle sat a rectangular black slate table topped with an assortment of microscopes, digital scanners, and a fourth computer. Another wall was lined with shelves that held beakers, flasks, test tubes, racks, microscope slides, and a bevy of chemicals both marked and unmarked, along with measuring equipment. A refrigerator was perched against the far wall on one side of the window, a much smaller freezer on the other. The same wall also held a smaller black slate table upon which rested a trio of centrifuges and pair of heating devices that looked like toaster ovens.

"Looks like something straight out of MIT," Michael noted.

"Which is where I got my doctorate before I went on to make a boatload of money. I still do, thanks to the patents registered in my name."

Michael again considered some of the newer buildings scattered around the village or currently under construction. He thought about the rows of Polaris ATVs in the storage barn and the home-model satellite dishes that still looked newly mounted to the sides or roofs of the houses—all likely stemming from Amka's generosity and desire to give back to the home she had abandoned for more than fifteen years.

"We have a doctor and nurse who staff the village clinic four days a week. On the days they don't come, or the weather keeps them out, that leaves emergency and routine medical care to me."

"You didn't mention getting an MD as well."

"I didn't, but tell that to the people who get sick or need medication. I can order pretty much anything I want through government vendors at no cost to the tribe. Nobody asks me who's prescribing it."

"Your secret's safe with me, Amka."

She moved toward the refrigerator and removed a tray holding what looked like one of the fish he'd seen piled along the shoreline. It was sliced apart, as if Amka had performed a detailed postmortem examination, a kind of fish autopsy. The odor reached him and Michael flinched from the stench.

"Sorry about the smell. You're looking at a salmon, Agent Walker. Various species of salmon make up the bulk of the fish that washed up on shore, but there were also cod, haddock, crabs, and rockfish. The fishing stock we rely on for our survival seemed to have been depleted virtually overnight and I needed to find out why."

"In order to point the finger at us?"

"At somebody, but not the Park Service, the federal government, or the state government. What I found was way beyond all of their capabilities. What I found was impossible."

Michael felt a brief chill, as he waited for Amka to continue.

"This is one of a dozen fish I examined and the cause of death was identical in all of them. I found no disease, no evidence of toxic exposure to something in the water, no signs of infection whatsoever." She stopped and held his gaze. "They froze to death, Agent Walker, each and every one of them."

‡‡‡

"In fifty-degree water? That's impossible."

"Tell that to fish," Amka resumed. "Fish take water into their mouth, passing the gills just behind its head on each side. Dissolved oxygen is absorbed from the water, and carbon dioxide is released into the water, which is then dispelled. The gills are fairly large, with thousands of small blood vessels, which maximizes the amount of oxygen extracted. Essentially, the gills of a fish function the way our lungs do. As the fish opens its mouth, water runs over the gills, and blood in the capillaries picks up oxygen that's dissolved in the water. In all twelve samples I examined, I was able to confirm the gills froze first, meaning the respiratory systems of the fish were the first to be attacked."

"Attacked . . ."

"Something did this, Agent Walker. Some form of biological or chemical agent that lowered their body temperature substantially below that of their surroundings. A fish swimming in forty-degree water would have a temperature of forty degrees, and so on. But the body temperatures of the fish I examined were all well below the freezing mark, even though the water temperature was twenty to thirty degrees higher."

Amka stopped, which gave Michael the opportunity to consider her words. He was no expert, but what she was describing appeared scientifically impossible, at least to a layman.

"I know what you're thinking," she said, "because I thought the same thing initially. That's why I kept at it, kept testing, and the results confirmed we're dealing with something here that known science can provide no explanation for."

"Any notion as to how the fish were infected by whatever it is we're dealing with?"

"More appropriate phraseology would be 'exposed.' And there are really only two possibilities: either it was absorbed by their respiratory system or ingested."

"If you had to guess . . ."

"I'm a scientist, Michael. I don't guess. I can surmise, offer a theory based on what I see, but right now I'm not seeing anything, at least not clearly. I need to run some more tests on both the respiratory and digestive systems of these fish and hopefully come away with at least a theory, or hypothesis, which is where all research starts."

Michael could only look at her and nod absently. Under the circumstances, Amka had done amazing work. His frustration lay in the fact that he needed to report this as soon as possible to Angela Pierce and get the word out about what was happening here, and he couldn't offer any indication of how it was happening, or what was causing it.

"Do you have that sample you took from the rear of the cave, those long, stringy hairs you found on the ice?" Amka asked him.

Michael had forgotten all about the plastic bag he'd zippered into an inside pocket of his parka. "It's in my jacket. Let me go get it."

His hand was trembling slightly when he extracted it from where Amka had hung up his jacket on a hook next to hers, but he managed to still the trembling when he handed the bag to her back in her lab.

"Now," she said, readying a microscope slide atop the slate lab table, "let's see if we can figure out where these hairs came from . . ."

CHAPTER 33

JOINT BASE ELMENDORF-RICHARDSON, ANCHORAGE, ALASKA

Montana has a much colder winter on average than this area of Alaska.

So much of investigative work was basic drudgery, reviewing data and findings in search of clues no one else had spotted. Gina believed her study and practice of demolitions had infused in her the kind of keen attention to detail that carried over into her career with the Bureau, speeding her ascent through the ranks because of her investigative skills. Simply stated, she saw things no one else did; not so much the conclusions, as anomalies that jumped out to her when scrutinizing files the same way they did when rigging explosive devices and det cord. Given the potency of the explosives she had rigged in Iraq, the slightest oversight on her part, from wind to temperature to the anticipated blast cone, could have cost American troops their lives. The same held true when she was called upon to defuse an IED or suicide vest. No two were exactly alike and the key was to look for what she didn't expect, since the enemy was often a step ahead of them.

Her role was similar here, only far less dramatic and dangerous. The nameless officer had allowed Gina to use his office to review the *Providence*'s computerized ship's log he'd brought up on his computer. It was amazing the kind of doors being a White House liaison opened. Although that shouldn't have surprised her, it did present a stark contrast with the cooperation, or lack thereof, she'd often received in the field in her capacity as an FBI special agent. In one sense, she had taken a demotion to work directly for the president, but in another she might well be the most powerful investigator in the country. Nobody said no to the White

House, at least no one had said no to her yet, since she'd begun acting in that capacity.

The sub's computerized log was far more voluminous than she'd been expecting and to understand all of it, she would need a submariner seated here by her side. Absent that, Gina had no choice but to perform her review to the best degree she was able and flag any entries she might not fully understand, but felt were potentially important.

The vast majority of the entries dealt with minor variation in levels of heat, air quality, oxygen content, weight distribution, engine function, climate control, temperature, and even minor spikes in electricity that might have indicated a power surge that could trip the system's breakers. These were color-coded in green, yellow, or red. And all of the computerized log entries early on showed green or, in a fair number of cases, yellow. In times past, such data would be reported in real time by engineers following old-fashioned gauges and even LED readouts. While that was still somewhat the case, the computerized logs offered the ultimate redundancy and had been adopted to counter the limitations of the human eye and ear.

Scanning ahead, she saw no entries in the vast ream of data that were marked red, so she confined her study, initially anyway, to those marked in yellow. There was an issue with a leakage in the laundry room, for example, that was the result of a faulty hose. Also, the quarters where the crew slept in shifts had suffered an electrical problem that left the private lights over each bed malfunctioning. The system utilized the latest generation of artificial intelligence to compose the reports in prose form, complete with time stamps and after-action reports of what was done to remedy the situation.

As was the case with the next yellow flag she came to.

This particular entry noted a clogged auxiliary condenser responsible for circulating a portion of the seawater pumped into the *Providence* to cool the sub down. Since there appeared to be another eleven such condensers, it was easy for the computer to take the clogged one offline and increase the intake of the other ones that hadn't been affected to compensate.

According to the log, Second Class Petty Officer Tom Massick had cleared the clog and reported no further complications. As far as Gina could tell, the auxiliary condenser in question went back online without incident and there were no further incidents reported regarding it. According to the log's time stamp, the condenser clog had been cleared just moments before the *Providence* had been hit by that World War II mine a salvage ship had brought up from the surface. But there was one item the log noted that caught her eye.

. . . seventy-seven-point-six gallons of water spilled out and were promptly cleaned up. No further issues noted in reporting period . . .

Gina halted her review there, her gaze frozen on the notation marked with a yellow flag. Over the course of the past few hours, she had covered every logged incident that rose to the level of yellow that had occurred over the past week while the *Providence* had been at sea. Given that the crew had been stricken with whatever had effectively frozen them to death so quickly, it didn't seem that the cause could have been rooted in something all that far back. Whatever had killed the *Providence*'s crew had to have been something more immediate and ultimately catastrophic.

Beyond that, the auxiliary condenser issue was the only logged incident in which something from outside the sub had gotten in while she was running silent and deep. Gina confirmed this by reviewing the remaining logged-in entries, which continued after the crew had died right up until the point where the log ended in favor of a report of the onboard findings by the rescue-turned-recovery crews.

Reflecting on that left Gina realizing the limits of artificial intelligence, how the computer had continued to go right on with its job without recognition or acknowledgment that the flesh-and-blood crew had died. She wasn't sure what she should have expected in that regard, but the notion that the computer's monitoring system had no idea what had befallen the crew brought home to her the stark distinction between man and machine, despite the purported advances made by the latter.

Gina reviewed the notepad on which she'd flagged any entry or notation that had grabbed her attention and, sure enough, none of the other incidents she'd noted dealt with penetration from the outside. She felt like she had down in the Everglades when she and Clark Gifford had both spotted that clothing tag hanging from the newly purchased shirt by the suspect in the murder of Jamie Bidwell.

Which, of course, begged the question of what the water that had poured out of that unclogged condenser might have been carrying with it, potentially responsible for the entire crew of the *Providence* freezing to death.

Still feeling a tremor of excitement, Gina was about to press the beeper-like device the officer had left her, when a knock fell on the door just ahead of him opening it.

"Perfect timing," she said. "I found something in the ship's log."

The officer seemed unmoved by that. "There's something else you need to see, Captain Delgado," he said, his face pale with what might have been fear.

CHAPTER 34

>-+0-0-0+-<

GLACIER BAY NATIONAL PARK AND PRESERVE, LESTER ISLAND, ALASKA

Southernmost of the Beardslee Islands.

"Well?" Michael said an hour later.

Amka had finished inputting the data of her microscopic review of the matted hairs found in the cave back on the Lamplugh Glacier and was staring at the results the computer had arrived at.

"This can't be," she told him, without lifting her gaze from the screen. "It makes no sense."

"You found out where those hairs came from?"

"Yes and no. That's what makes no sense. Or . . ."

Amka's voice fell silent as she said that, Michael taking note.

"Or what?" he asked her.

"How's your knowledge of history, Agent Walker?"

"Depends on which history you're referring to."

"The prehistoric Holocene epoch, specifically the Northgrippian Age that was known for vast cooling due to a disruption in ocean circulations that was caused by the melting of glaciers."

Michael nodded. "I've heard that referred to as the Holocene Ice Age."

"Good. Then what I'm about to tell you may not sound as crazy as it seems. The hairs you found in the back of that glacial cave came from a woolly mammoth."

‡‡‡

Michael had no idea what to expect when Amka had begun her analysis, but it certainly wasn't that. Her expression had changed, the flat resignation replaced by a dourer bent or, more likely, fear.

"The dead fish," she muttered, barely loud enough for him to hear.

"What about them?"

"They're not the only creatures to have perished inexplicably in Glacier Bay National Park, are they?"

"You're talking about the USGS team," Michael surmised.

Amka nodded. "There are numerous theories on what led to the extinction of woolly mammoths, just like there are about what led to the extinction of Neanderthals. Most involve primitive man's improved abilities to fashion tools, weapons, too, that made them the apex hunters, killing for food. And it wasn't just mammoths that died out at the close of the Holocene epoch, it was giant sloths, prehistoric rhinos, saber-toothed cats, and more. Plenty of experts believe something else was to blame entirely, as opposed to being hunted into extinction. One of the prevailing theories is that the warming trends of climate change destroyed the last patches of vegetation in their primary Arctic tundra habitat, which wiped out the animals' food supply. I think there's some truth in that, but it misses the point."

"What point?" Michael asked her.

"Imagine some kind of microbe, some organism, frozen in the ice since the original Ice Age sixty-five million years ago. Imagine the ice that it was frozen in thawing out ten thousand years ago."

"You're saying this microbe came back to life."

"Not exactly, Special Agent Walker, because it never died. It just became dormant, a kind of hibernation through the millennia. Then global warming melted all that ice and it was revived, resurfacing to infect animals with no natural immunity to it like prehistoric life almost surely had."

"Like the mammoth that died in that cave. It managed to crawl in there where it froze to death."

Amka nodded. "After the animal ingested vegetation that had been infected. And we can attribute this deadly organism's resurgence today to another extreme pattern of glacial melting, thawing the animal out and releasing the organism to spread once again. Following the natural runoff patterns, it could have ended up in the waters of Cross Sound. And, just like this organism froze the mammoth, it froze the fish that have been piling up on our shores."

"How is that even possible?"

"I don't know. We're dealing with a foreign organism here that operates on entirely different rules set sixty-five million years ago. It attacks any host it infects and kills by lowering their body temperature to create the optimal conditions for it to spread, like even the most mundane viruses."

"There's nothing mundane about this, Amka," Michael said, thinking along with her. "So the USGS team seeks refuge in the same cave as the mammoth did thousands of years ago and all six of them get infected, dying in a matter of hours. How is that possible? There's no infectious organism on the planet that can kill that fast, that uniformly."

"You mean, there didn't used to be."

"And if the Russians removed the bodies . . ."

"They will be able to isolate the organism," Amka completed, "toward whatever purpose they want. Those dead fish that froze to death in fifty-five-degree water . . . The organism attacked their respiratory systems first and spread from there. That's almost surely the same way the USGS team you came here to save died yesterday, and the way the woolly mammoth died thousands of years ago."

Michael had trouble processing all he was hearing, and yet through that, a realization struck him hard and fast. "Wait, this village must have been exposed, thanks to those infected fish that washed up on shore. And fish are a primary part of your diet, so you have ingested this thing, too. And yet no one's gotten sick."

"That we know of and not yet anyway."

"This thing, whatever it is, kills fast, Amka. If there was infection here, we'd know about it by now. . . . I need to report in to my boss. The government needs to be told what's happening up here."

"Really? The government did this. They're responsible because they didn't do enough to stop climate change while there was still time, while it still could have made a difference."

"We did this to ourselves, Amka. We warmed the planet to the point where this thing could be let loose on the world again."

"You know what this means, Agent Walker, you know what we're potentially facing."

Michael nodded. "An extinction event."

Amka didn't respond, her expression remaining flat, her mind clearly elsewhere. "You just made me think of something, something you said . . ."

"I barely got through biology and organic chemistry in college. What was it I said?"

"About how our people seem untouched by this, despite eating fish that may have been contaminated."

"That's because you said the mammoth must have absorbed this prehistoric organism in something it ate."

Amka nodded, finally ready to put words to what she was thinking. "So what did the fish that have been washing up frozen eat?"

‡‡‡

"What's the news from Lester Island, Michael?" Angela Pierce greeted him upon answering.

Michael had called her from Amka's lab after she excused herself to fix dinner for her brother.

"We found the cave where the USGS team sought refuge from the avalanche, but their bodies had already been removed."

"Wait, slow down. Bodies? You're saying they were killed?"

"I'm saying all indications are that they died."

"Even without the bodies being present?"

"I'll include the explanation in my report. It hasn't been verified, but there are signs that very strongly indicate that's the case."

"Okay. So what happened to the bodies? Any notion as to who got there ahead of you?"

"They were Russian, Angela. That's an assumption, too, but a safe one because we were attacked by a ten-man Russian commando team on the glacier."

"And you're still alive to talk to me?"

"Because the Russian commandos aren't. The Tlingit community supporting our efforts got me and a pair of local leaders to the glacier by helicopter. We were accompanied by a trio of *Kiks.ádi* warriors. They killed the Russians," Michael continued, elaborating no further.

"These warriors killed the Russians?"

"Most of them," Michael said, leaving it there. "We left their bodies on-site. I suspect whoever was behind their presence has already retrieved them. Otherwise, you may want to alert whoever handles such things in the military."

He could hear the scratchy sound of her scribbling notes. "There's something you need to hear, Michael: I saw a report that indicated a Russian trawler had been spotted south of Glacier Bay National Park."

Michael squeezed his eyes closed and then opened them. The presence of the trawler explained where the Russian commandos had come from.

"There's something else, Angela," Michael picked up. "Lester Island has experienced the largest fish kill I've ever seen. Fortunately, one of those tribal leaders I mentioned is a microbiologist. She's been able to determine that they froze to death in fifty-five-degree waters."

"How is that even possible?"

"Still to be determined, but we have strong reason to believe it's the same way the USGS team died. I don't have to tell you what all this adds up to."

"No, you don't," Angela said, her voice cracking a bit at the impact of what Michael had just told her. "Either the Russians are responsible for whatever's causing these deaths, or they showed up to bring it back home. Which brings me to something else, something I couldn't make any sense of until now: the man who shot the couriers and stole the Tlingit urn with that black powder inside."

"You've identified him?"

"Not by name. He's a ghost, Michael, and that's coming from the deepest databases maintained by the defense department and intelligence agencies. But the coroner who examined the body for the Alaska Bureau of Investigation noticed something you probably missed: severe yellowing of his teeth."

"You're right, I didn't notice that."

"Well, according to the FBI, yellow teeth are the norm in Russia, because their toothpaste lacks whiteners and cosmetic dentistry is barely practiced."

"So the assassin who killed those couriers might well be Russian, too . . ."

"What's going on here, Michael?"

Amka reappeared in the doorway just as his call with Angela Pierce was ending.

"Yehl's gone," she said.

‡‡‡

"If he snuck off to meet his friends, I'm done with him."

Michael followed her as she stormed outside to find her grandfather kneeling on the grass of the grove, just as he had been atop the rocky shore littered with dead fish earlier that day.

"Have you seen Yehl, Grandfather?"

Michael watched Chief Xetsuwu nod, speak briefly in Tlingit, and then point out toward the north. As far as Michael knew, not much was there besides wilderness holding barely a trace of civilization. Rugged land, especially at night when it was easy to get turned around and lost.

"Goddamnit!" Amka said to Michael. "He went on his spirit walk, decided tonight was the proper time!"

Michael remembered the boy telling him about that back in the cave. He should have realized what was coming. "He's about to turn sixteen, so maybe it is. But why now, tonight?"

"Because my grandfather says there's a storm coming and he wants to test himself. I'm going after him," Amka said, then turned and trotted off.

"Then I guess I am, too," Michael said, following in step behind her.

JOINT BASE ELMENDORF-RICHARDSON, ANCHORAGE, ALASKA

Incentive pay for soldiers working in conditions where it can get to -20 degrees Fahrenheit started in April 2024, and Joint Base Elmendorf-Richardson is one of those locations.

"We've got an AI computer simulation on how this thing kills, Captain Delgado," the officer resumed, as he led Gina back down the hall. "By the way, call me Bob."

"Bob what?"

"Just Bob. It's the best I can do and more than I should have. I'm making an exception here I never make."

Gina could feel the level of trust that was building between them. Colleagues forced together by something happening that was unprecedented.

Bob led her to a smaller, equally plain and sparsely furnished room farther down the hall. He knocked on an open door and entered without waiting for a response.

A single man was perched before a large wall-mounted flat-screen television, seeming to familiarize himself with the features of the remote control he was holding. He was tall and thin, and both his cheekbones and his Adam's apple poked out from beneath the skin.

"This is Special Agent Gina Delgado of the FBI, formerly *Captain* Delgado of the U.S. Army. But she's here on behalf of the White House."

The man turned his gaze on Gina. "Nice to meet you, Special Agent Delgado."

She shook his extended hand. "What should I call you?"

The gaunt man looked toward Bob, who nodded. "Atticus. It's not my real name, but I've always liked it. You know, from *To Kill a Mockingbird*, my favorite book of all time."

"Atticus, then."

Gina released Atticus's extended hand and then watched him use the remote to switch on the television. He took a seat behind a modular desk in which the chair was molded into the frame. As he typed, the figures and characters came to life on the big-screen TV that dominated the room.

"What you're about to see, Agent Delgado," Atticus started, "is a computer simulation of how the crew of the *Providence* died. I need to tell you right at the top that this is my field of expertise and I've never seen anything like this, nor can I explain it. Since you're already aware that they froze to death, we need to begin our discussion with water, which makes up, generally, sixty percent of the human body, significantly more than that in the blood and vital organs."

"Basic biology." Gina nodded.

"Indeed. Now, freezing water is actually a physical change rather than a chemical change. When water freezes due to a reduction in the temperature it's exposed to, its molecules slow down and come closer together, forming a crystalline structure. This process is a physical change because the chemical composition of water remains the same before and after freezing. Are you with me so far?"

"Yes, Atticus."

"Good. Now, watch."

He pressed a fresh sequence of keys, and a squiggly, indistinct shape appeared on the big screen in a soft red color.

"Picture that as a molecule of water, one of trillions inside the bodies of any of the crew members. Basic science, going all the way back to middle school, teaches us that one of the primary definitions of life is cellular division."

"I studied biology all the way through college, Atticus."

He smiled, not looking like a scientist who spent their time alone in a lab located several stories underground encased by ice. For some reason, Gina noticed for the first time he was wearing a white lab coat.

"Well, you've got a leg up on me, then, because I never took any courses in criminology. I still consider myself something of a detective, although this is a mystery I can't solve."

He returned his attention to the keyboard, striking a few more keys. A smaller blue shape appeared on the scene, circular in design but pulsing in a way that changed its size to larger before transitioning back to smaller. Gina wasn't sure what this denoted, but her rudimentary knowledge made her think it probably suggested the blue shape was a living organism.

Atticus looked toward her before continuing with the demonstration. "Can I ask you a question?"

"Of course, Atticus."

"Are you going to report what I'm telling you to the White House?"

"As close to verbatim as I can."

"Wow," he said, a boyish grin stretched across his narrow face. "Wow. Okay, watch . . ."

Atticus worked his keypad again, putting the smaller blue shape into motion toward the larger red one. For some reason, it made Gina think of a clandestine attack, someone jumping out from an alleyway when a hapless victim passed it.

Sure enough, the blue shape pierced the outer membrane of the red one that denoted a water molecule. Almost immediately in the simulation, the red began to change to blue, spreading outward in an irregular pattern that seemed to suggest tentacle-like extremities reaching out from the growing blue area as if to grasp for the diminishing field of red. When her father was sickened with the cancer that ultimately claimed his life, this was the way his oncologist explained what was happening to him as the cancer spread. The disease's cells would enter healthy ones and replace them as it continued to replicate itself, spreading beyond control. Gina shivered at the memory, missing her father the most in times like this, as always.

"It looks like cancer," she blurted, feeling stupid for making such an unprofessional response when she should have just let Atticus speak.

"Not quite," he said curtly. "Let's get back to water and the physical reaction that causes it to freeze. What you've just witnessed is a simulation of a chemical reaction that causes the same thing, a chemical reaction that forces clusters of molecules to rearrange themselves. Basically, cause and effect are reversed: instead of reduced temperatures in a physical reaction causing water to freeze, what we have is a chemical reaction that reduces the temperature of H_2O molecules to produce the same effect. Think of it this way, Agent Delgado. Water freezes from the outside in, while the water in the bodies of our one-hundred-and-twenty victims from the *Providence* froze from the inside out."

Atticus looked back toward the screen. "The red changing to blue—that's a simulation of the invading organism causing those clusters of water molecules to slow down and rearrange themselves, starting in the respiratory system because it must be airborne, although we haven't yet determined the precise chemical and biological methodology that explains how it manages a chemical reaction that mirrors the physical one of freezing. Theoretically, once the organism reaches the central nervous system it short-circuits the hypothalamus, adrenal glands, and mitochondrial network responsible for regulating body temperature. With each cell it transforms, the body temperature is microscopically lowered. And, as the cellular division advances geometrically, that process speeds up to the point where the body temperature of those infected, in this case the entire crew of the *Providence,* continues to lower until the infected host freezes to death from the inside out."

Gina felt cold herself, numb, too, upon hearing that. "How long would the process have taken?"

"There's no definitive timeline because we're dealing with an entirely unprecedented set of circumstances and an organism that's never been encountered before. But anecdotally, based on the reports from the sub, somewhere between three and four hours would be my best guess."

Gina looked toward the big-screen television where the blue continued to replace the red, before moving on to penetrate the walls of another cell to begin the process anew.

"The simulation you're looking at here," Atticus said, following her gaze, "has been slowed down for demonstration purposes. What you're watching unfold in moments would likely have taken no more than a millisecond."

"You called it an organism."

Atticus looked like he didn't want to disappoint her, but had no choice. "Since we have no living samples, that's all I can say. It would be safe to call it a microbe, which covers a broader range of possibilities. But it's not behaving in a manner like any germ, virus, bacteria, or fungus I've ever encountered, that anyone has ever encountered. Nothing like this exists on this planet."

"You mean until now, Atticus, right?"

"I don't believe it came from 'now,' so to speak. That's why its operational methodology is so unprecedented. This is an organism, or microbe, that may have existed millions of years ago, only to evolve out of existence in a normal cycle."

"And yet here it is, back again. How could that be possible?"

Atticus tapped his temples with his knuckles, as if to punish himself, frowning in the process. "I misspoke. The microbe didn't evolve out of existence because of time or factors that prevented it from replicating itself at the cellular level. More likely, it became dormant, like an extended period of hibernation lasting millions of years dating back, oh, maybe all the way to the dinosaurs."

"So this thing kills every person exposed to it . . ."

Atticus nodded. "I can tell you that is an accurate assessment. What I can't tell you is how the organism penetrated the submarine."

"I think I might be able to help you there," Gina told him.

‡‡‡

She wished she had the *Providence*'s computerized ship's logs readily available to show Bob and Atticus the entry about how unclogging an auxiliary condenser had allowed seawater to flood through the conduit onto the ship.

"How much seawater?" Atticus asked, the most animated he'd been yet. "Did the computerized log specify that?"

Gina couldn't recall the precise figure, but then remembered she had written it down in her notebook, which she still had with her.

"Seventy-seven-point-six gallons of water spilled out and were promptly cleaned up," she read out loud.

"More than enough," Atticus muttered. "Easily more than enough . . ."

Gina tried to make sense of everything she had just heard. "So we know how this thing kills, and we know how it may have gotten on board the *Providence*. What we don't know is where it came from."

"There's something else," Atticus said, softer and slower. "Once the clog was cleared, nearly a hundred gallons of seawater rushed into the ship. H_2O, right?"

Now Gina really did feel as if she were back in middle school, covering the most rudimentary of principles.

"You see what I'm getting at, Agent Delgado?"

She shook her head.

"Since we've established that this organism freezes the human body by causing a chemical change that slows down the molecules of H_2O, it's more than logical, likely actually, that it similarly produces a chemical change in water outside the body. That means similarly lowering the temperature of the sea once those waters are similarly exposed." Atticus's eyes widened, struck by a realization. "Have any measurements been taken of water temperatures in Icy Strait to see if there's been any decline, even a minute one?"

Atticus aimed his question at Gina, but it was Bob who answered. "Not yet. What do you expect we would find?"

"Since water temperatures vary in the abstract, we'd have to do a wide sampling to study consistent pockets of colder readings in order to determine the rate of spread and degree of decline. But the bottom line is that if this organism kills by lowering the temperature of water in the human body, it could potentially kill all life in the ocean the same way. Theoretically, if its infectious nature is based on hitching a ride on, say, oxygen molecules, the ocean would provide an ideal breeding ground for it to spread. But that means . . ."

"What?" Gina prodded him.

"Fish breathe through their gills, absorbing oxygen that way. Not so with people, obviously."

"You're saying this thing kills marine life by spreading through the water and people by spreading through the air."

Atticus nodded. "I guess I am."

Gina took a deep breath. "I need to call the White House."

CHAPTER 36

MICHOUD ASSEMBLY FACILITY, NEW ORLEANS, LOUISIANA

The original tract of land was part of a 34,500-acre French Royal land grant to local merchant Gilbert Antoine de St. Maxent in 1763.

Axel Cole was seated on the bridge of his starship, looking out the view window at all the previous space flight prototypes that had come before this one. He heard the clacking of Elizabeth Fields's high heels against the polished tile floor echo through the open portal and then the clang of her taking the retractable metal steps that would someday bring man to the surface of Mars.

"Getting ready for takeoff, Axel?" she said, upon entering the bridge.

"You tell me, Elizabeth, am I? Have a seat."

Fields did so, awkwardly sliding into the co-pilot's chair. "There's good and bad news to report. I'll provide the good first, if you don't mind."

"Proceed," Cole instructed, already wondering what the bad portion they would come to next might yield.

"We've completed our initial round of testing on Prometheus."

"Has a nice ring to it, doesn't it?" Cole grinned, hearing someone else call the black, crystalline power that for the first time.

"For what it's worth, you didn't exaggerate its potential, as well as its origins, in the slightest. All your claims have been proven true, with one exception."

"What's that?"

"The notion that one single drop could replace a tank full of gas. It's more like a single drop could replace five tanks of gas."

"I thought it best to err on the conservative side."

"And the substance does indeed appear to have originated with shale, as well as crude, oil buried deep within the Alaskan permafrost, but bears little resemblance to the oil it morphed from on a molecular level. In fact, it bears little to no resemblance on a molecular level to anything else on this planet."

Fields was wearing an unbuttoned lab coat. In his brief visit, introducing her to the lab he'd spared no expense to construct inside a smaller outbuilding on the Michoud Assembly Facility campus, Cole had watched her conduct a tutorial to the staff on how to keep the samples of Prometheus secure while remaining safe themselves. Many had never worked in such an environment and none had ever worked with any substance this unprecedented.

"How did it come to exist, Elizabeth?" Cole asked her. "I'm sure you've developed some ideas that no one else would even consider. You are the greatest molecular chemist and biologist in the world, after all."

"I guess you being the richest man in the world makes us the perfect team."

"I'm just getting started. And don't forget about your one-billion-dollar bonus when the *Death Star* sets down on Mars."

"I haven't, though the work itself is an even greater reward."

"You're a lousy businesswoman, Elizabeth."

"The world has already got more than its share of assholes, Axel. Now, getting to the matter at hand, how familiar are you with the most recent Ice Age, called the Pleistocene, that ended approximately twelve thousand years ago?"

"I couldn't even tell you how to spell it."

"Then I'll spare you the details. For our purposes, what you need to know is that the Pleistocene ended when the glaciers began to melt."

"Twelve thousand years ago?" Cole asked from the captain's chair.

"Climate change has been a regular feature of the planet, long before man accelerated and exacerbated things. Earth has been warming and cooling since its very formation, part of the natural environmental cycle."

"Okay," he said, his tone urging her on.

"When you think of life in prehistoric times, what comes to your mind first?"

"Is this a quiz, Elizabeth?"

"If you want to reach Mars, it would pay to understand exactly what's going to get you there."

"Then the answer is dinosaurs."

"Of course, just like everyone else. That's the norm."

Cole hated ever being remotely connected to the norm and uttered a sigh that sounded more like a harmonic growl.

"And dinosaurs," Fields continued, "don't exist anymore, do they?"

"Trick question?"

"Not at all."

"Then the answer is, no, they don't."

"But they weren't the only living organisms to go extinct sixty-five million years ago. Plants, trees, grasses, pretty much all types of flora and fauna died out thanks to lack of sunlight and a vast redefining of the environment they were ill-equipped to survive. So nature rebooted and, to a great extent, started over again. You know the one exception to that reboot?"

Cole thought for a moment. "I'm going to say the smallest organisms like germs, microbes, and bacteria."

"And in this case the theory I've long supported stems from the study of environmental DNA, or eDNA, in permafrost and lake sediments of hundreds of samples of salvaged remains of woolly mammoths in the region over thousands of years. They found that later samples of remains had eDNA measurements that varied distinctly from the earlier ones."

"And what do you make of that, Elizabeth?" Cole asked her, genuinely curious to hear not only her answer, but also how it was connected to the origins of Prometheus.

"You have given me strong reason to believe that the extinction of these species was directly due to this prehistoric organism released after millions of years in the ice." Fields stopped and held Cole's stare. "Axel, I am now of the opinion that Prometheus is that organism, that just as it transformed the molecular structure of the largest land animals of the time that were exposed to it when the glaciers began to melt to make them more fitting hosts, so, too, it transformed the molecular structure of oil. Basically, it solidified the oil on an immensely concentrated level I estimate to be somewhere around one hundred–plus parts per thousand, which explains why those tiny black crystals you've been smuggling out of Alaska might indeed be the ultimate fuel source."

Cole nodded, rendered speechless by Dr. Elizabeth Fields's assessment of his discovery. "Any theories as to how Prometheus managed to turn from liquid to solid?"

"Several, but one stands out. All oil, particularly older reserves, have some percentage of dissolved water at the molecular level, and I've always believed that percentage is higher than most believe it to be, as much as two to four percent. Again, the older the oil, the more water it contains and what you've been smuggling out of Alaska started out as oil that's about as old as it gets."

Cole smiled at her. "You could have just answered my question, you know."

"I'm about to, Axel. My working theory is that the oil was transformed millions of years ago by the microbe in question when the temperature of the water content was reduced to as little as zero degrees Fahrenheit."

"Are you saying the oil *froze*?"

"No. Oil freezes at temperatures between minus-forty and minus-sixty degrees Fahrenheit. The oil never froze. It was transformed into an incredibly concentrated solid form at the molecular level. Call it a new fuel source literally millions of years in the making, thanks to the same organism responsible for the woolly mammoth, and other creatures of the Pleistocene epoch, going extinct."

The excitement Cole felt was palpable—that is, until he recalled the circumstances surrounding the last shipment out of Alaska—the murders of his couriers and the theft of the Native funeral urn filled with Prometheus instead of ashes.

"The good news, Axel," Fields resumed, "is that Prometheus would render even the use of nuclear propulsion to reach Mars obsolete."

"And the bad news?" Cole posed, knowing it was coming.

"According to the inventory you provided, you are now in possession of approximately two hundred metric pounds—that's what your adventures in Alaska have yielded so far."

It sounded so little, given the planning that had gone into acquiring that amount, and yet portended so much for the future of man.

"And it's not enough to get your *Death Star* back and forth on even a single journey to Mars. You'd need twice as much to manage that, accounting for the experimentation use and the testing of prototypes. Far more than that, of course, would be needed for the repeated flights and multiple ships you envision. On the other hand, you'll be happy to hear we've already started work on how to develop a chemical means to allow you to utilize Prometheus in accordance with the design of the *Death Star*'s current propulsion systems, no easy task with a compound that has never been encountered before, but I assure you that we are making great—"

Fields stopped when an alarm began to blare throughout the cavernous space holding Axel Cole's private collection of spaceship prototypes.

"Was it something I said?" she tried to quip.

"That's the general alarm for the entire facility. Something's gone wrong somewhere, Elizabeth."

And, in that moment, her phone screeched with an incoming emergency text message. She pulled the phone from a pocket of her lab coat. Cole watched it start to shake in her grasp.

"It's our lab," Fields managed.

CHAPTER 37

GLACIER BAY NATIONAL PARK AND PRESERVE,
LESTER ISLAND, ALASKA

John Muir first visited the area in 1879.

Michael knew they never should have set out so close to nightfall aboard Polaris Ranger ATVs into the teeth of a looming storm, just as he knew they had no choice but to find Yehl before the storm hit. The last of the light bled from the sky when they were around five miles north of the village, just past the center of the island. Up until that point, the ATVs' LED headlights, designed for off-roading at night, sliced effortlessly through the darkness.

Then they hit a wall of white.

Amka didn't have to tell Michael to grind his Ranger to a skidding, screeching stop. He felt a blast of icy cold upon him. It felt like being draped in a blanket lifted from a freezer. Then he felt the assault of ice crystals mixed with a snow thicker and more blinding than any blizzard he'd ever experienced before.

"Looks like your grandfather was right!" he said, loudly enough to carry his voice through the storm.

"So was my brother, both of them born with the sight passed down only to males in the line."

"I don't need the sight to know a storm like this is rare this time of year," Michael said, his voice barely breaking through the wind.

"My grandfather said the storm came for my brother and called to him, sent by the spirits to either usher him into manhood . . . or away forever."

No matter which way he turned, Michael's face was subjected to an assault by the blinding blanket of white.

"We'll never find him in this. What do we do?" Then, as he climbed out of his ATV, he shouted louder, "What do we do?"

"Get back on your ATV!"

"*What?*"

"There's no way we can survive this exposed. We'll freeze to death. We've got to find shelter."

"Out here?" Michael posed in disbelief.

He was no stranger to weather like this, especially on Mount Rainier, but this was the first time he'd ever been stranded outside in such conditions.

"It's our only chance. Trust me. I grew up on these lands, I know these lands."

He knew he had no choice but to do just that, even though Amka's words made no sense to him.

"Now!" she cried out. "We need to go!"

Michael reclaimed his seat inside the ATV. With no windshield or side windows, though, "inside" was only a relative term. He felt the storm assault him as soon as he drove off in Amka's wake, banking to the left and falling in line behind her Ranger.

She was speeding along blindly, no better able to see what lay ahead than he was. Michael figured she was relying on a combination of instinct and her knowledge of the area, having grown up here. But how easy might it be for her to get disoriented, or even lose control of the ATV in a slick spot or in snow too thick for the tires to push through?

Michael felt fear tighten its grip on him and his breath slacken when he lost sight of her in the blinding sheet of white even his LED headlights couldn't penetrate. Finally, he spotted not Amka's Ranger, but a sliver of light piercing the storm, disappearing briefly only to reappear again. There was no way he could follow her ATV and counted himself fortunate to find a working alternative in the headlights reflecting off the white air ahead. Occasionally, he'd lose track of them to the sense of terror about to seize him, only to have the reflection reappear just in time to keep him from outright panic.

He thought of the weather the day Allie had been killed on Mount Rainier, the last time he'd been outside in such conditions. That, though, bore no comparison at all to this, the kind of storm that was truly the basis of Alaskan legend and myth and that turned out to be anything but. He lost all sense of time and, a few times, had to remind himself to breathe. Tried to compose himself and find a safe place in his mind, at least a rhythm to the ride, but his mind wasn't having it and neither were his hands, clutching the wheel in a death grip.

He lost sight of Amka's lights and realized he had backed off too much on his ATV's accelerator pedal, leading him to drift well behind her. He swore under his breath and felt the firm grasp of panic again at the same time he had to begin regularly mopping the pounding snow from his eyes in order to see.

Michael had been up close and personal with death several times in his life, but those came in sudden bursts that quickly passed. This experience lingered by comparison, as he gave the Ranger more gas, hoping he was headed in the right direction, while feeling as if he were riding inside the storm as its passenger. He was covered in snow and feeling it coat his throat from washing into his mouth and down his nostrils.

Where is Amka?

Despite running the Ranger as fast as he dared, he could find no sign of her at all. How long had he been driving since they'd set out through the storm? How much distance had he covered? Had the squall turned him all around and left him sidetracked?

Michael wondered if he should stop now and take his chances by sheltering behind the ATV in the storm, while leaving its engine on to avoid freezing to death. But he had no idea how long the gas in the tank would hold out. Amka was carrying the extra can in the back of her vehicle, along with other supplies he'd watched her pack before they set out. He had nothing, other than what the pockets of his parka held.

Michael ended up pushing the pedal all the way to the floor. His best chance, his only chance, lay in catching up to Amka. Fail there and he wouldn't survive, which made the best way to stay alive taking everything the Ranger could give him in the desperate hope he was still headed in her wake.

His ATV crested over knobby hills in his path and was launched airborne by berms that made for natural moguls. Each time the Ranger settled, he felt the crunch of the deep snow that would likely snare its tires before too much longer.

"Come on, come on!" he urged the machine, in a voice that sounded more like a whine.

Michael barreled on blindly, a few times absently wondering why the windshield wipers weren't slapping at least some of the snow from his eyeline only to remember the Ranger didn't have any. The world before him remained a vast, endless desert of white to the point where he didn't seem to be moving anymore. But he was, straight into a blinding pair of lights that suddenly appeared through the snow and the night.

Michael twisted his wheel to the left so hard that his ATV spun out of control and toppled sideways. He managed to unclasp his seat belt to free himself from the vehicle and struggle back to his feet. Through the spill of both the headlights of Amka's ATV and those radiating from his toppled one, he saw she was holding what looked like an ice axe in her hand.

"What kept you?" Amka said.

CHAPTER 38

─ ·─·─◦─◦─· ─

JOINT BASE ELMENDORF-RICHARDSON, ANCHORAGE, ALASKA

The Air Force's newest fighter aircraft is the F-22
Raptor, a leap forward in war-fighting capabilities.

Daniel Grant, the president's chief of staff, didn't pick up when Gina called the first time. So she asked the officer she now called "Bob" to dial the number again. By the time Grant finally picked up on the seventh try, Bob had committed the number to memory.

"This better be important," he said, annoyed. "I stepped out of a meeting with two cabinet secretaries to take the call."

"Oh, it's important all right: Operation Cold Burn."

"I have no idea what you're talking about, Delgado."

"Then put the president on."

"She's traveling."

"I'm sure there's a phone nearby. Get her on the line."

"Why don't you tell me what you're talking about first?"

"Listen to me. However bad the president thought it might be when she sent me up here to Alaska, it's worse. I'm calling from Elmendorf. The crew of the *Providence,* every single one of them, froze to death in a temperature of sixty-six degrees. They were infected by some kind of organism that reduces the temperature of water inside the body. By all indications, the organism penetrated the ship through a clogged condenser unit. Any questions so far?"

"No," Grant said impatiently, after a brief pause. "Keep talking."

"I just watched a computer simulation of how this organism operates that looked like something out of a science-fiction movie."

"Are you alluding to the possibility of enemy action here, Delgado? That Russian submarine was the lead item in the president's sitrep this morning. And if that sub had anything to do with the death of the *Providence*'s crew, it would constitute an act of war."

"It didn't."

Another pause, longer this time, that left Gina wondering if Grant was checking an incoming text or email.

"You sound pretty definitive about that, Agent."

"For good reason. The Russians didn't plant this organism in the water that clogged that drain on the *Providence,* any more than they did in the Everglades."

"What are you talking about?"

"Operation Cold Burn, the name of the project the United States Geological Survey team has been working on in the Everglades. It's what got Jamie Bidwell killed."

"Who's Jamie Bidwell?"

Gina fought to keep her frustration from spilling over. "Didn't you read my report?"

"This is the White House, Delgado. Yours isn't the only fire I need to put out."

"But it was the fire you sent me to the Everglades to find the origins of, and I think I have. There's a connection between what's happening down there and what killed the crew of the *Providence* up here."

"In the form of what?"

"I'm going to have to get back to you on that. For now, I'm just asking you to trust me."

"That's asking a lot, Delgado."

"This information is less than an hour old, so we're still in the realm of theoretical here."

A scratchy sound followed, as Grant must have put his hand over his phone's mic to address someone who had approached him. Gina heard a muffled exchange, but nothing she could clearly make out.

"Sorry about the interruption," Grant said. "Where were we?"

"The connection between what's happening up here and down in the Everglades, thanks to the murder of that intern."

"Are you trying to link an ordinary murder to the death of the entire crew of the *Providence*?" Grant posed, sounding incredulous.

"It wasn't an ordinary murder at all. It was handled by professionals who knew how to disable hotel security cameras and use a counterfeit hotel key card. And they tortured Bidwell first, then searched his hotel room, which means they were after something they thought he knew or had."

"You've seen too many spy movies, Delgado."

"No, I've worked on too many cases involving spies. Bidwell was planted there."

Grant sighed audibly. "By the Russians? Is that where this is leading?"

"It's one of the possibilities I'm considering. But the real key here is Operation Cold Burn. We can't ignore the connection between those crew members freezing to death because their body temperature fell off a cliff and an experiment that managed to lower the ocean temperature in the Everglades."

Grant hesitated. "You want to head back down there."

"I want to speak to the president."

"Since that's impossible right now, you'll have to settle for me arranging to get you back to the Everglades."

"Deal."

‡‡‡

Bob pressed the speaker button to disconnect the call.

"There's another call we need to place."

She gave him Rosalee Perry's cell phone number.

"It's Special Agent Gina Delgado, Rosalee," Gina greeted after Perry answered.

"Has there been a break in the case, Jamie's murder?"

"Maybe, but that's not why I'm calling. I'm calling about Cold Burn, how your team managed to lower the water temperature in the Everglades, even by a fraction."

"Okay," Perry said, clearly not sure where this was going.

"How'd you manage to do it, even incrementally?"

Gina could feel her hedging even over the phone. "I'm not sure I can tell you that."

"Even if it helps me find who killed Jamie?" Gina said, purposefully using only his first name.

"All right," Perry said, and then sighed. "Simply stated, we introduced an organism into that sample section of the Everglades to induce a chemical change in the water."

CHAPTER 39

GLACIER BAY NATIONAL PARK AND PRESERVE, ALASKA

The park covers more than 3.2 million acres.

"If I didn't know better," Michael said, looking at the ice axe in Amka's hand, "I'd say you were going to use that on me."

"If I can't find what I'm looking for here, I might as well, because we'll freeze to death before the storm passes."

"What are you looking for?" he asked, barely getting the words out through the snow that blew into his mouth every time he opened it.

"Old underground mines—copper, minerals, coal, even gold—dot this area everywhere. They were closed up, sealed after they were abandoned because of the safety hazard they posed. But some were still open when I was a little girl, and we kids used to explore them. They were all boys from the village, except for me. They didn't like me tagging along, but they were too scared to stop me."

Michael would have smiled if his face didn't feel frozen. "That's why you stopped here."

"GPS got me this far. I'll have to manage the rest on my own."

"How can I help?" he asked, crossing his arms in front of his parka to further ward off the cold.

"Watch where you step. This storm makes it hard to believe that we had a warmer than normal winter and the ice sheets that formed over the mine openings may not be able to support your weight."

Michael remembered Gina Delgado describe what it was like disabling land mines in Iraq, how careful you had to be with every step, and had a sense now of what that must have felt like.

"Actually . . ." Amka continued. Her long black hair extending out from her woolen cap was drawn down almost to her eyebrows, tossed about by the whims of the wind. "Stay close to me. Once I find an iced-over shaft opening, you can provide enough cover from the wind and snow to let me use this axe to break our way inside."

Michael didn't know what that meant exactly, but he nodded anyway. The storm showed no signs of abating. Amka didn't bother using a flashlight because the beam wouldn't make even a dent in such blinding conditions. They had only the LED headlights of the ATVs to guide the way, and the spill of his was limited because it had toppled over.

Amka knelt in an area she seemed to recognize and began to brush the accumulated snow aside with a gloved hand. The light and powdery piles offered little resistance and Michael watched her shift about in a crouch in search of a spot where her efforts would reveal ice instead of tundra, indicating the opening to one of the mines.

Michael hovered over her without being prompted, keeping as much of the storm away as he could to better enable her search. These kinds of conditions were the absolute worst for his prosthetic, especially since its plastic components didn't respond well to frigid temperatures. If the plastic fittings and composite straps froze through and gave way, his prosthetic would end up dangling from his ankle and he would lose the ability to do anything but freeze to death here. He was well equipped to start a fire in any conditions, so long as there was wood and kindling to be had. But the congestion of mines must have left the land so barren and decayed as to be blighted, no vegetation revealed anywhere through the fast-mounting snow. There were plenty of areas of Lester Island that were rich in flora and fauna, trees even, but not here where in years and centuries past the mines had dominated the land.

Michael started having trouble breathing and kept a sleeve of his parka pressed against his mouth to suck in air through the fabric, so taking in a breath no longer pushed air crusted with microscopic slivers of ice into his mouth to eventually find their way down his throat. That helped him maintain his position over Amka, but he knew the relief was only temporary.

He had lost all sense of time, no idea how much had passed when her clearing efforts revealed something that glimmered slightly in the spray of the LED lights that cut slivers through the storm. She pulled her ice axe from an inside pocket of her down coat where she'd secured it and tapped the edge along the spot she'd cleared, already with a fresh coat of snow atop it. The sound, which barely reached him, sounded like knuckles rapping against glass.

"Found an opening!" Amka said, loud enough to slice through the wind.

"You don't have another one of those, do you?"

She seemed to manage a smile that shone through the white sheen painted over her face. "More important for you to stand where you are and keep as much of the storm off me as you can."

Then Amka started hammering the axe against the ice, moderately at first to grow accustomed to the motion, but then pounding the ice hard enough to spray stone-sized chips into the air that disappeared within the snow. A few times Michael thought the chips actually hung suspended in the air for a long moment, an illusory trick of the storm, he thought, but maybe not.

As Amka continued hacking away with her axe, the chips grew into chunks and Michael glimpsed fissure lines that looked like a cracked windshield, indicating only a thin layer remained. It gave way in a single manhole-sized wedge and dropped downward into the darkness revealed below. Also revealed was a wooden ladder that whoever had sealed the mine up had left in place in case the time ever came to reclaim whatever lay within the shafts. If Michael's knowledge of mine construction in these parts was correct, below ground was a network of tunnels that wove in a honeycomb pattern. The role of a law enforcement ranger earlier in his career had forced him to become familiar with the general contours of all the parks, preserves, and memorials served by the National Park Service, since he never knew where his next assignment might take him.

The open abyss belched out a blast that felt like tropical air compared to the conditions of the frigid wasteland around them.

"Want me to go first?" Michael offered.

She unclipped the flashlight from her belt and handed it to him. "No. Get as low as you can and shine this downward to light my way. I've been using ladders like this since I was six, for thirty years."

"Okay, but when was the last time?"

"When I was Yehl's age."

"So twenty years ago?"

She smiled thinly as she started to lower herself down the ladder, testing the first rung she found with her boot. "Wish me luck."

"What am I supposed to do if the ladder breaks apart and you fall?"

"It won't and I won't," she said, and started lowering.

Seconds into her descent, all Michael could see was her woolen cap pulled down low. He aimed the flashlight beam on it, no trace of the bottom of the mine shaft revealed. She quickly dropped out of sight altogether, hidden from the weak spray of the beam, even when Michael backed away from the opening and positioned himself so he was actually leaning into the hole. The beam caught a flicker of motion, and he held it in place to at least cast a few blips of light toward whatever lay beneath her.

"I'm good," Amka called up to him, in a voice that echoed through the abyss. "Ladder's holding."

"How far down?" Michael shouted.

"Don't know. It's warmer, though. Still cold but nothing like the surface."

Twenty degrees compared to zero, he figured. Then he heard a thud.

"Amka!"

"I'm okay. Just dropped down the last stretch, maybe five feet. There's ground down here, at least until the snow follows. Can you see me?"

Michael moved the flashlight about. "No . . . Wait, I've got something. Yeah, I've got a glimpse. Looks like you're about thirty feet down."

"Some of these mines go down deeper than a hundred, right into the permafrost where the copper, gold, and coal was the richest."

"I'm coming down," Michael said, working to position himself for the climb down the ladder.

"Secure the flashlight first. We don't want to be down here in the dark."

Michael held either side of the ladder with his hands and felt for the easiest rung for his still whole foot, the right one, to manage. He secured it in place and then followed with his prosthetic, which felt like a dead weight attached to his ankle. The mechanism balked at performing the simplest, most routine motions. Everything else but the titanium portions must have frozen solid. He heard a creaking sound when he finally perched it on the rung beneath his right one and put weight on it for the first time. He resolved to keep as much of his weight on his right side, using the left only for balance, acting like a kind of piston.

Michael fell into an awkward rhythm, halfway down when his flesh-and-blood foot slipped off a rung, forcing all of his weight onto his prosthetic. He held his breath, certain the housing was going to snap then and there, but it miraculously held and even found the next rung without further incident. By this point the world had gone totally dark around him. Though he was focused on what lay below, he could feel the soft smack of snow blowing in through the hole Amka had chiseled above. The shaft felt like a wind tunnel, the swirls of snow dropping down to be whipped about in a building vortex of white powder and crystals. But the complete darkness was the worst, stealing all perspective from him and leaving his motions stiff and tentative.

"You're almost there," Amka called up to him. "Don't stop. Keep moving."

Michael didn't realize he had stopped, and started down again. Suddenly, there were no more rungs to find purchase on with his boots. He held himself still right there, unwilling to probe the air beneath him with either foot. Then he felt Amka's gloved hands close on either side of his waist.

"I've got you," she said. "Just drop down."

Michael did, after taking a deep breath, and managed a cushioned landing, thanks to her support.

"Thanks," he said, adding, "for saving our lives."

"It's nothing new. The Tlingit people have been improvising in order to survive for hundreds of years."

"Lucky for me."

Michael gazed about the chamber in which he had landed. It looked to be the original entrance to the mine. He was still cold but down here, absent the wind and the icy snow, he could breathe normally and his prosthetic already felt more normal, thanks in large part to the fact that the rest of his leg was no longer tensed up from the cold.

"What's that smell?" he asked, inhaling something bitter and sharp now that his nose was functioning properly again.

"Raw coal. I'm guessing this is your first time in a coal mine."

"There are a few relics left on national park property, but I've never been inside one."

"Mountain coal is different than the mineral that formed in the tundra amid the permafrost. More potent. Burns faster and hotter."

"Well, in that case—"

Michael took a step toward Amka and felt the mine floor give way underfoot, felt himself dropping downward, suspended in the air briefly before landing on something that cushioned his fall like an air mattress. He heard a click in the blackness and saw Amka silhouetted nearby in the glow of the flashlight she was turning about, as she climbed back to her feet.

Michael had trouble managing the task with his prosthetic still slowed by the cold and accepted her free hand to reach his feet. He watched her shine the flashlight upward toward the jagged hole where the floor had given way twelve or so feet above them.

"No way to climb back up," Michael noted.

Amka swept the flashlight around the level of the mine where they had landed in search of a passageway. "I used to explore these mines all the time as a little girl. There will be another way out—we just have to find it."

The beam traced the wall directly before them, illuminating the black, dull surface of coal layered into frozen tundra and permafrost. Michael knew the process to extract it was called longwall mining.

"Good thing I still have this," Amka said, yanking her ice axe from her belt.

"Good thing the fall didn't impale you."

She handed him the flashlight. "Shine it over here," she instructed as she positioned herself the way a miner might have in decades past. "I'm going to chip away enough to make a fire that will keep us warm through the night. We'll look for a way out in the heat of the day tomorrow."

"Heat?"

"Compared to now."

Michael coughed from the coal dust Amka's first strikes had released into the air, and he moved the flashlight to her right, illuminating another section of the wall. He froze it there, on a patchwork design of tiny crystal-line shapes that reflected some of the light's spray back at him.

Amka stopped her work. "What is it, Michael?" she asked, calling him that for the first time.

He held the flashlight in place. "Ever seen anything like that before?"

She moved closer and brushed a gloved hand over it. "No, I haven't."

"Well, I have, and now I know where it may have come from."

CHAPTER 40

FISHERS ISLAND, NEW YORK

Though it is in New York, the island is only two miles off the southeastern coast of Connecticut.

Hours later, after nightfall, Cole spotted his Fisher Island home rising out of the bluffs from the back of his armored SUV. All successful men hated failure, without being averse to it, since failure was an inevitable part of trying to do what no one had ever done before. Breaking new ground required busting a few shovels in the process.

This was different. He'd dug a deep hole for himself at Michoud Assembly Facility in New Orleans, one he might not be able to climb out of.

Cole and Elizabeth Fields had responded to the emergency at his lab on the Michoud campus to find a security perimeter erected, formed by men and vehicles arranged in a semicircle, and no one allowed to proceed farther. With Fields in tow, Cole approached the head of the facility's security apparatus, a man he'd met on several occasions, though he couldn't remember his name.

"What happened?" he asked the man in charge, stepping forward past the de facto barrier formed by the vehicles.

"Please step back, sir."

Cole remained in place. "You know who I am, right?"

"I do, Mr. Cole."

"Then you know the personnel in that lab work for me. Whatever it is that happened in there, I'm entitled to know."

"We don't know what happened, sir. We only know . . ."

"What?" Cole demanded, when the head of security's voice trailed off. "What do you know?"

"Please step back here, sir. That's an order. We have a hazmat team staging now."

Cole cast his gaze back toward Fields, who had opted not to advance with him inside the perimeter. "Hazmat team? What happened?" He scanned the inside of the security perimeter. "Where are the people who work for me? Are they still inside? What aren't you telling me?"

"Nothing's been confirmed yet, sir. We need to be sure."

"Sure about *what*, for god's sake?"

"Please step back, Mr. Cole."

Cole rejoined Fields and yanked out his cell phone to call the head of the facility. It went straight to voicemail, just as a pair of big SUVs arrived and personnel garbed in full hazmat gear with oxygen tanks strapped to their backs spilled out inside the perimeter.

Only when two of them emerged from inside the laboratory facility minutes later did the head of security approach Cole, his expression both dour and fearful after receiving an early assessment from the hazmat crew.

"The initial reports we received have been confirmed. There's no easy way to say this, sir, but all of your people are dead."

Cole had left Fields on-site while the investigation proceeded, then departed the grounds after learning the total count was twenty-one dead. No survivors and no details as to how they died. But Cole knew it could only have been Prometheus; he had taken a different kind of fire from the gods and was now paying the price for it.

Fields had called several times on his trip home to report on the obvious. His phone rang again, and this time he sent her call straight to voicemail, figuring he'd call her back once walled off in safety inside the confines of his impregnable home on Fisher Island. Then he'd need to go into damage-control mode, even as an investigation was carried out into his potential culpability. There'd be a swarm of lawsuits he'd have to fend off and a ton of bad publicity unleashed by the swarm who'd been rooting for him to fail ever since he'd begun achieving success on a virtually unprecedented level.

Approaching the bluff on which the sprawling house resided, Cole felt his stomach clench.

His perimeter guards were nowhere to be seen.

He'd grown so used to spotting the big men clad in black tactical gear patrolling their stations or manning their posts that they'd become ingrained on the landscape. Not so today. The driver of the SUV that had picked him up at the airport, seeing the same thing he did, slowed the vehicle to a crawl as they turned up the drive.

Cole saw the men seated next to him and in the front seat tense as they readied their pistols. Pulling farther up the drive, he saw the front door was halfway open, letting in the shrill air blowing off the nearby shore.

The SUV ground to a halt, jostling him slightly. The man in the front seat, Berk, turned and regarded him with an utterly flat expression.

"Stay here, sir."

Before he climbed out in the company of the guard seated by Cole's side, Berk nodded to the driver, surely a signal to burn rubber out of here if they didn't reappear or report.

The doors slammed closed, shutting out the cold air.

The two men fetched assault rifles from the rear of the SUV and headed up the walk toward the house.

They entered, leaving the door open behind them.

Time passed. Nothing.

More time passed. Still nothing.

Cole felt his heart hammering against his chest and his breath catching.

"Sir," the driver started.

"The hell with that! We're not leaving. My family's in there. We're not leaving. Take me inside."

"Sir—"

"Take me inside or give me your damn gun and I'll go myself!"

The driver opened his door and climbed out, covering Cole as he followed, then led the way up the walk.

Cole jogged ahead of him. The driver caught up and they entered the home together.

Empty.

Silent.

Cole felt the breath catch in his throat. He took the lack of bodies as a good sign, something positive, as he made his way to the stairs that led to the newly constructed basement level that held his safe room. Descending the stairs behind the former special operator with pistol testing the air ahead of them, Cole envisioned the scenario in his head: his family reaching safety behind the fortified steel doors as invaders did battle with his security force, none of whom were in evidence, including the two who had preceded him into the house.

At the bottom of the stairs, Cole spotted the heavy door sealed and edged ahead of his final special operator, a camera following his every move. He pressed his palm against the reader, then pushed his eyes closer to a scanner. A click sounded, the locks disengaging.

Cole heard a thud and glanced behind him to find the special operator on the floor, blood leaking from a head wound making a pool on the finished concrete. Turned back to find the door opening before him.

He saw his wife, saw his kids, gathered in a tight cluster on the floor, guns aimed down at them by big men with faces hidden behind black neoprene masks. Their eyes were wide in terror and streaks of tears ran down the children's faces as his wife clutched them close.

More faceless men filled the spacious safe room that wasn't safe at all, poking the air with their rifles, enclosing a short-haired man with an anvil-shaped, bald head, his face so rigid it looked more like a marble bust.

"Mr. Cole," the man said, managing a smile, "how nice to make your acquaintance."

The man rose from the chair he'd been seated in, stretching out the expensive suit he wore over a thick black turtleneck. He was not that tall but very thick.

"We have some business to conduct together. I am General Viktor Sergei Adamovitch, your new partner."

PART FOUR

—⬥—

Below us was the great land. Indeed, all
Glacier Bay is the great land, unique, wild, and
magnificent. It should exist intact solely for its
own sake. No justification, rationale, or excuse is
needed. For its own sake and no other reason.

—*Glacier Bay: The Land and the Silence*

—⬥—

CHAPTER 41

LESTER ISLAND, ALASKA

The Native village of Gatheeni provided labor for the canneries on Lester Island.

"Where have you seen it before?" Michael heard Amka ask him, as he continued to stare at where he was certain the contents of that ancient Tlingit funeral urn had originated from.

The crystals layered into the black shiny portions of the wall made those sections stand out from the ordinary coal beds pitched into the walls of what resembled a cave, but was actually the chamber of a mine. In his mind, Michael pictured the shiny portions being carved out and then ground into the crystalline powder that had cost couriers Olivia and Steve Morgan their lives.

"Yesterday in Sitka."

"Go on," Amka urged, as she continued to chip away at the coal, making a pile near her feet, still without explaining her intentions.

"That other investigation I told you brought me up here . . . I was trying to find out who was behind stolen Tlingit antiquities. But that was just a front for what was being smuggled out of Alaska inside them."

Amka aimed the flashlight she held in her free hand toward a portion of the wall that glistened in the light. "That?"

"In powder form, yes." Michael looked down at the pile of coal by her feet.

He watched her slide sideways and begin to work her ice axe in the area of the chamber wall Michael had indicated, working in subtler fashion to chip away smaller chunks, which fell at her feet.

"What's the plan, Amka?"

She stooped and retrieved a handful of the fragments of crystal-laden black rock. "I'll analyze this as soon as we get back to the village."

"I was talking about the plan for tonight."

Amka stowed the fragments in a zippered pouch on the inside of her jacket. "Not to freeze to death, Michael. It's time to build a fire."

†‡†

"Are you wearing an undershirt, like a tee?" Amka continued.

"A thermal."

"Then we'll use mine."

She waited for him to turn around to peel off the outer layers she was wearing to get to her T-shirt.

"Okay. You can turn around again. And pile these chunks in the center of the floor, while I chop away some more."

Michael's gloves came away black from moving the coal from around Amka's feet to the center of the chamber floor in as neat a pile as he could manage. The next chunks she chipped away with her ice axe were the biggest yet, and Michael dutifully added them to the pile.

"That ought to be enough to get us through the night," she said, hauling over the final load herself, the pile now about the size for a typical wood fire in a fireplace.

Michael watched her scrape her T-shirt against the coal to blacken it with dust. Coal itself was difficult, if not impossible, to light ablaze. But coal dust burned fast and hot. Amka blackened more of her T-shirt with coal dust and then wedged it beneath the pile they had made to use as kindling. Then she pulled a small box of matches from her pocket, struck one, and eased the flame up against a protruding edge of her blackened T-shirt. It caught with a *poof!* and almost instantly Michael could feel the heat rising off the pile of coal. Just a fissure of heat at first, but rising quickly as the flames spread upward, whitening the coal at the edges, which quickly turned red from the bottom up.

By the time the top of the pile began to whiten at the tips, he'd taken his gloves off and was warming his hands over the coal fire she had gotten lit.

"Stinks," he said to her.

"Small price to pay for not freezing to death," Amka said, rubbing her hands together close to his over the rising draft of heat. "If we're stuck here for a week, we'll have to start worrying about toxic exposure."

"If we're still down here a week from now, toxicity will be the least of our problems."

She managed a slight smile that slid away as quickly as she'd formed it.
"You're worried about your brother, out here in this, too."

"I'm thinking about him. I'm not worried."

"How can that be?"

"Because my grandfather wasn't worried. He knew the storm was coming and that Yehl was driving out to greet it. I could tell from my grandfather that he was going to return to the village a man, not a boy."

Michael tried not to sound skeptical. "Your grandfather can see the future?"

"He can read the signs. The future is predictable if you know what to look for."

Michael left it there. "Do you think he saw us spending the night in an abandoned mine under the heat of a coal fire?"

"I wouldn't put it past him."

"Then why didn't he warn us?"

"Would it have changed anything if he had?"

Michael shrugged, acknowledging her point.

Amka pulled her arms back through the sleeves of her heavy jacket and zipped it up. They sat down next to each other, as close to the coal as their sense of smell would allow. They had both turned their flashlights off to conserve the batteries, the mine's only light now coming from the orange glow of pieces of coal that reminded Michael of an old-fashioned backyard barbecue with meat grilling over charcoal briquettes.

Amka's gaze drifted off—in dreamy fashion, he thought at first, but then realized she was looking at the parts of the wall where the crystals embedded there twinkled ever so slightly. She began to speak without looking back toward Michael, her eyes still fixed on that part of the cave wall.

"There is a Tlingit legend about a raven named *Nass-aa-geyeil* who brought light to the world. He kept the light in a box, to be released into parts of the world only as he saw fit. In the legend, he comes upon a town where the people had lived forever in darkness and had come to fear and hate light. One day, the people were out fishing when the raven appeared on the opposite bank, box in hand, and asked the people of the village to take him across in one of their boats. When they refused out of fear, the raven opened his box just a little and shed so great a light on them that the people cowered and covered their eyes. He shut the box quickly, and demanded again to be brought across the river. When the people refused again, the raven became so angry that he opened the box all the way and let the sun fly up to the sky and the people lost the darkness they had come to welcome."

"I'm sure they came to welcome the light, too."

"That's not the point of the story, Michael." Amka's eyes were still fixed on the glimmering crystals. "The point is I'm wondering now whether the legend was speaking of something else that brought the light."

Michael could see her turn toward him.

"And if that's the case, what else can it do? The answer to that question explains why clearly two different parties want it so very badly: the Russians and whoever's been smuggling it out of Alaska for—how long is it?"

"Three years, by all indications." Michael fixed his gaze on the source of the crystalline powder he had glimpsed yesterday inside a Tlingit burial urn.

"I never told you that I'm sorry about your wife," Amka said suddenly.

"You had plenty on your mind already."

"Leaders must see to the edges, not only what lies directly before them. My people look to me as a leader."

"Is that the way you see yourself?"

"Sometimes it's hard to reconcile this world with the greater one beyond."

"Meaning the villagers aren't seeing the edges either."

Amka managed a smile. "Not always, but they're doing better at it, just as I'm striving to do."

Michael saw her teeth were chattering, the cold starting to have its way. He eased himself closer, wrapped an arm around Amka's shoulder, and drew her in against him. He could feel her shaking inside her parka.

"When I left this village for the world, I never thought I'd come back. That's how I thought about it—the world, as if my own village was on another planet. I saw it as the place where dreams died, nobody ever making anything of themselves, their entire identities defined by tribal traditions and lore."

She was still shaking, so Michael drew her tighter against him and wrapped a second arm around her. The shaking seemed to still a bit, and she looped her arms around him as well.

"You're freezing."

"Don't worry about me. I'm missing a foot, remember? Means there's less of me to keep warm." He hesitated, then picked up where he'd left off. "Why did you come back, Amka?"

"I told you: because of my brother."

"Yes, you did. And now I'm asking you again."

She sighed deeply and Michael felt the chill mist from her mouth against him, glimpsed the soft cloud it made in the air.

"I made a ton of money," Amka said. "Became renowned for my work in certain circles. And the whole time I hated it. Because they saw me as a scientist, an academic, a woman."

"Isn't that what you wanted when you left?"

"That's what I thought I wanted, Michael. Then I realized I had run from myself. A scientist, an academic, and a woman, but not a Native, not a Tlingit. In the years I was away, my heritage never came up. I should have been celebrating it, become an example to our people, but I couldn't. I'm not political, not an activist, but I realized all the people celebrating my achievements, the people who made me rich, had no idea who I really was and the closest I got to telling them was on whatever forms I had to fill out for the human resources department."

"You made yourself rich, Amka, and what's the difference whether they knew about your heritage or not? *You* knew—isn't that what mattered?"

"To a white man, I imagine it would." She stiffened and pulled away a little. "Heritage isn't something non-Natives think about. It doesn't define you, doesn't follow you. And when it stopped defining and following me, I realized I'd betrayed my own people. I hadn't only run away in body, I'd run away in spirit. I had to come back to find myself before it was too late, before I was lost forever."

"Sounds like the way I felt when I lost Allie," Michael told her.

"Allison," Amka said, calling her what the articles about the incident had. "Your wife."

"On the mountain, after it was over, I knew she was dead—I must have. But I told myself I could still save her and even with my left foot dangling, held in place only by my boot, I dragged her to a ranger outpost on a rise. Maybe a quarter mile away, maybe a half—I don't know, because I never measured it. But you know what drove me on, what pushed me all the way up the mountain? Hope, the hope that I could save her, that there was still a chance. I clung to that purpose and when I got her inside the outpost, and realized there was no hope, I lost that purpose and never really got it back."

Michael felt Amka's heartbeat quicken. "What happened to Allie wasn't the only thing I found out about you. Last year, you were involved with those domestic terrorists who were destroying national monuments and symbols."

If you only knew, he thought and let her continue without interrupting.

"Are you a man who finds trouble, Michael, or does trouble find you?"

"A little bit of both, I'd say. I envy you having something to come back to, Amka, because that's what I lost when I lost Allie. I never thought of it that way before, but I probably should have. I also never thought about attracting trouble but there was Rainier, those terrorists, and now whatever we're facing here. Do the Tlingits have a parable about that?"

"We have many, Michael, too many to tell. All of them about strength. I watched you on the glacier, watched you disappear into the fog, watched it welcome you as its own. Nature recognizes strength, nature welcomes strength. The fog helped you, made itself your ally."

"It was just a weather system, Amka. We got lucky."

"When I left Xunaa, I left myself behind. I came back to return to myself, not just the village. Outside the village, it was just me. Inside the village, it's me within the world, within nature. I realized how much the world was serving me as I served it, how much I missed that. You want to believe it was just a weather system back on the glacier; feel free. But you risk making the same mistake I did once I left the village, living apart instead of welcoming the world in."

Amka lapsed into silence, unbroken by Michael as exhaustion overcame both of them and they fell asleep intertwined in each other's arms.

‡‡‡

Michael had figured he would rotate shifts with Amka, adding coal to the pile to keep generating heat through the night. But when he awoke, stiff and cramped with her leaning against him asleep, he felt the heat and saw the fresh coal burning hot atop a hefty pile of ash that had accumulated overnight. The stench was overwhelming.

"Hey," he heard suddenly, "you guys down there? Hello? . . . Hello?"

Yehl calling to them from somewhere over the chamber of the mine they'd plunged into.

"We're here!" Amka called back to him, her voice echoing in tinny fashion.

They rose to their feet together and moved into a shaft of sunlight in the shape of the hole Amka had chiseled from the ice last night. A rope seemed to drop from the sun itself, dangling just short of the ground. Michael looked up and saw a grinning Yehl gazing down at them. Besides his eyes, every inch of him looked crusted with ice and snow.

"How'd you sleep?" he asked them.

JOINT BASE ELMENDORF-RICHARDSON, ANCHORAGE, ALASKA

The base's economic impact to the region in 2023 was
estimated to be over $3.6 billion.

Daniel Grant answered on the first ring this time, before Gina had even processed the import of Rosalee Perry's words.

"Simply stated, we introduced an organism into that sample section of the Everglades to induce a chemical change in the water."

There was nothing, of course, simple about it. That the crew of the *Providence* had all frozen to death suggested an indelible connection with the experiments the United States Geological Survey was conducting in Everglades National Park.

As part of Operation Cold Burn . . .

The scientists up here at Elmendorf had determined that the mystery organism they'd yet to isolate lowered body temperature by inducing a chemical reaction in water molecules, which was the basis of Cold Burn.

The connection to the deaths of the *Providence*'s crew to Operation Cold Burn meant she might have found a motive for the murder of Jamie Bidwell. Clearly, the USGS was up to something much bigger than she'd had reason to suspect.

"Why am I talking to you again so soon, Delgado?" Grant asked.

"Because I've got something to add about the connection between that murder of the USGS team member in the Everglades and the crew of the *Providence*. The USGS team in the Everglades reduced the temperature of water by inducing a chemical change in the molecules of H_2O. The crew of the *Providence* froze to death because a chemical change in the water in their bodies caused them to freeze to death, after seawater penetrated the sub."

"I fail to see what—"

"The seawater was carrying the organism or microbe that killed the crew, the same organism the USGS must be experimenting with in the Everglades."

Gina stopped, resuming when Grant remained silent.

"I think it's time for me to speak to the president directly."

"She remains unavailable."

"Put her on, Grant."

"Maybe you didn't hear what I just said."

"I don't work for you, I work for her."

"You work for the White House, Delgado, and right now I'm the White House."

"Then the White House is impeding the investigation the president herself sent me up here to conduct."

Another pause, one Gina couldn't tolerate.

"You still there, Grant?"

"Yes. I was just checking an important text that came in. We're running a campaign in these parts, in case you haven't been following the news, and the president's numbers are for shit. Two major polls have her down between six and eight points, dangerous territory even this far out from the election. We needed a game changer to rewrite the narrative."

Politics, Gina thought, *it always came down to politics for these people . . .*

"Don't tell me," she said, keeping her voice calm as Bob looked on, "the ability to lower ocean temperatures would represent the greatest weapon ever discovered in the fight against climate change. You think Operation Cold Burn could swing the polls back the president's way."

"Emphasis on 'could,' Agent. Lowering ocean temperature half a degree in a small sample area won't swing anything. We need to be in position to announce a much more dramatic achievement, something that will bring back voters who've strayed from the president. Our polling indicates a major climate change accomplishment like this is the game changer we need."

"You poll any of the crew members on the *Providence* before they died, Mr. Chief of Staff?"

"I'm not convinced there's a connection."

"Haven't you been listening to me? Well, you better listen now, because the microbe that scientists up here believe killed that submarine crew may be the very same microbe that wiped out a good portion of life on Earth around ten thousand years ago," Gina explained, doing her best to paraphrase the conclusions the scientist who called himself Atticus had shared with her. "Somehow it's gotten loose again and you should be focusing all of your attention on how to stop it instead of trying to use it to win an election. You're playing with fire here, Grant, so you couldn't have chosen a better name for this than Cold Burn."

Instead of a pause this time, she heard Grant sigh. "What would you like me to tell the president?"

"That we need to suspend all work on the USGS project in the Everglades. And run a check on hospitals throughout Alaska, particularly Juneau," Gina said, since it was the closest city to where the *Providence* had ended up at the bottom of the sea. "You're looking for spikes in hospitalizations, particularly involving the respiratory system because that seems to be what the microbe attacks first. The common denominator is water—that's what it attacks, by causing a chemical reaction that mirrors the physical reaction of freezing. We can't ignore the connection between those crew members freezing to death because their body temperature fell off a cliff and an experiment that managed to lower the ocean temperature in the Everglades. That means we need to uncover who had Jamie Bidwell killed and why, starting with uncovering who he really was and how he ended up part of that USGS team. Something made him a threat to somebody, Grant, and we need to figure out what that is. Because I think we're facing something even bigger here and whatever got Bidwell killed is somehow connected to it."

"How in God's name can that be, Special Agent Delgado?"

"What if someone intends to weaponize what killed the crew of the *Providence*, Mr. Chief of Staff?"

CHAPTER 43

FISHERS ISLAND, NEW YORK

Adrian Block, the first European to visit the island,
named it Vischer's Island in 1614.

When Cole looked behind him again, a trio of broad men who towered over him had appeared, one of them holding a still-smoking pistol that, no doubt, had been the source of his dead security man oozing blood onto the concrete beyond the safe room.

Before him, Adamovitch rose from his chair stiffly in a motion that looked almost rehearsed, as if every move he made was planned in advance. He shot one of his men a look and in the next instant that man was escorting Cole's wife and children from the safe room.

"You could let my family go," Cole said when the door closed behind the man.

"Yes, I could," the Russian said, "but I won't. Consider them the leash I have tightened over your neck. You are a man, Comrade Cole, who cares for nothing unless you are faced with losing it. That you see as an affront to your pride, an assault on your power."

Cole couldn't help but smile.

"You find this amusing?"

"You called me 'Comrade Cole,' like something from an old spy movie."

Adamovitch nodded as if he understood. "Depicting the Cold War, no doubt, when I was a mere boy. My father was KGB, in charge of a school that taught Russians perfect English and how to act like an American to make them perfect spies to plant in your country. Hundreds of them placed everywhere near the greatest centers of power. It was the most successful operation in the spy agency's history, thanks to my father. And when the Soviet Union fell he killed himself because there was nothing more to live for, nothing more to serve. You might say I'm doing this to honor his memory, by reconstituting the empire he watched crumble. And you are going to help me."

Cole had heard of Adamovitch, but knew little about him beyond the rampant speculation that he had successfully installed himself as Putin's eventual replacement, suggesting that was going to happen sooner rather than later, which may well have explained his presence here today.

"I must apologize for the execution of your couriers in Alaska," Adamovitch started.

"You wanted the powder."

Adamovitch nodded. "I did, indeed."

"How'd you learn about it?" Cole asked, immediately wishing he hadn't posed a threatening question. "If you don't mind telling me," he added.

"It's not important. Let's just say that I have my sources, too. And those sources were the ones who informed me that your discovery can do far more than help man reach Mars."

"So I've learned," Cole said, thinking of the deaths of Elizabeth Fields's entire team in their lab facility on the Michoud campus.

"Yes." The Russian nodded. "I heard about your misadventure in New Orleans. Learning the hard way is never easy."

"I've gotten no reports on how they died exactly."

"Because, I imagine, your American authorities are still trying to determine how they froze to death in comfortable seventy-two-degree temperatures. The explanation is quite interesting, but we have more important business to discuss. You have partnered with others in the past, of course."

"I have, yes."

"Then I propose we partner now, so that our mutual pursuits can be achieved, one helping to enable the other."

Adamovitch moved closer and extended his hand. Cole took it and squeezed lightly. Adamovitch squeezed back, just enough to let him know he could have crushed his hand had he wanted to. Another unspoken display of power.

"How do you propose we do that?" Cole asked him, regarding his hand as if to reassure himself that it was still there.

"We both need more of this compound than current reserves allow. We need to explore new opportunities for supply."

"I've already identified the location of massive reserves, only they're located beneath a populated area we can't access."

Adamovitch smiled in a way that left Cole chilled. "You mean *you* can't access them. That's where I come in. You see, Comrade Cole, you want to change the world," he said, smiling again, "while I only want to rule it. And we can both have our way. Just tell me where these massive reserves are located."

GLACIER BAY NATIONAL PARK AND PRESERVE, LESTER ISLAND, ALASKA

In the late 1800s, the canneries were closed due to a build-up of icebergs.

"Man, you stink," Yehl said, nose wrinkling when Michael emerged first from the hole in the ice Amka had chiseled the night before.

She insisted he go first and was already climbing the rope Yehl had dropped down to them. Michael saw that the boy had looped the rope around a trio of steel spikes he'd nailed into the ice to secure it. The ATV he'd rode out of the village the night before sat parked nearby, coated with a stubborn layer of ice.

"How'd you know to bring a rope with you?" he asked the figure encrusted in ice and snow everywhere but his face.

"I had a feeling I might need it."

"For your spirit walk?"

Yehl shook his head. "For this morning, for now. After I had proven myself to nature by surviving the night."

"Becoming a man is overrated, kid."

"Not when you're going to be the next chief. My grandfather's a tough act to follow. No one in the village can remember a time when Xetsuwu wasn't *aanñkáawu*. I see the way they look at me. After today, maybe they won't look at me the same way anymore."

Michael wanted to ask the boy how'd he managed to survive the night and the storm, but suspected that was a story Yehl would share only with his grandfather. He might not have believed in mythical monsters or put much stock in folklore, but the boy had managed to somehow endure the elements and prove himself worthy of becoming the next chief of the Hoonah Tlingit people in the line of succession.

"How far do we have to go before we've got cell service again?"

It turned out to be all the way back to the village. Outside his home in the grove shrouded by evergreen trees, Yehl's grandfather sat in the same position where Michael and Amka had left him, as if he hadn't budged all night. There wasn't even a trace of snow or ice anywhere to be seen, meaning the sudden storm had been confined to the center of the island, pushed away from the shoreline by the steering winds. Weather patterns could vary wildly in these parts, subject to the whims of atmospheric conditions even meteorologists were hard-pressed to explain.

Amka had drawn even with Michael when the boy reached his grandfather, the old man rising to his feet to lay his hands on his grandson's shoulders. He spoke softly, inaudible to anyone but Yehl, who nodded. As Yehl dashed inside, the old man looked toward Amka and spoke just a few words before turning around and heading for the simple home that was a twin of the one neighboring it.

"What did he say?" Michael wondered.

"He is a man now," Amka told him. "Let's go inside. I need to get back to work."

‡‡‡

Michael watched Amka moving about her makeshift lab, performing various tests on different samples of the crystal-laden rock they'd taken from the mine. She remained silent, not bothering to offer anything explanatory about what she was doing. For his part, Michael was too tired to ask, nodding off a few times until he shifted suddenly and nearly fell off the stool on which he was perched.

"That was close," Amka said to him, looking up from a test tube she'd been gently rotating.

Michael cleared his throat. "Imagine surviving last night only to crack my head open and bleed out on your floor."

"You wouldn't bleed out—I handle medical emergencies here, remember?"

She looked back at the test tube, the contents of which had turned yellow.

"Anyway," she resumed, "your timing is perfect."

"You managed to identify the substance so quickly?"

"You were asleep for longer than you think, Michael. And the answer is, yes, I did."

He spotted ground-up chips of rock from the mine, now resembling the crystalline powder he'd spotted in the Tlingit burial urn lifted from the Sheldon Jackson Museum.

"It wasn't hard," Amka told him. "A college student, even high school, could have done it. The basic parameters are that simple to collate."

"So what is it?"

"Oil, Michael."

He looked back at her. "Last time I checked oil wasn't a solid."

"That's because this isn't oil per se."

"But you just said . . ."

"I know what I said. Let me put it another way. This is a solid form of oil concentrated on an immeasurable level. Near as I can tell, it could be millions of years old, dating back to its molecular structure being altered."

"Altered by what?"

"Some stimulus. Potentially environmental, but more likely exposure to some kind of foreign organism."

"Foreign as in alien, as in from outer space?"

Amka looked at him the way a teacher might look at a student who'd voiced the wrong answer. "Foreign as in time, not space."

"I'm not following."

"The world's a much different place today than it was, say, sixty-five million years ago before the end of the dinosaurs—not just a physically different place, but also *physiologically*. If you looked at a map of the world from the Cretaceous period, nothing would appear the same. Many of the southern continents were still joined together as part of the southern landmass and the northern continents formed another great landmass. These two supercontinents shared many plants and animals dating from an earlier time when they were joined as one enormous landmass. Just as there were wildlife and animals—dinosaurs—that no longer exist today, there were also microscopic organisms. The difference is that during the Ice Age that wiped out animal and plant life on the planet, some of these microscopic organisms went into an extended stage of dormancy once frozen."

Michael's expression must have been enough to tell her he wasn't getting the point.

"What I'm getting at," Amka resumed, "is that we can't apply the scientific rules we live by when discussing whatever transformed oil from a liquid to an incredibly concentrated solid, because those rules don't account for whatever microorganism served as the stimulus for that."

‡‡‡

The gravity of that briefly distracted Michael from an anomaly he'd been wondering about since the previous night. "I never knew coal and oil could be found in the same place."

"The two being found in the same geological formation is actually more common than you think, since they're both formed from organic matter that has been subjected to heat and pressure over millions of years. It depends on the specific geological history of that area. While coal is typically associated with basins that produce natural gas, it is believed to be the source rock for commercial oil discoveries in some basins around the world. So it's possible that Alaska, with its massive coal reserves, contains large amounts of oil that were generated eons ago. We're talking about coal generating oil in a natural subsurface system, like the permafrost that dominates Alaska's ecosystem beneath the ground, making the coal mines on Lester Island breeding grounds for what we found last night. And I've heard of experiments that have produced crude oil from bits of Alaskan coal, which means coal-rich areas may contain undiscovered pools of oil in sedimentary basins. In this case, though, that oil is no longer oil as we understand it to be. It's essentially a whole new compound on the evolutionary scale."

"But the transformation occurred millions of years ago—that's what you were getting at before."

Amka nodded. "Speaking theoretically, yes. I'd need a lab more like the ones at MIT to give you a more definitive answer. But consider that, typically, oil is comprised of around eighty percent carbon, fifteen percent hydrogen, and as much as two percent oxygen with lesser amounts of sulfur and nitrogen. To create what we found in that mine last night, this outside stimulus must have somehow altered the chemical composition of that mixture."

"An outside stimulus like that microbe that's freezing fish?"

Amka's expression changed in that moment, eyes widening as if struck by a realization. "What was that United States Geological Survey team you came here to find doing in these parts?"

"I have no idea. I wasn't told and I didn't ask. It didn't seem to matter."

"What if it does? And what if they froze to death, just like the fish that have been washing up on our shores?"

"They had functional propane heaters and it wasn't that cold."

"You're missing my point. The fish froze in fifty-five-degree-water from the inside out. What if the same thing that's killing the fish killed those USGS scientists?"

"The same stimulus, you mean?"

"What do oil and water have in common, Michael?"

"Besides the fact that they're both liquids?"

"A simple answer, but the one I was looking for. Water freezes at thirty-two degrees Fahrenheit, while oil freezes at between forty and sixty degrees below zero Fahrenheit. The point is they both freeze."

"You think this concentrated form of oil *froze*?"

"No, because then, like water when exposed to higher temperatures, it would simply thaw out. But I think exposure to the same microorganism that's been killing the fish in Cross Sound somehow transformed the oil millions of years ago on a molecular level."

"The fish aren't the only thing it's killing, Amka. According to your brother, the members of that USGS team were alive and well when they reached that cave. A few hours later they were dead, after being in the same proximity as a woolly mammoth that died in there, too, five or ten thousand years ago. It died in there and froze, stayed that way until all the glacial melting thawed it out. And when it thawed out, so did the organism that might well have killed it."

"Lying in wait to resume its spread after thousands of years in hibernation . . ."

"So why are we still alive?" Michael challenged. "And if those dead fish were frozen to death by the same organism, why isn't everyone in the village dead by now?"

"I'd need that fully equipped lab at MIT to answer those questions definitively, Michael. But, theoretically . . ."

Amka started jotting down notes feverishly on a large notepad. Michael still couldn't grasp all the science behind what was happening on Lester Island, as it was of a magnitude now that far exceeded the rescue mission he'd come here to lead.

"Remember what we talked about before, how the mammoth that froze in that cave as many as ten thousand years ago must have ingested the organism?"

Michael nodded. "Just like the Russians who removed it must have come in hazmat gear, fully prepared for what they were going to find." In that moment, he realized that had saved his life; had he or any other rescue team shown up before the Russians, the same fate as the USGS team would have greeted them. "You also wondered what the dead fish who've been washing up on shore may have eaten," he recalled.

"I think I know now: plankton."

He waited for her to go on.

"I can't be certain without lots more testing," Amka resumed, "but it checks every box. Plankton feeds on small bits of organic matter that includes smaller bacterium-sized microbes."

"Or organisms."

"Exactly. The organism infects plankton, the fish eat the infected plankton, and we end up with thousands washing up dead. Then, before they die, the fish release more of the organism into the sea, which infects more plankton, to be eaten by more fish, and . . ."

Amka stopped there, no need to go on.

"So," Michael picked up, "if the organism manages to kill the plankton in oceans across the globe . . ."

"Then humanity dies, too."

"I need to make a phone call," Michael told her.

‡‡‡

"Michael," Angela Pierce greeted, "where have you been? I thought I was going to have to send a search party after you."

"Out of cell range since my last report."

"I forwarded that report up the chain of command. It turns out a Russian trawler was recorded on several satellite reconnaissance photos of the area. I guess that tells us where the hit team you and those warriors managed to take out on the glacier came from."

"Where's the trawler now?"

"We don't know, Michael. Officials at three-letter agencies believe it's using some kind of stealth technology that renders it virtually invisible to our satellites. It's been spotted sporadically during the day, only to disappear entirely at night. Aircraft have been scrambled on a few occasions but it's always gone by the time they get there."

"How long has this been going on, Angela?"

"As near as we can tell, several weeks at the very least."

Michael paused to process that. A Russian hitman back in Sitka, a Russian trawler, a Russian assault team . . .

"A Native scientist and I found an old mine last night with a wall of shiny black rock embedded with what looked like crystals."

"Sounds like that powder the Morgans were killed for."

"It's oil, Angela, oil in a form so concentrated we can't even begin to comprehend. But the Russians must have. That's why they're here, that's why they want the substance so badly they were willing to risk a covert mission on American soil to obtain it."

"You think the powder being smuggled out of Alaska originated in the same mine?"

"No, this mine had been sealed up decades ago. The crystalline powder I saw in that Tlingit funeral urn must have come from somewhere else."

"The Lamplugh Glacier maybe? That would explain the Russian interest in the site."

"Possibly, but I don't think so. The Russians weren't on the glacier for this substance. They must have gotten wind of what had gone down and got there ahead of us, because they thought that's what the USGS team must have been up to."

"In our last call, you said the team members were already dead when the Russians got there."

"And that explains why they removed the bodies, Angela, to find out how exactly this organism kills. It also explains why they took the body of the woolly mammoth, too, because it was the source. That means we can look at Lester Island becoming the site of of an ongoing fish kill of epic proportions as a harbinger of something much, much worse."

Angela hesitated before responding. "When I report this up the chain, what am I supposed to tell them this is?"

"The beginning," he said. "And I just happen to know someone who can bring it all to the attention of the White House."

JOINT BASE ELMENDORF-RICHARDSON, ANCHORAGE, ALASKA

Fisher House provides housing for family members
of the military undergoing care at a military medical
treatment facility on an outpatient basis.

Gina was waiting in the same outbuilding overlooking the tarmac that she'd entered after exiting the private jet hours before. A different jet was visible beyond the windows, but a mechanical problem had surfaced while it was being refueled for the trip back to Washington.

She used the time to call Clark Gifford on her own phone, having spotted a slew of voicemail and text messages from him when she had service again outside of the underground facility.

"We found the dock where the killers loaded Jamie Bidwell's body onto that boat our mystery man rented," he reported. "It belongs to a private residence the owner had already vacated for the season."

"A snowbird," Gina noted. "Something the killers were no doubt aware of."

"Well, they must not have been aware of the hidden security cameras that picked them up loading what looks like a heavy sack onto a boat that matches the one that was never returned. And get this, Agent: we got a front-on shot of the faces of two of the three men this time, one of them wearing the same shirt as the man from the marina. We're running them through the system now."

"I can expedite that from my end," Gina told Gifford, without elaborating further. "Text me the clearest shots you were able to lift."

"Already did," he said, referring to the texts Gina hadn't reviewed before calling him.

"And there's something else that occurred to me, now that we know James Bidwell wasn't the kid's real name," Gina told him. "Whoever he is, he's seriously into science, right? So maybe he attended conferences. I found several that have taken place in Florida in the past year. I'll text you the link to them, Clark. Start with the most recent because they're most likely to still have the security cam footage."

Gina pictured Gifford jotting that information down. "I should have thought of that myself. I'll jump on this as soon as I get your text. How are things going wherever you flew off to, by the way?"

"Enlightening," Gina said, leaving out the connection between the deaths of a Virginia-class submarine crew and Operation Cold Burn, and that she believed that Jamie Bidwell's murder was somehow connected to that as well.

Her phone buzzed with another incoming call, **MICHAEL WALKER** lighting up in the caller ID.

‡‡‡

"How's your day going?" she greeted.

"I'm investigating the impossible up here."

"Nothing new," Gina said, remembering that Michael had no idea she was actually in Alaska, too, at least for the time being, "for either one of us."

"Speaking of which, my investigation has turned things up you need to bring to the attention of the White House."

She listened to him explain what he'd uncovered in a cave on the Lamplugh Glacier where the USGS team he'd been sent to find had taken refuge, only to die from some unexplained cause inside. He mentioned the remains of a frozen woolly mammoth having thawed out and been removed, apparently by a covert Russian force, along with the bodies. Gina felt her skin prickle when he got to the part about fish freezing to death, the hairs on her arms standing up.

"Wait, did you say the fish *froze* to death?"

"From the inside out. Damnedest thing, right?"

"Oh my God . . ."

‡‡‡

Gina knew she was breaking operational security, but she had to tell him; he had to know in order for both of them to make sense of what was going on.

"You're saying the submarine crew died the same way," Michael said, when she'd finished.

"Virtually identical. I was sent up here to be the White House's eyes and ears. I'm still at Elmendorf now, at least for the next hour or so."

"Welcome to Alaska, Gina, Land of the Midnight Sun."

"More like land of mystery. That crew, and those fish, froze to death because of some organism that alters the molecular structure of cells. They froze to death from the inside out, starting in the respiratory system, because whatever this organism is, it causes a chemical reaction that reduces the temperature of water, akin to the physical reaction freezing causes. Listen to me, Michael, this organism reappeared ten thousand years ago, when the glaciers began to melt. Maybe it had been around a lot longer than that, forever maybe, only frozen in the ice until the ice melted and released it. Among other species, it wiped out the woolly mammoth."

Michael nodded. "The animal makes it into that cave, dies, and freezes. Then more ice melts, the glacier recedes, and it thaws out after thousands of years . . ."

"Freeing the organism," Gina completed before he could. "It ends up in the seas around Alaska thanks to glacial runoff. That submarine, Michael? I think it got on board through a clogged condenser bringing in seawater to cool the engines. The crew was dead within a few hours, because it spread through the air."

"The same way exposure to the woolly mammoth in that ice cave killed the USGS team. But there's more," Michael added. He proceeded to explain Amka's theory about plankton consuming the organism, only to be consumed by fish.

"Wait, you're saying you were exposed to the fish. You don't share the Tlingits' natural resistance, so why are you still alive?"

"According to Amka, because the fish ingested the plankton, I or anyone else would have to eat the fish to become infected."

"Makes sense. But she's hypothesizing about the potential end to life on Earth, isn't she?"

"Explains why the Russians want this thing so badly."

"Russians," Gina echoed, thinking of the submarine that had been spotted in Alaskan waters, along with that trawler she'd mentioned. "Keep talking, Michael."

"I saved the best for last. I drew this assignment because I happened to already be in the area pursuing the thefts of what the ISB thought were Tlingit artifacts."

"There's a lot of that going around, based on memoranda that I've read."

"But these artifacts contained something else, the reason why a pair of couriers were executed by an assassin I later encountered in Sitka Historical Park."

"'Encountered' as in . . ."

"Yes," Michael said, sparing Gina the need to complete the thought. "And early reports indicate he was Russian."

‡‡‡

She stayed silent after he finished, trying to process his words and make some sense of them and the connections to her own pursuits.

The crew of a Virginia-class submarine had perished in a matter of three or four hours while the sub was stranded at the bottom of the sea . . .

A few hundred miles away, huge amounts of fish washed up on the shores of Lester Island . . .

Both the crewmembers and the fish had impossibly frozen to death . . .

Scientists expert in such potentially hostile scenarios here at Elmendorf believed an unknown organism, in microbe form, was responsible for the death of the crew and, by connection, the deaths of the fish due to freezing, too . . .

While in the Everglades, a USGS team was conducting experiments aimed at lowering water temperature, which suggested a potential connection . . .

Might Jamie Bidwell's murder somehow explain how all this was connected?

"I need to get back to the Everglades," she told Michael, thinking out loud. "I can make sense of all of this, except for the Russian part. By all indications, this is a very sophisticated operation they've been running. Trawlers, submarines, assassins, commando teams—all that couldn't have been set in place overnight. So what were they already doing on-site, pursuing whatever's at the root of all this?"

"I think somebody told them about it, Gina, and I've got a pretty good idea who it must have been. You need to make a stop on your way back to Florida."

GLACIER BAY NATIONAL PARK AND PRESERVE, LESTER ISLAND, ALASKA

A popular site for clam digging.

"That's why we're talking, Michael, so I can make amends."

"No such thing."

"You may want to reserve judgment on that, because the country could be about to face something even worse than what you helped stop. Want to hear more?"

That marked the end of the last conversation Michael ever had with the disgraced former secretary of the Interior, Ethan Turlidge, who also happened to be his father-in-law, a year before. They had spoken at an undisclosed location in the Washington, D.C., vicinity that was so secret Michael had to be blindfolded to and from the site. Given that Turlidge had been a key cog in a conspiracy that had nearly toppled the U.S. government, it was quite likely he would never spend a day as a free man for the rest of his life, even though he wouldn't ever stand trial for his part in a plot the country could never be allowed to learn the complete details of. As a matter of course, and out of respect for the role his own actions had played in saving the country, Michael was informed that Turlidge had been transferred to the military prison at the naval base in Cuba's Guantanamo Bay. He had not requested further details and none had been provided to him since. As far as the world knew, Ethan Turlidge had simply vanished.

Michael never understood the source of the loathing the political hack who had transformed his position as secretary of the Interior into a money-making operation held for him. Turlidge had maintained a strained relationship with his daughter long before Michael had entered the picture, but

chose to blame him for that after he did. Turlidge had no respect for the
environment his lofty position charged him with both overseeing and preserving. By all accounts, he especially detested the National Park Service,
seeing the NPS as an impediment to his plans to similarly monetize those
wide-open spaces better left to drilling and development.

When he finished explaining the Turlidge connection to Gina Delgado,
Michael's gaze followed Amka's to the doorway, where Yehl stood next to
his grandfather, whose gaunt, almost skeletal form towered over the boy.

"Grandfather says he has something he must tell you."

‡‡‡

The boy and the man who'd served as tribal chief almost as long as he'd
been alive entered Amka's laboratory. Yehl looked to her to handle the
translating duties, since he was not nearly as familiar with the ancient
Hoonah Tlingit dialect their grandfather spoke.

"He knows what we found in that mine last night," Amka translated,
when Xetsuwu began speaking. "He knows we have many questions but
the answers are meaningless in the face of a great evil that is coming."

Michael held Amka's gaze until the old man started speaking again,
Yehl hanging on his every word.

"In a time long ago," Amka said, resuming her translation, "our people came to this land after ours became spoiled and the waters thinned.
The land here, despite its location, was empty because it was believed to
be cursed. Other peoples who settled here saw many die without cause.
Some called it a great sickness, but most believed the evilest of all spirits came
at night and blew his breath into the mouths of some of those who were
soundly sleeping. They did not awake the next morning and were found
dead in their beds."

The old man said more, but Amka stopped translating, as if she needed
to process the words for herself first. Her grandfather halted his words to
give her time to catch up, and Michael found her gaze meeting his.

"He says they had frozen to death."

‡‡‡

Xetsuwu began speaking again and Amka lagged only slightly behind him.

"Those who were here before us strung sage all around the village to
ward off the evil spirit, but still he came and more of their people froze.

They posted their bravest warriors on guard throughout the village with weapons made by the tribe's shaman to weaken and imprison the spirit, but still he came and more people froze. They packed more people into fewer huts to stand guard and keep watch, but still the next morning more of their people were dead."

Again, her grandfather stopped so Amka could catch up, then resumed once she had.

"Then the shaman gathered those who still lived and told them the evil couldn't be stopped because it was coming from within, not from without. The evil was coming up through the ground, traveling as no more than wisps of wind, invisible to the human eye. It did not want to share its land with the people and would not stop until all of them were dead. The only thing that could stop the evil was to leave so it could not reach them. The warriors resisted, saying this was cowardice, saying that they cowered before no evil, saying they would fight until the last man or until the evil was slain at last. Then, atypically, the women spoke up. 'It's not only about you,' they said. 'It's about the children. And if you stay and fight, you will watch your children perish because of your arrogance. Even if you live to vanquish the evil, you will be dead inside.'"

The old man stopped and laid a bony hand atop his grandson's shoulder, as if this story was meant more for him, as the future chief, than his grand-daughter and Michael.

"Then came one winter when the ice grew thick," Amka resumed again when he did, "and made peace with the land. It would not have with those who came hundreds of years before us, but it welcomed us into its fold be-cause we respected its wishes and paid the land the deference it deserved. We lived well and fed off the sea, and by the time the spring came, not a single one of our people had been lost to the cold the evil spread. Our peo-ple slept without fear or guard or talisman, and the evil claimed no further victims before the coming of a single dawn. Over the years, our people forgot the tales of those who had come before, and the story passed into obscurity more and more with each generation. It was passed first only to the elders and then, finally, only to the next chief in the succession, so he could be ready in the event the evil ever came back."

With that, the old man stopped and laid both hands on his grandson's shoulders. He spoke softly, addressing his words directly to Yehl, and this time Amka didn't translate them, convincing Michael even more that the story had been meant for the boy more than for them. And yet he had chosen to tell it now, because of what they had found in the mine last night.

His thinking stopped abruptly when Yehl addressed the old man in English.

"Grandfather, you said a great evil was coming. Has the spirit returned? Are the people of our village in danger?"

This time, the wait for Amka to translate proved maddening.

"This time the danger comes from without, grandson, not within. It comes from those who think they can control the evil and use it for their unholy purposes. But in unleashing it they will die, too. We cannot be like those who preceded us here and run. We must stay and fight for our land, because if we don't the world will die and us with it. We must fulfill our sacred destiny to save not just our land, but all lands."

Amka stopped there, even though her grandfather had kept speaking. She met Michael's stare, the fear on her face as evident as it must have been on his, the same realization having struck both of them in the same moment.

They looked down as if to peer through the floor toward what lay beneath the ground at their feet.

Looked up and found each other again.

"It's below us," Michael uttered, almost too softly to hear.

"What we found in that mine," Amka picked up, "what used to be oil, what killed before and will kill again."

"And the Russians are coming for it," Michael finished.

CHAPTER 47

Ⱶ•⧟•⊙•⧟•⊣

FISHERS ISLAND, NEW YORK

**Adrian Block later visited Block Island and named that
one after himself.**

"The highest concentration of reserves are located here," Axel Cole told General Victor Adamovitch.

He worked the cursor on his laptop over a land mass located within the borders of Glacier Bay National Park and clicked. And, with that, the map of Alaska displayed on his 120-inch television, recessed into a wall in his media room, highlighted an enlarged version of that area only.

"Lester Island," Adamovitch noted. "So what is our problem?"

"There's a Native tribe, the Tlingit, who currently live on the island directly over those reserves."

"Again, what is the problem?"

"The Tlingits would never allow the kind of operation it would take to mine the substance in question in that kind of bulk, and there would be no way to manage in secret. That's why I focused my efforts in more remote mines and never took more of the substance at a time than my couriers could safely smuggle out."

"You're a cautious man, my friend."

"I prefer 'patient,' General."

Adamovitch grinned, his head about even with where Lester Island sat projected on the giant flat-screen. "Well, I am neither of those. Life is too short to be bothered by such things."

Speaking of which, Cole had still not inquired about the fate of his security guards. There was really no reason to, since the answer was obvious. No point lay in pushing the Russian for information that would change nothing. Cole viewed this entire experience as just another transaction, the cost of doing business. And in this case, he had to admit, the cost he was paying was worth the return he might very well be receiving. If Adamovitch was able to extract the reserves of Prometheus from beneath the village of Xunaa, the Russian had promised him an amount of it far, far greater than what he'd been able to smuggle out of Alaska in dribs and drabs over three years. Enough to manage several trips back and forth to Mars.

Adamovitch turned back to the screen. "Let me see this village."

Cole worked his keyboard and brought up overhead shots of Xunaa harvested from the most recent available on Google. He watched the Russian back off to study the photos analytically, could see his eyes flashing like LED lights as he processed the information. Cole knew he was viewing the village from a strategic standpoint, where to bring in his troops that would be staging from a trawler and one of the most advanced submarines in the Russian navy.

"Dragging your finger across what you see will allow you to increase the scale and scope, as well as hone in on specific areas."

The Russian began doing just that, his mind recognizing and recording the logistics, as well as how those logistics would affect the positioning of his troops.

"My commandos will stage from the sea to the east and the tree line to the north. Those will be the primary points of engagement. Can you bring up the weather over the next twenty-four to forty-eight hours?"

Cole worked some more keys. The map overlay vanished and the expected conditions over the next forty-eight hours appeared on the screen visually through computer simulation as if they were happening now. Cole advanced the time slowly and, besides a few stray snow showers courtesy of a looming cold front, there was nothing in the forecast that posed any concern to the attack Adamovitch's commandos would be launching.

"Excellent," he said, again studying the screen.

"One thing to be aware of," Cole warned. "The weather in those parts can change on a dime without warning. Systems collide, wind currents change, storms pop up out of nowhere."

Adamovitch smiled thinly. "We will be prepared for any conditions we encounter."

"Do you expect to encounter much resistance?"

The smile vanished, replaced by an expression that looked like the Russian had just swallowed something bitter. "Members of this tribe have already killed ten of my men, catching them by surprise. But let's see how they fare against more than a hundred when surprise is on our side."

Adamovitch grinned, holding Cole's stare almost warmly.

"Killing is nothing more than a tool, as you have learned for yourself. And these people need to die, just as your brother did. Tell me, my friend, how did it feel when you pushed him off that mountain?"

CHAPTER 48

⊱━━◦━◦━━⊰

GUANTANAMO BAY, CUBA

The United States took control over the southern part of Guantanamo Bay in 1903.

"You need to sign here, here, and here, Agent Delgado."

Personnel at the American military prison at the base located on Guantanamo Bay had been advised Gina was coming. A ranking FBI special agent would normally possess the security clearance needed to access the better-known facilities of Camp Delta that had been steadily expanded from the camp's establishment in the wake of 9/11. Only a White House–level security clearance, though, permitted access to the part of the base where she'd be meeting with former Secretary of the Interior Ethan Turlidge.

Located a mile or so outside the main camp perimeter, the so-called "Camp No" was essentially a black-site facility enclosed by its own fence line. It had long consisted of nothing but interrogation rooms and what rumor had it were a series of virtual torture chambers where information had been obtained at all costs over the years. Gina didn't know herself whether they existed or not and didn't expect this visit to reveal anything either way. It had been explained to her that, as the lone American residing here, separate living quarters had been constructed within Camp No for Turlidge. He received no visitors, including lawyers, because his unique status didn't require any. As far as the world knew, he wasn't here at all, and anyone who took up even the most dedicated search would encounter nothing but dead ends.

The forms Gina signed were merely to attest to her presence and acceptance of the regulations set forth for visitors from stateside. A sergeant named Cartwright picked her up at the airfield and brought her to Camp No, where a guard manning an electronic gate stood on station. No explanations of anything had been provided and there was no need for anything like a blindfold. The only prevailing secret on these grounds was the presence of Ethan Turlidge, and he would be spending the rest of his life here.

He was waiting on one side of a steel interrogation table with his wrist chains looped through a hook that looked molded to the flat surface. The steel was dull with age, just like Turlidge, whose features were tinted with the yellow pallor well known to the incarcerated from lack of sunlight layered upon the effects of confinement. Gina had met him only once before, over another interrogation that took place when she showed up unannounced at his Department of the Interior office to accuse him of being part of a conspiracy to overthrow the United States government. The fact that he wasn't aware of his actual complicity paled in comparison to the vital role he had played as facilitator of a primary part of the plot. His hair had grayed, grown thinner and coarser. And as she entered the room after her escort had unlocked the door, Gina detected the rank scent of body odor from the limited shower time he was allowed, potentially no more than once or twice a week.

Turlidge's initial reaction to her presence seemed to be surprise, followed by a smirk and a slow shake of his head.

"Come to gloat, Chief Delgado?"

"It was chief before. I work directly for the White House now, so agent will suffice."

"The White House," Turlidge repeated, trying to goad her. "You must be coming up in the world."

"We're not here to talk about me. But if you cooperate, I'll do what I can with the president to return the favor."

"Well, you can't reduce my sentence, because I was never tried. What can even she do, then?"

"I'm not sure. I only said I'd try. You have my word."

"For whatever's that worth."

"It's worth a bit of hope, Mr. Secretary."

"Thanks to you and my son-in-law, I'm a civilian incarcerated in a military prison."

"And thanks to you ten million Americans almost died."

Turlidge leaned back in his chair and started to cross his arms, only to have the chains stop him less than halfway. He laid his arms back on the table, the metal clanging on metal.

"I cooperated with you before, Agent. I've got nothing to lose by cooperating again. What is it you want to know?"

"Your son-in-law sent me."

Turlidge's eyes flashed at that. "He couldn't come himself?"

"It was easier for me," Gina said, leaving it there. "The last time the two of you spoke you hinted that there was another threat to the country looming, but you weren't specific."

"It's the one card I have left to play. I can't squander it."

"Well, this may be the last opportunity you get. You specifically told Michael the country could be about to face something even worse than what we managed to stop."

"And since you're here, I imagine 'could' is no longer the operative word. Happened faster than I was expecting."

"Play your card, Mr. Turlidge. I'm guessing it involves a substance found in Alaska," Gina said, paraphrasing what Michael had described to her. "A substance derived from ordinary crude and shale oil."

Turlidge nodded, looking pleased, back in his element for however long their conversation lasted. For a man who'd had no power over anything for a year now, it must have felt especially good to have value and importance again.

"And, since you're here, I assume we don't have to go into detail about the unique capabilities of this substance, both as a weapon and a fuel source—a game changer in both regards."

"It was discovered during your watch at Interior," Gina said, in what had started out as a question.

"By a United States Geological Survey team entirely by accident. They were studying the degradation of the Alaskan permafrost when they literally stumbled upon it. Samples were sent to Lawrence Livermore National Laboratory for a detailed analysis. I red-flagged it to assure the results of the testing were sealed and reported only to me. Needless to say, I was shocked by those results."

"Shocked or pleasantly surprised, sir?"

"A combination of both, I suppose. Early experiments identified the substance as an oil-based fuel source of unprecedented proportions beyond anything the world had ever known."

Gina recalled what Michael had told her about the timeline, the thefts of Native antiquities going back three years. "How long ago would this have been?" she asked Turlidge, testing him.

"Around four years, not long after I was chosen to run the Department of the Interior. Sorry I can't be more specific, but you lose track of time in a place like this, Agent Delgado."

"And what did you do upon learning of this substance's potential?"

"I contacted someone who had two things going for him: he was ultra-rich and was building a spaceship to reach Mars."

"Axel Cole," Gina realized.

‡‡‡

It was falling into place, but some big pieces remained a mystery. "What about the Russians? When did you sell yourself out to them, Mr. Turlidge?"

He looked unmoved by her criticism. "As soon as scientists uncovered that the substance could be weaponized. That came three years later, not long before you showed up at my office. I never even got to collect all the money due me."

"My apologies."

"Because I hadn't been paid in full, the Russians I was dealing with never got all the information I had. Since you're here, I'm guessing they figured out the rest for themselves."

Gina recalled the demonstration the scientist who called himself Atticus had provided at Elmendorf, figuring Russian scientists must have arrived at comparable findings. "Did they manage to isolate the organism responsible for all this at Lawrence Livermore?"

Turlidge nodded. "But I made sure their work was shut down before they could compile and circulate their findings. They called it a microbe, said it had come close to wiping out all life on Earth once before. Their working theory was that this microbe had been dormant in the ice potentially for millions of years, only to be released when the ice melted ten thousand years ago. An entire ecosystem of animal life was wiped out from drinking water and eating vegetation contaminated by it. Millions of years earlier, they believed, it had also seeped into oil reserves layered in the Alaskan permafrost and changed the molecular structure to a concentrated form of fuel that could power the planet forever, as well as provide the fuel source for deep space travel. In short, maybe the greatest scientific discovery man has ever made."

"You mean like the atom bomb?"

Turlidge chuckled. He hadn't sounded either guilty or remorseful as he explained all of this to Gina, and why not? Developing a conscience wouldn't change the fact that he would spend the rest of his life in isolation and captivity.

"I had the information I needed at that point," he continued. "Priority two was to keep anyone else from getting it."

"Priority one being to find a buyer. Did you have the Russians on speed dial?"

"Pretty much, through a middleman who brokered the deal."

Gina couldn't believe how routine Turlidge was making this sound. Then again, he had no reason to hide anything and every reason to give up everything he knew on the chance Gina might, at the very least, get him reassigned to a supermax prison stateside.

"How many times can one man sell out his country, Mr. Turlidge?" she asked anyway.

"As many times as it is profitable to do so. Don't be naïve, Agent Delgado. It doesn't suit you."

"Who was the Russian you sold the information to a year ago?"

"I honestly don't know. I told you, everything was handled through an intermediary."

"Did you tell them about Axel Cole's involvement?"

"I told them where to look. I imagine they figured out the rest for themselves."

Gina processed all she had heard. Something was still missing. None of what Turlidge had told her explained what led a USGS team to conduct experiments in the Everglades to lower water temperature. Someone had sent the team down there for that express purpose. And they must have been in possession of the microbe Atticus had described to her because the experiment had produced results that could be quantified in lowered water temperatures, on a minimal basis at least.

"Someone else knew what this microbe was capable of, Mr. Turlidge," Gina said, forming the conclusion as she spoke. "They knew about its potential maybe not as a weapon or fuel source, but certainly to reverse at least some of the effects of climate change, particularly the warming of the oceans by chemically lowering water temperatures."

Gina could tell her remark had caught Turlidge entirely off guard. It was clear he had no idea what she was talking about.

"I can't help you there. I kept the circle tight."

"Who else might have known?"

"Someone at Lawrence Livermore, that's the only possibility."

It made sense, Gina thought, since that facility would have had access to samples that could have been transferred to the USGS team down in the Everglades. By whom, though? If not someone at Lawrence Livermore, then it could only be someone whose role had made them privy to their work on the microbe.

"You weren't lying, right?" Turlidge said suddenly, sounding weak and pleading. "You will do what you can to help me, get me relocated out of this hellhole."

"Only to another hellhole, Mr. Turlidge."

"On American soil at least."

"I'm still missing information I need, sir."

"I've given you everything I've got. The only other possibility I can think of is that someone from the President's Council of Advisors on Science and Technology was monitoring what Lawrence Livermore was working on as a matter of course."

Gina knew that the members of that council consisted of distinguished individuals from sectors outside of the government who advised President Cantwell on policy matters pertaining to science, technology, and innovation.

"Any names on this council of advisors stand out?"

"No names stand out because I don't remember any. I never dealt with PCAST, to use the acronym, directly."

"Is that all, sir?"

"No," Turlidge said, with a smile born of the corrupt and greedy government official who had sold out his country on multiple occasions. "Please tell my son-in-law that I'm still thinking of him."

›—‹•—‹•—‹•—‹

GLACIER BAY NATIONAL PARK AND PRESERVE, LESTER ISLAND, ALASKA

A hydrophone cable was laid in very shallow water
along the shoreline to listen for humpback whales and
other underwater real-time sounds.

Michael called Angela Pierce first to bring her up to date.

"You think the Natives are in danger?" she asked him at the end.

"I'm certain of it. The Russians aren't coming, they're already here—in the area anyway. A small army."

"Now down ten men," Angela reminded him.

"There is that, yes. And it's eleven, including the assassin who killed the Morgans in Sitka."

"Thanks for reminding me, Michael. They could still fit an awful lot of men on that trawler, not to mention the submarine that's been lurking about."

"We can't let them get their hands on this, Angela. If they figure out how to turn it into a targeted weapon . . ."

"Game over, I get it."

"We need to build a wall around this village—figuratively. We need police, soldiers, heavy equipment. Whatever it takes to keep the Russians out and make sure we can deal with them if they show up anyway. The Army has Northern Command troops stationed in Elmendorf. They can chopper in the soldiers we need to mount a defense."

"Active-duty military deployed on American soil, Michael? Only the White House could authorize such a move."

"I know," Michael said, leaving it there.

He heard Angela sigh in realization. "You can handle that from your end with Delgado, right? Because the head of the National Park Service doesn't have enough influence to organize a parade."

"I'll reach out to her immediately to get things going."

Michael was about to hang up, when Angela resumed.

"I just got a report from hospitals in Anchorage and Juneau, Michael. They're dealing with a sudden influx of patients over the past week, spiking in the last few days, all suffering from an as-yet unidentified respiratory virus, by all accounts. Anchorage especially, where some of the patients are now critical, with Juneau a close second. Spikes in hospitalizations and emergency room traffic have also been reported in pretty much every other hospital."

"It's moving from north to south, Angela, following the currents and steering winds. But I think there may be a way to stop it."

‡‡‡

Michael laid it all out for Amka first.

"And we are supposed to invite these soldiers onto our land?" she responded flatly.

"If you want to keep the Russians from taking what's beneath it, yes."

"A difficult prospect for my people to accept, all the same."

"Offering the best chance you've got to preserve the land in the long term."

"No one has ever come to our aid before."

"This is different," Michael told her. "Hospitalizations are spiking across the state. It won't be long before a full-scale pandemic breaks out. But no one's gotten sick or reported symptoms here in Xunaa, have they?"

"Not since the initial years after the Hoonah Tlingit people settled here, as my grandfather told us."

"There's only one explanation for why there hasn't been an outbreak."

"We're immune . . ."

Michael nodded. "The Tlingit people have been living over stores of this substance that used to be oil for centuries. You've been breathing the air, drinking the water, and eating the fish that live in those waters that whole time. And, even now, with the organism wreaking havoc across the state, the effects are nonexistent here, because you've been coexisting with the microbe for so long."

"You're talking about active as opposed to passive immunity or, potentially, some sort of mechanism of resistance that's evolved over the years."

"There's more," Michael said, stopping there to let Amka pick up his thought.

"Our blood could be the basis of a vaccine . . ."

He nodded again.

"We'd be saving a world that's done so little for us over the centuries."

"We've got to survive the Russians first, Amka."

Her gaze grew distant, looking more through than at him. "We lost our last battle against them almost two hundred and twenty-five years ago, Michael. We aren't about to lose this one."

PART FIVE

This natural beauty-hunger is made manifest . . . in
our magnificent national parks—nature's sublime
wonderlands, the admiration and joy of the world.

—JOHN MUIR

CHAPTER 50

〉-◦-〈

MIAMI INTERNATIONAL AIRPORT, MIAMI, FLORIDA

America's busiest airport for international freight.

Clark Gifford was waiting for Gina next to his park ranger-issue Ford Expedition when she emerged from the Gulfstream 850 and clamored down the metal stairs that extended from its frame.

"You look tired," he noted.

"Exhausted." Gina gave him a longer look. "And I could say the same thing about you."

"I always look this way. It just stands out more because I've been reviewing security camera footage from science shows and fairs for the past twenty-four hours. Your instincts were right, Agent. Those links you sent me were spot-on—we've already gotten hits on two of them. Get in and I'll show you."

‡‡‡

Gina had called Michael Walker as soon as she was back on the plane headed for Miami.

"You were right, Michael," she told him. "Turlidge was doing business with both the Russians and Axel Cole."

"What's Axel Cole got to do with this?"

"He wants to go to Mars and must see this mystery compound as the fuel source that can get him there."

"But Turlidge served it up to the Russians, too."

"On a silver platter and for obvious reasons. There's more but that's the gist of it. It wasn't hard to get your former father-in-law to talk. I think he enjoyed every moment of it."

"Because it made Turlidge feel like he was in control again, even if only for a few minutes. That's why Allie broke away from him: every time they talked, he tried to get her to do what he wanted. Follow the plan, which never included his daughter becoming a park ranger. Beneath her station in life, in Turlidge's mind."

"I'm going to call the White House now, Michael. Turlidge has confirmed the worst-case scenario. We need to get troops to Xunaa."

‡‡‡

Gina climbed into the Expedition with Gifford, figuring she'd hold off on calling the White House until she heard the rest of what he had to say. She watched him fire up his laptop, after starting the engine to get the air-conditioning going.

"Like I said," he resumed, tilting the laptop so Gina could see it, too, "we've got two positive hits already, but I'll focus on the one that gave us what we were looking for from the VRARA Central Florida Immersive Technology Summit. It was held at Full Sail University in Winter Park three months ago."

Gina figured the timeline in her head. "Not long before the man we know as Jamie Bidwell joined the USGS's work in the Everglades."

"His real name is Jackson Delaney." Gifford hit the laptop's enter key. "Check out the screen."

Gina saw a front-end still shot of their murder victim Gifford must have lifted off the security camera footage. A yellow badge dangling from a lanyard looped around his neck was marked PRESS in bold black letters beneath his name and picture. Unlike Jamie Bidwell on the fake driver's license, the young man identified as Jackson Delaney was smiling in the picture, as well as the still security cam shot.

"So he was press. Any leads on which outlet or outlets he worked for?"

"He was freelance as far as I've been able to learn. Wrote extensively for the kind of places that don't pay a lot, if anything. Environmental issues were his specialty and until recently he made his real living on the Geek Squad from Best Buy."

"Don't tell me, he left that job after getting the internship gig with the USGS team at the Daniel Beard Center."

"Right as rain, Agent."

Then Gifford posed the question Gina had already asked herself. "You figure Rosalee Perry knew who he really was?"

"No. And I think the relationship happened so he could pump her for information for a story he must have been working on."

"I'm sure she'll be thrilled to hear that."

"No hits on the identities of the men that backyard security camera caught loading Delaney's body onto that boat?"

"Nothing yet."

Gina had hoped to have something positive to share with Rosalee Perry. "Let's head over to the Daniel Beard Center," she said, raising her phone to her ear. "In the meantime, I need to make a call that's supposed to be classified, so close your ears, Clark."

‡‡‡

"You must be back in Florida," Chief of Staff Grant greeted, when he answered her call.

"Just in time," Gina told him. "It turns out our murder victim is really a journalist named Jackson Delaney."

"That changes a lot."

"Only everything, Grant. We need to find out what exactly Rosalee Perry told him, what he might have shared already or been about to write about. It means there's a much straighter line leading to his murder, because either someone must have wanted to know what he did or to stop him from writing about it."

"I've read the reports, Delgado. Cold Burn is at best a marginal success, and at worst incidental to naturally-occurring cyclical temperature swings. Not even enough we can use to help the president's campaign yet."

"But enough to get somebody murdered, it would seem. I'll keep you informed."

"Do that. What's next?"

"I'm heading to interview Rosalee Perry again, while you get the president to approve a troop deployment out of Elmendorf to Lester Island."

"Alaska was United States territory last time I checked. No way we can scramble active-duty military that fast with all the red tape. You'll have to settle for the Alaskan National Guard."

"So long as there's a lot of them, Grant, a whole lot. But we're going to need more than weekend warriors to go up against the Russians. Talk to Colonel Beeman," Gina said, referring to the special ops commander still attached in an advisory capacity to the White House. "He doesn't just know where all the bodies are buried, he knows who put them there."

"Meanwhile, we've pulled out all the stops to locate that submarine and the trawler the Russians must be staging out of. Our aerial surveillance satellites and reconnaissance planes are working overtime."

"Good to hear. Oh, and one more thing, Grant. Ethan Turlidge mentioned that samples of this substance in concentrated form were transferred to Lawrence Livermore for testing when he was still secretary of the Interior. You know anything about that?"

"No. Must have happened before I became chief of staff."

"It did, but Turlidge also suggested that something called the President's Council of Advisors on Science and Technology, or PCAST, might well have been made aware of what was happening. You might want to do a deep dive into all the members at the time to see if any of them might be the link to how a sample of the stuff got from Alaska to the Everglades as part of Cold Burn."

"I'll have to track them down, which is no small order. I'm not really familiar with this council."

"Just let me know what you find out," Gina told him. "It might be the missing piece in all this."

"Like I said, I'll see what I can do but it'll take some time."

"Something we're already running low on."

"I can't make miracles here, Delgado."

"Maybe not, Grant, but you're the president's chief of staff. That means you can move mountains."

◄─◄●─◇─●►─►

CHAPTER 51

CRAZY HORSE MEMORIAL, BLACK HILLS OF SOUTH DAKOTA

At the time construction started in 1948, the artist estimated the work would be complete in thirty years. As of 2022, there was no timeline for when the monument would be completed.

A pair of Lakota Sioux manually lowered Blaine McCracken on a platform down the sheer face of the mountain where the monument to the great legend Chief Crazy Horse was being carved into the granite face. He knew work on the monument had begun in 1948 and, after more than seventy-five years, was nowhere near completion. He knew this and much more because his oldest friend in the world for more than half a century—since they'd served together as part of the Phoenix Project in Vietnam—had committed himself to finishing it at long last.

McCracken's platform came to a rest next to the one occupied by Johnny Wareagle, who didn't look away from working his hammer and chisel to regard him. McCracken unhooked the carabiner that had fastened him to the platform's housing, and looped it through a safety hook before joining Wareagle on the platform he worked from with no such protection.

"I'm not going to call you Indian," he greeted. "I'm not allowed to any-more."

Wareagle rose from a crouch, where he'd been working a fine tool to add lines to the statue's skin, to his full height, which still reached seven feet. Blaine remembered when Johnny's ponytail was coal black. Now it was mostly silver, with dark streaks sprinkled in. It wasn't much different from his own beard and still-thick hair, the black starting to lose the battle with the gray.

"Normally you call before you come. That tells me this isn't a typical visit, Blainey."

"Nothing's typical anymore, In—" McCracken caught himself just in time and smiled. "We've been dinosaurs since we got back from the jungle, but it looks like the rest of the world finally figured that out. At least it took them long enough. When was the last time we got the call?"

"Before I started adding lines to the statue's face."

Blaine looked at how many of those there were. "When we got our start, SEALs were called Frogmen and Delta was nothing more than a Greek letter. I'm tired of being told we paved the way for them. Being called a legend makes me feel like I've got one foot in the grave."

That drew a smile from Wareagle. "We've had both feet in the grave more times than either one of us can count."

McCracken grinned, too, reminding himself not to look down. "Always seemed to claw our way out, though, didn't we?"

"It's not like you to speak in the past tense, Blainey."

"It feels like that's all we've got these days, Johnny. I'm seventy-two and I don't even know how old you are."

"Around the same."

It was a good answer. For McCracken and others who knew of him and his exploits, Johnny Wareagle was ageless, like he'd been dropped into the world exactly as he was now and, besides the silver-streaked hair, never changed.

"Care to join me, Blainey?" he asked, extending a scraping tool toward McCracken.

"No, thanks."

"Why?"

"Because I never want to start in on something I can't finish. That's the one thing we differ on, Johnny."

"And yet you came here because you can't finish something else you started."

"Not a lot of opportunities lately. I never realized how much I'd miss giving bad guys what they deserve."

"It's harder to recognize them these days, Blainey. They've found new places to hide, the kind our skills don't translate well to."

McCracken nodded. "Sure, like cyberspace." He pulled out his latest satellite phone model, coal black like his and Johnny's hair used to be. "Best thing about this is there's no internet. It rings and I answer. The problem is that it's stopped ringing. The call doesn't come anymore."

As if on cue, the phone rang, drawing a whimsical look from Wareagle, as McCracken answered.

"Been a long time, Colonel," he said, the phone pressed against his ear. "If you're calling about my retirement party—"

McCracken's expression tightened when the man on the other end cut him off. "Yes, sir," he said, "loud and clear. Alaska." His eyes found Johnny Wareagle again. "Hope you don't mind if I bring a friend along. . . . That's right—him."

McCracken returned the phone to his pocket, smiling.

"We got the call, Indian."

CHAPTER 52

›‹‐‹‣‐‑○‐‣›‹‐‹

GLACIER BAY NATIONAL PARK AND PRESERVE, LESTER ISLAND, ALASKA

The northern part of Lester Island is surrounded by
Secret Bay, named by the U.S. Coast and Geodetic
Survey in 1939 because the bay is so well concealed.

"My grandfather says help isn't coming," Amka said to Michael through the overcast gloom of the day.

"My boss just told me the National Guard's been granted approval to deploy," Michael countered. "They should be here by nightfall."

"They're not coming, Michael. No one's coming."

"This isn't 1804, Amka. The Russians don't get to win this time."

"Now, as then, we will be fighting this battle alone."

Amka's conviction, her certainty, was starting to make Michael think. "How many *Kiks.ádi* are actually in Xunaa?"

"Eighteen. They are already preparing, making sure 1804 doesn't repeat itself. This is the chance they've been waiting for."

"Revenge?"

"More like justice. We lost our land once. We will not lose it again."

"No, you won't. As many as a thousand National Guard troops are coming to make sure of that. And all stops are being pulled out to track that Russian submarine and trawler."

Amka's expression remained flat. "My grandfather is never wrong about such things. But this time we're going to be prepared."

CHAPTER 53

DANIEL BEARD CENTER, EVERGLADES NATIONAL PARK, FLORIDA

The Nike Missile Site HM-69 closed in 1979, and the
Daniel Beard Center was the command center.

"I'm sorry," Gina said to Rosalee Perry.

Perry's expression was dour, her frown frozen in place as she processed everything Gina was telling her. "That doesn't mean what I had with Jamie wasn't real," she gasped.

"His name was Jackson, Rosalee."

She swallowed hard.

"And, of course, it's possible his feelings for you were genuine. But I need you to tell me everything you shared with him about Cold Burn, all the details."

"To ascertain how much damage I may have done, right?"

"More to help us to determine who may have killed him. The fact that he was a science journalist instead of a scientist changes nothing about that."

Perry's expression had turned utterly blank, glazed over in shock as if the truth Gina had shared with her about Jamie Bidwell's actual identity had just struck her with a delayed effect.

"I need to think," she said, her words aimed beyond Gina and Clark Gifford, who were seated in the chairs before her desk again.

"Take your time."

"There wasn't a lot to tell that he didn't already know from working in the field. I can't remember all of the specifics because it felt like two people who loved science just talking. He seemed to genuinely share my passion for it. I don't get to meet a lot of people like that."

"As Jackson Delaney, he wrote a ton of articles that are way beyond my pay grade, so I think you're right there. But don't limit yourself to Cold Burn. Tell me what the two of you discussed in general."

"The climate, of course, because that was what we were both passionate about. You know, saving the planet even though that may sound cliché."

"It doesn't, Rosalee, and you should know that his best and most well-regarded articles that drew the most comments online centered on climate change and global warming. His interest was real and so was almost all of his résumé. Very little of it seems to be altered, other than his personal info. You recommended him for the opening to your superiors because he appeared to be a great candidate for it and he was. Now, we need to find out how that got him killed."

Gina's last statement seemed to strengthen Perry's resolve. Her expression scrunched up, digging furrows out of her cheeks as she reviewed the many conversations she must have had with a young man she'd believed to be someone else entirely.

"Well, he was definitely interested, very interested, in how we had managed to lower water temperature in a small sampling of Gulf waters. He didn't join the team until much of the groundwork had already been laid, until our work in the Everglades was already underway." Perry stopped and took a deep breath. "Do you think he used me?"

Gina nodded. "I believe he did, yes. Did you ever get a sense Jamie wasn't being honest with you about anything?"

Perry managed a sad smile. "You mean Jackson, not Jamie, don't you?"

Gina shrugged.

"And the answer's, well, no. Nothing stands out that I can remember. He never asked too many questions and his interest in the environment seemed very real."

"Because it was, Rosalee. His writing more than bore that out."

Her face seemed to pale. "I told him everything. I feel so damn stupid . . . What was I thinking, for God's sake?" She shook her head and settled herself with a deep breath. "What do you think happened, Agent Delgado?"

It was a question Gina had been asking herself since learning the truth about Jackson Delaney. His actions had clearly run afoul of someone with the resources to dispatch what by all accounts appeared to be professional killers. Extraordinarily few people, or groups, had access to such people. Even then, ordering anyone's death was a drastic step to take under any circumstances. Clearly, Delaney had done or uncovered something that posed a grave risk to somebody. Whatever he had learned had come during his six-week tenure with the USGS team based here, so whatever that was, it figured that Rosalee Perry knew it, too.

"I'd really rather not speculate," Gina told her, "and, technically, I'm not allowed to share anything with you that isn't in the public sphere already."

"I understand. I just want to help you find who did this. What can I do? Just tell me."

"Did Delaney," Gina said, using the victim's real name now to make him feel like a different person than the young man Rosalee Perry had clearly fallen in love with, "give you any indication he had learned something about Cold Burn you weren't yet aware of?"

"No, nothing like that."

"Did any line of questioning he used to get information seem odd to you?"

"No, not at all."

"Jackson Delaney wasn't killed because he was a journalist who infiltrated your team. He was killed because of something he uncovered. Are you sure he never mentioned, or asked you, anything about that?"

"No, and I would have remembered if he had. We talked a lot about the ramifications of Cold Burn being successful, what that would potentially mean to the world. The ability to lower ocean temperatures would be the ultimate game-changer. That's what we talked about."

"And you never left out any documents or reports of a secure nature he might have spotted?"

"Of course not. The only thing I remember him asking that stood out to me was where and how we had obtained the substance we had released in that sample area of the Everglades. That was information I alone was privy to, so I had no choice but to dodge his question, which was easy because the sample was provided by the United States Geological Survey itself: a black rock no bigger than a baseball, full of crystallized spots. Our instructions were to ground it into a powder and release a small sampling into an area of the Everglades of our own designation. Wait a day, then return to take measurements and samples. Then repeat the process until we achieved quantifiable results."

"How long did it take to achieve those results?"

"The temperature registered a minute drop on the third day, after that particular sample was released. We've been exposing additional sampling every third day since in the same amount, the temperature continuing to drop and the sample area expanding in a quantifiable spread."

Gina considered that in relation to what Michael had told her about the massive fish kill happening in the waters off Lester Island. If the organism had reached the waters of Cross Sound, as they must have Icy Strait, the fish might have been infected in the same manner as the crew of the *Providence*. Her instincts about a connection between these dual inexplicable occurrences had been correct, though the spread had only just begun down here. And, at this point, there was no way to determine how many more humans, and fish, were going to die, if the spread of the microorganism wasn't stopped in its tracks.

"How long into Delaney's tenure did the results begin to occur?"

Perry had to ponder that, her eyes sweeping about as she backtracked in her mind. "We registered the first breakthrough three weeks ago, so that would be three weeks after he joined the team."

She dabbed her eyes with a sleeve at that. Gina backed off for a moment, using the time to collect her own thoughts. Now that she had the victim's actual identity, she'd requested a dump of his cell phone records to see who he had called and who had called him. Clues to the identity of who had ordered his death, and why, might well lie there.

"How did you come by that sample exactly?" Gina asked Rosalee Perry next.

"Like I said, the USGS supplied it, along with as much detail as they could provide about its capabilities. Because of the rapid increase in temperatures the Gulf waters have been experiencing, the Everglades were deemed to be the perfect site for running the test. That decision was made at a much higher level within the USGS and, I suspect, beyond it."

Gina knew she had reached a crucial tipping point here. Turlidge had told her he'd been doing business with Axel Cole and the Russians. He had mentioned nothing about the USGS in that respect. So how had they become aware of the microbe's existence and come to be in possession of at least a small sampling of it? A definite anomaly that might well answer the question of who was behind Jackson Delaney's murder.

"And who would I contact at the USGS to find out how they came to be in possession of the sample you were provided in the first place?"

"The director himself, I imagine. We're working directly with the chief science advisor who had previously served as USGS's associate director for water, overseeing all aspects of the bureau's programs in water science. He's been down here to monitor our work on numerous occasions. He came to the USGS from the Department of the Interior where he served as science advisor to the secretary there."

Gina nodded, as another crucial piece in the puzzle she was methodically assembling fell into place. In that capacity, the USGS's chief science advisor would have worked with none other than Ethan Turlidge. But Gina still didn't have what she was looking for, the smoking gun that would indicate what had gotten Jackson Delaney killed and who was behind it.

"I'll need the name and contact info for this chief science—"

Gina stopped in midsentence, feeling a sudden chill not related to the blast she felt from the air-conditioning system. The crew of the *Providence* had perished just hours after the sub was penetrated by the very organism the USGS team down here was releasing into the Everglades, which fed into the Gulf Stream itself, which could only mean . . .

"Can you reach your team in the field, Rosalee?"

"Yes. Why?"

"Because you need to tell them to cease all operations and get the hell out of there." Gina looked toward Clark Gifford. "We need to shut that area down."

Perry's cell phone rang and she looked back across the desk at Gina.

"That's my team in the field now, Agent Delgado."

"Pull them out, Rosalee. Get them back here."

Perry answered the call, her face paling as she listened to the person on the other end of the line.

"Oh my God . . . No, don't do anything. I'm heading there now."

She ended the call, looking back at Gina with eyes glazed in shock as she rose from her chair. "I've got to get out to the field. Something's . . . happened."

CHAPTER 54

CHICHAGOF ISLAND, ALASKA

Fifth largest island in the United States.

General Viktor Adamovitch stood on the deck of the Russian trawler *Lucretia Mru,* dressed uncomfortably as a fisherman. They were docked at Port Althorp, on the north coast of Chichagof Island, hiding in plain sight under the name and registration of a Canadian fishing vessel. To anyone observing, the main deck appeared as any would for a vessel of this type returning from a stretch at sea. Adamovitch had even watched as the Russian captain supervised the off-loading of a substantial catch an actual Russian fishing boat had transferred aboard that morning before she sailed into port.

Port Althorp was only a little over twenty-three nautical miles from Lester Island, which made this the perfect setting to await the looming attack. The timing was limited, since the submarine could only surface close to the far side of Lester Island at high tide where she would off-load men instead of fish: fifty members of Russia's elite Spetsnaz commando force, the equivalent of America's Delta Force or Navy SEALs. They would supplement the seventy-five troops currently hiding in concealed holds of the *Lucretia Mru.* While all activity on deck purposefully appeared normal, belowdecks held not just men but a heavy store of weapons that included handheld rocket launchers and light explosives. There was also an impressive supply of heavier weaponry tucked into conveyors and risers that could swiftly be brought into position on the main deck to provide cover for the troops advancing on the Tlingit tribe that lived over the reserves of what Axel Cole called Prometheus.

If all went according to plan, the *Lucretia Mru* would be leaving with reserves of it on board, more than enough to weaponize in a way that would tilt the balance of power in the world Russia's way. Once the landing party was in place, ready to stage the attack, it would fall on the submarine to deal with any attempted response from the sea in the form of the Coast Guard, whose ships lacked the firepower and whose men lacked the combat training to prove much of a hindrance. In addition to offloading troops well away from any populated region, the trawler had an extraction team on board whose job it was to proceed straight to either of two entrances to the mines beneath Xunaa and chisel out as much of the compound as possible in the limited time allotted. By the time they had finished extracting and using their accompanying machinery to ferry the reserves back to the surface, the trawler would have docked at the harbor the American Natives called their own.

The logistics were challenging but with all contact to and from the island cut off, and attacking under cover of darkness, Adamovitch believed he would have around three hours to harvest ample reserves of Prometheus, more than enough to establish Russia as the world's preeminent superpower. And there would come a time, at that point, when his forces could return to a decimated and conquered America to harvest more reserves.

It was without question a deadly serious provocation, an act of war for which Putin's government would be blamed, bringing the world to the brink of World War III. Adamovitch not only anticipated that, he intended to use it as the catalyst to propel himself to power in the new Russia under his more determined and aggressive leadership. Putin had retained his power while losing his passion for it. He had gotten old and rich, where Adamovitch cared nothing about his own gains. Russia's gains were all that concerned him.

The plan's timing and complexities invited disaster, but Adamovitch had made his mark as a superb strategist who factored every conceivable response and event into his planning. The only resistance his men could be expected to encounter on the island was from a small force of fighters who saw themselves as the keepers of the tribe's warrior traditions. But they had received no formal training, maintained only a limited cache of weapons, and would be hopelessly outnumbered.

For his part in this, Axel Cole expected a significant portion of the reserves to be transferred to one of his ships at sea, once the *Lucretia Mru* was back in Russian waters. Cole was about to learn he had been lucky to emerge with his life and the lives of his family. Adamovitch wondered how he would respond to having the tables turned on him, but he did intend to leave Cole some space by providing limited reserves of Prometheus and not destroying the ship he was supposed to be rendezvousing with just miles from Russia's shores.

It wasn't much, but it was more than he had allowed all the other men he had conquered. And if Cole proved ungrateful for the gesture, he would not live to see his *Death Star* ever take off, much less reach the red planet.

Red planet, Adamovitch mused. *Has a nice ring to it . . .*

CHAPTER 55

EVERGLADES NATIONAL PARK, FLORIDA

Many scenes of the classic television series *Gentle Ben* were filmed in the park.

The only way to get to the site in Everglades National Park where the USGS team was collecting samples was by airboat. It had been cordoned off by oil booms strung in an oblong pattern over a half-mile radius to contain a purported oil spill. For that made-up reason, pleasure- and other craft had been prohibited from entering the area since the USGS team attained their first breakthrough several weeks back.

The isolated nature of this tributary of the Everglades, well off the beaten paths tourists were known to frequent, might well have rendered such precautions moot. The USGS team members were ferried to and from the area every day by the same airboat Gina and Rosalee Perry would be taking, since regular boats couldn't manage the task due to their submerged motors. Airboats, on the other hand, can traverse even partially submerged marshy areas, like the Everglades, and do so in a fast and agile fashion. A number of anchored platforms had been towed in and placed strategically to serve as staging areas from which the USGS team could conduct their experiments without having to remain in the swampy waters more than was absolutely necessary.

Gina accompanied Rosalee Perry to a base with a small outbuilding the team had appropriated for their use twenty minutes from the Daniel Beard Center. It was convenient to Highway 41 and just off Krome Avenue, just a slight walk along a path that remained safe and dry except after the worst of the area's storms when alligators tended to perch there. An airboat and its driver were waiting for them on the dock, Gina getting her first look at one up close and personal.

Made from fiberglass or aluminum, airboats were built to glide across the surface of the water with the help of its giant airplane propeller, powered by a 400 horsepower engine. The propeller pushed huge volumes of air backward, resulting in the boat skimming the top of the water, unhampered by vegetation or collections of muck gathered below the surface. Airboats were by far the most common means of covering the 1.5 million acres the Florida Everglades occupies. The one real drawback was the noise. Environmentalists complained bitterly about the harm that did to the native wildlife species, seldom acknowledging that the damage potentially done to the area by other types of crafts would have been much greater.

Fifteen minutes into their ride, the oil boom came into view, uncoiled like a giant snake riding the top of the water, enclosing the wooden staging platforms, but there was no sign of the USGS team members on station.

Then Gina spotted the first of the dead fish floating on the surface.

Drawing closer, she saw it wasn't just a line of them, but a blanket that blocked out much of the water. Michael had described a massive fish kill that had washed up on the Lester Island shoreline. By all appearances, the one down here was just getting started.

"It's worse than I thought," Rosalee Perry noted, her voice cracking.

"And this is the area your team's been working in?"

Perry managed a nod.

"Then where are they?"

"I don't know. Let me try to raise them. . . ."

Gina watched Perry unclasp a walkie-talkie from her belt. She tried hailing her team, tried again, and then a third time, only silence or static coming in response all three times.

"Something's wrong, Agent Delgado."

Gina had already pushed her jacket back to ease the process of drawing her pistol.

Something was indeed wrong.

They hadn't been able to converse during the ride because of the noise levels. Rosalee Perry even donned earplugs and offered Gina a pair, which she declined, not wanting any of her senses to be diminished. Now, with the engine idling, they could hear the birds and light splash of the currents.

"I've got a friend at the White House who can help us," Gina said, readying her phone. "I have to tell him about the fish, too," she added, needing to make Daniel Grant aware of the fact that whatever was happening off the coast of Lester Island in Alaska was happening here now, too.

Gina finished dialing. "Come on, Grant," she muttered, "pick up . . ."

"Daniel Grant?" Perry posed.

"Know him?"

"Sure, for years. Before he became chief of staff he was associate director of the White House Office of Science and Technology Policy and then oversaw the President's Council of Advisors on Science and Technology."

Gina felt her stomach sink. *PCAST,* she realized, everything falling into place, including the man responsible for Jackson Delaney's death.

"I'm not really familiar with this council."

There was only one reason why Grant would compose such a lie. She ended the call to him and a moment later another came in, Clark Gifford's now-familiar number lighting up in the caller ID.

"You're not going to believe this," he greeted.

"Try me," a still shaken Gina told him.

"I've got positive IDs on two of the men captured on that backyard security cam, but it makes no sense."

Nothing does right now, Gina almost said, waiting for him to continue.

"They're both Secret Service, Agent. You mind telling me what the hell—"

The call dropped, hardly unusual in the Everglades. Instead of calling Gifford back right away, Gina redialed her dedicated White House number. Only this time, she had to figure out a way to get President Jillian Cantwell on the line.

The call didn't seem to go through. No ring followed. Then a click and she was disconnected.

Gina tried again. Same result. Then a third time, with a slightly different result in the form of a disembodied mechanical voice coming on the line.

"This is not a working number . . ."

She needed to reach Michael, tell him no help was coming his way either.

The call didn't go through, garnering only the annoying chirp of a dropped call. Gina checked her bars. There were none, SOS lit up where the bars should have been.

Her phone had been deactivated.

"Get us back to the dock," she ordered their airboat driver.

CHAPTER 56

⊢•❄•⊣

GLACIER BAY NATIONAL PARK
AND PRESERVE,
LESTER ISLAND, ALASKA

Other Beardslee Islands nearby include Spider Island,
Strawberry Island, Flapjack Island, and Kidney Island.

With twilight approaching, Michael and Amka continued to walk the village, observing the *Kiks.ádi* warriors preparing for the coming siege.

"Where are your National Guard troops, Michael?" she challenged him
with the light starting to bleed from the sky.

Amka was right; they should have reached Lester Island by now and he
hadn't been able to reach Gina Delgado. He took out his phone to call her
again and saw he had no signal.

"Check your phone," he said to Amka.

She did. "Nothing."

"The signal's been cut. Either we're being jammed or the Russians took
out the cell tower."

Amka didn't look surprised. "Good thing my grandfather and the
Kiks.ádi knew this was going to be our battle alone to fight."

They had been preparing, Michael realized, since the night before,
sensing what was to come. He had spotted groupings of them lugging
wheelbarrows and ATVs loaded with gear throughout the area surrounding the village, both inside and outside the tree groves that formed the
village's rear as well as closer to the shoreline. Michael recognized some of
what they were laying the groundwork for, from his extensive knowledge
of Native American history. Apparently, while the vast majority of traditions and practices varied from tribe to tribe, the construction of primitive, but extremely effective, defenses did not. At this point, he could only

hope they would be enough to help repel a vastly superior force in both numbers and weapons.

In his mind, as night fell Michael could clearly picture a woolly mammoth, dying from exposure to the organism, taking refuge in that Lamplugh Glacier cave thousands of years ago where it froze to death. When the rise in temperatures thawed the remains of the animal out, the organism it had carried was freed to wreak havoc on the world once more. Was it only this one animal or had climate change released even more of something that could wipe out much of the life on Earth today as it had ten thousand years ago? He thought of the ongoing fish kill here and pictured similar scenes throughout the country, the world. If the organism managed to kill all life in the oceans, humans wouldn't be far behind.

He followed Amka in a slow sweep of the village, spotting her grandfather and brother kneeling across from each other on a flat patch of land centered between their matching homes. Their eyes were closed and they seemed to be chanting softly.

"What are they doing?"

"Their part," Amka told him, leaving it there.

"Well, I'd like to do my part, too. Take me to the entrance of those mines that lie beneath the village."

‡‡‡

"Here," Amka said, standing beyond the last of the village's homes lying along the farthest reaches of the rise just short of the forest line.

"Where?" Michael asked, noticing nothing that particularly stood out.

"You're standing where the primary entrance was before it was sealed centuries ago."

"Who dug it up?"

Amka just looked at him.

"Why?"

"To blow it up, Michael. At this entrance and another closer to the village itself. To stop the Russians from claiming what's beneath it. This time we're going to stop them."

And that's when they heard the echo of gunfire pushing through the trees.

CHAPTER 57

EVERGLADES NATIONAL PARK, FLORIDA

The Everglades receives an average rainfall of sixty inches a year.

The airboat rode the surface of the swampy water smoothly, almost like it was flying. Gina was still processing Clark Gifford's report that Jackson Delaney's killers were Secret Service, at least in name, since their primary role must have been to serve as Chief of Staff Daniel Grant's personal soldiers. The shape of what had fallen together before her was maddening. Delaney must have been on the verge of revealing exactly what the USGS team was up to. Operation Cold Burn was supposed to make up the formidable distance President Jillian Cantwell had fallen in the polls, but that revelation would lose the vast bulk of its relevance and impact if exposed by a science writer. Maybe Delaney had also somehow figured out the White House connection and political nature of the project. If that were the case, such a scandal would sink the president's reelection bid in its tracks, more than enough motive for a Rasputin-esque character like Grant to act in the fashion he had.

It all made a twisted, terrible sense.

Gina was the problem now. The president herself had ordered her dispatched to solve a murder Cantwell had no idea her chief of staff had ordered. Gina was a loose end, but not the only one. Grant had no idea what he had inadvertently unleashed with Operation Cold Burn. The fish were now dying here just as Michael reported they were in Alaska where the spread of the microbe was significantly advanced. It had already claimed a United States Geological Survey team that had gone missing in Glacier Bay, the crew of a Virginia-class submarine, and now Alaskan hospitals were beginning to get overrun. But the fish dying made for the scariest proposition of all because if that cycle continued, the death of marine life would signal the inevitable death of man and civilization as it was known today. The oceans would become vast burial grounds for the organisms at the root of life itself.

The airboat driver wheeled agilely around the bend, straight into the path of an airboat with gunmen poised in the front.

Gina was certain she recognized one of them as the killer who had rented the boat used to dispose of Jackson Delaney's body. He and what must have been a second agent opened up with sidearms, firing straight on toward her airboat. She grabbed hold of Rosalee Perry and dragged her as low as the airboat's seats would allow and felt the bullets whiz over them as they surged past the converging boat and heard their driver groan, the airboat suddenly losing speed.

She swung to find him slumped in the pilot's seat he was buckled into, the airboat still slowing and heading toward a mangrove nest on its port side where it would become hopelessly tangled. Acting on instinct, Gina grabbed tight hold of Perry with one hand, as she grasped for her pistol with the other.

"Get help! Go!"

And with that she pushed her into the shallow, muck-riddled water, hoping there were no alligators about. Then she twisted her frame over the seats and dislodged the driver from his seat. He'd taken at least two bullets and maybe more—there was so much blood pumping through his thin life vest it was hard to tell. Believing he was dead, she nonetheless lowered him across the seats directly before his chair and took his place behind the controls, which amounted to the rudder stick that controlled steering and the accelerator pedal that controlled speed, no brake pedal or anything resembling a gearshift in evidence.

Gina could hear the powerful whir of the second airboat's engine, along with fresh gunshots, as she jammed the pedal to the floor at the same time she worked the rudder stick to the left. She had just heard the *thwack!* of the airboat's bow crunching atop exposed mangrove roots, when it jerked suddenly away, back into the open channel. More gunfire traced the boat the whole time Gina was struggling for control and rhythm, falling into it and speeding on with the trailing airboat coming fast and bullets clanging off the cage enclosing the powerful propeller.

▸•◦•◦•◂

GLACIER BAY NATIONAL PARK AND PRESERVE, LESTER ISLAND, ALASKA

The kelp beds along the shoreline can grow up to six inches a day.

General Viktor Adamovitch loved nothing more than leading his troops into battle, believing wholeheartedly in the notion of never ordering anyone to do something he wouldn't do himself. He was walking at the head of the contingent of commandos encircling the team that would extract the precious ore from the vein that ran beneath the village of Xunaa, when the face of the man on his right erupted in a red mist. Adamovitch hadn't heard the shot, nor could he glean the angle from which it had been fired. Along with the other troops clustered behind him, he hit the bare ground dotted with stubborn patches of thin snow and ice that the sun had ignored.

His approach from the north of the village, effectively its rear flank, was meant to draw all the attention away from the troops who had deployed off the submarine and were now approaching from the east and west. He had expected the element of surprise to be his and hadn't anticipated losing a man this early in the fight to what could only be a sniper.

Adamovitch had studied not only the 1804 Battle of Sitka, in which Russia had finally prevailed over the Tlingits, but also the years that had preceded it, which had seen the tribe hold their own against vastly superior manpower and armaments. They had used the advantages the land provided to tip the scales in their favor, but Adamovitch fully believed those days were long gone.

Perhaps he'd been wrong.

During the initial months of the war with Ukraine, the generals in charge had made the mistake of vastly underestimating the enemy's resources, tactics, and, most of all, resolve. As the blood of the commando who'd been walking next to him soaked into the hard ground, Adamovitch found himself fearing he had made the same mistake they had. He had rescued that war from disaster, establishing a foothold from which he could restore Mother Russia to its roots. A foothold that was to be cemented with what he had come to Lester Island to obtain.

While he had underestimated his enemy, this initial setback was nothing more than an inconvenience. If anything, it strengthened Adamovitch's resolve not to be merciful with the villagers. The Tlingits would fall and he would relish the sound of their screams.

Still lying prone on the ground, Adamovitch heard crackling around him and felt his heavy uniform jacket being pricked. He realized it was pellets of ice falling in sheets from a sky that had been clear when they'd begun their advance with no storm fronts anywhere on the radar. While weather patterns in these parts were known to shift on a dime, this felt like something different. A sudden squall of ice that would pass quickly and pose only a minor hindrance.

Still, the advance of his group, here in the open, had effectively been stopped. He unclasped the old-fashioned walkie-talkie from his belt and raised it to his lips.

"Group Two, report your position."

"Holding at the forest tree line."

"Begin your advance now."

"Group Three, come in."

"Group Three here."

"Continue your advance and secure the mine."

"Acknowledged. Group Two out."

Adamovitch lowered the device, chipping away with a gloved hand at the coating of ice that had formed on it during the brief duration since he'd yanked it from his belt. He felt the skin exposed beneath the hood of his Russian military jacket similarly coated from the conditions that could best be likened to Siberia. He knew hypothermia was a very real possibility in such an ice storm, as was frostbite. But the sudden fall of thick blankets of sleet that had sprung forth from the crazed oddities of Alaskan weather would pass soon.

At which point, Adamovitch would continue his advance into the center of the village. He smiled at the sound of screams erupting from beyond the frozen world in which he was encased.

Until he realized they were the screams of his own men.

‡‡‡

Yehl chanted with his grandfather, feeling the ice they'd summoned from the sky pattering against him. The slivers of ice numbed his skin, its cold burn starting to penetrate the multiple layers of clothing he had donned. The frigid feel didn't so much soak through, as radiate inward after forming a crystal sheen over him.

It was an entirely different sensation from what he had encountered in the midst of the spirit walk that had left him a man. Last night he had felt the cold in every bit of his being, as if he were freezing from the outside in. A few times he had felt his heart to make sure it was still beating and had spent the night believing he had actually died and could only hope he was worthy of being reborn.

Manhood was a rebirth that meant him returning to the village in an entirely different form than when he had embarked on his spirit walk. He may have looked the same on the surface, been confused for the boy he had been, but the spirit and soul that had broken through the storm that should have killed him bore no resemblance to those that had previously been shielded by the warmth of childhood. He was now worthy of manhood, and becoming chief, as evidenced by his grandfather enlisting him in his call to the Old Ones who had walked the hallowed ground of Hoonah Tlingit tribes in centuries past to aid their forebearers' efforts to keep this land as their own and vanquish those who would seek to despoil it.

"We must summon the ice, grandson," Chief Xetsuwu had said, speaking in the ancient Tlingit tongue Yehl had never understood until today, following his spirit walk. "I am not strong enough anymore to manage such a feat alone. We must do so together so the *t'éex* may fall from the sky and steal the enemy's advantage away."

It was as if his grandfather could see the events of the future on a viewing screen in his mind, while there was still time left to affect the outcome.

"Their triggers will not pull, their barrels will not warm, their bullets will not fire, if we do this."

And now they were. Yehl should have felt cold, but he didn't, in spite of the thin layer of ice encrusted over him. He felt warmed by the words he continued to chant with his grandfather, hearing them in his mind a moment before he spoke them in perfect cadence with the chief he would someday replace. The import and responsibility of that succession, that legacy, had made no sense to him in that moment, this battle that was his to help fight completing the process his spirit walk had started.

His grandfather continued to chant, and Yehl continued to chant with him, his words mirroring the old man's.

‡‡‡

"You may want to cover your ears," Amka said to Michael, after the first of the screams rang out. "You can't unhear the horror that will follow."

They were just outside the woods that rimmed the village to the north, keeping watch over the entrance to the mines she had shown him earlier. The contents of those mines were the key, had to be protected at all costs.

In the next moments, the mere lapse of time between breaths and heartbeats, Michael saw it all happening in his mind in conjunction with the screams that continued to come, the images conjured from the preparations he had witnessed the *Kiks.ádi* making for the battle to come.

The first line of defense the *Kiks.ádi* had laid in the woods was their own deadly version of the old deadfall traps used to snare game animals. The traditional deadfall trap was a simple mechanism made of sticks supporting a heavy weight pivoting on the tip of the more upright one. A trigger would be planted at the base of the lower stick that, when jarred, would collapse the weight atop the animal. The *Kiks.ádi*'s more modern version used the identical principles with triggering branches instead of sticks and foot-long wood tips shaved to a thin, pointed edge instead of mere weight. The Russian soldiers advancing into the woods who were unfortunate enough to trip these outlying traps would send the others scurrying through the dark in shock and confusion.

The next series of screams told Michael that was exactly what had happened an instant before a pair of arrows buzzed the air, seemingly within milliseconds of each other, downing the Russians desperately retracing their steps from the woods, their weapons turned into frozen hunks of steel by the sudden ice storm.

The horrible screams of the men impaled by the deadfall traps continued to pierce the night. Fresh wails joined those as the next rush of Russians, funneled into what was essentially a layered obstacle course of pain and death, fell victim to more of the *Kiks.ádi's* ancient traps.

Tree limbs, lashed high between trees with heavy rope, dropped in a speed-gathering arc once the camouflaged rock holding them in place as a contact point was struck.

Buckets of road tar heated by open flame, and then nailed on a swivel atop branches, spilled their thick, oozing contents upon anyone who so much as jostled the lower-hanging connected branches, while seeking cover behind the tree that held them.

The hardness of the earth rendered the old covered hole trap infeasible, so the *Kiks.ádi* opted instead to hammer more razor-pointed wooden spikes into the ground, camouflaged by brush. The ice tumbling from the sky created a blanket of crystals stretched over the scene, accompanied by the clacking of ice pellets as the layers mounted. Add to these what amounted to tripwire strung in tight strands of twine and tied between stakes. Those Russians lucky enough to avoid them could still find their boots and feet pierced by the sharpened spikes, and those who fell victim to the tripwires were almost certain to fall forward into the deadly snare waiting to pierce flesh and muscle as if they were pudding.

Michael thought such traps to be no more than weapons of terror meant to turn the orderly Russian seizure of Xunaa into complete chaos. While they were every bit of that, they also served the dual function of disabling, or outright killing, untold numbers of the invading force. Their retreat made them fodder for the Tlingit warriors' own sniper fire with weapons wrapped tightly in wool fabric with the texture of steel wool so they could be fired through the ice.

The Russians not caught in the kill box, meanwhile, were met with the simplest snares of all—basically, just a wire noose suspended in the likely paths of the Russians rushing desperately through the woods. Once a boot hit the center of the noose it would snap into place, tightening over the foot or ankle the more the man tried to free himself. Unless the victim decided to chew his own leg or foot off, the wire would hold him for as long as need be.

Shapes flashed in the spill of darkness, aglow in the fall of ice from the sky, specks of motion more than men, with their faces blacked out with ground tar the falling ice left intact. A number of the *Kiks.ádi* that kept shifting before Michael's eyes followed the Russian soldiers into the woods, firing arrows through dark hardwood bows methodically as they moved. The rhythm of the process so smooth and graceful that it belied the death held at the tip of every arrow shot off. Thunks, grunts, and groans replaced the screams as the tribe's modern-day warriors continued to turn the tide in a battle over two hundred years in the making.

It felt surreal, more like a dream. His prosthetic foot barking at him inside his boot brought Michael back to reality. It had never been subjected to conditions like these and he feared the plastic housing would freeze and crack, separating from the titanium prosthetic itself. He reached down and tried to rub some heat into it with friction through his gloves.

"Michael," he heard Amka say softly, and followed her gaze to the tree line to the east where another phalanx of Russian soldiers was advancing toward the entrance to the mines that ran beneath the village.

⊢•⊢◦⊣•⊣

CHAPTER 59

EVERGLADES NATIONAL PARK, FLORIDA

The airboats run between 25 and 30 mph for tours, but
are designed to operate up to 60 mph.

The airboat bounced along the surface, jarring her. Gina held her pistol in her free hand but didn't dare risk a glance back to steady her aim for fear of losing control. Having never driven an airboat before, she was amazed at the sensitivity of the controls and how the slightest twitch on the rudder arm could force a near complete change of direction.

Gina settled into an awkward rhythm, just as the trailing airboat raced to draw even, and one of the gunmen opened up with an assault rifle on full auto, kicking up fissures of water on both sides of the airboat. More bullets clanged off the propeller housing and she tensed at the thought of how close they were coming to her. The fact that the trailing airboat had five people on board, compared to only one, gave the speed advantage to her. Outrunning her pursuers offered one option, but they still held an immense advantage in firepower, and the ease with which she had taken to the airboat's controls gave her other options to trim their advantage.

In that moment, she jerked the rudder stick to the left again, easing off the gas and then again slamming the pedal all the way down while she worked the rudder stick more to the left and then rightward. Turned back toward the narrow channel she had just left, she surged past the airboat carrying the gunmen.

Gina locked on the five gunmen twisting to resteady their weapons, Secret Service agents all, no doubt. Hers was already poised their way when they passed each other, Gina firing seven times. Certain she had hit one of the enemy and maybe two, but airboats didn't come with rearview mirrors, so it was impossible to say. She gave the boat more speed to buy some time, though the clear expert nature of the trailing boat's driver left the enemy with a distinct advantage she could in no way overcome. The alternative was making the landscape of the swamp-riddled Everglades work in her favor.

Gunshots had begun ringing out behind her again, bursts of automatic fire among them, when Gina spotted a tighter, winding channel it would normally take someone far more adept at piloting an airboat than her to negotiate, but right now the contours offered her the best chance for survival. She nearly lost control as she banked into it, leaning into the turn as she adroitly worked the rudder stick right and then quickly jerked it back left. She glimpsed alligators scurrying beneath the surface and a few more of the massive reptiles seeming to follow her path with big sunken eyes from the muck-rich shoreline.

Neither outrunning nor outgunning her pursuers was a viable option, leaving Gina to consider others. She could abandon the boat and take her chances in the thigh- to waist-high water, but that too seemed a fool's errand for someone hardly used to such difficult conditions, not to mention the gators and even pythons lurking about in the shadows. Gina's mind trailed to where she was most comfortable, specifically explosives, even though she had none of those handy either.

Or did she?

Recalling how the pilot now lying across the seat had filled the airboat's gas tank, she knew at least a portion of it lay directly beneath the pilot's seat. Since no parts of an airboat dipped below the surface, that meant the tank was relatively small, no more than ten gallons, and long and low-slung as opposed to the contours of a car or regular boat's tank.

Gina leaned heavily sideways to press her pistol against the aluminum flooring and fired three times. Her experience indicated that the spilled fuel would cling to the surface and, even if it didn't, plenty more of the recently filled tank bubbled out through the holes to be sprayed in all directions atop the surface by the powerful propeller. The craft had already begun to handle more sluggishly, but still with enough power to maintain the gap between her and the airboat chasing her, the pool of gas spreading in her wake.

An emergency kit lay within easy reach and she plucked a flare gun from inside. Hearing fresh gunshots cutting through the roar of the trailing airboat's engine, Gina glanced backward long enough to aim the flare gun down into the fuel-rich wake she was leaving and pull the trigger.

The flare thumped out and burst aglow on impact with the surface. For a moment, Gina thought the move had failed. But then she heard a massive *poof!* as sheets of fire erupted behind her. In a perfect world, the airboat holding the killers Daniel Grant had dispatched would have exploded. Instead, the pilot maintained the wherewithal to twist his craft away from the worst of the flames. But the motion was so sudden it lifted the airboat from the swamp's surface, tilting it sideways in the process. It crashed back down with a crackling thud that tossed all of the gunmen overboard.

Gina only had a moment to celebrate, though, because her own craft, bled of gas, coughed, bucked, and coasted to a stop. She dropped into the swamp up to her thighs, spotting four of the killers righting themselves enough to fire wildly her way.

Not wanting to waste any of her precious remaining ammo, Gina waded into a thicket of reeds and bramble, listening to the splashing the killers made as they gave chase, more gunfire tracking her into the swamp.

GLACIER BAY NATIONAL PARK AND PRESERVE, LESTER ISLAND, ALASKA

In 2022, Alaska mines produced $4.5 billion worth of minerals.

The air itself felt frozen with the endless fall of frigid crystals as the ice storm continued to rage around them. No scientific, or meteorological, explanation existed for its sudden and lasting appearance. Michael recalled the sight of Yehl and his grandfather, present and future tribal chiefs, kneeling across from each other, eyes closed and lips moving, and gave the storm no further thought. He was in unchartered territory here in more ways than one, coming to grips with the fact that the Tlingit belief in the power of the spiritual world was well-founded.

Though some advance warning from Amka would have been appreciated, the fact that the ice had rendered all firearms exposed to the elements useless, was more than enough for him. He knew the shots he heard sporadically piercing the eerie clack of the hail against ground and flora came from *Kiks.ádi* warrior snipers.

"Stay here!" Amka ordered him.

And, before Michael could argue, she had advanced ahead of him, straight into the view of the approaching Russian force, which appeared to number around thirty men, more as they drew closer. A few harmless shots flashed toward her, the bulk of the weapons already frozen solid, as she twirled what looked like an old-fashioned slingshot, set aflame, overhead. Even through the storm, Michael could hear the wind whooshing in the circular path it sliced through the air, no more than a blur when Amka finally released it. The slingshot creased forward, landing in a patch of flat frozen land between the advancing Russian force and the entrance to the mine, but with the flames extinguished.

"It won't ignite, the gas won't ignite!" she cried out, as much to herself as to him.

"Let me," Michael said, freeing his SIG Sauer pistol for the first time since the onset of the battle.

That meant it was totally dry and he might be able to empty the entire magazine before the conditions rendered it inoperable. He assumed a ready stance with both hands holding the pistol, tempting the still occasional and even more desperate fire, as he eased in on the trigger again and again. He'd fired nine shots before a massive pillar of flames shot up from fuel pooled in a shallow trench dug earlier that day. Any number of Russian soldiers were caught in its grasp, their screams horribly loud and strong enough to pierce the storm. Still more took cover or launched into all-out retreat, visible in the mounting flames they could not breach to reach the entrance to the mine it was their charge to guard.

Amka stripped the backpack from her shoulders and crouched next to him, drawing out what looked like tightly wrapped, softball-sized wedges of cloth.

"Gunpowder, Michael," she said when his count had reached eight of them. "The Tlingits lost the Battle of Sitka in 1804 because their supplies never reached the fort. Things are different today."

‡‡‡

General Viktor Adamovitch was living in the midst of the impossible. A small band of resistance fighters using primitive weapons laying waste to the best soldiers Russia had to offer. It was a story that would leave his name in infamy should it ever be told. But the force at his command was still almost entirely intact, forty men, in stark comparison to the others that radio traffic indicated had been decimated.

He had resumed his advance on the village, propelled by the certainty he could still prevail and emerge with what he'd come here to retrieve. Maybe not as much, but still enough until he located more reserves elsewhere amid the frozen grounds of the American state he would someday reclaim as Russian territory.

The beginning of his tenure in Ukraine had started out badly as well. But he had stuck to the plan, stayed the course, and the results now spoke for themselves. While the ice had rendered the assault rifles useless, the pistols tucked beneath their heavy jackets along with an ample supply of RGN hand grenades retained their punch. Plenty of weaponry to still conquer Xunaa tonight, just as the Russian troops had conquered Sitka in 1804.

With that, Adamovitch led his men forward into the forest. He would widen the spread as they neared the village and launch an all-out attack, sparing nothing. The sudden burst of engines roaring froze him in his tracks, the sound seeming to come from everywhere at once. Then he caught glimpses of what looked like ATVs tearing through the forest from all angles, a driver behind the wheel and a gunner somehow standing erect in the rear. As one of them whizzed by through the trees to his right, Adamovitch saw the gunner had strapped himself in to avoid being thrown from the vehicle as it sped in a winding, improvised route.

Gunfire erupted and he watched waves of his men cut down before they could free their sidearms or get to the grenades clipped to their ammo vests. An eternity passed before the survivors, who had managed to elude the ATVs and take cover, were able to return the fire with their pistols. Adamovitch unzipped his jacket and stripped a pair of grenades from his own ammo vest, hurling them one after the other into the path of ATVs streaming through the woods. The twin blasts sounded barely a second apart, both vehicles launched airborne with ruptured fragments and flaming carcasses plunging back to the ground in smoking heaps.

He watched more of his troops get mowed down by gunfire from the remaining ATVs before they were taken out by RGN grenades tossed in expert fashion by his surviving men. A dozen men were all he had left when he emerged from the tree line to find an old man and a boy seated cross-legged apart from each other, encrusted by the ice that rained down without pause. At first, he thought they had frozen to death in that position. Then he saw their lips were still moving and, as he drew closer, heard them chanting in what must have been this cursed tribe's ancient language.

The chanting continued, until Adamovitch pressed his pistol through the air still heavy with ice against the boy's head.

"*Stäp,*" he ordered in Russian.

The chanting ceased and, as quickly as it had begun, the ice storm slowly waned before the sleet stopped falling altogether.

CHAPTER 61

─•─○─•─

EVERGLADES NATIONAL PARK, FLORIDA

Ernest Coe, a landscape architect, started the push to
recognize the Everglades as a national park in 1928.

The first thing that struck Gina as she waded through the thick black oozing waters of the swamp was the stench. She'd read somewhere that as much as a third of the Everglades had been contaminated by sulfides that had soaked into the nutrient-rich sediment to produce the sulfur-like odor of rotten eggs. It was strong enough to first turn her nose, then to leave her queasy and on the verge of nausea, likely explaining why this area was utterly deserted except for her and her pursuers.

She backed herself in deeper amid the cover of the bramble and mangroves, spotting three surviving gunmen approaching through the water, one wielding the assault rifle she had detected earlier and two others only pistols, steadied with two hands the way Secret Service agents were trained to do when advancing in such situations. She had managed to keep her own pistol dry, but not her spare magazine, leaving it useless. Gina had lost track of exactly how many shots she had fired herself, figuring she had only three or four bullets left at the most. She didn't dare make a run for the shoreline where the line of alligators that had been chased there by the explosion snapped at each other, as if angry over being disturbed from their perches in the water.

That sight formed her next move, opted for before she could change her mind, when she fired what turned out to be her three remaining bullets into the shoreline. Enraged, the giant reptiles hissed through gaping jaws and then dropped into the black waters.

Her fire had drawn all of the gunmen's attention at first, their gazes seeking her out amid the mangroves. The one wielding the assault rifle had just twisted in that direction, about to open up again when the splashing sound of a horde of gators dropping back into the swamp turned his gaze that way. Instead of firing on Gina's position, he sprayed the water with fire, hitting only the surface the gators had already dropped below.

For her part, Gina broke off the thickest, longest piece of a cypress branch she could find from an overhanging tree providing her cover and dropped low into the black water until only her face above her nose was revealed. She was busy steadying her breathing when a horrible, high-pitch scream sounded, as one of the gunmen was dragged under the water and swarmed by a host of angry gators that turned the water into a splashing, red froth.

The other two gunmen lit out desperately through the narrow channel, no heed paid any longer to her position, concerned only with escaping before the gators descended upon them. Gina let the first one pass by her hiding spot and then lurched up and out when the second drew within range, swinging her cypress branch like a baseball bat. It shattered across his face, obliterating his nose and cracking his cheek and orbital bones.

He sunk below the surface, unconscious, as the second man whirled around with pistol in hand, just as Gina dropped below the surface, too. Holding her breath, instinct propelled her in the proper direction, almost straight ahead through waters too black with muck to see below the surface. She felt bullet fissures, like tiny breaks in the water, speeding past her, saved as much by fortune as anything.

Gina glimpsed the man's shape when she was only a foot or two away, grabbing hold of his belt and dragging him under with her. She heard a plop that could only be the gun he'd lost his grasp of. She surfaced while struggling to hold him under, but he was too strong and ended up cresting over the surface with his hands at her throat, driving her backward into a nest of mangroves.

It was the man from the marina security footage, the one who'd forgotten to clip the tag from his newly purchased shirt!

Back up the channel, gators continued to thrash about in the area where one of the gunmen had been pulled under, igniting a feeding frenzy. That left her with no help coming again from that quarter, even as the breath bottlenecked in her throat and the world started to turn cloudy around her. The man's grip was incredibly strong, and Gina spotted his enraged glare through the blood and wounds that dotted his face. He snarled in determination, continuing to choke the life out of her, when one of Gina's flailing hands grasped a pencil-sized piece of mangrove root and snapped it off, driving it forward and up.

Straight into the man's right eye.

He gasped, screamed, released his grasp. Still wailing in agony when Gina pushed him under and, this time, lent all her strength to the effort until the black waters around her stopped bubbling and she felt the man sink farther into the darkness.

Gina steadied herself on her feet, measuring the distance to the shore-line when an alligator coasted by with sinewy, blood-riddled flesh stuck to its teeth. It seemed to regard her with a smile, then swam on atop the surface.

GLACIER BAY NATIONAL PARK AND PRESERVE, LESTER ISLAND, ALASKA

The area gets around sixty-eight inches of rain, and ten inches of snow from October to April each year.

Michael and Amka poured the gunpowder in twin rows along the floor of the old mine, enough to last them all the way until they were fifteen or twenty feet in. Plenty to collapse the entrance for the foreseeable future, if not forever. She held one of the tightly wrapped packets back, in order to serve as the detonator once lit aflame and dropped down.

Michael climbed the ladder out of the mine first and then extended a hand down to help Amka the rest of the way.

"The storm has stopped," she said.

Michael realized that only when she said it, both of them discovering why when footsteps crunching ice drew their gazes back toward the forest, where a Russian with a chest the size of a beer keg advanced with a pistol pressed against Yehl's head, while another soldier yanked Chief Xetsuwu across the ice-strewn ground.

"Drop what you're holding," he called out in English laced with a strong Russian accent, "or the boy dies."

†††

Michael put the count of soldiers clustered behind the Russian at around a dozen, looking much the worse for wear and likely making up the last of his functional force, all with pistols drawn in place of assault rifles that had likely frozen up solid thanks to the ice storm. Yehl and his grandfather being taken hostage explained the sudden end to the ice's fall, removing the advantage the Tlingit forces had enjoyed until that moment.

Michael knew he was facing the man in charge of the Russian operation to pilfer the microbe from the ore tucked within this mine he and Amka had been on the verge of sealing forever. She stiffened alongside him, trapped between emotions and intentions.

"Let my men and me finish what we came here to do," the Russian continued, "and these two will live."

Amka dropped the packet of gunpowder she'd been holding.

"Now drop your weapons!"

She and Michael both discarded their pistols and let them clack to the frozen ground.

"Raise your hands into the air."

The Russian gestured for a few of his soldiers to advance and search them, finding no further weapons.

"You are to be complimented on the efforts of your people," Michael listened to the Russian say, more directed at Amka than him. "Very impressive."

"We've had over two hundred years to prepare for this day," she told him.

"And yet the results will be the same. We will take what we want and then we will burn your village. The only question now is whether we burn your people, too, and the level of your cooperation will determine which outcome I choose."

‡‡‡

The Russian left a trio of soldiers above the surface with the old chief, while Amka and Michael led what remained of the Russian forces down into the mine that weaved its way beneath the village at its outer reaches. Yehl was kept farther back, held hostage to dissuade them from doing anything more than leading the way. Michael thought he recognized the big bear of a man as General Viktor Adamovitch, whose taking over command of the Russian Army in Ukraine had turned the tide of that war. Western journalists were fond of speculating about Adamovitch's political ambitions, and his presence here seemed to confirm them.

"You should try a Russian prosthetic," Adamovitch said, grinning at him after noticing Michael limping from the stress placed on his foot. "They are much more forgiving of the cold."

The winding trail through the old mine spilled out into a chamber with walls laden with black rock formations speckled with crystals, identical to what he'd spotted in the mine he'd spent the previous night huddled in. This substance had come very close to ending all life on the planet once before, ten thousand years ago, and, in Adamovitch's possession, might well do so again.

"*Poydem na rabotu!*" he ordered his men in Russian.

Instantly, they stripped off their heavy coats to reveal pickaxes clipped to their ammo vests that doubled as body armor. Removing their outer layers released the smell of sweat and fear that had collected over the course of the battle. It made sense, Michael thought, that Adamovitch would have held the crew selected to handling the extraction duties back until the village had been reasonably secured and, following his instructions, they immediately set about chiseling away at the mine walls under cover of lantern- and flashlight. The lanterns were battery-operated, not fuel-based, so there would be no toppling them and setting their contents ablaze.

Michael looked toward where Yehl and Amka were being held at gunpoint by one soldier, while another kept watch over Michael, freeing Adamovitch to supervise the process of packing the black ore-like, fragmented rocks into sacks the Russians had spread out on the floor, one per man.

"Why did you remove the Americans from the cave on the glacier?" Michael asked him.

Adamovitch grinned again. "To study how they died, of course, since it was obviously the result of what I intend to weaponize." He studied Michael's uniform. "Who do you work for exactly?"

"The National Park Service."

The Russian's eyes narrowed. "It was you who killed my man in Sitka."

"Guilty as charged."

Adamovitch seemed to regard him a different way. "He was good. That makes you better. I might have to kill you, after all."

The clacking of the pickaxes hammering away at the black walls of the chamber echoed faintly in hollow fashion. The soldiers wielding them worked fast and expertly, obviously selected for their experience working in one of Russia's many coal mines. At this rate, they would have several of the sacks of what someone else had been smuggling out of Alaska in

Tlingit burial urns full in no time. No need for such subterfuge or patience here, leaving Michael to wonder how much damage to humanity such a large amount could do in the hands of a proven madman like Adamovitch.

Michael's eyes found Amka's. She was protectively shielding Yehl as best she could from the soldier with his pistol steadied upon them. He held her gaze for a long moment, trying to communicate his plan to her by flexing his prosthetic foot. She nodded in understanding, sliding protectively closer to her brother.

Michael put all the weight on his left leg and felt the already cracked plastic housing attached to his prosthetic splinter audibly with a resounding snap. He collapsed to the mine floor in a heap, much to the delight of Viktor Adamovich.

"That's why you need a Russian model," the general taunted, as the soldier guarding Michael hoisted him unsteadily back to his one good foot.

Then Adamovich's eyes gaped at the pair of RGN grenades Michael was holding in either hand. The soldier watching Amka and Yehl turned his gun on Michael, about to fire when she barreled into him, struggling for control of the pistol. With all but two of the general's troops working with their pickaxes, there was only Adamovitch himself and the soldier whose grenades Michael had stripped to offer immediate resistance. The general pulled back his bulky jacket to tear his own pistol free, as Amka managed to aim the pistol held by the soldier she was grappling with across the chamber, aimed straight for the soldier steadying his pistol on Michael.

Two shots, deafening in the chamber's closed confines, poured out, the first missing but the second slamming into the soldier's skull. Adamovitch managed to get his pistol raised as the soldier fell in his path, in the same moment both grenades flitted across the mine floor, stopping near his feet.

"Come on!" Michael screamed.

An instant later, Amka and Yehl were on either side of him, supporting Michael in the moment the first flash erupted, consuming Adamovitch. The flash faded to reveal the sight of what was left of him lying in a clump on the cave floor, when the second blast sounded, sending the walls caving in on the remaining pair of gunmen along with the troops wielding handheld pickaxes.

"Come on!"

Michael, dazed by the percussion of the twin blasts, felt Amka dragging him out of the chamber and along a winding path that steered for the village. The sensation around them felt like an earthquake, the ground shaking and tunnel ceiling giving way, collapsing in their wake.

Yehl joined his efforts with Amka's, pulling him on to outrun the collapsing pile of debris. Michael found an awkward rhythm to dragging his left leg, while his right one propelled him onward with Yehl and Amka on either side of him, barely managing to stay ahead of the wall of rock, ledge, and earth chasing them down.

Finally, the flashlight Amka had the foresight to grab revealed a ladder up a slope straight ahead. They reached it with the thunderous roar of the collapsing tunnel bubbling their ears, Amka thrusting Michael onto the rungs when he'd intended to do the same to her.

"Shove him up!" she screamed to her brother, pushing him onto the ladder next.

Michael felt Yehl shoving until he emerged through the manhole cover–sized gap and then reached back down from the rim to help the boy follow him to the surface. Michael had just pulled him free of the mounting rubble and managed to hoist Yehl into the cold dank air, when the hole closed up with Amka trapped below.

"No!" the boy cried out, as he dug futilely at the rubble. "No!"

Then a single hand clawed free and broke the surface. Michael pulled as hard as he could, lifting Amka enough for her to poke her second hand through the debris entombing her. Yehl grabbed hold of that arm and, together, he and Michael used all their strength to hoist Amka upward in agonizingly slow fashion that left him wondering if she might suffocate in the process.

But she emerged gasping for breath, collapsing between the two of them with the mine buried forever.

‡‡‡

"My grandfather!" Amka blurted out, once she regained her breath, struggling to sit up.

She found the strength to rush on ahead, while Yehl supported Michael in her wake. She drifted out of sight in the night, only to reappear near the entrance to the mine that had collapsed as well. She stood with her grandfather amid the downed bodies of the three Russian soldiers left there to guard the scene.

Michael started to wonder if the old chief had worked another miracle when he spotted a third figure sporting a tight growth of beard hanging back a bit in the darkness. The rugged-looking figure held a high-tech military-style pistol with an elongated barrel. Michael recognized it as a Desert Eagle, a gas-operated semiautomatic that fired the largest center-fire cartridge of any magazine-fed, self-loading sidearm. He stood in the shadow of an even larger figure who was certainly Native American and, just as certainly, not a Tlingit.

He regarded Yehl helping Michael along and seemed to smile through the darkness.

"Welcome to the party," said the man, scratching at the thin beard that was an equal mixture of gray and black, just like his wavy, wind-mussed hair. "Looks like I missed most of the fun."

He came forward, holstering the weapon as he approached the three of them.

"I was never here, if anybody asks. Easier that way." The man, whose beard looked more like a few weeks' worth of unkempt stubble, swept his gaze about as if taking in the entire scope of the village and its surroundings, almost like his eyes could pierce the night. "You did great work here. I'm impressed." He looked toward the huge figure just behind him. "Looks like our work here is done, Johnny."

And, just like that, he turned and walked off.

Minutes later, a sleek helicopter like nothing Michael had ever seen before rose over the tree line and sped away, seeming to melt into the night.

"Who the hell were they?" Amka watched it vanish.

Her grandfather muttered something, following the helicopter, too.

"What did he say?" Michael wondered.

"*Haadaa gooji,*" Yehl repeated. "Which means lions."

THE WHITE HOUSE

"I don't know what to say, I just don't."

President Jillian Cantwell sat down in the chair of her office in the residence next to the one already occupied by Gina Delgado. They were alone in the room, except for a uniformed figure Gina knew and trusted standing in the corner like a statue with arms crossed behind his back.

"This is all on me because it originated in the White House where I'm supposed to be in control."

"Daniel Grant genuinely believed he was serving your interests, Madam President."

"Not Jillian anymore, Gina?" the president asked, her tone ringed with guilt.

"That depends."

"On what?"

"On whether I can trust you, ma'am. Trust you to truly have the best interests of the country in mind."

The president looked almost hurt by Gina's words. "And you don't think that's the case anymore?"

"Not when your campaign gets in the way."

"I can't do any good for the country unless I'm in office, Gina," Jillian Cantwell said, her gaze hardening.

"Does that mean having to bring the likes of Daniel Grant into the fold?"

"I didn't know he was a killer."

"He did it for you, Madam President. And good intentions don't mean the next person you bring in, and the person after, won't end up going down the same road."

"I'll have to be reelected to bring in anyone. That's actually why I called you here today. How would you like the job, Gina?"

Gina felt like someone had shaken her chair. "Chief of staff?"

The president nodded.

"Wow. I don't know, ma'am. I'm not sure it's for me."

"Your intentions indicate otherwise. Instead of putting bad guys away, you'd be keeping them from surfacing in the first place. A line of defense against precisely the proclivities Grant fell victim to."

"Power, ma'am?"

"You can't do good unless you have it, and as chief of staff you can make sure it doesn't get abused."

Gina decided to change the subject. "Speaking of which, the only guards I saw on the White House premises are wearing Army uniforms."

The president looked toward the similarly garbed figure in the corner. "I've asked our old friend Colonel Beeman to take over all security matters while the Secret Service undergoes a thorough investigation to determine how many more agents may have been compromised by the likes of Daniel Grant."

Gina nodded in satisfaction, exchanging a long gaze with Beeman, whom she had fought alongside the year before to save the country from another threat.

"Your new job wouldn't really be all that much different from your old one, when you think about it," the president resumed. "Dealing with politicians instead of criminals. So what do you say to my offer?"

Gina gave her a long look. "Give me some time to think about it . . . Jillian. Meanwhile, what about Axel Cole? After what he's done, what he'll continue to do, we can't leave him out there. The threat he poses is too great."

The president turned her gaze on Beeman again and nodded. He emerged from the room's shadows into the light, hands remaining clasped behind his back.

"That's being handled, Captain Delgado," he assured, addressing Gina by her military rank. Then he smiled ever so slightly. "I've got just the man for the job."

‡‡‡

Cape Canaveral Space Force Station, Cape Canaveral, Florida

Axel Cole sat in his private viewing suite in Space Launch Base A, overlooking the launchpad where the *Death Star* prototype would be lifting off in just a few hours. He'd paid for the entire complex's construction on the grounds of Cape Canaveral Space Force Station with his own funds, christening it "Base A," because it was the first such partnership the station had ever entered into. Cole didn't want to use a number because Elon Musk had used a number for his base out at Vandenberg from where he launched his SpaceX rockets.

The good news was that Viktor Adamovitch perishing in Alaska had allowed him to wriggle out of this whole mess scot-free, no accusations or recriminations whatsoever, since by all accounts no one knew of his role. The bad news was that any further reserves of Prometheus would be hard to come by indeed, what with the existence of his magical fuel source no longer a secret. The one sticking point remained the debacle at Michoud in New Orleans where botched experiments with Prometheus had led to twenty-one deaths. Fortunately, no one, it seemed, wanted the truth to come out, and Cole had even managed to secure the reserves from the closed-off facility before anyone knew they were missing. He had convinced Elizabeth Fields to remain on board by advancing her promised billion-dollar bonus without waiting for the promised Mars landing. Having learned from her mistakes, Fields had managed to turn enough Prometheus into the fuel that would power the *Death Star*'s maiden voyage into the Earth's orbit, leaving plenty for further testing. And by the time the ship was ready to make the journey to Mars, Cole would find a way to harvest additional supplies from the Alaskan tundra no matter what, or how many lives, it cost. He had changed the results of the simulations his team had been running to make it appear the *Death Star* was 100 percent flight worthy, which it was until getting back to home was taken into account.

He genuinely believed he had survived all this to fulfill his destiny. It was the only explanation for why he remained standing, while the likes of Daniel Grant and Viktor Adamovitch were out of the picture.

He sat alone in Space Launch Base A's viewing suite. From this distance, the view cast the illusion that he was at the same height as the *Death Star*, which sat mounted on the massive solid rocket booster that would blast the ship into orbit before detaching. There was no one Cole wanted to share this maiden voyage with. He wanted to be without distractions, without company, without anything but a view of the launchpad. The launch itself was still hours away, but Cole wanted to be here to savor every minute of the preparation, and communications from launch control emanating from the suite's hidden speakers made for the only noise.

"We are at T-minus three hours and counting . . ."

No crew was on board the ship and the flight would be totally remote. That had already been his preference, even before it was revealed the heat shields wouldn't survive reentry, meaning this was a suicide mission for his *Death Star* prototype. Well worth it, though, since two successful orbits around the Earth, powered by Prometheus, would be more than enough to prove the efficacy of his vision and help him secure the reserves he needed to reach Mars. What money and power couldn't buy, dreams could, and Cole would find a host of willing partners to mount fresh expeditions into the frozen Alaskan wilderness to get more of what he was after. Even if that meant accepting the cost of doing business with someone like Viktor Adamovich again, the price would be worth it.

The viewing suite looked like something lifted from a spaceship itself, with a rounded design and modular, built-in furniture. It looked like an expanded version of the bridge from the *Enterprise* of *Star Trek* fame, the newer version with all the bells and whistles special effects could conjure. And, truth be told, he really did feel a bit like James T. Kirk, soon to go where no man had ever gone before.

His private elevator chimed, signaling the cab's arrival at the suite level. Strange because he had locked it into place, so no one could find their way up here. Cole turned around to see the door had already slid open and he approached to find the cab empty. He peeked inside, as if to make sure no one was pressed against the wall or something.

Nothing.

Just a malfunction, a ghost in the machine, Cole thought as he swung to retake his spot by the window to find a pair of shapes that were little more than blurs converging upon him, one big and one bigger.

‡‡‡

Cole awoke to find himself in the passenger bay of the *Death Star*, tilted upward in a seat that would someday cost upwards of $100 million. He tried to move and couldn't, realizing he had been fastened to the seat by straps his own scientists had constructed out of an indestructible poly-carbon material. He could taste the fibers from a strip of tape across his mouth.

Suddenly the viewing screen switched on, revealing a grizzled-looking figure with ice-blue eyes and a thin beard colored with the same mix of gray and black as his hair. Cole noticed a second figure, massive in size, filling out the background. His hair, clubbed back into a ponytail, was an equal measure of salt and pepper, too.

"The name's McCracken," the man said, with a smile that chilled Cole to the bone, "though I don't expect that means anything to you, Axel. How's it feel to be the first man to ride on your own creation?"

Cole's eyes bulged. He tried to speak but his words were swallowed by the tape fastened across his mouth.

"*T-minus one minute to liftoff . . .*"

"Hey, this is nothing. I hijacked a space shuttle once. But I won't be joining you on this flight. It's yours and yours alone. You're going to see the world a whole new way, twice from orbit. Too bad the heat shields failed testing. That ought to make for an interesting reentry."

"*T-minus thirty seconds to liftoff . . .*"

Cole tried desperately to speak, managed some mumbling.

The man named McCracken just looked at him. "A man like you probably just offered me a fortune to call this off. Since you don't know who I am, you can't know money means nothing to me. You know what does? Moments like this when people like you get what's coming to them."

"*T-minus ten, nine, eight, seven . . .*"

"Payback's a bitch, isn't it?"

‡‡‡

Glacier Bay National Park and Preserve, Lester Island, Alaska

"We've still got problems, Amka," Michael said, in the wake of the Tlingits defeating the Russians on Lester Island.

Mass fish kills in both the seas off Alaska and waters of the Everglades continued to appear, effectively charting the organism's expansion— toward the mainland up north and the Gulf Stream in the south.

"Using Tlingit blood as the basis for a vaccine won't stop this microbe from continuing to spread through the ocean," he reminded her.

"Maybe it can, Michael," she told him, the microbiologist in her speaking. "You remember the Deepwater Horizon oil spill in 2010?"

"I was a park ranger at the time. It's something I wish I could forget."

"Then you may recall how a microbe was employed to clean up the lingering effects of the spill, actually billions of hydrocarbon-munching microbes. Almost a million gallons of chemical dispersants were exposed to the oil slick both above and below the surface of the sea to break the oil into microscopic droplets that bacteria could more easily absorb. And it worked."

"Why is that relevant here, Amka?"

"First, because it forms a precedent we can build on. And, second, because I engineered that microbe."

Michael did a double take.

"I was at MIT at the time. The discovery launched my career and made me rich. And the same principles can be applied here. Only this time, instead of genetically constructing the microbe to attack oil, we construct it to absorb the organism that's infecting fish. So long as that organism is reasonably contained, there's a clear way we can do that."

"By using Tlingit antibodies as the basis for what you'd be concocting in the lab."

"Exactly! Look, I'm not saying it's going to be easy. But given the unlimited resources we should have available to us, I know it can be done, and done before the spread reaches population centers in the upper northwest, based on projections of the organism's current spread southward."

"A fish vaccine? That sounds impossible."

Amka shook her head. "You're forgetting about the plankton. Plankton was able to infect the fish that ingested it because it had ingested the organism. We can engineer the vaccine to be the perfect food source for plankton. Figure out how to do that, and the plankton won't be killing all the fish, it will be saving them. The only thing we need is a lab advanced enough to handle all this."

"Let me make a phone call."

‡‡‡

Joint Base Elmendorf-Richardson, Anchorage, Alaska

Two days later, Michael and Amka had relocated to the very same secret, underground facility at Elmendorf that Gina Delgado had visited where scientists had finally managed to isolate the prehistoric organism from the corpses of the crew of the *Providence*. One of those scientists, who called himself Atticus, worked alongside Amka in simultaneously developing a human vaccine and organic microbe constructed to attack and destroy its prehistoric cousin, both based on antibodies drawn from Tlingit blood.

Except for the electron microscopes, Michael didn't recognize a single piece of the futuristic equipment they employed or understand any of the terminology they used as they worked around the clock on experiments to test the various microbes they created. It all culminated a month later in a computer simulation conducted by Atticus before a room full of scientists who'd been working under him and Amka.

At last, Michael found something he could understand. On-screen, an army of microbes the size of tiny black dots penetrated the cellular wall of a blue mass representing the prehistoric organism. As he watched, the black dots expanded, slowly at first and then in blinding fashion, until they had absorbed all of the blue. The scientists crowded into the room rose and applauded.

"Does this mean what I think it means?" Michael asked from alongside Amka.

"It means the microbe we engineered works, Michael," she told him.

Thereby saving marine life in the oceans and preserving life on Earth, he thought.

"Within three weeks, a month at most," Amka explained to him after the meeting had broken up, "the first million gallons of dispersants containing our microbe will be ready for release in the infected areas of the seas off the Alaskan coast, bioengineered to be absorbed by plankton. And the more plankton the fish eat, the more resistant they become to the organism. Production and release will continue until there's no sign whatsoever of our prehistoric friend in the waters here or in the Everglades approaching the Gulf Stream."

"We dodged a bullet this time, didn't we?"

Amka nodded, looking considerably less celebratory. "But what about the next one, Michael, what about the next one?"

‡‡‡

Guantanamo Bay, Cuba

Ethan Turlidge was jarred awake by a key rattling in the lock of the incarceration section of Camp No where he might well be spending the rest of his life in one of two twin cells few outside this facility even knew existed. The clock on the wall told him it was the early morning hours, a strange time for a visitor, and Turlidge rose from his bunk in expectation.

A pair of military policemen he was familiar with entered, dragging a man whose wrists and legs were in chains and who was already wearing the orange jumpsuit reserved for noncompliant prisoners kept on these grounds, in contrast to the white one he donned. Turlidge didn't recognize the disheveled, worn-down figure but reveled in the sight of someone who looked worse than he did.

As Turlidge watched, one of the MPs pulled the neighboring cell door open, while the other clung tightly to the prisoner. Then both of them shepherded him inside.

"Meet your new roommate, Mr. Turlidge," one of them said, "Daniel Grant."

The neighboring cell door clanged closed and the other MP checked to make sure it was sealed tight, then fit a key into the lock and turned.

Click.

ACKNOWLEDGMENTS

Writing these National Park thrillers is a cowriting venture, but it takes a village to turn an idea into a finished story.

Thank you to Terry, Greg, and Samantha for the support and love.

Keith Kahla, Grace Gay, Hector DeJean, Mac Nicholas, Sara Beth Haring, Kelley Ragland, and the fantastic team at Minotaur Books. We could not have dreamed of a better experience writing and publishing these National Park thrillers, and we are excited to continue working with you.

Literary Agent Extraordinaire John Talbot for the advice, enthusiasm, and encouragement. Knowing we are in such great hands makes all the difference.

Dr. Jill Behm for the help with prosthetics and feedback.

These terrific park rangers, retired park rangers, and ISB agents—James Montgomery, Geoffrey Walker, Sanny Lustig, Caden Wilson, and Tim Giller—helped us get the details right.

Javier Morejon for details on the Everglades and airboats.

To help make the science semi-believable, David Levin and Matthew Tracey.

Claire Cerne and Greg Wiles are responsible for glacier assistance.

Michael Taylor, Mayor of Gustavus, for insight into the town and the area around Glacier Bay National Park.

Marc Cameron, Brian Weed, and Rodger Carlyle for help with Alaska geography and history.

Brian Andrews for assisting with the submarine scenes.

Jim Patton, Tammy Patton, and Patrick Yearout for terrific suggestions and National Park advice.

Kristoffer Polaha and Samuel Octavius, thank you for inspiring us.

The National Park Conservation Association team, thank you for your support and for helping us launch *Leave No Trace* in a terrific way.

Thank you for taking a chance on events for us, Becky Walsh at Third Place Books, the team at Wakefield Books, and the terrific folks who work at Murder by the Book.

River, your friendship helped keep us accountable.

AUTHORS' NOTE

The indigenous people of North America and the stewardship of her lands are inextricably combined. You cannot tell stories involving the National Parks of the United States without acknowledging the massacre and forcible removal of native people from their homelands. There continues to be separation from sacred sites and traditional hunting and gathering locations, and ongoing challenges to the preservation of their cultures and traditions. Equally important to recognize is that native people and tribes have endured, with resilient and vibrant connections to the land in the present day. Since 2022, the National Park Service has developed new policies that call for direct engagement and involvement with tribal governments and native communities in the planning and management of the parks. With these partnerships, the history, values, knowledge, and priorities of indigenous people will be a key part of managing the parks for generations to come.

In writing *Cold Burn,* we researched the diverse culture of Alaskan Natives, visiting important historical sites and talking with local people. The stories of the modern-day Tlingit people are theirs to tell, and so we opted to create a fictitious Tlingit village on Lester Island, revising both geography and landscape. Although we sought to celebrate the history, traditions, bravery, and endurance of the Tlingit in our characters, we used creative license in the folklore and legends in our story. The facts at the beginning of each chapter about Lester Island are accurate, but any resemblances to actual locations or individuals are not intentional. We hope readers will be moved, as we were, to learn more about Alaskan Native culture and people.